SONG OF ALL SONGS

BOOK ONE

EARTHCYCLES

DONNA DECHEN BIRDWELL

Wide World Home

Song of All Songs: EarthCycles, Book One

Copyright © 2020 by Donna Dechen Birdwell

Cover design by Robin Vuchnich, mycustombookcover.com
Author photo by Lucero Valle Archuleta

Published by Wide World Home.
8944B Parker Ranch
Austin, TX 78748 USA
wideworldhome.com

First Printing—August 2020
Second Printing—June 2021

Publisher's Note: This is a work of fiction. Names, characters places, and incidents are either the product of the author's imagi-nation or used fictitiously.

Birdwell, Donna Dechen
Song of All Songs: EarthCycles, Book One
375 pp.
1. Science Fiction – Fiction 2. American – Fiction
I. Donna Dechen Birdwell
II. Song of All Songs: EarthCycles, Book One
ISBN: 978-1-7355569-0-1

Printed in The United States of America.

PRAISE FOR *SONG OF ALL SONGS*

"When anthropologist Donna Dechen Birdwell turns her keen sense of how societies evolved in the past toward imagining a post-apocalyptic future, the result is a thoughtful, nuanced, intelligent thriller."—Robert J. Sawyer, Hugo Award-winning author of *The Oppenheimer Alternative*

"Song of All Songs is a beautifully written and richly realized vision of the future, informed by a deep understanding of humanity." — Christopher Brown, Campbell and World Fantasy Award-nominated author of *Tropic of Kansas* and *Failed State*

"Song of All Songs is a lovely book. It is sad and hopeful both, and I thought about it long after I read the last page." –Patrice Sarath, author of *The Sisters Mederos* and *The Unexpected Miss Bennett*

"The creativity in the language, phrasing, world-building and plot make the book an immersive pleasure to read. The author has an obvious gift with words..." – *Self-Publishing Review*

To all the possibilities.

"Deep song is a stammer,
a wavering emission of the voice…
Deep song is akin to the trilling of birds."
–Federico García Lorca

"If you want to find the secrets of the universe,
think in terms of energy, frequency, and vibration."
– Nikola Tesla

1.

THE OLD MAN PICKS HIS WAY through the darkened hallway of the columbarium. A scent of burnt wood stains the stale air as he listens for the chirps and hums and breathy purrs. The three stones in his pocket pulse warm against his hand, indicating that he's drawing near to another of their kind. He passes his hand along the seal of the niche and opens it, smiling at the bright turquoise that winks at him from among the ashes inside the urn. He cradles the stone in his hand, relishing the notes it sends coursing through his body, the longing for home and family. But this isn't the stone Abél is looking for. He puts it back into the urn and replaces the urn in its chamber. With a single syllable, he re-seals the niche.

Humming softly in harmony with some of the stones, in counterpoint to others, Abél moves on. Day is coming and he knows he must get well away from the temple grounds before the sun rises. He's been accused of theft before. He knows he's not the thief. A sigh of regret sifts through his head as he turns toward the space outlined in sepia light. The way out.

A sudden buzzing between his brows draws him up short. The stones in his pocket quiver and squeal, directing his attention to a chamber to his left. A purple glow emanates from within it. This one is newly sealed and easy to open. The urn inside is particularly elaborate—unusual for these austere days. Is that real gold outlining the figure on its lid? The figure looks like a tree in flames.

Abél looks back at the cover stone he removed from the niche and squints hard at the writing on it, trying to make sense of the letters. A name comes into focus.

"So it's you," he mutters. "And this is how they try to own you?" The little stones resound to the silken clarity of his voice. He lifts the lid from the urn and is overwhelmed by a steady brilliance. The purple stone fills the palm of his hand. It's warm to his touch and resonates with more colors deep in its core.

He knows this stone. Not long ago, it was his own.

But something is wrong. He places the stone in his pocket and reaches back inside the urn, digging into the ashes. He digs deeper and lets the ashes run through his fingers. And then he knows. These are wood ashes. There are no remains here.

"This one has continued," Abél whispers. The space between his eyes pulses and his throat constricts around the unvoiced words. *This one is still among us.*

2.

IT COMES IN FRAGMENTS and pieces, thoughts that catch in my throat. Things I see with my eyes closed. It's like that.

I'm called Meridia Einkorn, and this is where I live, here where everything is the color of earth, all browns and rust and dull yellow streaked with gray. This room has no hard corners. I know the number of slats of my simple wooden bed through the thin mattress beneath my body. There's exactly the same number of beams in the ceiling as slats in the bed. I know this without counting. I also know the table, the chair, the chest where my earth-colored garments lie folded and waiting to shelter my skin from the sun's assault. I know the cupboard holding food, the jug of fresh water.

I thirst.

I know the small pale birds outside the window. They shake the sleep from their feathers and chirp a tuneless song to the day that's come.

My feet touch the rug and know the cool earthen floor beneath. I know my face, warm, alive, every crease that deepens when I smile, how the muscles sag as the smile goes.

What was it I have to do today? I reach for yesterday, across the chasm of dreams that reach to draw me back toward sleep. Forgetfulness. Awareness.

Damon. The smile comes and goes. Lungs inflate and release. I promised Damon I'd meet him this morning. I hear myself saying this though my voice and ears are still. The taste of eggs. Bread streaked with butter. Damon's dark eyes, deep voice, rough hands, gentle touch. Not that. We are to talk about something. No, he's going to show me something. Something he found. My head moves up and down, acknowledging that I have claimed this day and may proceed.

I take my nakedness to the far corner of the room and douse my body with water, letting it run cool through my hair, over my face, my arms, and trickle down my legs. Between my legs. Between my toes. Water drains away through the opening at the low corner of the room. It carries bits of my skin into the out-of-doors, soaking into the ground, taken up by plants, always becoming something else. Not really. There is no else. I scrub my hair and body dry with a gray cloth, soft with age. It was once a new shirt.

I clothe my body—trousers, shirt, a neck scarf, and sandals are all I need. I attack my unruly brown curls with a comb. Give up. Stuff it all under my hat.

When I open the door, I'm overwhelmed by the town waiting outside. Everything is as it should be, though not to my liking. Too loud, too bright, too busy. The sun is barely breaking over the line of low buildings across the street. I blink and cower under my hat. Others are on the street before me, chattering, talking. I know this way of speaking.

A pedaled vehicle whooshes by, too close, and I jump back, knocking into someone.

"Good day, Meridia," she says. She means *Why can't you be more careful?*

"Fine day, Londra," I say, meaning *I'm sorry, I didn't mean to.* My voice sounds shrill and unnatural. I prefer the voice of thought and dreaming.

Most people don't speak at all when they see me. Pretend they don't see me. I pull my hat down and watch my feet. Sometimes I chafe at my invisibility. But when what you are is something hateful, isn't it better to be invisible?

There's dust in the air, glittering, etching into my nostrils and throat, floating, defying gravity. I pull the scarf up over my nose and mouth. Droplets of sweat gather, trickling down the sides of my face. Too hot for a winter day of Fifth Stint. Every passage brings worse heat. Seasons make little difference.

There it is. The café where I promised to meet Damon. I catch the scent of fresh nutbread, carried on the windless currents stirred by moving bodies.

The door of the café stands open. Flies, glinting blue and green, buzz at the windowpanes.

A room like any other. Low ceiling, soft corners, scent of earth. I recognize Damon, the spaciousness of him. Open fields lush with grass, running streams. Fecund. No, that's for women. Only not for me.

His smile says he sees me. What does he see? My strange color and bulging body? I concentrate on the hardness of the floor beneath my feet, the arrangement of tables, chairs, bodies. Damon is sitting in a back corner, an area reserved for people like me. His height and dark skin look out of place. He could have sat anywhere.

"Fine morning," I say, settling onto the hardness of the angular wooden chair. Not a chair you can sit in, only on.

"Too hot."

I like how Damon scowls with that smile in his eyes. Is there a word for that?

"I've ordered eggs and bread for both of us," he says. "I hope you don't mind. It was getting crowded and I was hungry. I didn't want to eat without you." Now the full-on smile, which I return. Which is returned by mine. I didn't will it.

He pours tea from the jug into a cup and pushes it toward me. Tepid. Tea used to steam. I'm sure I remember that.

My face is still smiling. "How's the work going?" That's good. A good thing to say. Besides, Damon's work interests me. I want to know about it.

"Slow," he says. He draws the word out, as if that is how it means what it means.

Damon photographs photons. Well, what else is there to photograph? What's different about Damon is that he photographs what he calls biophotons. Light that comes from living things. Living people. He's telling me about his latest pictures, painting them for me with his words. I struggle to follow. Sometimes he uses words I can't see.

"So the new process is really no better than the old one," his words sigh. "On to the next trial, right Meri?" A weary look. "But that's not why I wanted to talk with you this morning. I have something to show you."

We've finished our eggs. I spread another dollop of yellow grease on the last crust of my hard bread. We call it butter. I bite, chew. Wipe oily fingers on the stained cotton napkin.

"Well, what is it? Show me."

"Not here. It's something I found." He glances around at the other patrons. "It's probably better not to show it to you here. Can we go back to your house?"

I swallow the last of my tea as Damon picks up a battered attachycase from beside his chair. It isn't heavy.

We walk back down the dusty street to where I live. Inside, he places his case on the table. I sit across from him, leaning forward on my elbows. Latches resist, then spring open. The lid blocks my view, but I see him unwrap something. He pushes the case aside and sets the object down in front of me.

I see a rock. A squarish rock. It's mostly green but with layers, veins. It's shiny on one side.

"It's a rock," I say. "Maybe a healing stone?"

"Only that?" Damon is looking at my face, but not in my eyes. A little above my eyes. More centered. "Is that all?" He invites me. He's giving me permission.

She's beautiful. Her clothing wafts across her body, hiding nothing. Green scarves. No, blue. Now purple. Bright and glowing. Her eyes laugh. Her mouth mocks. Her hands, her hands…

Damon's hand is on mine. "Stop. Enough," he says. "That's what I needed to know."

I take the stone from where I held it against my forehead. There are tears in my eyes. I hand the stone to Damon. He may have what he needed, but I need so much more. I need this woman to tell me who she is. To tell me who I am.

3.

MOTHER WOULD EVER ONLY SAY that he was a madman. The space my father occupies in my memories is mostly blank. My heart remembers gentleness.

When I told Mother what I thought, she bristled. "You never really knew him," she said. "He was gone long ago."

How long she wouldn't say. I knew that he was how she got me. I'm sure he was still here when I was very young. I think I knew a lot then. But I wanted more. I hadn't yet learned to keep my questions to myself.

"Was he from here? From Temur?"

"No, child. Not from Temur."

I didn't know any other towns, so she'd just as well to have told me that he'd dropped down from the sky. Sometimes I thought he had. Sometimes I thought my mother had. I didn't understand how hard life was for her. There was only my mother and me, nobody's kinren. In this world, everyone is either a Sidayen or a Sidayen's kinren. Or a Shoon. Mother and I were nobody. I was less.

When I was small, I didn't understand how different I was. I'd spend hours chasing colored hoops and spheres that my mother insisted weren't there. How was I to know I created them with my own laughter? Whenever I could, I wandered off into the woods with the birds. The birds understood me. They sang strands of colored jewels, tossed gleefully to one another and occasionally to me. I tried to sing with them. Sometimes I searched for pebbles and arranged them according to their sounds and colors. Some of them I gave to Mother. I don't know what she did with them.

That scrubby scrap of woods was my forest. My refuge.

I was always a disappointment to Mother. She wanted me to learn to read, but reading was impossible. The words wouldn't sit still, wouldn't stay in order. Each word wanted to show me things and wouldn't let me move on to the next. I memorized poems easily enough, the music of them, the pictures the words painted, but I couldn't read them. Mother scolded and made me sit with the books and struggle, doing battle with words scratched on paper.

"Meridia, you'll never be anything if you can't read!" She would shout and strike me on the side of the head with a book, as if that was going to help me understand all those stacks of words.

I shouted back, just noise. I stomped my feet and pounded the table with my fists. I ripped pages out of the book. She picked up the ladle hot from the soup pot and hit me with it. Again and again she hit me. She covered me in burns and bruises. I screamed and ran away into the woods.

She didn't come after me.

I wandered in my woods, scuffing dusty bare feet against stones. I picked up a few pebbles and saved them in my pocket, worrying them with my fingers as I walked. Listening. I sat down finally in a clearing and the birds gathered around me. Little things, pale and plain like me. They were afraid, too. We watched the hawk at the top of a dead tree.

We watched her fly away, soaring, sun on her head and back, wind soft across her belly where her talons lurked, hungry for her next meal. When she was gone, the birds chirped and twittered their way back to their perches, high or low according to their customs.

I would go home.

I saw my mother through the window. She was crying. I watched as she glued another torn page back into the book, smoothing it ever so gently. Lovingly. She closed the book, examining it to see if the restored pages lined up with the rest. Tears still trickled down her cheeks as she clutched the book to her heart. She wasn't crying for me.

After that I tried harder with the reading. The best I could do was never good enough. I learned to cook and to clean. I was good at tending my mother when she was sick and soon neighbors wanted me to tend their sick ones, too. They said I had a knack. Mother became more tolerant. I spent more and more time in the woods with the birds, always looking for something but never knowing what.

"Do I look like him?" I asked.

"Like who? Oh. I don't remember much anymore. I guess you have his eyes." My eyes are as yellow as my skin; my mother's were deep brown. But I knew I had more than that. Mother was tall, and her face was slender, her nose and mouth small and well formed, her hair almost black, skin dark as polished bartlenut. People said she was pretty. I wasn't like her.

"What was his name?"

"Abél," she said. She turned away, refusing me anything more.

It's almost an entire passage since Mother went away. I took care of her through the illness that took her mind long before it took her bodily and completely. It was all I did for many passages. Neighbors brought food and our clothes grew worn. I grew tired. I tried to know her but there was always a wall and what was behind the wall I couldn't comprehend. She was like the books she tried to make me read.

It wasn't long after I lost her that Damon came to Temur.

4.

"WHERE DID IT COME FROM?" I ask Damon. I've always seen colors from rocks, felt vibrations, heard sounds. Imagined I saw and felt and heard such things. Is that it? But those were only small healing stones, tiny pebbles. Far less than the fist-sized stone Damon showed me.

Damon and I are walking outdoors along the alley behind my house. He says the movement will bring me back to myself.

"You know I went traveling a six ago." He has to remind me.

"Where?"

"Over to Brightlea."

A town larger than Temur. Craft shops behind colorful doors in whitewashed walls. Marketplace. Dogs barking. Red and yellow and blue umbrellas. Parasols.

"How far is that?"

"No more than twelve fellspans."

I try to see that. Distances and their measure never make sense to me. "In a shop? Or the marketplace." Damon knows I'm back to my first question.

"Yes, the marketplace. I got it from a surly old fellow who was already packing up to leave barely past midday."

"Why?" I ask.

"He was grumbling about people all wanting things for free and how was he supposed to make a living like that?"

"Not what I meant."

"Oh. I didn't buy it on purpose. What I bought was a sack of old plates and I found the rock lodged in the bottom of the bag. Caught behind a tear in the lining."

I know he means photographic plates. "Hidden," I say.

"Do you think so? I didn't find it until I began sorting through to examine the plates."

"You paid fairly?"

"The plates you mean? The old fellow thought so. He said he didn't get much call for that sort of thing. But now I'm thinking I got a great bargain. When I found the rock, I suspected it might be something exceptional, so I went back to the market to see if I could find the seller. But he was gone. I asked around. People said he doesn't come often. One woman told me he'd said he was going to Fayredell."

"Where did he come from?"

"They said he's a vagrant. A vagabond. Buys and sells as he goes."

"A name?"

"Nothing anyone could say. One fellow called him Chapling, but somehow I don't think that's his real name. More like something that follows him."

"Maybe. How do we find him?"

"We?" Damon's eyes tease. Eyebrows lifted. Lips tilted. Soft lips.

"I need to ask who she is, how he knows her."

"Knows who? Ah. You need to tell me what you saw. I saw vague color, some hints of movement, but nothing clear. You saw a person?"

"A woman. I'm glad you didn't see her. You'd be smitten."

"As beautiful as that?" He reaches for my hand.

We've turned along another back street, not minding where we go. Birds chirp along the verge, collecting seeds, crumbs, insects. We're nearly back to my place so we go there. I bring the jar of tea and pour it into cups. Tea brewed by the sun from leaves I gather near the woods. Near where the woods used to be.

"Can you show her to me?" Damon asks.

I walk to where he sits on the opposite side of the table and he turns to face me. He spreads his knees as I approach. Close, I draw his forehead against my throat. I close my eyes. Humming, I conjure her in all her colors, all her beauty. Why did I say beautiful? I see now that she has amber skin and straw-colored hair, full features, rounded hips and bulbous breasts. Not beautiful after all. Or am I making her this way? I remember the eyes and the lips and hands. No, this is she. She is like this. I remember.

I long to reach out for her, to ask her things. I'm sure there was a song. I try to recall the sound of it.

"She looks like you," Damon says.

"Does she? I didn't think so." But I know she does. She's a Shoon.

He takes my hands and pulls them down near his waist, drawing me closer. Not for seeing. Something else. Our lips meet. Joy without images.

I sit down on his right thigh.

"I suppose we could go to Fayredell and ask about him there," Damon says.

"That would begin it. We can't know where it would end."

He nods and places his two arms around my waist. My heart and belly quiver and I lean into him.

"I have some work to finish," he says. "Give me two days."

The days are there. I can neither give them nor take them away. "Good," I say. "How far is Fayredell?"

"Nearly twenty fellspans." He sees my brow furrow and laughs. "Three days walking. We can get there in three days if we move diligently."

I haven't been more than a fellspan outside Temur in many passages. Never been to Fayredell.

Damon says goodbye and returns to his work. His kiss lingers on my lips and in my heart. I think about clothes and shoes.

I think about the woman.

It will be a full six on the road, there and back. Maybe more if we don't find the old vagrant there. Or if we do.

The woman *was* beautiful. There was a song.

My sandals need new soles. Do I have coins for that? I can sell some tea. People say my tea has healing powers. It's only tea. Tomorrow's cooking day. I'll bake some sweet flatbread to sell. Nutbread for the journey, too. I will have coins. I will have new soles on my sandals.

5.

MERIDIA'S RESPONSE to the odd stone was more than Damon had anticipated. He'd hoped she might be able to pick up something from it, though he wasn't sure what that something might be. All Damon had experienced was a faint greenish glow when he glimpsed the stone at the margins of his field of vision. When he looked at it straight on, he saw nothing out of the ordinary. But then he'd brushed his hand over the spot where he'd left it sitting on his table overnight, and he thought the spot felt vaguely warm.

He acknowledged that it could all be his imagination. Damon had always been accused of having a vivid imagination. But his curiosity was piqued. He re-examined the photographic plates he'd acquired along with the stone. They'd come inside a thick black photographer's bag, gray with age and heavy with dust. On a couple of the plates he discerned ghostly images superimposed over more ordinary ones. This was not his imagination. Something was definitely there. His researcher's mind quickly formulated two questions: What kind of photographic plates were these that could record images in this manner? And did the stone have anything to do with the unusual effect?

The guiding principle of what Damon privately (and somewhat self-importantly) referred to as his life's work had been the notion that certain living things, and especially certain people, emit not just biophotons but, under certain circumstances, biophotonic images. He conceded that calling them "images" was probably a stretch. What he could see was usually no more than vague colors, indistinct patterns. He acknowledged that it wasn't exactly "seeing" but he doesn't know how else to describe it. He could almost remember having discerned more distinct images when he was a child. He cautioned himself that this was likely no more than fanciful memory. He tried hard to be a good scientist.

The old man Damon bought the plates from reminded him a bit of Meridia. And not just because he was a Shoon. Damon detested that term, the way it was used, but it's all he had to describe these differences. Of course, Meri was only half Shoon, or at least he supposed that was what she was. Damon never knew her mother, but Meri had said she was as dark as Damon and almost as tall. Meridia had to get her ochre skin and abbreviated stature from somewhere.

Damon had come to Temur almost a full passage ago. After working four passages apprenticed to a photographer in Benbridge, far to the south of Temur, he'd finally decided it was time to strike out on his own. He was good at what he did and confident he could make a living at it. He'd secured a property just outside the Temur town center that included what had once been a reasonably well-equipped photographic shop. Much of the paraphernalia was still there, stacked haphazardly in a back closet, some of it broken, but most of it salvageable. The place had most recently been a shop for the restoration of wood furniture. It still smelled of glue and wax.

Before the Great Fires, people had been accustomed to photographs printed on paper, but these days they demanded more durable media. Damon's stock in trade was his technique of printing on ceramic plates and tiles. He was skilled at it and people liked it, coming to him in steady streams for photographs of their old people, their sick family members, someone who was moving away to another town—anyone they thought might soon be gone forever.

In the back of his studio, beneath some discarded containers, Damon had discovered a metal box full of the old-style prints on paper. They were scorched along their edges but still showed clear images of babies and birth anniversaries and ceremonies subsuming young women to young men—all kinds of celebrations. These days, it was only the sadness of parting that people commemorated with photographs.

Damon had been glad to leave Benbridge. His parents were both dead, and he had no other family, nothing to tie him. His apprenticeship had made him kinren to his Sidayen mentor, though he doubted the man adhered very assiduously to the principles of the Sidaya. "Sidayen" was just a status these days rather than a matter of faith or practice. Becoming independent from his mentor, Damon would be able to claim Sidayen status for himself. Or rather, as a man, the status would fall to him, whether or not he subsumed a woman or took servants or apprentices of his own. His own kinren. More important than status to Damon was the fact that he'd be able to pursue his own admittedly idiosyncratic interests more freely. Benbridge had become an unpleasant place to live, ruled as it was by a faction headed by Zibal Palinj. His cultish followers were called

Palinjians and Damon found them without exception to be hateful and arrogant.

The first time Damon saw Meridia, she'd been having an argument with a shopkeeper, a leading Sidayen, about something or other. Or rather, she was standing there muttering and stammering while the Sidayen lectured her on simple math. When Damon looked at her—not straight on, but a bit to one side—he could see not only quivering waves but well-defined, pulsing spheres of red and orange bouncing and bursting around her. He'd never seen a display quite like it. Damon knew most ordinary people didn't see such things at all. Or at least if they did, they didn't mention it. Damon usually didn't mention it either.

Urged by his sympathetic heart, Damon had gone to Meridia's rescue, attempting to intervene on her behalf with the shopkeeper. She didn't seem to appreciate it. She tried to tell him she was on the verge of finding the right words and would've been able to take care of things. But even in telling him this, her words tripped over one another and got wrong way 'round. She thanked him politely and went on her way. Her brief words of gratitude had felt more like grudging forgiveness. Damon was intrigued by this Shoon woman, though, and he began to look for her whenever he was out and about.

Now they are planning to be in one another's company for a full six or maybe longer. Damon understands why Meridia has always claimed to hate traveling. Out there she's only a Shoon. Here in Temur at least people knew her mother, even though, as she says, she and her mother were nobody.

Damon doesn't share the prejudice against Shoons (or at least he tries not to) and he thinks it's because of Oriel, the man who worked on his parents' farm when Damon was a boy. Oriel taught Damon all kinds of fascinating things about plants and animals. The man had a stringed instrument and sometimes Damon would hide and listen to him playing and singing in the evenings. Oriel's songs felt more like stories, and even though Damon cannot now recall any of the words of the songs, he still remembers some of the characters as vividly as if they were someone he'd met in real life. Oriel didn't stay long. The other kinren made no secret of their resentment of this Shoon's presence. Damon missed him when he left. He missed him for a long time. There were hardly any Shoons in Benbridge, where Damon's family moved after their farm burned.

Oriel was the one who had explained to Damon about destiny stones. "Boys of your kind, sons of Sidayens, always go out in search of their destiny on the day marking the twelfth passage since their birth. They have to find a stone that speaks to them."

"Stones can't speak," Damon said, as he tried to ignore the pulsing pebbles in his pocket. But Oriel argued that they can indeed speak and that some of them can even sing a little bit.

Oriel's words came back to Damon when, on his twelfth birth anniversary, his father sent him out in search of his destiny. His family had left the farm behind by this time, so Damon wandered out of Benbridge, taking a path that led toward the Markham Clauster. He walked and wandered, listening as much as looking because of what Oriel had said. He hadn't been allowed to take any food along, only some water, so by midday he began to feel dizzy. Perhaps that was what made him hear that humming sound, but at the time he was convinced that it was coming from a smooth chunk of pale marble. Because he was hungry, he picked up the stone and took it home and told his father it was his destiny stone. Damon's father seemed pleased.

Damon started thinking about Oriel again after he met Meridia. He guessed that Oriel must have been half Shoon, too. Full-blood Shoon like Chapling have a clearer amber color to their skin whereas Meri is more of an ochre. Oriel had this crazy head of red-brown hair and eyes like spring goldiflor. Meri's eyes are like that.

Damon is eager to set out on this adventure with Meridia, but he's worried, too. There have been disturbing rumors from Fayredell about conflicts between the Palinjians and more traditional Sidayens, the ones still loyal to Prophet Amos Quint. Damon pushes such trepidations aside. In a six they'll be safely back in Temur with answers from Chapling about those extraordinary plates and the stone that affected Meridia so strongly. He looks forward to the break. His work printing photos of the soon-to-be-departed on ceramic tiles ticks along busily enough, but his work with biophotons has hit an impasse. The biophotonic imprints that he still believes he captured one time have begun to seem like nothing but flukes as he utterly fails to reproduce what he thought he'd done. The plates and the stone acquired from the old Shoon offer him a glimmer of hope.

6.

TURNING SOUTHWEST from Benbridge, Abél had approached Markham the first time on a clear fall day that felt more like Suntide. He moved in the margins, avoiding the attention of those who might object to the presence of an old Shoon like him near a sacred Palinjian precinct. He was searching for the Old Mica Benison, the great stone imbued with a song known as Calling the Rains. He hoped he might find it in Markham. Pieces of it, anyway. Were any of the old monuments whole anymore? Abél doubted it. He'd heard rumors of some pieces of mica being found near Markham. Perhaps placed in some of the cremation urns. And although the stories were vague, Abél found them plausible. So he'd come to see for himself.

Sometimes even Abél didn't know when a day was about to veer off in a different direction.

The Markham Clauster had been a monastery at one time, but there were no monks there now. Nobody took monastic vows anymore. Nobody kept them. For many returns the place had been little more than a subsidiary temple with a columbarium for the dead. The temple itself was seldom used except for some of the more esoteric rites of the Palinjians' inner circle. Under the leadership of Zibal Palinj, they had finally banned all kinren from temple precincts, reserving such places exclusively for Sidayens. So Abél was surprised to hear the murmur of women's voices from inside the walls as he approached.

He knew by the sound that they were in the garden; at least the women weren't violating the interior space of the temple sanctum. They were reciting poetry, their voices fluid and rhythmic. Abél strained to hear the words within the undulating cadence. Then one voice began to recite, braver and more melodious than the others. Abél was mesmerized as the voice of his own mother resounded in hers. This was one of Avienne's songs. The words this woman put to it were unfamiliar, but the song within it was the same. It was a Carnelian song, the Song of the Wide Path.

A shout intruded, and then a grumble of male voices, rising angrily. The woman's voice became louder, clearer, more resolute, as she continued reciting the notes of her story. The other women's voices stirred in alarm and there was the sound of scuffling.

Roused from his reverie, Abél searched frantically for a gate by means of which he might enter the temple grounds and perhaps put a stop to the impending violence. Or inflame it. He was a man, but not the right sort of man. Suddenly the voice of the poet strangled into silence. Abél's blood ran cold.

"You kinren go now," a deep voice commanded. "This sacred ground is forbidden to you. Go. And leave this traitor to her fate. She has brought this upon herself."

Abél sees the women, some nearly hysterical as they are hurried out, herded out, through a back gate. And then over his head comes the body of the poet, hurled unceremoniously out of the temple grounds and onto the path. Her body lands in a crumpled heap at his feet.

From the group of women hurrying away, one individual detaches herself and runs toward Abél.

"Keira! Keira!" she cries softly as she approaches. She falls to her knees and bends over the broken and lifeless body. The distraught woman's thick, coarse hair has escaped its bindings and curtains her face as she sobs.

Abél utters no words, instead humming a canopy of protection into existence so that this stranger might grieve for a moment in peace.

After a while her sobbing subsides, and she looks up at Abél as if seeing him for the first time. She studies him with squinting eyes and seems not at all put off by Abél's amber skin and frizz of straw-colored hair. "Did you know her, too?" she says.

"No, but I know the poem she was reciting."

"It was always her favorite." The woman tucks a handful of hair behind her ear and wipes her face on her sleeve. "She said it was part of her destiny, and that her mother knew the woman who composed it. Kinren have destinies, too, you know."

Abél saw then, in his mind, a group of pilgrims at the edge of a forest, brown and amber together, singing and telling poems. Two small boys at the feet of an amber woman listen and learn. "What was her name?"

"Keira. Keira Landry of Quint. I need to take her home so that her family can perform the rituals."

"And your name?" Abél needed to know. He wasn't sure why, but he heard the voice of his mother asking the question, so he spoke it.

"Vidvana," she said. She didn't say where she was from or who was her father or what Sidayen had subsumed her as wife. She didn't think that mattered.

"I can take her," Abél said, "if you trust me."

Vidvana looked at him truly then, and her eyes brimmed with trust.

And that is how Abél breth Avienne came to travel many fellspans taking the body of Keira Landry of Quint back to Fayredell, to her father Lambert Quint and to her grandfather, the great Prophet Amos Quint.

7.

TWO DAYS, AND MY BACKSACK is packed and ready. I sit on the front stoop, listening to the birds' dawn chorus, waiting for Damon. I scatter a few breadcrumbs and the birds descend, hungry. I wiggle my toes inside my sandals, admiring the thick new soles. A cat lurks around the corner; I chirp a quick warning to the birds. They drop crumbs and flutter up to the rafters and fenceposts, just higher than a cat can jump. Cat narrows his eyes at me, looks away, pretends he wasn't interested. Was too. I've seen him spit feathers.

Damon is coming. Tall and lean. Wavy dark hair bound into a braid at his neck. Rich brown skin like my mother's. His hat sits low on his face, looking as if it's held up by those bushy eyebrows. We exchange a smile and I shoulder my sack. We set out in the direction of Fayredell. I know this trip will take longer on account of my short legs. Damon can cover half again as much as me in a stride. He's unhurried. Patient.

As we leave Temur behind, the land undulates, barren and empty. Tufts of wiry grass occupy low spots. There's a scatter of bushes and an occasional solitary tree, sparsely covered in leathery leaves. We'll travel from spring to puddle to milparinka. Under the rocks and between the stones we'll find sufficient water to keep going. The road is dusty and soon I feel it hot right through my sandals.

Midday we stop where some other traveler has constructed a rough shelter. We rest in its welcome shade.

"How far do you think we've come?" I ask.

"Far enough. No need to push too hard. An extra day coming and going I'd accept easier than getting sick from exhaustion." I know he means me.

I brought some roots I know about and we keep pieces of them in our water sheaths. They give us more stamina, protect us from things in the water. It's called bitterroot and Damon calls the water bitterwater. Not so bitter, I think.

Drowsy, I rest my head on my backsack. Damon sits straight up. Keeping watch, he says.

"Watch for what?"

"For whatever's coming."

"Birds tell us that. Listen to the birds." There aren't so many birds in these barren stretches, but I hear them even at a distance. They're resting now.

"You understand the birds better than I do," he says. "I listen, but I feel like they never quite finish what they want to say. They just start over again."

"Nothing finishes," I say. "Everything goes on and on." I don't know why I say that, but I know it's right. I doze off, listening.

My eyes open to longer, sharper shadows. Birds have awakened from midday naps, too. I hear them chippering among themselves. Easy, colorful sounds.

Damon is on his feet, stretching long limbs, limber back. Not smiling.

"It's time we got back on the road," he says.

We drink from our sheaths, ready to go. Plod.

"Next milparinka should be only an hour or so. Drink what you need," he says.

We meet few people along the way. Once a cart pulled by an equid overtakes us and we choke and cough in the dust it raises in its wake. Another time someone on a pedaled vehicle passes by, going toward Temur. But most people are on foot like us. Simple greetings suffice as we pass.

"Good afternoon," Damon says.

"Fine afternoon," they say.

We never stop moving.

We pass a few paths leading out to old farmsteads and once I see a house in the distance. No crops, only open fields. Too dry for farming. No fences. No need for fences. This morning I saw a cavouti and just now a couple of cabras. All gone feral. People used to keep cabras for milk and cavoutis for the meat of their strong haunches. Cavoutis are not much bigger than a housecat but their meat is delicious.

My steps form an irregular syncopation alongside Damon's. I count. Five of my steps, and we both hit the left foot. Six more matches my right to his left. I hear a hawk cry overhead and I lose count.

"Did you hear it?" I ask.

"Was it a falcon?"

"Hawk. Bluetail. Are there trees near here? They never go far from nests."

"Not so very near, but not far. It's where we're headed for the night."

There will be woods. Leaves crunching into cool softness underfoot. Branches that creak and sway, taking breath from the wind. Photon showers filtered through shifting leaves. "I haven't been in a woods since Temur woods finished," I say. "So many passages ago." Even then there were burnt stumps dotting the spaces between trees.

"It must have been one of the last to go. How did it happen?"

"Cut for cooking mostly. Last few trees died isolated, coppiced. Windstorm took them." Mother cooked almost every day back then. Soups rich with meat and onions and garlic and savory herbs. Sweet delicate cakes. Yeast-fragrant breads baked in blazing ovens. Now almost everything's crunchy and cold. We cook only a few times during each stint, using communal stoves to save fuel. Flatbread mostly. Quick to cook. Hard to chew. Tea is all sun brewed.

Sun slips toward our left shoulders. Shadows stretch and dim.

"Do you see it?" Damon asks.

I look where he points. There are a few scrubby trees low on the horizon. Not exactly a woods. My feet and legs cry for rest and my head tweaks inside. Clothes cling wet with perspiration. I swing my water sheath around and slow my steps to take a drink.

"It'll be nearly dark by the time we get there," Damon says. "But no need to hurry. I know a good spot where we can sleep."

"You've been here before."

"I grew up near here. No town, of course, only our farm and a few others nearby. It's where we raised cavoutis and wilderfruit."

Lines of verdant trees heavy with brown fruit. Nittering striped creatures hopscotch below. Teeth dig into fallen fruit. Some spoiled sweet, soft, juicy, intoxicating. Some hard and sour and dry. A small boy sits on a low branch. "That was nice," I say. "Lots of trees to climb."

"My favorite thing."

By the time we reach the line of trees, the sun is below the horizon. Sepia light without shadows. Not much cooler beneath the paltry foliage. I follow Damon. His feet are confident. Mine try to remember walking in woods, stepping higher over roots and fallen branches. A few birds make familiar roosting noises. I always went home at dark. Always going out of the woods, never in.

Damon stops as we enter a space sheltered by three scrawny acorn trees and a half dozen meskies. There are charred stumps. He pauses, surveying, and then sheds the pack from his back.

"The place is changed from what I remember," he says. "This was at the edge of where the fires came through." He's sad for the trees that are no longer there. "Looks as if even these survivors have been cut one too many times. That one won't survive another season. On our farm, we tried to protect the trees and took to burning fireblocks instead of wood."

Fireblocks are made from waste stuff. Manure, grass, all kinds of things, soaked in groundfat and bound up tight. They smell awful, but they burn hot.

Damon takes a sheet from his pack and unfolds it, spreads it across a flat piece of ground.

"I'd rather sleep in the grass," I say. Soft grass. Fragrant, dew-wet. Cool. I look down at sparse clumps of dry yellow-brown grass.

He chuckles. "That would be risky. There are billbugs galore. Used to be anyway. They may still come out at night looking for blood." His eyes open wide and his brows twitch, trying to frighten me.

I shrug. Billbugs are no bigger than a silphy seed. How much blood could they need? My arm itches, remembering. I'll sleep on the sheet.

"Do you have water?" Damon asks. "There used to be a spring nearby. Better if we can wait until morning to go there. I'll share with you if need be."

We each eat a few mooli root and some of the nutbread I brought. I take a second sheet from my pack and we lie down and pull it up to our chins. Not for warmth. It's still too warm and will be all night long. It's for protection. There could be more than billbugs.

The ground is not as flat as it appears, and I rearrange my body several times before it rests. In the distance a patkány screams into the night and I listen for answering yelps. There are none and I relax. Patkánies only attack in packs. Or in defense. My eyes close and at last I melt into the freedom of sleep-space.

The fragrance of ripe wilderfruit fills my head. The sun is warm, not hot, on bare arms and legs. Its light catches on the evaporating dewdrops outlining a spider's web. Grass is soft on calloused brown feet. Butterflies gather, sucking the last juice from an abandoned wilderfruit core. A russet raven croaks from a high branch.

I run barefoot among the trees, chasing a sniggering cavouti. I won't catch it. I never do. They're no faster than I, only quicker as they twist and turn, hopping, leaping. My quarry dashes around me to the right as I lean left. I drop to my knees, laughing. I turn and see him stop, looking at me, teasing. I spring to my feet and take off again. He darts into a hole under some rocks. I have him now, silly creature. I plunge my hand into the hole. At the same moment that I see him bound away the other side, I feel a sharp pain in my wrist. I jerk my hand back. There are two dots, oozing blood. I stumble backward, holding my left hand over the holes. What did Father say to do for snakebite? I don't remember. Go home. Father will know. Mother will know. Go home. I run. Careless, my foot catches on a root and I fall. Get up. Hurry. Go home. My ankle hurts. First step I hear a pop and fall again. Get up. Hurry. So much pain.

My eyes are open. The image remains. A little boy lies in the grass clutching his arm, breath coming hard, eyes wild. He tries to sit up. He gags, shoulders hunch as he retches. He falls back. His eyes close, oozing tears. *Damon. Damon, wake up!*

"Damon!" My cry shakes the stars overhead.

Damon startles and sits up, wild-eyed. His hand covers his mouth. We reach for one another in the starlight.

"I'd forgotten," he says.

8.

WE SLEEP THE REST OF THE NIGHT wrapped around one another. We wake together but I lie still, waiting. The air glows. Not quite dawn.

Damon rises and soon I hear his piss on the leaves, out of sight. I go the opposite way and squat next to a bush. A rivulet traces its way downhill, turning dry leaves shiny gold, redolent with my scent.

Damon is folding our covering sheet. I take the food packet down from the branches where we stored it overnight. Jerk meat and nutbread. And bitterwater.

"Were you really snake bit as a child?" I ask.

"It would seem so. But if it happened, it's something I'd forgotten. How could I forget something like that? You saw it too?"

"Not saw. I was there. It was me. I was you."

Damon frowns, trying to understand what I'm saying. Trying to hold onto the images. "I'm wondering how old I must have been when that happened. What do you think? Maybe five?"

I'm not good at such guessing. "That could be," I say.

"It's already fading for me. It's almost like it's something I'm not supposed to know about. You hold the memory for me now, though. I'm grateful for that." He pauses. "I guess it was being back in a place I know from long ago that made me remember."

I don't think that's it, but I don't know for sure, so I say nothing. I tell myself he could be right.

We pass the second day much like the first. We meet no one on the road all morning. We start again after resting midday.

"Someone's coming our way," Damon says. "A whole group of travelers."

I rise up as tall as I can and look down the road. They look so small in the distance. Dust hangs in the air behind them. I can make out two Sidayens and several kinrens, two of them only children.

"Why do you suppose such a large group would be traveling somewhere?" Damon asks.

"Odd," I say.

"They look to be carrying heavy packs, too. They must be going on a long journey. A distant journey. Or at least they're expecting to be gone for a long while."

"Be careful," I say softly, as we and they draw closer together. "They're not pleased to see us."

"Good morning," Damon calls out when they're close enough to hear. He stops, hoping they'll do the same. "Are you coming from Fayredell?"

My feet want to keep moving, but I stop. I retrace a couple of steps to stand close to Damon.

"Fine morning," the lead man grumbles. He's older than the other Sidayen. Older than either of the two women. One is kinren, the other Shoon. I see that the Shoon woman is holding a nen, wrapped close to her body. The younger man has taken the smaller of the two children on his back. She's barely more than a nen herself. They're all tired. Anxious.

The man doesn't want to say more. "From Fayredell, yes." His voice growls flat and colorless. His eyes remain fixed on the road ahead, wanting to move on. The woman with the nen glances back down the road behind them. She has tawny skin like me. I want to offer her a smile, but she won't look.

"We're searching for a trader you might have met in Fayredell. They say he's called Chapling."

I try to sort out the different things they're feeling. They're annoyed. Some are frightened. There's anger, too. The woman with the nen holds it closer. The older man's thoughts try to recede behind a dark veil. "That name is not one I know," he lies.

"Well, thank you anyway," Damon says. "We wish you good journey."

At last the man looks at us. His eyes rest on me. Sad. "Good journey to you. Go carefully."

"Go carefully," we reply, our words not quite matching.

They move off in the direction we've come from, their steps quicker than before.

Damon sets a faster pace, too.

"Odd bunch," he mumbles.

"They were frightened," I say. "Some of them angry."

"I thought so. But what were they frightened of? You and I are not exactly a terrifying apparition." He laughs quietly and re-centers the pack on his back. "I think they may be Chanters."

"Why do you say that?" I don't know much about Chanters, though I've heard talk of them. People say they're barely better than Shoons.

"Did you see the wrap the old man had around his wrist?"

"Yes." I call it to mind. It was strips of cloth or maybe leather, all knotted together with some orange-red beads.

"Chanters wear wraps like that. The knots are supposed to mean something."

I think the red beads mean more. "The man lied about Chapling. He knows something."

"I thought as much. Maybe we should be more cautious in our inquiries."

"Did you see the one woman who looks like me? The one with the nen?"

"I don't pay much attention to such things. But, yes. I saw."

"She was the most frightened. She was frightened for her nen." I want to say more but the words won't come. Women like her, women like me, we're not supposed to be able to have nens. Everyone knows we're infertile except with our own kind. "Do you think it really was her own nen, Damon?" He knows what I mean.

"I guess that would be unusual," he says. Damon won't say anything more, but I know he's worried.

I want to go back and beg the woman to unwrap the nen so I can look at it. Does it look like her? We plod on.

"Why are they called Chanters?" I can't stop thinking about the travelers.

"Because they chant." Damon laughs. "Supposedly they believe that there's some kind of power in groups of people speaking the same words together. The same words, over and over. Not like the anthems you hear in the temples or the ballads people sing in the brewhouses.

There were some Chanters who lived near Benbridge, off the road leading to the old clauster at Markham. I used to like listening to them. Their chants were nice."

Another fellspan down the road and we stop at a puddle for water. It's cloudy.

"They stopped here, too. Water hasn't settled out," I say.

"No matter. We need the water. That's what the mud filters are for, right?"

We fill our sheaths, trying not to disturb the water further, and affix the filters.

"Where do we stop tonight?" My sore legs make me think of stopping.

"We should look for a place soon. I don't know this area, so we need to start watching. We'll stop when we see a good place, even if it's still early."

"I heard a canyon wren. A canyon could give us some protection." Hard rocks and pebbles pressing into my hips and shoulders. It won't be easy sleeping.

We find a dry creek bed below a high bluff. A stingy spring drips water from a crack in the rock. Travelers before us have rigged up a ledge where a water sheath can be attached to collect the drips. Good water comes slow.

There's a raggedy nutcone tree and Damon clears a space for us to sleep next to it. I find a few cones and shell out half a handful of nuts. We sit on the groundsheet and eat our supper.

"I need to ask you something," I say, trying to fathom what I'm about to ask, uncertain why I want to ask it.

Damon nods and looks attentive. He takes a swig of water from his sheath and hands it to me. Mine is on the ledge, collecting fresh drops.

I hold the sheath in my hands. "Where's the rock?" I start with that.

He knows what rock I'm talking about. "It's in my pack. I thought I should bring it along. To show to Chapling if we ever find him. It might jog his memory about where he acquired it."

"I want to put it in my pack," I say. "Only for tonight."

"You think that's why I dreamed what I did last night?"

"Wasn't a dream."

"No, I guess it was something more than that. So you want to protect me from more nightmares? From remembering anything else that might terrify us both?" He's smiling. Mischievous. Hiding his concern.

"Partly. Let's say I'm curious."

"It's an experiment, then. Okay."

I try not to look directly at the rock as he takes it from his own backsack and places it in mine. But I see flashes of something in my peripheral. I shiver, anticipating.

Darkness closes around us and we settle side-by-side, not quite touching. I rearrange the backsack under my head, feeling for the rock inside. Are my eyes closed? I see lights. Lights of all colors.

She emerges from within the light, takes form from the light.

Hands dancing, tracing patterns in the air. Hips swaying, head erect. A river of colored light coils around her. Fireseed sparks at her crown, forehead, throat, and palms. I hear her voice, like the song of a lulark. She sings and I melt away. All night long she sings to me, the same song, time after time. A song without words. Painting a world beyond words.

I stand high on an outcrop and the song becomes mine. It bursts forth, more powerful than anything I've known. It comes not only from my throat, but from some deeper place inside and it soars higher than the trees that surround me. The trees sing, too, in glorious chorus. This song has no words, but I think I know what it's about. It's about everything. As we sing, the colors swirl, reaching out in every direction, carrying me along all the paths of their undulating brilliance. I am the colors, the light. Birds gather in the trees, joining their voices with mine. We sing and sing.

"Meri! Meri, be careful. Come down!" It's Damon's voice. Its deep resonance pulls me earthward.

I open my eyes, the ones that see the ordinary world. There are no trees, no birds. I see where I stand, high on a rock, perilously high, facing the rising sun.

Damon is frightened.

I smile his fear away as I glide down the steep side of the rock. Weightless, I run to his arms. He holds me as the song echoes in my head, reverberates through my body. I tremble, wavering like heat rising from a distant landscape. Damon's arms give me substance. I step back and hand the rock to him, the rock I still clutch in my right hand.

We walk back to our camping place. At the spring he stops to retrieve my water sheath. It overflows. The drip has become a steady stream pouring down the rock and onto the earth below, offering itself to the parched ground. We both drink deeply from the water sheath and fill it again.

Damon puts an arm around me and pulls me close. My head rests against his shoulder; he kisses my hair. "I have no idea what this is about," he says, "but this morning you are the most beautiful woman in all the world."

9

ABÉL WRAPPED Keira's broken and bloodied body in a sheet and placed it in the back of his cart, hiding it among baskets of the small household goods that he sold from one town to the next as a way of explaining his wanderings. He also enveloped it in a cloak of blue-white light that produced a faint layer of frost along the bottom side of his baskets. He hoped no one would notice that.

He was troubled by the violence he had witnessed. He knew about the rivalry between different factions of Sidayens and their mounting hostility toward Shoons such as himself. But Keira Landry of Quint was no Shoon. She was the granddaughter of a recognized prophet. Had the one who attacked her known who she was? Abél couldn't answer that.

Somewhere he had heard the name Vidvana before encountering the woman of that name in Markham. He thought she might be someone his mother had told him about, and he tried to remember what it was she'd told. It felt like something important.

Instead of the well-travelled road from Markham through Benbridge to Fayredell, Abél took another route, a way known only to people such as himself, existing only for such people. It was slower, but it skirted Benbridge and avoided difficulties. It used to be a track through the great southern forest of Cesta, back when Cesta extended all the way from the forest of Cödweg in the east to Serani in the west. Back when there was forest all the way across. Now the path wended its way inconspicuously among stands of bushes and along dusty old stream beds.

The cart had only two wheels and Abél had to pull it himself. With the added weight of the woman's body in it, one wheel or the other kept getting lodged in the sand or between stones and stumps. Abél sang some songs that he knew, trying to make the way easier but the necessity of keeping the preservation cloak in place made it almost impossible. He added another half day to his estimate of how long it would take to reach Fayredell.

His intention was to arrive at night so as not to attract attention. As it happened, it was nearing daybreak when Fayredell finally came into view and by the time he found the residence of the Quint House the sun was oozing faint pinks and orange onto the horizon. He knew the front gate would not be available to him, so he made his way to the back.

"Stop there, peddler," the guard said. The man was tall and looked strong, in a wiry sort of way, his dark skin pocked by some old illness. He sounded as if he'd just awakened.

"I'm bringing a package from Benbridge to your masters, Sidayens Amos and Lambert Quint," Abél said.

"Give it to me then and be off with you."

"That won't be possible. The package is rather large and comes with a message that must be relayed in person."

The guard yawned. "Well, I'll ask the Sidayens if they'll accept what you bring."

"Give them this," Abél said, handing the kinren guard a silver bauble he'd taken from the ear of the dead woman.

The guard let the object rest in his open hand. "I don't think a bribe this small will do much good," he said, looking up at Abél as if expecting something more. Then he shrugged and made his way up the path to the rear door of the great house.

The Quint House was the grandest in all of Fayredell, the only remaining wooden structure in the entire town. The fact that it had been spared when the Great Fires swept through had contributed in no small measure to the rise of Amos Quint as a revered prophet. *Better than that idiot Zibal Palinj*, Abél thought. Why people in Benbridge honored Palinj so highly was a mystery to him. If it was true that the New Obsidian was his destiny stone, it was also clear that he had corrupted the intent of its Song of Embracing Death. That song was intended to be about a peaceful, natural end of life, but now it had been infected with a more sinister meaning. Rumor had it that, here in Fayredell, Keira's own husband Rolang Landry had been converted to the Palinjian cult. Abél hoped to avoid any encounter with Rolang Landry.

Shortly the guard returned. He opened the gate and motioned for Abél to enter. "The master is just rising and will accept your visit after prayers. He says I'm to keep an eye on you so I guess you can come in and have some tea and bread." The guard looked perplexed and kept glancing at the cart.

"Thank you but I'd prefer to stay here," Abél said.

The guard grunted. "Suit yourself." He went back inside, returning a few moments later with a mug and a plate. There was an instant of open curiosity on the guard's face, a look almost of comradeship, that made

Abél wonder if the man might belong to one of the weftreds, the secret networks that passed rumors and gossip among kinrens. The weftreds often included Chanters.

Abél sat on the ground, leaning against a wheel, and stretched out his legs. It felt good to stretch. The tea was sweet and the bread heavy with bits of dried fruit and nuts. Abél consumed it all, sending gratitude to the guard and the cook and all the other kinren of the House of Quint. He was aware of the guard watching him, seated in the kitchen, peering through a curtained window.

The guard came out again as the sun was sending its first beams into the upper limbs of a dead peppertree in the enclosed yard. Amos and Lambert Quint's prayers hadn't taken as long as Abél had expected. Perhaps they'd cut them short.

"You can come now. And bring your package with you."

"I'll require a little help with that," Abél said. The body was well wrapped but as they lifted it, the guard could tell what it was. He didn't like it. He didn't like how cold it felt. But he said nothing.

Amos and Lambert Quint were waiting. Father and son sat with regal composure in oversized wooden chairs next to a long table. Lambert's delicate features contracted into a scowl when he saw Abél. The guard hadn't mentioned that the messenger was a Shoon. His pale brown eyes widened as Abél and the guard laid their burden down on the table. Abél began uncovering the body, starting with the face.

"Oh, my precious Keira!" Lambert cried, throwing himself upon the body, embracing his daughter's cold and lifeless form.

Amos stood apart, bearing his sadness in silence, his lips twitching with restrained grief.

Lambert looked up at Abél in sudden alarm. "Does her husband know?"

"I've told no one but you," Abél said.

"Then you should go at once, because he's due to arrive here soon and he will surely hold you to blame. Can you tell us how this happened?" It was impossible to miss the injury to Keira's neck.

"It happened at the Markham Clauster. Your daughter was with some other women reciting poems and songs inside the grounds. They were doing no harm. I didn't see whose hand took her life."

"I tried to warn her." Lambert's voice was wracked with misery as he brushed back wisps of hair from his daughter's face. "I tried so often to warn her to keep to herself, to let the chanting and poetry go. But she persisted. Tell me no more. It doesn't matter. She'll be held guilty of her own death in the eyes of the Palinjians who hold sway in Benbridge."

In his mind, Abél heard Amos say, *And here in Fayredell, too, of late*. He's wondering who will convey the sad news to Keira's daughter.

Abél stepped back from the table. "I'll take my leave then. My task is done. I promised her friend I would bring her here and here she is. Home."

But Abél knew that Keira considered the town of Woodclasp to be her true home. Her mother's town, the town where she was birthed. That is where Abél would go next. But first he went to Amos and touched his hand, placing into it an Amethyst stone to offer him comfort and hope.

10.

I HUM THE SONG softly to myself. My legs no longer ache. Breath comes easily and I hardly feel the sun. Damon doesn't ask about what happened, about what the green rock showed me. I think he knows that I have no answer. Maybe Chapling will have an answer. Today we will reach Fayredell.

I ask Damon, "How much farther do you think?"

"At this pace, we should arrive well before sundown, even with a good midday break."

We take only a short rest after lunch and then resume our journey. We're seeing more gallekrels, more sandy pips. The kinds of birds that prefer the convenience of towns.

"I see it," Damon announces. His extra height gives him a moment's advantage over me. "And there's a bothy up ahead, too. With a sign. It looks like a place where we might get a meal."

My stomach rumbles. Fresh bread. Maybe soup.

It's a plain sort of place, built of earth like everything else. Walls a patchwork, repaired many times over with different colored earth. There's a broad porch sheltered from the sun. The sign is one even I can read. It says, "Food & Drink."

The floor inside is level with the ground outside. It's the same ground. I blink as my eyes adjust to the dim. Greyed curtains flutter in the breeze at open windows. The place is fragrant with cooking.

The woman behind the counter puts on a stiff smile. She studies me and glances toward the door. She's not much taller than me, dark and slender and wide-eyed as a child. Her hair is an unnatural shade of deep purple, its curls coerced into two rough plaits. She wishes us a good day, but she sounds doubtful.

"Fine day to you, keeper," Damon says.

We sit at the bar on stools with seats made of worn leather.

There's no one here but the woman. She squints toward us. "I'm Rita," she says. "Rita Harper. And you?"

"I'm Damon Mikelson."

"Meridia Einkorn," I say. The Einkorn part is what Mother gave me. My mother, Madelyn Einkorn.

Rita Harper points to a framed handwritten menu behind glass.

"How about the bread stuffed with meat and onions?" Damon asks. I nod and he orders that for both of us.

Rita offers wine and we accept. It comes in tiny glasses that honor its preciousness. The wine is sweet and goes down warm and gentle. A few minutes later she brings in two plates. Is that steam rising from the food?

The stuffed bread is delicious and comes with a pile of greens seasoned with peppers and vinegar. I close my eyes, savoring the memory of such meals. Mother always put in too much garlic. This is perfect.

Rita wipes her hands on a threadbare apron and leans against the counter. "Where are you pilgrims coming from?" she asks. "From the looks of you, I'd say you're about three days from home." She laughs but her eyes are solemn.

I'm not sure what she means by "pilgrims." When she said it, it almost sounded like a joke. Or an insult.

"We're coming from Temur," Damon says. "Three days is right. We expect to pass tonight in Fayredell."

"Is that so?" she asks, looking at me with narrowed eyes. Her gruff voice grows softer. "We have a room here where you could stay. Out back. Away off the road."

Damon looks at me for approval. I nod. My tired legs relax a bit.

"I'll show you," Rita says. "My Sidayen husband will be back shortly. You come with me, Meridia. Your man can stay here." She hurries me out a side door.

We walk through a shady canopy of surprisingly green trees that I don't recognize. "What kind of trees are these?"

"They're a variety of chincha. My mother brought the seeds from up north where it had already turned drier than here. They're doing well, don't you think? Did you see my laurel over there past the well? Crispin fusses at how much water I waste on her, but she's such a pretty thing." She's smiling as she reaches out to caress a low hanging branch.

The room is far back. It isn't much, but it's shelter. There are hammocks.

"Is Temur your home?" she asks. "I'm thinking your friend is originally from somewhere else. By the way he speaks."

"Yes, I was born in Temur. Never lived anywhere else. Damon's been there most of a passage." I don't say where he's from.

Rita looks thoughtful. There's something she wants to ask. "I've always heard Temur is a nice town, even though I've never been there. What work does your House have there?"

Houses belong to Sidayens. To fathers and husbands. I refuse to say that I have none. "My mother was a teacher," I say. "She's gone now. I mostly make my way taking care of sick folks. There's always sick people needing care."

"That's true." Rita scowls and looks at me sideways. "And your father?"

This is what she wants. She already knows. She's being mean.

"Gone long since." I say only that.

Rita doesn't answer, but there's an odd buzzing in my head that tries to resolve into the contours of something I can't quite catch. "You should stay here," she says. "If my Sidayen husband Crispin sees you, he'll send the both of you packing. And I can see you're tired from the road. It'll be okay as long as you stay here in the room."

I don't stay. After she leaves, I walk back to the bothy, but I don't go inside. I lean against the wall next to a window and I listen. Crispin is there, and he's talking to Damon. I peek at him through the curtain. He's tall with hair slicked into a tight plait. Razor-scrubbed face. He's even darker than Damon. Stiff, rigid. I think it's because of his battered body. He wears a faded, checkered shirt, sleeves rolled up almost to the elbow. Shirt buttoned tight over his thin chest, buttoned right up to his neck.

"This place looks like it's been here for quite some time," Damon says. "You must know this area well. Have you always lived here?"

Crispin adds another few drops to Damon's wine glass. "Answering that is going to require a bit of telling." His laugh is a deep rumble as he leans his arms against the bar. He winces and stands up straight again. "I haven't always been as I am now, though I was born here. My parents ran a proper inn when I was a boy. A bigger place, with six rooms for guests, wood floors, nice furniture. Stairs to an upper floor and more down to a cellar. We were a House of five. I had an older brother and a younger sister. The blaze came in the third passage of the Great Fires and it came right through the last of the forest here and took our place with it. I'd barely completed twelve passages. That was the first time I died."

I sense Damon's astonishment. I swallow mine into silence.

"That may require some explanation," Damon says. "What happened?"

"The fire was all around us, so we children took shelter in the cellar. My parents kept trying to protect the building and they were caught, surrounded, burnt up. I remember choking, struggling to breathe, fighting for the last air in a low spot on the floor, then going to sleep. Next thing I knew, I was awake again in a strange house, alone in a dark room. I started to call out for help and when the woman came in, she was all shouting and crying about miracles. They told me I was dead when they brought me in. My brother and sister were lying on the floor near me. They were still dead."

I listen to his story, but I don't sense anything behind his words. Strange. As if it's someone else's story.

"There you go, telling your story again." Rita's laugh is high-pitched and nervous.

"He asked," Crispin says.

"Well go ahead, then." She knows he does this with certain strangers. He tries to convince them of something.

My heart beats faster and my breath goes shallow.

Crispin is speaking again. "We buried my brother and sister here on the land, along with what bones we could find of our parents. The family that took me in couldn't bear any more burning for a proper cremation. They helped rebuild this place, but only as big as it is today. They had a daughter."

Rita takes up the story. "He was an odd one," she says. "When we first took him in, he'd talk about things that he couldn't possibly know about, being from right here local like he was." She stops. She's not sure how much to tell.

Crispin's voice again. "Rita was always kind to me, but we didn't get close until after the next time it happened. This time we'd been playing out by the old well, just Rita and me, and she'd brought along a little grampo pup that someone had given her. When the pup fell into the well, she climbed in to save it. There was more water in that old well than she thought. She started hollering, so I jumped in to help her."

Crispin is laughing, so I think this time there's a happy ending. I'm still trying to catch the story. Something is clouding my senses.

"Well, wouldn't you know, we both drowned. One of the kinren pulled us out and neither of us was breathing. No heartbeat, nothing. Dead. But he worked on us a bit and first me and then Rita, we started to breathe again, puking up that rank well water. The funniest part was that the grampo had somehow held on and when they pulled him out, he was fine. But that's when I knew I was going to subsume this woman," he says. "A woman is hardly ever able to accomplish what my Rita did. She has a strong will."

I'm beginning to understand. They have the vision, but not like me. More like Damon. But not exactly like that either. I strain to understand.

"But that wasn't my last time," Crispin says. "Three passages back I was helping some neighbors rebuild a house and the ridgepole slipped from its moorings and fell right across my chest. By the time they got it off me, I'd stopped breathing. No heartbeat, nothing. Dead. Again. Rita was crying and shouting at me to come back. Yes, I heard all of it. Every bit. So I came back. But it wasn't me exactly. For a six or so, I knew I was more than Crispin Harper. But then I settled into being the man you see before you. I still call myself Crispin Harper. I *am* still Crispin Harper. But Crispin Harper is not *all* of who I am."

"You needn't add all of that," Rita says softly. She thinks he's showing off.

"I think this man here understands," Crispin says.

Damon pushes his empty plate away and wipes his mouth with the napkin. He's skeptical about Crispin's story. No, suspicious. But he'll let it pass.

"You're traveling alone are you?" Crispin says.

There's a sharp intake of breath from Rita. "Would you like anything more to eat?" she says. "We could pack you some bread and pickled mooli root. Everybody says my pickled mooli root is the best. I know you're likely tired from your journey. I'll show you to the room where you can stay. It'll be getting dark soon."

"Thank you for that." Damon hesitates a few more seconds. "We're going to need some supplies in town. Is there a market there?"

Crispin frowns. "There's a market on the southwest edge of town. Sometimes." He picks up a chart from behind the bar and studies it. "Yes, it should be open tomorrow. Traders come there from all around. They're a mixed lot and generally welcoming, although there's no guarantee you'll find what you're looking for on any given day." He sets the chart down. "But you said 'we.' So you're not traveling alone. Who's with you?"

"Already gone to the shelter to rest. I saw to that," Rita says.

"Rita met Meridia." Damon is confused. I'm understanding more and more.

Crispin sees at last. "A Shoon? A Shoon whore?" He roars at Rita. Then he turns to Damon. "That's who you're traveling with? And looking for another of 'em in Fayredell. Chapling!" He spits on the ground. I hear all of this. And even though my eyes are tight shut, I see it. He strikes Rita, calls her a sully kinren. She begins to cry.

"She's just a woman tired from the road, Crispin. And only half Shoon. Her mother was people." Rita whimpers like a beat pup.

I run back to the shelter to collect my pack. We won't be staying here tonight. Why is Crispin like this? And why would he want Damon's rock? No! I shouldn't even have thought that. At least I didn't think of its hiding place in Damon's backsack. Oh!

A cave. Filled with rocks of all shapes and sizes. Ordinary rocks. Falling, rolling into crevices and pits. Shattering against one another. A cascade, a stampede of rocks.

I'm already well down the road when Damon catches up to me. I'm no longer tired. Shame and anger energize me.

"I'm so sorry, Meri. I had no idea it could be this bad. He has no right treating you like that, calling you names. I guess living in a smaller place like Temur made me forget."

But even in Temur it happens. "Nothing I haven't heard before," I say as I scrub the tears from my face. "Crispin is dangerous. I should've seen that. Rita isn't so bad. She would've let us stay."

"Crispin wanted the rock, too, I think. Though I'm not sure how he knew about it." He stops, sighs. "Why do I ask such questions? What do you suppose he wants with it? We don't even really know what it is yet. Only that it's somehow able to hold images."

He wants it because he thinks it's important to Shoons like me. Is that it? He thinks Shoons use it to harm people like him. He calls it a banestone. He hates me because of what I am. He hates Damon for not hating me. We need to keep moving.

"Crispin told me this weird tale about how he'd died and come back," Damon says.

"I heard."

"Do you think it was the truth? Could all that happen like he said? Crispin acted like it was some great achievement, like he ought to be admired for it."

I have nothing to say. I don't admire anything about Crispin Harper.

"I'd heard stories before, but nothing first-hand." Damon falls silent, thinking.

It's almost dark, but we walk on. He tries to cheer me by telling about Fayredell, painting it for me with his words. Dusty streets, wider than in Temur or Brightlea. Some buildings have staircases and upstairs rooms. Wooden furniture from long ago. He doesn't mention the people who hate Shoons. The people like Crispin. There are many more like him in Fayredell.

As Damon speaks, he takes the rock from his pack. It's still wrapped in cloth and I try not to look at it, try not to think it. He says nothing. He wants me to take it. I tuck it inside my blouse, under my left breast. The brightness of it almost stops my breath. It's warm.

I mustn't think about the rock.

I had a kitten when I was a girl. I slept with him next to me. Warm and soft. I'd wake with his tongue scraping my cheek. At breakfast he rubbed against my legs under the table. I saved milk for him. I kept him fed so the birds were safe.

Damon walks fast and soon I'm struggling to keep up. My legs remember how many fellspans we've already walked. I try to recall the lady's song and a vibrant warmth radiates through me. I float on a river of color and silent song.

"It's okay, Meri. No need to keep running." It's Damon's voice. His hand on my shoulder pulls me down. Pulls me back. The colors melt into the earth. Song becomes a whisper. The still air vibrates all around me.

He's speaking again. "There's a rock formation over here where we can rest out of sight for a while. I don't think Crispin is following us. I feel like he just wanted us gone. We should be safe."

He's right. Almost right. They're sleeping. Waiting.

The place Damon found is good. Tall rocks. Broken ground riddled with crevices, deep and wide. Once there was a vast forest rising and a stream surging through a canyon. White flowers like fallen stars in the moonlight.

I take the rock from inside my blouse and put it into my backsack. I look again. No forest. No stream. No flowers. Moonlight on a few twisted bushes and bare rocks. Darkness collects in the depths of the crevices. Damon spreads the sheet and we settle. I rest my head on my backsack and close my eyes.

The forest is magnificent. Scent of pine. Branches creak and sigh overhead. Bed of soft pinefall. The soothing murmur of a stream. In the distance, a rumbling. Leaving my clothes on the bank, I walk toward the stream and wade into its cool water. Tiny creatures nibble at my toes and ankles. Raindrops splash cool on my skin. I find a deeper pool and dive into it. Water covers me. So much water. I blow bubbles and they burst, each a clear note, a vivid color. The rain is full of laughter. Even the trees laugh. A night fowl chuckles from high in a tree and then falls suddenly silent.

Everything silent.

My eyes fly open. *Damon. Where is Damon?*

I sit upright, probing the pale landscape. Silence. Stillness and silence.

Then a tumble of rocks. A shout.

"Run, Meri!"

Damon!

"Run!"

I grab my backsack and stand. Run where? Sounds of a scuffle. As I clutch the backsack to my breast, I notice a dark opening in a rockface. I run toward it.

Hot tears sting my eyes. I choke back screams of anger, sobs of impotence. *Silence, Meridia. Run. Hide.*

There it is. It's not a cave. Only a small overhang. Not enough. At one end it leads downward. A sheltered niche. Walls too steep. Too far to jump or fall. I grab a branch that lies on the ground nearby, test its strength, lay it across the top of the crevice. Holding tight, I lower myself into the niche and bring the branch in with me. Voices. Shuffle of feet. I swallow everything into silence, eyes closed, barely breathing, heart thumping hard and fast.

"No, this isn't where we hid it. It's a bit farther on." Damon's voice. More shuffling feet.

"Why do I think you're lying to us?" Crispin's voice. He's holding Damon's arms behind his back. He shoves and Damon stumbles.

I force my mind to fly away. Up out of the rock shelter. High above the forest. I know what I mustn't think about and I try not to know. Fly higher. Clouds. Trees. Birds of all sorts. Some I've never seen before. I settle among them. They'll hide me. We peck at seeds, twittering, whistling, leaping. Innocence dissolves fear. A noise and we rise, fluttering up as one into the trees. I see who made the noise and launch alone into the sky. *Run, Meri. Hide.* Be quiet. No, quieter than that. I perch in the top of the tallest tree and gaze skyward. The sky is vast, empty, quiet. I go there. I linger.

Willful quietness settles into true silence. Still I linger.

Sharp stones press into my back and buttocks. I'm clinging stiffly to the far wall of the niche. Out of sight. I inhale the acrid animal scent of the shelter. I listen. I exhale.

My face is damp. My neck and shoulders ache. I need to relax. To think.

A prickle of fear and I reach for my backsack. I hold it close and feel the contours of the rock. It's there. I didn't lose it. It's what they want. That and me. What will happen to Damon? I clutch the stone more closely and listen.

"Did you really expect me to believe this was the banestone the Shoon whore meant?" That's Crispin. "What do you take me for? I'm not ordinary. I'm Revelant. Like you, only more so. Three times over."

"That makes no sense." Damon is speaking. "What's relevant about it?" He's still with Crispin and with someone else I don't know.

"Not 'relevant,' you fool! 'Revelant'." Laughter. Not Damon's.

All of this is because of me and because we're searching for Chapling. Looking for a Shoon. They hate Chapling even more that they hate me.

"You really don't know, do you?" Crispin's voice again. "You don't know why you're able to see things others can't. It's what happens to those of us who have died. It's what happens with our return. It's how we return."

"But I've never died."

"You must have. Only Revelants and Shoons have such powers. And you're sure the void no Shoon!"

The cavouti. The chase. The snakebite. A little boy lying in the grass. He retches one more time. He falls back. Eyes wide. Pleading. His body shakes violently. Head jerks back. Eyes roll up. Painful intake of breath. Breath leaking back out. Nothing more.

Now I've told him. Now he knows. We know.

Voices fade away. I huddle against the wall of the crevice, willing myself once more into silence, breathing the song the lady taught me, feeling it reverberate in my throat and chest, sensing that somehow it will protect me, wanting it to protect Damon, too.

I brush clean a small space and spread my sheet, place my backsack under my head. My hand seeks out the shape of the stone through the canvas. The notes of the song caress me. Weary and watchful, I sleep.

I see her now.

Her childhood was filled with warm days running through meadows in a warbling tumble and tumult of children. She drank from cool springs under clear blue skies.

I know this the way one knows the contours of one's own face without a mirror.

The laughter quieted as she grew, crafting itself into shimmering songs.

I see her as a young woman. Her brow is furrowed, her song muffled, though it pulses in my throat and between my eyes.

Cries of pain hang in the air.

"A healthy nen," the aproned woman says, holding aloft a squirming, crying nen slick with blood and fluid, shining iridescent.

Another cry, and the mother convulses again. Attendants scurry about, tending the nen, yes, but hovering over the mother as well, feeling her belly, peering between her raised knees.

The aproned woman wipes her hands and places her fingers inside the woman. She nods and smiles. "Push, my girl," she says. "Yes, it's time to push again."

More cries. The nen cries, too. Such a hubbub. Confusion. One more shout of release.

And then the sounds of two nens crying.

11.

I LEAN THE BRANCH against the lowest wall of the cavern and use it to climb out. The early morning air is warm and still as I strain to take deeper breaths, trying to settle my mind still fragmented by fear and visions. Damon feels far away. I feel far away. My heart longs to go to him, but I know I can't. That would be even worse for him. I'm the reason they took him. I could go home. But Temur without Damon is empty. I can't abandon him. I have to finish what we started. To find Chapling. Can I do such a thing alone? Why do I think Chapling will help me find Damon?

My eyes probe the pale light. How did I get here? I was running, flying. Before that I was with Damon. I choke back a sob and turn in what I think is the direction Damon and I were headed, which I have to trust is toward Fayredell. I walk. I'm so confused. Who are these people who can read me and Damon so easily? Temur had hateful people, but not people like Crispin Harper.

Scenes of Damon's ordeal and visions of the beautiful woman float in the shimmering air as real as the gravel that litters my path. I know they're coming somehow from the green stone Damon found. I remember the song and it begins to thrum in my throat. I'm grateful for the song. Grateful to the woman for giving it to me. Did she give it, or did I only find it, take it?

I need to find Chapling. Can I trust him? Mother said Shoons are devious. Not quite right in the head.

Like me, I guess. But who else can I trust? There was only Damon. I have to help Damon. Surely Chapling knows how.

The road is there, off to my left. The road to Fayredell. The road back to Temur. There's nothing for me in Temur. I continue toward Fayredell, but stay off the road, keeping it in view. The lady's song echoes through me, giving me strength.

The town comes into view suddenly. I've been looking down and when I look up there it is. My heart beats faster and there's a familiar ache between my eyes. I wrap my scarf around my head to hide my face and hair, pull my hat down lower. Maybe they won't notice my color. Where did Crispin say the market was? Southwest? Yes, that was it. I'm arriving from the south, maybe southeast. Avoid the center. Go around. Circling.

Rows of low earthen houses look much like Temur. A fountain in a small square. I fill my water sheath. In the meagre shade of a building I drink deeply, letting the water fill my belly. Hunger will have to wait.

There are people on the street. I watch their dark brown feet, and I think they know where they're going. I follow. A passing pedaled vehicle raises dust and I pull the scarf more tightly over my face. I try to blend into the crowd. I watch my feet. My pale feet following in their steps.

Shop doors stand open. A broom sweeps some steps. The smell of fresh nutbread grabs at my belly. A cat peers at me from behind a water jug. People greet one another with names I don't know. So many strangers. No, I'm the stranger. I become smaller.

Then I see it. The marketplace is huge, filled with colorful carts and canopies and caravans. Dusty. Noisy. People haggle with venders of meat and vegetables, leather goods, clothing, metal blades, baskets. How to find Chapling? Don't ask. Look for an old Shoon.

Food aromas from a nearby cart. My stomach begs. I feel inside the pocket of my shirt for coins. Do I have enough to buy a stuffed bread?

"How much?" I ask the vender.

"Two coins."

I count out a coin and two half-coins and lay them on the counter. He puts the stuffed bread on a scrap of paper and pushes it toward me. I nod in gratitude. Why? I paid for it. He didn't want to sell to me. He wants me to move on. He doesn't want to be seen serving someone like me.

I step between a tent and a caravan. Behind the tent I sit on the ground, grateful for a moment's rest. I bite into the stuffed bread. Hardly any stuffing. Bland. Hunger doesn't care. Eat slowly. It seems like more when I eat slowly. Sip water. Another bite.

Deep voices, angry and rumbling. I risk looking around the corner of the tent. Where? Over there, just beyond the stall selling old chairs.

"We don't need your kind here!" I sort this out from the clamor. I know at once who they mean.

I keep watching as the blood boils hot through my head. The last bite of stuffed bread goes down hard and tasteless. I lick the grease from my fingers, keeping my eyes directed toward the commotion. I fold the scrap of paper and tuck it away in my backsack. One more swig of water from the sheath, held in my mouth for a moment before swallowing.

The old Shoon is leaving. His tent is folded badly. It flaps awkwardly as he shuffles away angry, pulling a cart. Both he and the cart limp. I'll follow, but not too close. Sidayens and kinren hurl insults as he goes. One hurls a clod of earth that explodes into dust against the side of his cart. Chapling looks over his shoulder. But not toward his harassers. Toward me.

I stand, brushing crumbs from my shirt and trousers, my eyes fixed on Chapling. I arrange my backsack and sling the water sheath over my shoulder.

I walk cautiously. Disinterested.

Invisible.

The marketplace is empty. Quiet. No one here but Chapling and me. He nods to me and I return the gesture. I follow.

A rough hand on my shoulder. Heavy. It pulls me back, jerks at my scarf.

"Here's another one of 'em!"

I shrink and try to cover my head again. My face. But he's pulling on my scarf. Pulls it away and flings it on the ground. Steps on it.

"There's nowhere for you to hide here, you sully Shoon!"

I look at the man. A dark man. Dark eyes. Darkest I've ever seen. Even the whites are almost brown. More people gather around. Sidayens and kinren, too. I feel so powerless. Exposed. I hear a shrill cry from another area of the market. People turn and run toward the cry. Except the man who still holds me roughly by the arm. I twist and strike at him.

Not like this. Gather yourself, girl. Don't fight his way. Drain his strength.

What does that mean?

His grip loosens.

"Psssh!" The sound comes from somewhere behind a stall. A voice hisses, "Come this way. I'll help you."

What else can I do? I twist out of the man's grip and run toward the call.

It's a girl. Young, but taller than me. Her dark hair droops in soft waves around a darker face. The eyes beneath her silky brows are kind. She has a pungent scent I can't place.

"Come quickly." Her voice is soft but angry. She's not angry at me.

I follow. She grabs my hand and we run.

Pickles. She smells like pickles.

We hurry down a narrow track leading away from the main road. I feel the stones on the path right through my sandals. Sharp stones. Not a well-travelled way.

After a while, she pulls me into a collapsing shed and sits down. We're both breathing hard. I sit, too. My body trembles and I try to breathe it calm.

"I'm sorry for what they did," she says.

"Not your fault. You helped me. Thank you."

She takes a thin scarf from a pocket of her shirt and hands it to me. "You might need this," she says. "I'm sorry they took yours."

"Not your fault," I say again. Why do people do this? Say 'sorry' for things they didn't do? She fidgets with the wrap around her left wrist, with its knots and red beads. She pulls her sleeve down over it.

Something feels strange. I listen. Breeze scrapes some weeds against the side of the shed. Nothing else to hear. No birds. Why are there no birds? Then I hear it. Shrill cry like the shriek in the marketplace. The voice of a hawk.

The girl jumps to her feet and steps outside. She cries out, just like the hawk. The bird answers, then swoops toward her. It lands on her arm, delicately, on the centers of its feet, holding talons aloft. I know by the big bird's short rounded wings and long tail that it's a thrushawk. I've seen their work in the woods at Temur and I shudder.

The girl and the bird murmur to one another, face to face. She gestures and the hawk flies away. It makes a circle, then settles on the roof.

The girl is smiling. "She'll keep watch for us."

Yes, and all the birds will hide while she watches. This girl's hawk makes me nervous. Herself seems friendly enough.

I offer my name. "I'm Meridia."

"Ann," she says. "Ann Landry."

"Why are people in Fayredell so angry?" I have to ask. I need to know.

"They're afraid of you. Afraid of your kind."

"But why?"

Ann sighs. Perplexed. Her father was one of the angry Sidayens who attacked Chapling. One of the angriest. I don't know how I know this. I only know it's true.

"You're afraid of your father," I say.

The bird on the roof flaps her wings. Ann fidgets, scowling.

"It's the Palinjians," she says. "He's joined up with them. Palinjians think they run everything. Or ought to. They blame Shoons for anything bad. They say Shoons are deceitful. Shifty."

My mother thought that.

Ann scratches with a finger in the dust on the shed's floor. "They say Shoons ought to go back to where they came from. So they run them off or beat them up or…"

"Or kill them." I say what she doesn't want to say. My spine goes cold, but my head is burning, temple to temple.

"Sometimes." Ann's voice is an unwilling murmur.

"Tell me about your father." I need time to think. Distance. Quiet.

"He wasn't so bad before. When Mother was alive." There's a hitch in her breath as she says this. She wipes a sleeve roughly across her face. "They worked the business together. Making the pickles. Mother had the best pickle recipes. But father started making fun of her because of her books and because sometimes she met with other kinren to share poetry and stories. And I think he hates me because I'm not a son." Ann slaps her hat against her thigh and exhales loudly.

I see her father. He'd be taller if he stood erect. He walks off kilter. That broken leg wasn't set properly when he was a child. It pains him still.

Ann continues, not looking at me. Just talking. She talks because there are things she needs to say, and she thinks I'll listen. No one else listens. Not since her mother's death. Her murder?

"I heard things, hiding outside the door sometimes when my father met with some of the other Palinjians.

They're all Sidayens, of course. Well, some kinren are sympathizers, even a few women. Anyway, I hid and listened. They say Shoons do evil tricks. They say they have no language of their own. They call them ugly, the color of barren earth."

"Do you believe that?" I say. Do I believe it? Mostly.

Ann shrugs and looks away. "Not really." She sounds doubtful. "They say it's Shoons' evil that caused the earth to go hot and dry. Shoons never honored the sun like people are supposed to, hiding in their dark forests. There used to be forests, you know. But that was before my father's time. Before the Great Fires. Well, I don't even know how long ago. It's not anything we learned in school. School is all numbers and crafts and instruction books. And girls only go to school for a few passages anyway. They see no point in educating kinren. I was always good at reading but awful at numbers." She's wandering. Remembering things.

"My mother was a teacher." I don't know why I say that.

"Really? I thought for a while I might like to be a teacher. To teach reading. Do you like books?"

I shouldn't have brought it up. Now *I'm* remembering things. "I was never good at reading." Leave it at that.

"My mother had so many books. I read all of them many times over. Her books were different from the ones at school. School books were all boring numbers and instructions. Mother's books were full of lovely stories and poems."

My own mother had a few books like that.

"When she died, Father got rid of them. I don't know what he did with them."

He burned them. He put them in the fire, a few each night, while his own anger burned. I see what Ann doesn't.

"I can't stay," she says. "Father will wonder what's happened to me. I'll think of something to tell him on my way back to town. You'll be okay here for a while. I don't know where you're going and it's probably best that I don't know. You can stay here as long as you like. Well, overnight anyway. There's a map in that chest over there, along with some other things you might need." She's on her feet, brushing the dirt off her trousers.

In the doorway she stops. "I wish you good journey, dear stranger." She's already forgotten my name.

"Thank you. Thank you for your help, Ann Landry."

She starts to respond. The hawk cries.

12.

I'VE ONLY EVER BEEN ALONE inside my own house or in the forest outside Temur. Ann has gone and I'm alone here in this place I don't know. Alone without Damon. Afraid to think about Damon. Afraid of Crispin. Afraid of Ann Landry's father and those Palinjians she spoke of. Hot tears rim my eyes. I refuse them, scrubbing them away with the scarf Ann left for me.

Outside, the birds chirp quietly to one another. The day is still and hot, the sky a clear yellow green. Stories say it was blue once.

My heart aches for Damon, but I wrench it away. His trouble is all my fault. If I can find Chapling, maybe he can help. I try to remember the direction he went. The moon is just past full; I can travel tonight.

My body droops with fatigue. So tired.

The map. I should look at the map while it's still daylight.

The chest Ann showed me is not large. It's thick with dust. No lock or latch. Leather hinges. The lid is heavier than I imagined. Solid wood. Maybe linden. Tall trees branching broadly. Leaves as big as my childish hand. Fragrant blossoms and deep shade.

Inside the chest I find a metal cup and a small cooking pot. There's a cloth with faded green and blue stripes, brown stains. And a folded paper.

I take out the cloth first and spread it on the ground. Then the paper. It's a thick paper, deeply creased. I lay it on the cloth and unfold it.

I stare.

A map is a picture of things on the ground. Things and places. I need to make sense of this. I think the reddish circles might be towns. There are words next to the circles. I sound out the letters. This one sounds like "Temur." That's a start. That's where we started, Damon and me. My hand jerks at the thought of Damon. I force my mind back to the map.

The black twisty lines might be roads. I follow one of them and sound out the letters beside the next red circle. It sounds like "Br..." Wrong direction. Go back to Temur and try again. Track another black line to a different red circle. Sound it out. "Fayredell." Good. But where am I now? I close my eyes and think of how I got here with Ann Landry. I think of the marketplace at the edge of Fayredell. On the southwest. I try to think where the sun was as we left to come here. Almost directly overhead. That's no help. We didn't come far. And we were coming away from the town. I study the area all around Fayredell on the map. There's a small brown X, almost lost next to a crease. That's where I am. A thin line of faded dots connects Fayredell and the brown X. I'll need to find the main road to find Chapling.

He's stopped now.

He's waiting for me.

I study the map a little longer bird struggle to sound out a few more names. None of them sounds familiar. I strain to imagine the landscape described by the map. I think the blue triangles may mean water. I need to memorize where they are. All this effort makes me weary, clouding my perception with words and unfamiliar symbols. I fold the map and the cloth and lay both of them back inside the chest. I stretch out on the ground and close my eyes. I listen to the birds. I try not to think of Damon, but he seeps through my fear.

It comes in sepia tones with streaks of brightest orange. Clots of gray dust. Muted sounds rise and fall.

"Half Shoon is still Shoon." Crispin's voice irrupts through the muffled hubbub, heavy with disgust.

Damon sits on the floor, slumped to one side, hands bound behind him. Red stains mark his shirt and streak his face. Blood oozes warm from his nose.

My own heart wrenches in my chest and my head throbs with his. Through Damon's eyes, I see Crispin. He's sitting erect in a chair. Other men we don't know stand around. They're angry about a temple burned. A prophet killed.

Angry at Damon.

Angry at me. At me, Damon.

They lean toward me. Menacing.

"You can't claim you were unaware," one of the men says. "Revelants always know."

I raise my head to look the speaker in the eye and my head explodes with pain. My left eye is swollen nearly shut. Vision blurs. *Focus.*

"Of course I was aware. I thought it could help me with my research." The words taste of blood and have to be pushed out past bruised lips. I shouldn't have said that.

"Research? What kind of research might that be?"

I have to say it. My brain hurts too much to lie. "Bio-photons. Images from biophotons."

Scoffing laughter.

"You're a bigger fool than we thought. But what's that got to do with the rock?" They don't understand the connection.

"It emits biophotons."

More laughter. "He thinks the stone is alive!" They laugh even louder.

I can't say that I wanted the stone for Meri. Because I know it's something important to her.

"I'll ask you one more time: Where is the Shoon whore? Where is that sully banestone?" The speaker moves closer. He holds a leather sandal in his right hand and slaps it against his thigh. Another man stands behind him. I can't see what's in his hand. There's a glint of metal.

"I hid the rock. In a cavern. Let me go and I'll find it for you." I can't let them know that Meri has it.

"Liar!"

The blow across my left temple starts the flow of blood again. I swallow some of it, almost choking.

"We know when you lie! You gave it to the Shoon. You just said so."

"No… No, I hid it." I'm not used to this. Who are these people who can see inside my mind?

Meri? Meri, if you can hear me… Run! Hide! Don't let them find you!

An explosion of white as the piece of metal cracks Damon's skull.

"Damon!"

My own cry of pain awakens me. My hand clamps over my mouth. Eyes frantic. Searching.

Danger. Even more than I knew.

"Damon?" Only a whisper.

My eyes close again. Breathe. Lungs inflate. Release. Again. Silent tears. Trembling heart. Damon's pain draws away from me.

I fall into loneliness. Despair.

Moonlight slants through cracks around the window. It's time to go, time to find Chapling. But he feels…gone. Like Damon. I'm so confused. But I have to go. I can't stay here. I call to mind the map. I gather my belongings and open the door.

I pause, listening to the quiet. In the distance an owl. Nearer at hand a night lizard's bark. All this is as it should be. I close the door behind me. The moon is still low and helps me find my direction. There's no path to where I'm going. Wary, I watch for obstacles. Big rocks. Old stumps. I go slowly.

I'll need water.

The light goes strange. It feels brighter.

A grassy path winds between rows of bushes laden with ripe berries. Cabras graze just beyond, little bells tinkling around their necks. They raise their heads to look at me as I pass, flicking droopy ears. Wrens flutter and scold. They have nests in the bushes. Young ones. Another path joins this one and it grows wider. Well worn. Tinkling bells merge with the murmur of water. There it is. A stream tumbles over rocks into a pool where living things wriggle, glinting silver. On the far side, a spring flows. I wade across.

Stones slippery beneath my sandals.

I stop.

I stand on dry ground. Barren ground. There's an echo of water. I shift a large flat stone and find a milparinka. Barely a trickle. I can't even submerge my water sheath. Can't fill it. I drink greedily. Body is grateful. Scoop more water.

I study the angle of the moon and keep walking.

Damon said *run*, but I can only walk.

Damon said *hide*, but there's nowhere to hide.

The scarf Ann left me is a mottled brown print. Something dark to shield my Shoon face and hair, to shield my ugliness from their anger.

Ann is in trouble. Her father is furious. How can he know she was with me?

Scraping sound. Shifting rocks. My spine goes rigid. I squat next to a boulder, listening.

More scraping. Stone on stone. Shuffle of feet. Four of them. There it is. Silly nightvark. Digging for grubs. I sit until my breath comes even. Nightvark shuffles away.

The moon is almost directly overhead. Pay attention, Meridia. Don't lose your direction. This landscape is so plain. Everything looks the same. A cloud floats across the moon and features dim. Which way was the wind blowing? I'm not good at this. There are only dark and darker things. One of them is a tree stump. I sit on it to rest a while.

I need Damon.

Damon's eyes are closed. Swollen shut. Surrendered. His body rests awkwardly. Blood soaks into the earth under his head. A flutter of wings. A carrion crow lands.

No! Damon, wake up!

Crow cocks its head. Flutters up and lands on Damon's shoulder. The bird looks at me.

Follow me, Meridia. What voice is this? Not Damon's.

A harsh call and I startle. A crow sits on a rock nearby. Other birds twitter. Sky's begun to brighten. That smear of pink is east. I've gone off course.

Crow is still there. He cocks his head. Shakes his feathers. Looks at me. I want to question this, but I can't. My heart breaks for Damon.

I'll follow.

Whenever crow gets too far ahead, he lands. Waits until I catch up. Takes off again. Flies zigzag. Back and forth, up and down. Stops. Watches. Launches.

In the morning light, from far overhead, I see that Chapling is not far past the edge of town. When crow flies high, the outline of the buildings is just visible. Chapling's dragged the cart off the road and into a thicket of struggling trees. Barely more than bushes.

My steps slow as I near where he sits leaning against the cart. Crow rests on his shoulder. His silvered red-gold hair lies in a tangle around his ears. He scowls as he rubs sore shoulders.

I stop at the edge of the cart's long shadow. "Good day," I say.

He looks at me with yellow-green eyes. Says nothing. Says colors. A cloud of color rising between us. Pulsing. I blink at the brightness. Colors congeal into images. A woman. Is it she? And a man. Not Chapling. Forest. Trees filled with birds. The man chirps and a bird flutters down to land on his hand. Mountains strewn with massive boulders. Lush grass. Running streams.

Rain. Drenching rain. Clouds. Stars. Moonlight. Sunshine. Mother?

"Please stop." My voice squeaks. "You're confusing me."

Chapling inhales deeply and the images, the colors dissipate. Recede. As if he's breathed them back into himself.

"You're Chapling," I say. I don't know what else to say.

"So it's said. But my true name is Brân. And you're Meridia." His voice sounds strange, almost like a bird imitating the speech of people.

I nod and don't ask how he knows. "Yes. Meridia Einkorn."

He looks at me and I see my mother. My mother Madelyn Einkorn. Can he see her, too?

"Einkorn," he says. "Please. Come and sit down. You've brought the stone with you. I wasn't sure who would come, but I'm glad it's you. I didn't mean to overwhelm you. I have to remember that those who've been raised out of contact with the rest of us are like caged birds. You know they never learn their full songs properly when they're kept isolated."

His smile sends a wave of golden warmth through me. I sit. I try to think a question to ask. I have so many questions. "Us? Shoons you mean?"

Brân sighs and his head drops to one side. Eyes skyward.

His voice is soft, but I feel its resonance at the center of my forehead. It's a pleasant feeling.

"That's what they call us. But we know ourselves as Melfar. That's who we've always been. Melfar."

The word itself is streaked with blues and golden orange. It stirs something in my mind. I hear it in my mother's voice. Did she know this word?

"Of course, you're only half Melfar. I have to remember that."

"Because my mother was…" Is there a word?

Brân supplies it. "Mundani. Your mother was Mundani." Another word formed from colors, this one purple and gray.

"Like Damon," I say, remembering why I'm here. Brân starts to speak but doesn't. "I need to find Damon. Crispin Harper took him. They beat him."

Brân clears his throat. "Have you looked to find where he is?"

I know what he means. "I saw what happened and I'm afraid. I'm afraid to look again. Crispin could find me."

"Mmm. So…" He inhales deeply. Crow flies up, perches on the side of the cart. "I think you know how to tell when they lie. Dissemble."

"Yes," I say. I'm not sure how I know, but I know that I know.

"You know that what they speak is not always the same as what they verberate."

Verberate. I understand at once what the word means. It's the sense of a thing, the message within and sometimes underneath the words.

"You know the difference. You know when they lie." He directs his gaze from the sky to the ground and then angles his eyes up at me. "Now you need to learn how to lie to them."

I remember how I thought about cascades of falling rocks to hide what I knew about the stone.

"That's one way to fool them," Brân says. "But it's best to learn how to shield your own verberations altogether. I can teach you."

I sit and wait. Anticipating.

"No, it's not like that. Not like a classroom. Not like trying to learn to read." He chuckles, then looks sad. "If you stay with me, we'll synchronize. You'll learn."

"Can you find Damon for me?"

"Yes." He closes his eyes for a moment. "You're right to be concerned about Crispin. He's a strong Revelant. Several times. This will be harder than I thought."

More questions. "Revelant?" It's a word Crispin used. I'm still not sure what it means.

"Dear child," he says. "You have so much to learn. And I'm so tired. I was speaking Mundani words all day and then had to drag this cart away in the hot sun. And I spent most of the night looking for you. I'm an old man. We should have some breakfast. We have time."

"I have a few scraps of nutbread and some mooli root. It's gone a bit withered." I fumble in my backsack and pull out my humble offering.

"And I've got some shreds of dried meat and a couple of fresh guavacots." He spreads a cloth between us. Hunger makes a feast of simple food.

"Where are you going?" I ask. I'm afraid to think of Damon. His impression has gone faint and I don't want to know why. I cling to something purple that feels like hope.

Brân looks up at me, chewing. His eyes close. Wind. I grab my hat and Brân chuckles without opening his eyes. Another gust. Gentle hills. Soft pine needles underfoot. Glorious scent. *Look up.* Taller trees than ever grew at Temur. Swift-scudding clouds. Blue sky. Truly blue. More trees. Barely discernible path. I approach a clearing and find a village. Hodge-podge of unpainted wooden cottages. Large animals. Equids. Men and boys move along the paths, carrying water in large jars. The people look a lot like Brân.

He's watching me, curious.

"What's it called?" I ask.

"Try again. Breathe." He closes his eyes.

I follow his breath. And then I hear it. Myriad colors rise from their voices, reverberating along the paths and sweeping among the cottages. An ululation. Sound arranges into a word.

"Beni..." I say.

"Close enough. It's called Beniford." There are more colors when he says it. "It's my home. Well, one of them. I was born in another place called Lindmor." Where his mother was born, too. Lindmor no longer exists.

"But what about Damon?" I grasp my hands together to keep them still. I need to know. Brân's presence makes me braver.

"Sit quietly," he says. "And breathe. Breathe with your mind."

I'm under a canopy. Inside a bubble. It reminds me of a mirror Damon showed me once. I can see out, but no one can see in.

Damon.

I breathe. I see his body. Why do I think *Damon's body* and not just *Damon*? I hardly recognize his bruised and swollen face. Drying puddle of blood beneath his head. Awkward attitude of arms and legs. But different now. Right arm straighter along his side.

"Take quiet breaths. It takes some getting used to."

Damon moans and stirs.

My eyes fly open. "Oh! I thought he was dead!" I say this to Brân.

"He was. But now he's Revelant. Again?" The colors of another word stir underneath this one. *Token?*

"You talk so strangely. Revelant. And what is Token?"

"A Revelant is someone who dies and comes back in the same body. They are known to…well, sometimes they're known as Tokens."

"You mean like Crispin?"

"Yes. And I think your Damon was already Revelant. Is that true?"

"The snakebite. When he was a child. Yes, he died then. How does it happen? Does it happen to everyone?" He wants to say that people like us are Tokens from birth. He thinks I won't understand.

Brân laughs. "No, child. It's.. What's the word? Complicated. It's complicated."

"Do you know where Damon is? Can we go to him?" Where are all these questions coming from? I remember asking questions as a child. I learned to stop.

"Yes, I think I know where he is. But we can't go yet. I'm waiting for someone else." He brushes crumbs from our meal onto an edge of the cloth and invites the crow. Crow devours his meal. Another gesture from Brân and crow flies off to look for more breakfast on his own.

Shall I ask Brân who he's waiting for? "You said you were waiting for me. How did you know?" I ask that instead. An answer comes. "The rock. Is that it? The rock brought me to you."

Brân nods and looks off into the sky where the crow went.

"The rock, as you call it, finds its own. It must have been your Damon bought it from me. And he gave it to you." He closes his eyes. His eyebrows twitch. His hands tremble and flutter. "You saw her." He looks at me with bright eyes. "You learned her song. Well done, Meridia."

"Who is she?"

"She's my mother, Avienne." His eyes seem to have gone slightly turquoise.

"How did her song get into the stone?"

"That's a long story. Let's wait and I'll tell it once for both you and the one who's coming next."

"When will they come?"

"Soon, I think. You must be weary. We both had a tiring night. We should rest."

13.

MY WORRIES NESTLED into their own space and I slept. The hard ground felt like the softest mattress, the shade like deepest night. Cool breeze blowing all the while.

The mind is a powerful thing, Meridia. I hear this in Brân's voice, but when I open my eyes, I find he's just returning to camp. He carries two sheaths, heavy with water, and a kerchief half full of ripe berries. The slant of the sun tells me it's nearing midday.

"Yes, thank you," I say, even though he didn't ask if I'd slept well.

He accepts my remark. "Good. We'll likely want to travel tonight." He walks over to the back of the cart and picks up a glass jar full of a golden liquid.

"Yes, please." Did he offer tea or didn't he? "When will he get here?" I ask.

Brân nods approval. It is a man after all. Someone he knows. He's pleased. But worried, too. The traveler is leaving the main road, coming our way.

The tea is sweeter than the tea I brew in Temur. He shows me the leaves he uses, explains to me where they grow at the base of stifflebriar bushes where they're protected from afternoon sun.

"I like it," I say. I wonder if it has any healing properties.

"It helps the body sustain itself, evens out the energy," Brân says.

There's a flutter of birds and we both turn toward the sound of distant footsteps. Not careful steps. Brân rises to pour a cup of tea for our guest. He sets it down on the edge of the cloth and we wait.

The man who enters our circle is not what I expected. He's a little taller than Brân and looks unusually strong. His skin is a color similar to mine, but his face and arms are covered in tiny brown speckles. His hair is a mass of russet curls. It's thinner on top and reminds me of a bird's nest. He should wear a hat. As he comes closer, I notice that he has one green eye, one light brown.

Brân is on his feet. Curiosity lights his eyes. He doesn't speak, instead sends the same colors and sounds that welcomed me. Our guest stares and blinks, looking annoyed. Colors recede.

"Welcome," Brân says. "Please join us for some tea."

"Who are you?" the man says. "Why am I here? I thought I was going to Fayredell."

"You almost did," Brân says. "It was necessary to bring you here instead."

"I'm going to say it again: Who in the void are you? And why the sully void would you bring me here?"

"Well, yes, I suppose introductions are in order." Brân deflects the traveler's rudeness. "My name is Brân and this is Meridia. And you're Malaki. Malaki Milburn, if I'm not mistaken."

"You know me?"

"Not well," Brân says. "I knew your mother once."

He knew her many times. I didn't want to see this.

Brân gestures toward the space between him and me. "Now. Will you join us for some tea?"

Malaki is still standing. He removes the sweat-soaked kerchief from around his neck. Looks hard at Brân.

"You said your name is Brân? You're obviously Shoon. You knew my mother." He laughs.

Why does he find it so funny to meet his own father? Malaki is unreadable. For me, anyway.

Brân's eyes twinkle but he remains silent. Malaki's laughter subsides to a soft chuckle and he sits.

"Mother told me stories about you," he says. "I never thought to meet you face to face. Certainly not like this. I was never sure I wanted to. Great void, I was never sure you really existed."

I catch a faint tremor of fear. Is that coming from Malaki or from Brân? Malaki's lips tighten and a dullness shrouds his mismatched eyes.

"Whatever the stories were, they were likely true," Brân says. "Mindrel was one of the most honest women I ever met." He glances at me. "I was sorry to have to leave." His words shiver a deep brownish purple.

"Oh, she always told me it was for our own good you left. When I was a boy, I had my doubts." He was a resentful child. Moody and difficult. "But these days, with the way these Palinjians are acting toward people like us, well, maybe I get it."

"How is your mother?" Brân asks. He knows. He's making conversation.

"She closed the shop in Camberton two stints back. People stopped coming in and I knew it was because of me. She's gone to live with her sister. I stayed on to pack up her things to send to her. That's when I found this rock and remembered that she gave it to me a long time ago. I'd almost forgotten." He takes a black rock out of his pack and lays it on the edge of the cloth. "I have a feeling you're going to tell me about that."

The rock glistens and a deep hum rises from it. I feel it quavering blood-red and orange in my chest, exploding like a drumroll between my eyes. A man emerges, tall and dark with broad shoulders and arms thick as logs. There's a rough sash slung diagonally across his chest and stitched into it are stones and pieces of metal. The sound forges itself into a somber chant and I feel compelled to join in.

"Stop, stop!" It's Malaki. "The colors are nice enough, but what's this noise Meridia's making?"

Torrent of hailstones. The man disintegrates to black sand. Particles fall heavy as boulders. Choking, I open my eyes.

Brân scowls at Malaki. The scowl fades into a half smile as he looks at me and then back at Malaki.

"You two are quite a pair," he says. "This is going to make it harder."

I remember what Brân said about the caged bird. We know different parts of the song, Malaki and I.

Malaki is angry. I only know that by the expression on his face. He won't tell why.

Brân picks up the black rock, bounces it in his hand as if he's weighing it. He sets it down and makes a gesture over it. Glances at Malaki.

"Tell Mal what you pertanged, Meridia."

Pertanged. I don't know the word, but I know at once what it means. It's how things become tangible without seeing or hearing. I close my eyes and call to mind the colors, the figure, the chant.

"No, not like that. Mal needs words." Brân shoots another sharp glance at Malaki.

"I'm not sure… Words are hard for me." He knows that. Why is he asking me to do this?

"I'll help," he says.

I take a deep breath, eyes wide open.

"Well, there's colors," I say. "A swirl of colors." That's a good word. Swirl.

"I guess I saw that much," Malaki says.

"Go on," Brân urges.

"A man," I say. "A large man. Not like us." I remember what Brân called such people. "A Mundani man. Wearing a scarf sewn with stones and pieces of metal. Drums." I hear them again, pulsing, rumbling, and the sound carries me away.

"I saw no man." Malaki's voice cuts through. The drums scatter into disarray. "How can a rock do that? Project an image of a man."

Brân picks up the rock, cradles it in the palm of one hand. *This one wasn't supposed* to, he says. He looks at me and I hear—no, I pertange a name. *Zibal Palinj.*

Brân gestures toward me. "May I?" he says. And I hand him my rock as well. "You and Meridia keep calling these rocks, but they're more than that. Each one belongs to a Benison. Each is a waif of a Benison."

More words I don't know. I repeat them, trying to pertange their tones and colors. "Benison. Waif."

Malaki picks up a pebble and skips it toward the rocks. The Benison waifs. Brân frowns and a dark bubble rises and falls, deepest maroon.

"A Benison is a special sort of stone. A container, of sorts. Almost like a book but filled with sounds and images rather than words. It's how we Melfar preserve and share our stories, our songs, our truth." He has to explain again about Melfar and Mundani. "The Benisons these waifs belong to were great monuments, crafted of materials that absorb the verberations of Melfar, inscribe them into the very substance of the stone. They hold our stories. Make them available to those capable of pertanging them. A new Benison is erected—well, used to be erected—at the beginning of every Marble Return to celebrate a new meed with a song commemorating the meed just completed. The composite of the Benison also intensifies the residue of past events and conditions. They can show what used to be in any given place. They also resonate with one another." The colors of Brân's own words threaten to carry him away.

I struggle with the words. Each one straining to reveal something. *Craft*. These stones are crafted? *Inscribed*. But not with words. *Return*. That seems the same as a passage, a period of time containing all the seasons. *Meed?* How many returns in a meed? I let the words in, let them tell me things. No, that's Brân. Brân verberating in accord with the words he's chosen to try and help us understand.

Malaki struggles even more than I do. He has little more than the mere words. "So this is an artifact?" he says, nodding in the direction of the rock. The waif. "Who made it?"

Brân sends a golden surge toward the waifs. It compiles into an image. A man. A different man this time. A Melfar man. Sturdy. Golden beard and hair all streaked with silver. Face crinkled from laughter. A strange smell that reminds me of Damon.

"These two are recent ones, from the present Amber Meed, the current cycle of Benisons that have been erected. A New Obsidian and a New Jade. They were made by my mother's brother. My Uncle Fannan. He learned the skill of crafting Benisons from his own uncle. Melfar have crafted Benisons for many turnings, many generations." *Yes, Meridia. I learned the craft.*

The waifs shudder and purr. A fibrous, transparent pulse wavers between them.

I look up at Brân. We rise together.

"We need to go, Malaki," Brân says. His crow takes off from the cart's roof, flying high and silent. "Someone's coming." Not friends.

Malaki is doubtful but he nods.

I hear Brân's protection canopy before I see it. A tone so low I can discern—pertange—the contours of each vibration. But this tone is gentle, unlike the tone from Malaki's obsidian stone. His waif. This tone is blue, as blue as long-ago sky. Malaki takes up the cart, following Brân. Our pace is quick but unhurried. Purposeful.

Where are we going? Brân knows. I have to trust him. Everything disappears into the blue canopy.

14.

THE SWELLING IN DAMON'S FACE has gone down. The medicine the woman gives him helps with the pain. The taste reminds him of something Meri gave him once when he'd burned his arm with some of his photographic chemicals. He tries to sit up and his vision blurs. Placing his hand against the wall helps a little.

"Careful," the woman says. "That was a nasty blow you suffered. You're going to feel unsteady for a while. You need to rest." She places a pillow behind him, and he leans back. "Are you hungry?"

He's not, but he can't remember when he last ate so he says, "Yes, thank you."

She offers him a small glass of tepid tea and some squares of almost fresh nutbread on a chipped green plate. Maybe he's hungry after all. He chews slowly, dipping the bread in the tea to soften it. His lips are swollen and some of his teeth hurt. One or more of them may be missing. He tries to remember how he got here, to think how he knows this woman. Does he know her? He has this odd feeling that he and she are the same person.

He studies his surroundings. It's a small earthen house, sparsely furnished. Open windows invite soft breezes fragrant with some kind of flower. "Where are we?" he asks.

"Our house," the woman smiles, looking a bit confused. "My house." Somewhere Damon remembers a smile like hers. "The nearest town is called Blanton. It's where we found you."

Damon looks around to see if someone else is here but sees only this woman. An ordinary looking woman. Old, but with an almost childlike air. She was probably considered pretty when she was young. "Could you tell me about that, please? I'm having a hard time remembering what happened."

"I don't know much," she says. "You were still mostly dead when we found you. Just coming back, but badly damaged. You required urgent care for your wounds."

He recalls an explosion of white light, unbearable pain. Then a darkness devoid of breath. Free of pain.

He remembers remembering Meridia. Did he really hear her voice? He remembers thinking, *I can't leave Meri.* He inhaled forcefully, then, painfully, choking on clotting blood and a desperate sob. He feels again how his whole body tingled and how he lay quietly, remembering to breathe, aware of the vastness of existence seeping into his singular body. His broken body. Knowing he had to get well. Knowing he'd failed Meri. *Oh, Meri, I'm so sorry! I should have fought them. I should have protected you.*

"Meri..." Her name on his lips is only a sigh. Tears burn his swollen eyes. He turns his face aside and whisks them away. "You haven't told me your name," he says. He's trying to remember his.

"Maddie," she says. "And yours?"

It comes to him like a whisper from a friend. "Damon. You're telling me I died?" He needs to know what she knows.

"So it would seem. I've only seen it happen once before. But you had the look of it. You were badly injured, as you can see. Attacked, I suppose. By someone you'd met before?"

Damon recalls his skepticism regarding Crispin Harper's stories. Crispin was there. Crispin was one of the men who beat him. Killed him. Murdered him. Damon waits for Maddie to tell him more about what happened, but she offers nothing more.

"How far are we from Fayredell?" Damon remembers now where he was going. Where he and Meri were going. What happened to Meri? Did she get to Fayredell? Did she find Chapling?

I'm okay, Damon.

He hears Meri's voice and wonders, *Who is Brân?*

Meri's voice merges into Maddie's. She's cocked her head to one side and has a faraway look. "Blanton is about ten fellspans northeast of Fayredell. Where we are is another couple of fellspans farther east. There are only a few houses here, not even a village. It's called Shadham." Maddie puts their used plates and cups into a pan for washing. Sunlight slants through a window, but since Damon doesn't know which way the window faces, that doesn't tell him the time of day. At least he knows it's day.

"It's afternoon," Maddie says. "You've been here a whole day already. You can stay as long as you need."

Maddie sits down at the table and pours water from a jug over the dirty dishes. She turns toward Damon, leaning forward, and a ray of sunlight illuminates her face.

Mother! Meri's voice again.

Maddie. Madelyn.

Damon gasps. "I thought you died. Meridia told me you went away, and I thought…"

"You know Meridia?" Did she ask a question, or merely state something she already knew?

"I was traveling with her when Crispin and his men took me. She got away, but I don't know where she's gone."

15.

I DON'T KNOW HOW LONG we walked. Brân set the pace so we didn't go fast. It felt like a short time, a long distance. I'm not tired. We haven't said much. Birds weave litanies of color from the trees overhead.

There are trees.

I look up and see blue sky, clear and deep and endless. No, that's the protection canopy.

Damon's presence lingers. Damon and my mother. My mother is alive! And somehow she's with Damon. She's not like I remember. Different. That difference must be why I never found her again after she went away. I grasp at the fleeting image of her, persuading my reluctant mind to believe that she truly is alive. And that she's with Damon.

Brân's limp is worse. He leans on the cart.

Even with Malaki's help, the canopy grows thin and there are gaps where it's disappeared altogether. Like a soap bubble in the dry air. The trees shrink to bushes.

"When do we stop?" I say.

Malaki and Brân stop. It's early morning. We're in a rough clearing next to an abandoned shelter. Eroded earthen walls and charred remnants of a roof. Malaki drags the cart alongside one of the walls. Brân stretches, massages his hip, then his shoulder.

"Damon is alive," I say.

Brân knows.

Malaki says, "Who's Damon?"

"My friend. He died."

"But I thought you just said he's alive?"

"He is." I appeal to Brân.

"Yes, I'll try to explain all of that," he says. "But first let's have something to eat. I think we'll have to build a small fire and do some cooking."

I follow Brân's lead, picking up sticks from under the bushes. I'm inexperienced with building fires in the outdoors like this, so I watch.

Malaki rummages in his pack and pulls out something wrapped in a piece of old quilt, tied with a ragged string. He pulls the string, unfolds the quilt. His face shines golden. Inside the bundle there's a long hollow stick with holes. He places one end of the stick in his mouth and exhales.

Tones rise in colorful eddies, dancing and circling around one another as his fingers move.

"What is that?" I whisper the words, not wanting to disrupt the design he's weaving.

Brân looks up from his fire-building. "Haven't you ever seen a flute?"

I shake my head. I can't take my eyes off Malaki, can't turn away from his tapestry of sound.

Another tone joins in, a whining, droning sound, a deep solid green, building ground for the dance. And then a third line, sketching paler arcs through it all. Where is this coming from?

Brân's fire begins to blaze. He sits back, breathing evenly, deeply.

Somewhere inside the cart, Brân's waifs resonate and soon we're enveloped in a whole symphony of sound, surrounded by a company of dancers, turning, stepping, swaying in colorful rhythmic profusion.

I'm captivated. I've always secretly believed that stones could sing, but I've never experienced anything like this. There are prickles of wonder all down my arms and puffs of wind at the center of my forehead. I feel compelled to add my song, the song the woman taught me. It merges perfectly. We become song, dance, pattern. Beyond substance. Beyond eyes and ears and body. Singing. Dancing. Being.

A dissonant buzzing. My throat constricts and I open my eyes. A sharp pain resolves into a tingling at the center of my brow.

Malaki is staring at me. Irritated. Staring at Brân. The flute in his lap still emits a shimmer of colors.

"What's going on?" he says.

Brân doesn't answer. I have no answer.

Malaki shakes his head. Shakes the residue of moisture and breath from the flute. Wraps it again and returns it to his pack.

"Where did you get the flute?" Brân asks.

"I made it myself," Malaki says. "I learned the craft from my stepfather. Well, mostly from him. I added the reed as an experiment."

"And the vocal humming?"

"There weren't many musicians in Camberton, so I guess I kind of tried to be my own one-man band." He grins. "I had to leave my foot drums behind."

It's only music to him. He doesn't see the colors or the dancers. Doesn't pertange them. Not the way I do. The way I do ever since I came into possession of the jade waif.

"It's an excellent instrument," Brân says. "You play well."

"My own compositions mostly."

Brân and I know otherwise, but we don't say.

The pot bubbles. Brân covers it and rearranges the fire. I don't know what he put into the pot, but it smells delicious.

"So who is this Damon you were talking about? The fellow who's dead and not dead."

Brân explains again about Revelants.

"How does that happen? Why doesn't it happen to everyone?" Malaki wants to know. I do, too.

"Mostly, the dying person decides." Brân stirs the pot and replaces the lid. "Many are ready for death, welcome it. Some are taken by surprise and have no time to reflect. Some die by their own will, of course. By their own hand. But others reach out with a strong desire to continue living. Those are the ones who can become Revelants." I think this sounds wonderful, but Brân finds it troubling. "Once someone knows they're Revelant, they may be more likely to reach out again, though many people forget."

Like Damon did after he died of snakebite. He was only a child.

"But what is it exactly? What is it that restores their life?" Maliki asks.

"Mundani say it's 'the Creator' or 'the Restorer.' We call them the Migrant, although they really need no name." There's a shifting pattern of colors at Brân's throat. "It's how we conceive the inconceivable. How we try to name what can't be named." The colors pulse with a few soft notes like Malaki's flute, like breathing. "Ultimately all our names, all our words, are Mundani words, you know, but we Melfar choose differently. We select the words that suit our thinking, the ones that carry the right colors and tones." The pot threatens to boil over, so Brân moves a couple of sticks. "Mundani normally forget about becoming Revelant within a tide or so of their renewal." He shakes his head slightly and passes a hand across his eyes. "A tide is about as long as a stint but linked to the moon's growth and decline. Anyway, whether Mundani remember their renewal or not, their sensibilities are heightened. The amazement of the moment of renewal causes that. Never equal to Melfar, of course. Our aurynx and gnosic orb are fully developed."

They have names. Aurynx says colors with sound. Gnosic orb pertanges them.

Malaki is puzzled. He's skilled with the aurynx. His orb is weak. I think I'm probably the other way around.

Brân takes three wooden bowls from a box inside the cart. He ladles stew from the pot into each. He hands one to me and one to Malaki. He cuts up some nutbread and passes that to us as well.

"Thank you, Brân. This is delicious." It's simple scurfpeas with onions and purslane, but it is delicious.

"Where are we?" Malaki asks. "Or maybe I ought to ask where we're going."

Damon. Brân has found Damon.

"We're just south of a town called Blanton. We're heading for a hamlet nearby, but I don't know if it has a name."

"Shadham," I say. "It's called Shadham."

Brân is pleased.

"I need to look for some brink thistle," I say. "The stems are strong medicine. Damon needs it." Mother means well, but she's let the wound on the side of his head get infected.

"We can do that later," Brân says. "Better to stay close by for now. Better to stay together. Mal and I will take turns with the canopy."

I'm grateful for the canopy. It provides at least the semblance of a roof for this broken-down cabin. I find an old mattress and when I lie down, it exhales dust and a smoky herbal aroma. I take Damon's rock, the Jade waif, out of my backsack and I cradle it near my heart.

16.

MOTHER'S WANDERED OFF again. I've checked with all the neighbors. Morgan says he saw her picking up rocks in his garden a couple of hours ago.

"I didn't mind," he says. "I've got plenty of rocks." He thinks he made a joke.

Morgan's older than Mother, but not so unstable. He doesn't understand how fragile she is these days.

"Not about the rocks," I say. "You should've brought her home. She loses her way."

He promises me he will in future. I know he won't. He thinks I worry too much. If I do, I learned it from her.

Mother's always been difficult, but now she's impossible.

I continue walking, looking. Wondering where she could be. Trying to reach out for her and finding nothing. The last time it had taken me most of a day to get her back. Ambia had found her then and brought her home.

"Where was she?" I needed to know. Her wanderings never seemed to have any pattern.

"In the woods," Ambia said. "That's what she told me, anyway. You know, up past the ovens where the trees used to be."

That was odd, because Mother never went to the woods. Gathering firewood was always my job. My favorite job. It would take me hours.

"She said she was looking for her daughter." I remember Ambia's nervous laugh as she glanced at Mother.

"I don't know what's happened to that little girl," Mother said then. "She's never around anymore. She doesn't like me, you know. Always running away, off into that forest. I tell her the forest is too dangerous. There could be patkánies and even zakis. She shouldn't go there." Mother began humming a scrap of a tune, watching a stray wasp buzzing around the eaves of the house. Gone again.

"Thank you, Ambia," I said. My heart was wrung dry. Only a remnant pang of hurt. She's right. I never liked her. Was never like her. I love her with all my heart.

"I've made tea," I said, meaning to invite Ambia.

"Oh, that would be nice, dear. Is this your house?" Mother said.

Ambia demurred. Waved goodbye.

"Yes, please come in," I said to Mother.

She entered. Looked around absently.

"My name is Maddie," she said, as if she'd just thought of it.

We'd done this so many times.

"Nice to meet you, Maddie. I'm Meridia."

For an instant she looked as though that name might have stirred something. She sat down at the table, waiting patiently for the tea. It was the same chair set at the same angle as always. Somewhere she remembered such things. I gave her the tea in her favorite blue glass. She smiled. Gulped the tea. Thirsty. No wonder. So hot outside. How long had she been gone this time? Longer than usual. I offered some nuts and fresh wilderfruit. She chewed, gazing blankly out the window. She had no thoughts. At least none that I could fathom.

"You're tired. You could lie down."

"Oh, that would be nice. Are you sure you don't mind? I don't want to impose."

"No, it's fine." I guided her over to the bed. Her bed. She sat. Slipped off her shoes. Winced as she lay back onto the mattress. She fingered the threadbare blue quilt, the one she made herself, long ago.

"Would you read to me?" That pang again.

I picked up the book that always lay at her bedside.

"I had a little girl once," she said. "I don't know what became of her. She wanted to learn to read, but I wasn't a very good teacher. She never learned. It made me so sad."

She'd never told me that before. I'd never known that she blamed herself for my inability to read. Yes, sad.

I opened the book, turned a few pages, and began reciting poems. In the middle of the third poem her eyes closed. By the time I finished the fourth she was sound asleep.

That was the last time she came home. This time I wouldn't find her. I would try to see where she was, at night when all was quiet. But she'd grown so faint. There was hardly anything left of her.

I see myself take a book from the shelf. It's the one with the glued-in pages that never quite fit back in. I open it and stare at the words until they dissolve into my tears.

Everything dissolves.

I lie there half asleep, remembering. That was my favorite book, the only one I truly wished I could read.

But since I couldn't, I memorized almost every poem in it. There were a couple of other books of poems. But mostly she tried to teach me from the schoolbooks, the books with numbers and instructions.

Poems rise up in my mind and I recite their images to myself in the dark, drifting between memory and sleep.

I'm overcome by a blankness and forget which poem I'm reciting. I see a man walking toward me.

Damon!

"Damon, you're okay!" My heart leaps.

He says nothing. Just gazes at me from where he sits on the edge of my small bed. I reach for him, pulling him down to lie beside me. I cling to him, to the solidness of his body.

"I thought you were dead," I say. "I thought you were sick."

"I've come for you Meridia. You see how strong and healthy I am. You see how I want you and how you yield to my wanting."

Damon is not usually like this. Not so desire filled. But we've been apart. We've been through so much. Seeing him strong and whole, my heart is beyond joy. I do yield. I find his soft lips and he finds my nether lips and presses insistently until he enters, pressing, pressing. I yield and yield. I rise up toward him, toward his wanting. Wanting more. Quivering bursts of light edged with all the colors, my body surging with the colors, exploding at last. Exploding the whole world. Erupting. Disrupting.

I feel the weight of Damon's spent body on mine and I open my ordinary eyes.

A shriek of flaming orange. Every muscle of my body contracts as I wrest myself out of his grasp. Not Damon. Not Damon! My fists pound against Malaki's strong shoulders. "No! No!" I shout for Brân. "Get off me! Beast!" Where is Brân? Where has he gone?

"Brân isn't here. Besides, you know you wanted it, Meridia," Malaki says.

"No!" Tears congeal into cold hate. My face contorts into one word. "Liar!" All my strength converges into one mighty heave as I push Malaki off me and onto the floor.

He's laughing. "You liked it," he says. "I liked it. Where's the harm in that?"

I pull my trousers up, grab my backsack, and run. I hurl one final word toward him. "Liar!"

17.

I RUN. NO PATH APPEARS. I crash through brush and stumble over rocks. Where is Brân? Why did he let this happen? Colors burst in discordant clangor all around me. Spinning disks of color chase me. Assault me. Grabbing at my eyes and ears and orb. Suffocating my heart. Strangling my throat with fire. Where is all this coming from?

From me. It's coming from me.

I stop. I squeeze my eyes shut for a moment and breathe. Tears leak through. A surging spring of tears. Ordinary Mundani tears. A moan, soft brown tinged with blue. I breathe through it, surrounding myself with its mournful colors.

I have to go on. I have to go on alone. Damon needs me. Thinking this, a wave of shame overwhelms me, submerging me in a dark, blood-red place. How can I face Damon? I allowed myself to make love to a man who was not him.

"No!" Not love. Nothing of love! Truth imprints itself, dispelling shame, inflaming anger. I was deceived. This lying is Malaki's twisted use of his Melfar gifts. I refuse it. He lied. He deceived me. I gave myself only to Damon. I had Damon in my heart. Only Damon. I would never betray Damon.

And yet I feel stained. Stained by the blood-red truth of Malaki's lie. His theft. I hurl the full weight of truth into the void as I finally call this what it is: "Rape!" I shout. "Rape! Rape! Rape!"

I emit a quivering brown sigh that settles on me like dust. I beg for cleansing as well as protection. I feel my face blood-red, streaked with blue. I take out the scarf, the gift from Mundani Ann. I soak it in my tears. I scrub my face, my arms, my violated place with the tear-soaked cloth. I throw the cloth on the ground, grind it into the earth with my feet. Stomping, tearing. I find a large rock and pound the cloth with that until my shoulders ache and my throat is raw from my angry cries. I search in my pack for the tools Brân gave me for building fires. I gather some dry sticks and wind them with the shredded cloth and set my fire. I sit and I watch it burn. I watch until the last embers of the cloth have gone to ash.

As the ashes cool, I begin to hum, my voice uncertain and out of tune. I hum the green song the woman taught me. Then I remember Brân's canopy. The feel of it. The tone. Green merges through turquoise into a soft blue eddy that quiets into a cool presence, breathing with me. I sing the canopy into existence. It vibrates and shimmers.

It's really more like a cloak than a canopy.

I think Brân.

"You can't lie to me, Malaki." Brân's anger heartens me. "I know what you did. Rape by deception is still rape. Don't you know who she is?"

"She liked it, old man. Of course I know who she is. She's a crazy half-Shoon like me." Malaki is holding the left side of his face where Brân struck him. I'm glad it hurts.

"More like you than you know. Why are you so blind, Malaki? Meridia is daughter of my brother Abél. My brother twin."

I freeze into stunned silence. Brân is my uncle. Brother twin to my father.

"She's my cousin sister?" Malaki doesn't sound so arrogant now.

My stomach heaves and I'd retch but my throat is clenched shut.

"Yes, your cousin sister."

Why had I not pertanged this already? I should have seen that Brân was my father Abél's brother twin. The two sons birthed by the beautiful lady of my visions. I recognize her now as their mother, Avienne. My own grandmother.

"I can't deal with you, Malaki." Brân's voice is flattened by sadness. "You're my son, but I no longer believe you're worth my trouble. I'm leaving to go find Meridia and I forbid you to come along. You're on your own."

Should I dispel my protection cloak so that Brân can find me? No. That would only make me tangible to Malaki. Brân will pertange me wherever I am, regardless of the protection cloak.

Where am I anyway? I look around and find nothing but barren ground, a few bushes dead or nearly so. The air buzzes with a crimson hate that burns my eyes and rasps in my chest.

I take a deep breath and try to think Damon. My thoughts retreat behind a curtain of shame. I can't think Damon. Not yet. I think my mother instead. I catch a brief glimpse, just enough to choose a direction. I gather myself and rise. The cloak rises with me. Like a solitary bird wrapped in sky I go, my tread soft among the stones.

In the vague distance, a woman appears, a Melfar woman. Behind her a whole group of Melfar, both women and men, emerge from the dim. They're singing together. Walking toward a great stone. Each person holds a bell and with every step, every bell rings. Such a pulsing clangor of bells and voices. There's joy in their voices. No, triumph. I merge with the colors of their song and feel release like water bursting from a broken jug. Tears rim my eyes as the splendid notes flood across the barren earth, overwhelm the hateful buzzing in the air. The singers walk circles around the stone. The Benison. It glows indigo blue and sends out sparks that snap in time with their steps, the notes of their song.

Not now, Meridia. Brân's voice.

I trip over the chant and stop. Look around with my ordinary eyes. No Melfar. No Benison. The tears are real. The song still rings in my head, but the notes have gone flat. Colorless.

I'm on a small hill. Below it, a great expanse of dry, yellow plain strewn with gray-brown rocks and boulders. From beneath a bush, a small stone winks at me, bright blue. Crystal-clear tone like a bell. Sustained.

I descend the hill, my eyes and orb cleaving to the stone, attuned to the Benison waif.

I grasp it in my hand, and I become the sound, ringing, vibrating. I cling to it, to the surge of power and freedom it offers. The waif in my backsack sparks hot against my back. I breathe deeply, holding this new stone near my heart.

I need to rest. Rest and think what to do next. Where to go.

I sit in the brindled shade next to the bush and set my mind loose. It flies to Damon. Damon needs the medicine.

"It's only the heat," he says.

Mother has her hand on his forehead. "No, I'm afraid you have a fever." She soaks a cloth in water and lays it on his head. "Mer would know what to do," Mother says.

I do know. What I don't know is how to find them.

I take the Jade waif from my pack and hold the two stones, one in each hand, touching. Like a bird I fly, launching from the bush here in front of me, rising high in the sky. To the north I see a town and beyond it a cluster of a few simple cabins. Shadham. That's where Damon and my mother are.

I open my eyes, blinking in the bright sunlight. A bird is there on the bush, a gray echo thrush, perched carelessly on a swaying twig. Head cocked, bird studies me first with one eye, then the other. Its tail and flight feathers are a deep blue, like the waif.

"Wake up!" The bird speaks. That's how echo thrushes got their name, but I've never heard one talk before. "Wake up!" it says again.

"Okay," I say. I've always talked to birds, so this part isn't strange.

"Look around," bird says.

I look and find that the bush is surrounded with brink thistle. I gather some for Damon's medicine. I shake the dry soil from the roots and place them in my pack.

"Come along," bird says.

I rise and hoist my backsack. I've tucked the two waifs into my pockets, the Jade waif on the left, my new indigo-colored waif on the right. "Coming!" I say. I remember the crow that guided me to Brân. This is different. The crow belonged to Brân. I think this bird belongs to me. It came to me with the waif. I don't understand, but I go. I follow.

Should I put on the pale blue cloak or not? Will I lose touch with this bird? I think of Malaki and I know I have to do it. Even the brief thought of him is fraught with fear and rage. The suffocating weight of him. I see his face so close to mine. The shock of seeing that it was not Damon's face. Malaki's laugh. My voice is thin, and it cracks as I hum the shimmering cloak into existence around me.

Bird disappears, but as I'm about to lose heart, I hear him again. "Come along. Wake up." He sees me. Pertanges me? Can birds do that?

"Coming," I say. There's the faintest whiff of lilac in my voice. A hint of hope.

Soon I recognize bird's natural call. *Chrrr-eep. Chrrr-eep.* Delicate blue bubbles of sound. I answer back as best I can, and after a while I realize this is his companion call. We call back and forth and I don't have to see where he is. We're companions, traveling together.

Within the safety of my cloak, pierced only by the reassuring bubbles passing back and forth between bird and me, I permit myself to uncover the morning's horror, to peek at the tangible fact of it. I'm no longer afraid to call it by its name. Rape. Malaki raped me. Shards of crimson rage threaten to rend my cloak. I try to remember Brân's canopy. It felt like a mirror where I could see out, but no one could see in. I let the shards fly toward Malaki.

I didn't mean to look, but I see him. My cloak remains intact. It's his canopy that's in tatters. Heavy brown scraps of it hover around him. People are there, too. They've hurt him. Choked him. Damaged his aurynx. His head is injured, and he's barely conscious. A touch of pity subdues my anger, but I don't want to know more. I grasp the blue stone more tightly in my right hand and let the sound of its bell course through me.

I stop suddenly. Did they find Brân, too? Did the ones who hurt Malaki hurt Brân? I look for him and find nothing. Cold thorns of yellow-green horror prick my orb and the back of my neck. Brân! I sit down right there, close my eyes, cover my ears, shutting out everything but the thought of him. Nothing. "Brân!" I shout his name. And then I feel something like amber honey dripping into a jar, seeping from a melting, waxen honeycomb. So many chambers. Brân stirs, inhaling the thick golden stuff, choking on it even as it nourishes him. He groans in pain. I see him there at the bottom of a gulch. They didn't get him. He tripped and fell into the gulch, knocked his head. They left him for dead. His leg is broken. And his wrist. But he's not dead. Not anymore.

"Where are you, Brân?" I say the words out loud and try hard to verberate them, try harder to pertange his location. The heaviness of his pain repels me, preventing me from seeing where he is.

The colors in my head knock back and forth in confusion. Damon needs me. Brân needs me, too, but I don't know where he is. Besides, I'll need help to get him to safety. Where can I find help? Maybe Mother knows. I will go to Damon.

"I'll come for you, Brân. Soon I'll come for you. Please stay strong." I say the words aloud, my eyes clenched shut as I grip the stone in my left hand, the green one that brought me the peaceful song of the lady, the song of Brân and Abél's mother. My grandmother.

She's there with him. Avienne has been there all along.

I keep going. I'm tired and still fearful, but I push my body onward. A little cony sits by the path ahead of me, trying to be invisible, as fearful as I. My steps are soft, but his big ears stand suddenly straight up. He hears me and he's gone.

It's midafternoon and my legs scream for rest. The bird and I stop next to a low bluff. Beside it there's shade enough when I sit huddled under an overhanging rock. I notice bird pecking at a stone and when I move it, we find water. I let bird drink first, then I fill my sheath and drink, too. I scoop out another handful of water to wash the brink thistle. Preparing it. Keeping it fresh.

"Do you have a name?" I ask bird.

He looks at me, first one eye, then the other. Scratches his head with a foot. Shakes his feathers out. Raises wings like a shrug.

"Well, my name is Meridia," I say. "If you're staying around, I think I'll call you Duende." It's a word I remember from a poem I knew once. I can't recall exactly what it means, but I remember an exalted feeling. It seems right for this exuberant little companion. "Okay?"

Bird's head bobs up and down as if he approves.

I take the last of some very dry nutbread from my pack. I tear off a piece for Duende and another piece for me. He pecks and I chew.

If I rest much longer my legs will go stiff and I won't be able to go on at all. I've been walking most of the night and now most of the day. I've run out of roots to make bitterwater. I think about the song the lady taught me, but I can't ask for Avienne's help. She needs to stay with Brân.

"Let's go," I say to Duende.

"Come along. *Chrrr-eep.*"

There's an urgency in my heart and I move faster than before, despite my aching legs and blistered, burning feet. Duende and I call back and forth less frequently. I sense where he is even when I don't see or hear him. Through his eyes, I see that we've passed by the town of Blanton and are nearing Shadham. As we get closer, I see that of the six cabins in the hamlet, only two of them are inhabited. Damon and my mother are in one of those.

Duende rests on an old fencepost to which no fence has been connected for many passages. The sun is gone, and I've drunk the last of the water from my sheath. But we've arrived.

18.

I GO TO THE DOOR AND KNOCK obediently. What else would I do? A face appears at an open window. Her look mystifies me. Surprised, yes, and happy. But something else, too.

The door opens and we embrace without words. She's different. I'm different. Despite my exhaustion, I can tell that her mind is clearer. There's more depth. Less certainty. Regret?

"How did you find us?" she begins, then shakes her head. She thinks I came for Damon, not her. I came for both. But Damon is the one whose need is urgent. Mother walks with me to where Damon lies on a bed near the open window. He's asleep but his face is tense. There are wet cloths on his forehead, chest, belly. I can almost see a rusty steam rising from them. My heart sinks with the weight of what I know I must tell him. But that can come later. When he's better.

Mother brings me a glass of water. I drink a few swallows. I notice that her dark complexion is more lustrous than I remember and that her topknot of wavy hair seems a little less gray. Is that possible? Her Mundani eyebrows are as thick and dark as ever. My heart holds back. I have so many questions.

"I know you can help him," Mother says.

I ask for a grinding bowl. I take the brink thistles from my pack while Mother finds the bowl and its stone pestle. I trim the plants down to the part where stem becomes root and grind these to a paste, extracting resistant woody fibers. I concentrate on my work, pushing aside questions, feelings, worries. My arms are heavy, and my hands shake.

"Meri?" Damon is awake.

A burst of gold between us. It's weak from his side, but it's there. I've never seen this before.

"We'll need water," I say to Mother. It feels odd, giving her orders like this. It feels good how readily she complies.

We help Damon to a limp sitting position. I place a bare spoonful of the bitter paste into his mouth and he gags. "Here, drink." I put the cup to his lips. He gulps it down with a grimace. He drinks a few more swallows before we let him lie down.

I bathe a few of the brink thistle leaves in the diluted paste and apply the leaves to his wounds.

He offers a wan smile. "You found me," he says.

"I couldn't let you die."

"Again?"

"Again. Rest now," I say. "Let the medicine work. We'll talk when you're stronger."

He pats my hand, closes his eyes.

My heart screams with despair, but no tears come. Exhaustion has consumed them. I sit with Damon, bathing him in weak blue light. He needs more, but this is all I can manage. I sit until his breathing evens out in sleep.

I go to the table where Mother sits, writing in a notebook. That secret thing she's always done. I sit down across from her. My legs quiver and my mind is a torment of memories, old and new.

Mother closes the book and looks up at me. "I'm so happy to see you, Mer."

I think she looks more sad than happy, but I say the expected thing. "I'm happy to see you, too." Am I happy? I can contain the questions no longer. "Why didn't you come home?" There's gray-brown hurt in my voice. It dusts across the table toward her.

She looks down at her hands as she clutches the notebook, the receptacle of her words. She's searching for the right ones to say what she wants to tell me. Words are such frail vehicles.

"At first, I simply didn't remember. The renewal, the coming back, it didn't heal me all at once." She pauses, riffling the pages of her notebook with a thumb. She's uncertain how completely it's healed her even now. She knows that I know she died. "I didn't even know who I was for a while. Had no idea where home might be. I felt so disconnected. By the time I began to remember Temur, to remember you, I was already settled in here. My friend Gerd helped me so much with that. She and her weftred."

I've heard about weftreds, but I don't really know what they do. I think Mother was part of one in Temur, long ago. It feels like another one of Mother's secrets.

Mother keeps talking. "Gerd says I was pretty helpless when her son Fergus brought me in. He's the one who found me. She says he had to carry me, I was that weak." She riffles her pages again. The sleeve of her blouse has drawn back to reveal a wrap around her wrist, a wrap with red-orange beads. She touches one of the beads, turning it with her fingers. "Maybe I was wrong," she says, "but as I began to come to myself, I felt like you'd be better off without me. I was such a burden on you for so long. I'm sorry for all that, Mer." Her eyes study my face, searching for something.

It's a struggle for my tired brain to follow her story, to make sense of the feelings it stirs inside me. To figure out who my mother has become. Who she was. The burden of her regret is heavy. She's thinking about that time she beat me with the soup ladle. It was not the first time she'd hit me. And it wasn't the last.

"Why?" I say, and she knows what I mean.

Behind the sadness in her eyes there's a flash of something. It passes. "I shouldn't have let myself go like I did," she says. "But your father had left us, and I knew this time he wouldn't be coming back. I couldn't let you go on being like him. Your life would be too hard."

A deep sigh rises up from my heart, tinged with longing. I'm remembering her illness. Is that when it began? That long ago, as she tried to withdraw from a life that had left her stranded? I remember my own worry as, passage after passage, her condition worsened. How I used to go looking for her when she wandered off. And finally, the gradual letting go when, day after day, she didn't come home at all. I try to say that I understand, but the words won't come. A pale trickle of turquoise light reaches from my aurynx to embrace her as I say, "It wasn't so bad, Mother." The verberations don't exactly match the words. I want to know more about how she died, how she came back, but I'm not sure she has answers to such questions. I'm not sure I'd have the strength to hear her. My eyelids are heavy, but I know the gyrating confusion in my mind won't let me sleep. Not yet.

Mother feels so Mundani to me.

We sit in silence for a while, starting over.

"Damon said you and he were on your way to Fayredell when you got separated. He didn't say why you were going there."

I try to explain. I owe her some truth. I always hid my visions and strangeness. It was to protect her, but now I think she may be ready. So I tell her about the rock and about the beautiful woman and a little bit about the song.

Mother nods thoughtfully. "Did you find the man you were looking for? This Chapling fellow?"

"I did," I say, but I don't tell her his true name. Not yet. I feel as if saying his name might drain his strength. Is that really why I don't say it? I know he needs all his strength. "He was coming with me to find Damon and you, but there was trouble. He's been injured. I need to find him and help him."

"Why didn't you say so earlier, Mer? Where did you leave him? How badly hurt was he?"

"He was fine when I left him. The accident happened after. And I don't know where he is." But I do know. Suddenly I know. And I know Duende can guide me there. All I say is, "I think I know where to look. But someone would have to come with me. He may need to be carried."

"Of course. I'm sure Gerd can go with you. She helped me bring Damon here from Blanton. I can go early tomorrow morning and send her here with her cart. Will that be soon enough?"

"I think so." It will have to be. I'm glad Mother has a friend. I remind myself that she's been here almost a full passage.

She keeps talking as my eyelids grow heavier and heavier. She tells me about how she found work at a small bookshop in Blanton. I think she says she works there two days in each six. Just sufficient to pay for her simple needs. She likes working among the books.

"I work in Blanton," she says, "but I decided to live here in Shadham. It's so quiet. You always loved the quiet, Mer. The quiet of the woods."

Mother sees that I can deny my tiredness no longer. She spreads blankets on the floor next to Damon's bed so I can keep watch over him through the night. I lie down gratefully, exhausted. I place my two waifs under the edge of my pillow.

19.

THE WOMAN HUMS SOFTLY as she walks along the path. It's an old path, not much used anymore, overgrown and difficult. She stops to pick up a sparkling pink pebble, caresses it with a swollen finger, tucks it into her pocket. The pocket is already heavy, bulging. There's a hole in one corner and a smaller pebble has fallen through. She doesn't notice.

She also doesn't notice the sun's heat nor the stone in her sandal nor her parched lips, her thirst. She's amused by the dryness of her tongue and sticks it out, waggles it. Laughs a little. Tries to make clucking noises with her dry tongue. She shakes her foot, the one with the stone inside the sandal, and almost falls.

A sound draws her up short. A cry. A nen's cry, faint and weak, but unmistakable.

The woman is suddenly alert, her broken brain and pounding heart a maelstrom of competing images and emotions. "Mer?" the word comes hoarse, a barely intelligible squeak. *My nen,* she thinks. *My little girl!*

She struggles to focus on the sound, so faint and small. Her hands and legs are scratched and bleeding as she pushes her way past the clutches of dry grass and brush toward the sound.

"Mer, Mer," she murmurs. She doesn't see that the whimpering nen is still tethered to its mother. She doesn't see that a wild animal has already been at its tiny limbs. She hardly notices the woman at all, doesn't notice her golden color fading to gray, doesn't see that the woman's head is covered in blood, or the pool of drying blood between her legs. My mother doesn't see the thinning canopy of soft, clear colors. All she sees is the nen, a tiny, pale thing with dully iridescent skin, struggling to breathe, lying next to the woman's bloody breast. The woman's last effort was to draw the infant to her breast, to nourish it with her dying body.

My mother lies down next to the dead woman and takes the nen into her arms, exposes her own withered breast, offers it to the nen. But the nen is too weak, barely breathing. Mother moans softly and strokes the tiny body, murmuring "Mer, Mer," her eyes stinging with tears that do not form. She doesn't hear the heavy footsteps coming back, the man thinking to finish the job he thought he'd accomplished. He's annoyed to find a second woman by the one he's already murdered.

Mother sees the man, sees his intention just before she closes her eyes, just before her heart stops.

Just as breath ceases.

But not before her own anger congeals into a knot in her throat.

Unacceptable.

Impossible, really. Not merely the inertness of absence. This tiny body is broken, savaged, torn beyond usefulness. The one it's attached to was ready to go. A Token reunited. Reconciled. The woman beside her is injured, yes, but she expired from extreme sadness, sudden rage. Yes, she is the one who reached out to us. Reached out with anguish and regret. She will be our Token.

I stare at the stone in my hand, wide-eyed, grasping after the fading vision. I need to remember this. Is this what happened to Mother? Does she love me so much after all? Does she have so much regret? It makes no sense, but I know I need to remember.

Through the rest of the night I toss and turn, moving between oblivious deep sleep and wakefulness, never yielding to dreams. Near morning, I hear Damon's cries and thrashing about. I sit up and see that his eyes are still closed.

"Damon?" I'm whispering. "Are you okay, Damon?" I feel his brow and find that the fever has abated.

His eyes open. They're wild and confused. "Meri," he says. "My poor Meri."

He takes my hand and cradles it on his chest. I kneel next to the bed and he holds my hand the rest of the night as I slump into slumber beside him.

20.

MOTHER LEFT FOR WORK EARLY today, promising to send Gerd right away. I couldn't look at her, trying hard not to see in her the broken and desperate woman of my dream.

Damon is better. He sits up and eats a little proper food. His wounds no longer ooze. He's been looking at me strangely ever since he woke.

"I dreamed about you last night," he says after we've said goodbye to Mother.

"Yes?"

Waves of reddish light pulse above his chest. "It was terrible, Meri. I dreamed that a man forced himself on you. I saw at first that you seemed to comply but then you woke up and saw who it was and turned into this fierce zaki of a woman and fought him off. Why would I dream something like that?"

Brân was right. The renewal from death does give Mundani some of the Melfar abilities. My heart swells to know that he saw me as a zaki, the biggest, fiercest cat beast of all.

"You dreamed it because it's true," I turn my reddening face away even as I long to probe his eyes and heart. I'm trying to suppress the zaki that wants to rise again. "I dreaded telling you." My body contorts into a gray-blue sob of release like the slump of wet sand. I bury my face against Damon and let the tears come. I let the images of Malaki's assault rise up in me so that Damon can know the whole truth.

"You believed it was me," Damon says, anger pulsing through his body. Not anger at me. Anger at Malaki. "How could he deceive you like that? What kind of man is he?"

"He's half Melfar, like me."

"Melfar?"

"It's what people like me are properly called," I say.

He grips both my hands almost too tightly. "Oh, Meri. I should have been there to protect you. I'm so sorry."

"Not your fault. Malaki is a sully beast." The zaki again.

Gradually Damon's grip loosens. We breathe together more calmly.

Then I explain in the best words I can find about locating Chapling who is called Brân and about what I learned from him. I tell Damon about the Benison waifs and I show him the indigo-colored waif I found on my journey. "Malaki is Brân's son." I can't say yet that Brân is my father's brother twin.

"And Brân let him do that to you?"

"He wasn't there. He'd gone out looking for food and firewood. Brân is angry, too. He's left Malaki behind."

Damon is quiet. Struggling to grasp all of this.

"I think deception is all Malaki's good at," I say. "He uses it to get whatever he wants. Brân says we've developed different parts of the Melfar gifts. I have a strong orb. Malaki's aurynx is stronger." Then I have to explain about the gnosic orb and aurynx. About how the aurynx verberates sounds and colors that the orb pertanges.

"So these are actual physical organs?" Despite his weakness, despite his distress over what happened to me, Damon is energized by this knowledge. It's something he's been trying to figure out in his research.

"I have no idea how they work," I say. "I only know what they do." I recall how I'd learned to help Damon pertange my verberations by placing my throat against his forehead. My aurynx against his weak Mundani orb. We don't seem to need that anymore.

Damon takes a deep breath, his eyes wide, his heart beating more calmly. He knows I don't want to talk about Malaki anymore. Don't want to think about him. "This is related to the Benisons, isn't it?" Damon says. "The waifs. Crispin and his comrades were demanding our waif. I didn't want them to know you had it, but somehow they knew. They claimed to be Revelants. Are Revelants able to do what Melfar do? They're people who have died and come back, right?"

"Like you," I say, reminding him.

"I guess since I was so young the first time it happened, I didn't realize what a difference it could make. Do you suppose that's why I was able to sense your...your...?"

"Verberations." I supply the word. "Yes. I think that's it."

"Do you know why they were so interested in getting hold of our stone? The waif? I know about destiny stones, but Crispin and the others were hardly boys marking their twelfth passage."

"Some women I took care of had things they called healing stones," I say. "I always thought they had different colors. Different tones. Maybe that's it." But I don't think so. Not really. "Probably they just know the stones are important to Melfar." They don't want them for themselves so much as they want us not to have them. They're afraid of what we can do with them. What we can do is far more than I would have imagined. I'm certain that it's more than I know even now.

"I think being near the waifs is making your perceptions more acute," Damon says. "And I sense stronger...what did you call them? Verberations? Your verberations are stronger."

"That could be. But you're twice Revelant. You pertange more." Really, I've been feeling weaker lately. I've spent so much energy healing Damon. And trying to find Brân.

There's a brief spark, a current between us, the color of fresh violets.

"I know what happened to Mother," I say.

"She's Revelant, too, right?"

Damon does notice more. "Yes," I say, and I tell him what I saw. I try to. I leave out the part about the Migrant. Is that what that was? The presence that brought her back? I can't find words for that part. "She's different now. Her brain is mostly healed. She still doesn't remember everything."

"Nobody remembers everything," Damon says. "What became of Brân?"

"He's hurt. Gerd and I are going out soon to fetch him. He's not far away."

"Will you be okay?" He scowls, thinking of Malaki. "Promise me you'll be careful. It will be good to have Gerd with you. Gerd seems to be a good friend to your mother. And a strong woman. Very capable."

I give him another dose of the medicine and clean his wounds. I make some tea that I know will help restore his strength. I'm glad we're able to talk about things other than Malaki. The horror of what Malaki did still hangs between us, but we have to go on. I want to put it behind us. I want it to be just something in the past that we've forgotten about.

A soft knock on the door announces Gerd's arrival. She's a tall woman, even taller than Damon. Not quite so dark. Her black hair is flecked with strands of gray and hangs in a long plait down her back. Her eyebrows thick as mats of wickmoss. I like her eyes. They reach out and pertange me gently, asking permission. That's odd for Mundani. I feel guilty having a word for the ones who are not like me. I've always been the one labelled. The rest were just people. Sidayens or kinren, but all of them people.

"You must be Meridia," she says, extending her hand in greeting. Her bare arms are muscular, and her wrist is wrapped in knotted cloth and orange-red beads.

"Gerd," I say as our fingers touch. "Please come inside."

"Your mother said we need to go rescue an injured man, but she didn't say who it was. A friend of yours, I gather."

"Yes. Damon met him in Brightlea." As if that explains anything. "He's my uncle."

"What?" Damon sits up halfway in his bed. "Brân is your uncle?"

I hadn't got to that part yet. "Yes, he's brother twin to my father, Abél." Now I'll have to tell Mother.

Damon lies back down, then springs up again, his eyes flashing anger, red sparks bursting from his chest. He's put it together. *Yes, Malaki is my cousin brother.* I can't look at Damon. My face flushes hot. This is going to be harder than I thought.

"I've brought my equid and cart," Gerd says. Her voice is deep, but soft as a feather pillow. "I've also brought my son Fergus to stay here with Damon. In case he needs anything. Fergus is minding the equid. Do you know the way to where your uncle is?"

"I can find the way," I say. "We'll have help."

There's a sharp tapping on the window next to Damon's bed. "Come along," Duende says.

Gerd turns toward the window, looking puzzled.

"Do you trust a bird?" I say.

She chuckles softly as she opens the door to leave. I walk to the bed and lean down to kiss Damon goodbye. He grips my hands again. I try not to see the pain in his eyes. I'm glad someone will be here with him. I don't like leaving him alone. He doesn't like where I'm going. Neither do I. But I have to go.

21.

"HOW ARE YOU FEELING TODAY?" Fergus says as he closes the door behind himself.

"Better, thanks," Damon says. Fergus is young, barely a man. Not the kind of companion Damon wants today. In fact, he'd prefer to be alone, but he knows they're still concerned about his health. His strength. He's feeling better but he's still weak. Probably too weak to be left alone.

Fergus takes a book out of his pocket and draws a chair up near the window, arranging and rearranging his gangly form, still managing to look uncomfortable. "Let me know if you need anything," he says.

Damon settles back onto his pillow, relieved to know he's not going to be expected to make conversation. One of the things he's always liked best about Meri is how she only speaks when she has something to say. Not like most Mundani, who will rattle on endlessly about nothing, filling up time with meaningless strings of words.

The silence leaves Damon time to wander among his own thoughts. Fuming, angry thoughts about "that bastard Malaki" and what he did to Meri. He hopes that his desire to confront Malaki, to give him a few good whacks, might help him to regain his strength faster. At the moment, it's giving him a headache. He knows there's nothing to be done about what happened. Trying to report such an assault to authorities would do no good. A Shoon raping a Shoon would be of no interest to them.

Damon was so careful with Meridia. They were friends for many stints before he approached her physically. She'd lived her whole life as a single woman, or so he'd thought at the time. Eventually, as trust grew between them, Meri told him that at one time, when she was quite young, barely a woman at all, she'd been promised to a young man. He was the son of one of the local shopkeepers. Meri said that her mother had been pleased because the boy was the son of a Sidayen. Not an important Sidayen, but a Sidayen, nonetheless. The boy had insisted on coupling even though Meridia didn't want it. Meri confessed that he generally treated her badly. She said he was short and blind in one eye, disfigured from a childhood accident. Even so, he constantly reminded her how lucky she was that a Sidayen's son like him would be interested in a Shoon at all. Then it was discovered that the young man had gotten another girl in town pregnant and, rather than backing out of the arrangement with Meridia gracefully, he'd publicly denounced her for being barren. It was an unnecessary insult, because Shoon women are known to be barren. That's why so many men use them as they do. Damon was grateful that he'd had the sense to be patient with Meridia.

Meri is different in so many ways, and Damon loves her *because* of her difference. Unlike most women he's known, who seem to revel in playing guessing games with men, Meri is honest. He thought at first that maybe this was a Shoon characteristic. *Melfar,* Damon tells himself. *I need to start saying Melfar.* But that must not be true. This Malaki fellow is Melfar and Damon can see how disgustingly adept he was at deception and lying.

Fergus shifts awkwardly in his chair as he turns another page in his book.

By the configuration of the words on the page, Damon sees that it's a book of poetry. "Would you mind reading me a little of that?"

Fergus looks surprised, but he nods and clears his throat. His voice still has that uncertain register characteristic of boys becoming men. But the words are beautiful. It's one of the poems Meridia knows and Damon closes his eyes, hearing Meri's lilting voice among the words.

22.

"WAKE UP! COME ALONG," Duende says.

Gerd's equid is almost as tall as me at his shoulders. The black stripes across his haunches contrast with the golden tufts along his spine. His ears are small and rounded, hardly bigger than his flaring nostrils.

The cart is a large basket on a wooden frame. Its two wheels are wrapped in metal, pocked and dented from many rotations over stony roads. The vehicle looks none too sturdy. Gerd offers her hand and I climb up, settling onto the piece of smooth-worn board that serves as a seat.

Duende is well ahead of us, perched on a stump, bobbing his head impatiently and calling, *Chrrr-eep.*

I point toward him and answer. Gerd looks amused. She climbs into the cart and urges the equid in the direction the bird indicates.

The hard toes of the animal seem better suited to the rough road than the cart he's hauling. He wants to go faster than Gerd allows. She's not sure how far we'll need to go before the day's end. I'm not sure either.

I've brought both of the waifs with me, the green one that connects me to Brân through his mother Avienne, and the blue one that connects me to Duende. I rub my thumb across the surface of the green stone, thinking Brân, reaching out, opening. Breathing with my mind.

Brân is resting despite the awful pain. The break in his leg is clean and the bone remains in place. His hand is a bigger problem. Twisted and shattered. I'm wondering how we'll get all those small bones put back together. I hear him humming and recognize the tune. It's the one Avienne taught me, the one from the Benison whose waif I hold in my hand. Avienne has been with him all night.

Gerd has asked a question. Something about my mother. How long it's been since we've seen one another? Yes, that was it.

"Nearly a passage," I say. "She was ill and lost her way one day. She never made it back home."

"You must have been worried."

"I tried to find her, but it was impossible. I wasn't very good at such things. Not back then." I chirp at Duende and he replies from well down the road where he's indicating the left fork at a turning.

"You know she was worried about you. After she began to remember, she spoke about you often."

I didn't know. I wonder what she said of me.

"Our weftred here was happy to take her in," Gerd says.

"Weftred." I repeat the word. "I've never really understood what that is."

"Weftreds are networks of kinrens, mostly women, that share information. News, warnings. And stories. Even songs and poems. Chanters have their own weftreds in many places."

Like the one Gerd and Mother are part of. "Why are they called weftreds?" Words have to come from somewhere. I'm trying to anchor this one.

"Oh, I think it's because of how they weave in and around the Houses and Sidayens who, you might say, form the warp of things. You know about weaving?"

I don't, so this doesn't help much. At least I know what weftreds do.

Duende chirrups and I answer.

"I take it your bird is a recent thing," Gerd says.

I nod. I try to think of something to say. I've never been good at small talk, and stones and birds aren't much help with that. So mostly we sit in silence as we bump along in the cart while the sun edges higher in the sky. The road gets narrower and bumpier the farther we go.

Just as I'm about to think the road is becoming impassable, I hear Duende chirruping insistently from a small bush off the road to the left.

"We'll have to leave the cart here," Gerd says. "It's bad enough on the road. I'm afraid we might break a wheel out there."

I shoulder my backsack, which contains water and medicine and bandages as well as some sticks for splints. I hope that will be all we need. I hope it's not far.

Past the bush where Duende sits, I pertange some greenish bubbles rising from a gulch and I break into a run. "Brân?" I shout. "Brân, I'm coming." Avienne vanishes in a swirl of colors and a soft arpeggio as I reach the edge of the gulch. I find a way down and kneel next to Brân, reaching out with blue light to pertange his injuries. The leg won't be a problem, but the hand is a mess. And I don't need my gnosic orb to see that his head wound is covered in flies.

"You found me, Meridia." His voice is barely more than a whisper. I give him some water from my sheath, offering it in measured drops so he won't choke. He's so thirsty. Once I can tell that his mouth is no longer dry, I place a dollop of medicine on his tongue, followed by more water. He gags a bit, just like Damon did. Medicine isn't meant to please, only to heal.

First I cleanse the wound on his head, applying brink thistle leaves and a bandage. Then I take his wrist in my two hands, close my eyes, and feel for the bones and tendons and ligaments. So many tiny parts to a wrist and hand and they all have to fit together exactly so. The medicine has begun to give him some relief from pain, but I know this is still going to hurt. I press firmly, right below the thumb and feel him wince. Then I massage the hand all over, pressing harder where I find things out of place. There are tears in Brân's eyes. But I pertange something else. Sadness. Regret.

Gerd watches me work. She's seated on a rock near Brân's feet, ready to help.

So I ask for help. "Could you cut a piece of this board about so long and work off all the corners?" I need something to support Brân's hand, which I lay across his chest while Gerd works. I fasten splints around Brân's broken leg. I'm surprised to find that it's already partially healed. I bind the splint tightly to the leg. Then I take the splint Gerd has crafted and bind it to the hand and wrist.

"How will we get him to the cart?" I ask.

"Wait here."

I wait. Soon Gerd returns with the equid. She's detached the wheeled basket. The two lengths of wood that connected the animal's harness to the cart drag on the ground behind him. Gerd has brought a blanket, which she spreads out on a flat area of ground. Then she climbs back down into the gulch. She lifts Brân in her arms as if he weighs no more than a child and climbs to the surface, where she lays him on the blanket. Brân only cries out once. Gerd maneuvers the equid into position and secures the edges of the blanket to the lengths of wood. It forms a sort of bed that the equid can pull. Just as I'm about to object that bouncing my patient over the rough ground is not a good plan, Gerd lifts the ends of the frame, lofting Brân's body off the ground and hoisting the whole contraption onto her shoulders. She makes a clicking sound and the equid moves forward.

"We'll have to leave the cart here," she says. "Fergus can come and fetch it later. Are you okay walking back to the house?"

"Yes," I say. "But can you carry him that far?"

"Your man is not so heavy. Besides, I carry things for a living." Gerd takes a deep breath and sets off at a brisk pace behind the equid, carrying the contrivance that supports Brân on her shoulders. I follow.

We know our way now, but I keep an eye on Duende all the same, trusting him to keep watch for us. Once in a while he soars skyward and then dives back toward us. He does this as much for fun, I think, as to get a broader view of where we are. I'd do that if I were a bird. He has nothing to report.

We stop twice to let Gerd rest and to let me check on Brân's splints and injuries. The second time we stop I notice that the head wound has begun to bleed again, though not badly. I think it can wait for a new dressing until we reach Mother's house. We drink water and eat the gorseberries I brought. I should've brought bitterroot for Gerd. I crush a couple of berries and Brân sucks the juice. Gerd interrupts the equid's grazing to offer the animal some water.

Mother is there waiting for us by the time we arrive. Fergus helps Gerd to transfer Brân to the bed that Mother has prepared for him. It's her bed and I wonder briefly where she plans to sleep. I notice the way Mother looks at Brân. Does she see a resemblance to Abél, to my father?

"How bad are Chapling's injuries?" she asks.

"He'll live," I say. "But his name isn't Chapling. It's Brân."

Mother's eyes widen and she looks at him again, studying his face. She's seen that he's Revelant. If she sees anything more she doesn't say so.

"I've made soup," she says.

"That would be good. Let him rest a bit first. The journey wasn't easy." I leave Brân and go to Damon.

He says he wants to go outside.

"A little walk," I say. "Around the garden?" He wants to find out how strong he is.

I help him up and hand him his hat. So far, his walks have only taken him to sit on the pot in the corner but this time we walk all the way to the door. He steps outside and trembles with the first breath. He sways and places a hand on the door jamb. The other hand is on my shoulder. He takes another breath and is steadier. There's a breeze, and he turns to let it caress his face.

"Can you go as far as that bench?" I ask.

He nods. Step by step we go. He stands taller. Reaching the bench, he sits down heavily, breathing hard, clearly relieved. Pleased with himself.

"How did Mother find you?" I ask.

"I'm not sure. I was in a shed in Blanton. They left me for dead. Well, I guess I was, wasn't I? But I heard your voice, Meri. I heard you calling me, and I think that's what brought me back. I'm sure that was it. I kept wanting to tell you to run, to hide. I was so afraid for you, afraid of what they might do if they found you. I'm just glad you found Chapling. Brân." He's not at all glad about finding Malaki.

"It's good that Mother had a friend who could help her bring you here. Gerd seems a good friend. She's very strong."

"Your mother trusts her. She seems younger than Maddie."

"Mother is younger, too," I say.

Damon tires quickly. His color wavers and then sinks greenish-brown.

"We should go in," I say. "It's getting hot." It's not really so hot, but Damon has begun to sweat. He doesn't resist. It takes longer to go back than it took to come out. He's breathing fast and shallow. The sweat is cleansing but it's draining his strength.

He sits on the bed and I get him a cup of water. His hands shake and it almost spills. He asks for more. My heart is happy to see him stretching to recover. He lies back down and soon sleeps.

Mother leaves to walk with Gerd and Fergus, as Gerd instructs her son how to find the cart. She's put a folded blanket over the equid and set Fergus astride it. The big animal seems hardly tired at all from his journey.

I walk around Mother's house. It's all one big room, broken up only by a few curtains and some low shelves of books. Near the corner where she sleeps, where Brân lies snoring softly, the stones in my pockets pulse. I open the door to a small cupboard next to the bed and find inside a jar half full of stones. I take them to the table and spread them out. Some of them are healing stones like the ones I used to collect in Temur. I now recognize them as waifs, though some feel stronger than others. Some of the stones are just pretty stones. Or maybe they've forgotten their songs. I sort them out and put the inert rocks back into the jar. I collect the waifs in front of me. I take Damon's green waif and my blue one and add them to the pile. I place an open hand on either side of my construction.

There's a tingling in my hands and something sparkles in my peripheral vision.

Mother is singing over the breakfast dishes. Her voice is unexpectedly melodic. Have I ever heard her sing before? I hear another voice. The pitch is nearly the same, but this voice is more resonant. They harmonize.

I see him sitting at the table, his chair pushed back, arms akimbo, chest expanded in song. His physique—stout and sturdy—and his amber-colored skin are like Brân's. But this Melfar man has straw-colored hair and, although I can't see them, I know he has amber eyes. He rises and walks toward Mother as their song softens and slows, final harmony drawn out, sustained, embraced. He puts his arms around her waist and nestles his bearded chin against her shoulder. I see how young she is.

So this is my father. This is Abél, son of Avienne, Brân's brother twin.

I steady my vision, studying him more closely, clinging to the image before it fades.

He's not as tall as Mother. He's not pretty, but his song was exquisite. It resonates in my heart. I think Mother felt this, too. I begin to understand.

23.

ABÉL SITS ON THE SHADY SIDE of a spindly meskie in the old town of Woodclasp. He'd come to tell Keira's family that their daughter was no more. Her mother was Fia Pritchard, born and raised in Woodclasp before being subsumed to Lambert Quint. Abél has found that Keira's only family remaining in the old town is her mother's brother, Orban Pritchard. In fact, Orban and his Melfar partner Emba are the only residents remaining in what was once a vibrant community. Abél should have known. He leans against the tree's rough bark and feels the town all around him. Feels its absence. Sometimes he forgets to ask the right questions.

Orban and Emba are happy to have a guest, even one who comes bearing sad news. They've told Abél that Fia had indeed been staying in Woodclasp, but that she'd passed away only a few tides back. They'd meant to send word with the next visitor, but there had been none until Abél arrived.

In the sparse shade of the meskie, Abél spreads a cloth on the ground. On it, he arranges his stones, sorting them by color, breathing in each stone's hues and tones. Occasionally he catches a wisp of song and echoes it back. Most of the stones are too small to contain more than a few notes, a few scraps of images. There are four Mica fragments, and he picks these up, one by one, holding each one to his forehead, trying to pertange its song. Three of them are clearly from the most recent Mica Meed, whistling the clear notes of the Song of

Reflection. He wills the reflection to be a pool of fresh water, but it isn't.

The fourth fragment is the smallest of all. It belongs to the Old Mica and its layers are fragile, threatening to flake away if he handles it too roughly. That's always been a problem with the Mica Benisons. It's said that the Old Mica still exists. Its song was Calling the Rains. Somewhere that song still lives. Somewhere it is still whole and complete. Finding the Old Mica Benison, finding its song, has been Abél's quest for the past few meeds. Could it be as many as three? More than thirty Mundani passages. It's hard for Abél to keep track according to the Melfar calendar ever since Melfar abandoned the Benison rituals. Part of the ritual was a recitation of all the meeds and the singing of all the songs, even when all anyone remembered were floating scraps of the oldest songs, the ones known as Ancients and Preterits.

Abél's fragment of the Old Mica was given to him by his father, who was named after the stone itself. Mica, partner of Avienne and father of the brother twins, Brân and Abél, was a keeper of the song of Calling the Rains and had tried to teach it whole to both of his sons. The song had many layers, resonating and reflecting tones and images, surging like the thrum of raindrops on a forest canopy. Brân had found its complexity too difficult, but Abél eventually mastered it. Now he's forgotten as much as he remembers.

It was just before the Marble Return of the New Quartz Meed that Avienne had called Abél and his brother to Woodclasp to bid farewell to their dying father. Mundani counted it as the passage 630. Mica had been caught in the fires that consumed the last remaining stands of forest in the region of Cödweg and east Cesta. Abél hardly recognized him. The left side of his body was covered in bandages and Abél could see that one hand and most of a foot were gone. His face seeped vivid red and parts of his scalp were singed right down to the skull. He should have been dead.

"Come here, my sons." Had he spoken the words? His voice was a harsh rasp, but it contained a smile that his face could no longer express. Brân sat in a corner of the room, his body collapsed into a chair that could barely hold his sadness. He rose in silence and approached, standing with Abél on Mica's right side, the side where their father still lived.

Avienne, bring my cache, Abél said, speaking wordlessly. A moment later she held out to him a heavy leather bag. *Please open it for me.*

Avienne did as she was asked and began taking the waifs out, one by one. As she did so, Mica designated which of his two sons would be its keeper. Brân received a Quartz, a Turquoise, two Jades, an Obsidian, a Lapis, and several smaller stones. Abél, in his turn, received a large Amethyst, two Granites, a Turquoise, an Amber, and two Micas. The smaller Mica he knew well. As each stone was placed into a waiting hand, Abél heard a sigh of parting and whether it came from his father or from the stone itself he couldn't say.

When he was finished, Mica strained to look into his sons' eyes. *We must come together. Somehow this disaster must end. Promise me.*

And in that moment, Brân promised to collect Melfar together once more so that their songs could rouse the people to harmony. And Abél knew that he must find a way to restore the earth itself; he must find the parent of the small Mica that was entrusted to his care, the Old Mica with its song of Calling the Rains. This time they would sing in more supple chorus and the rains would fall gently. It was a difficult song and Melfar were few. Those who knew the song, fewer still.

Abél said his farewells to his father, his mother Avienne, and his brother Brân. He departed hopeful but far from confident.

Abél had returned to Temur, to his beloved Madelyn and their young daughter Meridia. He tried to explain to Maddie what he had to do. He spent endless hours singing with the tiny Mica waif, trying to pertange where its parent stone might be found. At times he caught glimpses of it, weathered but still whole, covered in accretions of... what? He couldn't tell. It was a substance he found unfamiliar. Almost like something living. And then the vision would fade, submerged in forgetfulness, its song overwhelmed by a surging, sucking nothing. For the time being, he'd have to rest content in the knowledge that the Old Mica Benison still existed.

All of this happened in the early returns of the New Quartz Meed. There had been no Benison for the New Quartz, although pieces of Quartz were sent out among the Melfar, each invested with maps and messages, something to hold them together, to help them find one another. Since then another meed, the New Carnelian, had come and gone. This one was marked not by the dedication of a new Benison, but rather by taking pieces of the Old Carnelian with its Song of the Wide Path and working the pieces into red-orange beads. Hundreds of beads. The New Amber Meed, which would soon draw to a close, was not marked at all except for evoking the powers of the Old Amber and its Song of Turning.

Everything seemed turned around wrong these days.

Abél doesn't know where to go next. When he followed the rumors about the Old Mica to Markham all he'd found was the desecrated body of Keira Landry of Quint. A sadness sifts through him, dusky and heavy.

24.

I DON'T KNOW WHETHER to confess to Mother that I've raided her store of stones. Sometimes I still feel like a little girl around her. She keeps wanting to take care of me again. At times I still see that look in her eyes, the look that took her mind into unknowable places. The places that took her away from me.

Damon and Brân have both awakened from their naps by the time Mother returns with Gerd. The cabin feels crowded.

Mother busies herself making supper. Gerd lifts a book off the shelf and shows it to me. It's bound in leather with words stamped on the spine and cover.

"What is it?" I say.

"Your mother never let you read the Story of Razak?" Gerd's eyebrows rise up like a couple of startled caterpillars.

"I can't read." I'm no longer ashamed to admit that. It's just part of who I am.

Mother looks at her feet and smooths her apron. "I told her that if she wanted to know the history of our people, she would have to read it herself. I thought it would motivate her."

"Not a question of motivation." I say this a bit too harshly. I'm reminded that for Mother "our people" means Mundani. She needs to remember that I am also Melfar. I'm as much Melfar as Mundani. And that isn't a bad thing.

"Well then let me read it to you." Gerd glances at Mother, who doesn't object. Gerd's voice is round and resonant as a temple bell as she begins to read.

"In the darkness before time, people were only a memory in the mind of the Creator. That which passes away comes again. That is the will of the Creator. That is the will of the people." Gerd pauses, allowing the words to congeal into meanings.

"I've never understood what that meant," Damon says. "It doesn't make sense."

I think Brân understands it.

Gerd shrugs and continues. "Out of the struggle between darkness and light came all the plants and animals and a wealth of cunning tools and vehicles, all the gifts of the Creator. But the tools and vehicles failed and the devices the people were able to craft for themselves were poor and simple. They were left with only the sun, the rain, and the plants and animals. They made gardens and traded with forest beings for meat slain in its secret depths. Through many generations their numbers grew. They began to compete with one another for land and resources. They began to quarrel.

"In a passage of a double eclipse, a baby was born, darker and more beautiful than any who had been born before. His eyes sparkled like black sand on a beach and when his hair began to grow it was shiny and wavy like the surface of an obsidian blade. He was born to the House Caloyer and was called Razak. When he was weaned, he refused to eat the meat of the forest and instead subsisted on the grains and fruits his family grew in their gardens. His reputation as a strong and skillful fighter spread from an early age and whenever there were contests to determine who was fastest or strongest, Razak always won. His gardens also grew more and better produce than any others. He was generous in training and instructing the people. He lived many happy passages and died in old age. That was the first time he was among us.

"For more than one hundred and eighty passages, Razak was mourned and revered as people sought to follow the ways he had taught them of personal strength and wise and diligent cultivation of the earth. The people made water offerings to the Creator and they ate well and were healthy and happy and had many nens. But then a time came when the rains hid from the people for twelve long passages and they called upon Razak to return to them and tell them what to do. While they waited and entreated, they made more and greater water offerings. Out of great hunger, they began to eat meat. When the rains did come at last, they came with such force that the lands were inundated. Crops and towns were destroyed, and many people died. They left off their water offerings, but their prayers for the return of Razak never abated. The lands dried out again and it was as if the rains had spent themselves in the time of floods. For twelve more passages, the rains did not come.

"So it was that in the passage of another double eclipse, Razak returned. This time he was born into House Pherson and everyone knew at once that it was he, because on the day of his birth, while great storm clouds formed across the land, the only place where rain fell was on the house where Razak's mother lay in seclusion with her nen. There was great celebration and the child was fêted and nurtured and protected as they waited for him to be of an age when he could instruct them.

"Before Razak Pherson's fifth birth anniversary, he became gravely ill. All the healers came to his bedside, but none could restore his strength. As they were about to lose hope, a bird came into his room during the night and left a piece of ripe florapple in his hand. When they rose the next morning, they saw the child eating the fruit and they were mystified. He began to get well, and the wise men declared that it was the florapple fruit that had restored him. After that, every passage at the time of Razak Pherson's birth anniversary, rains would come, and they were especially abundant in the passages when the florapple trees bloomed.

"Young Razak grew strong and was sent to study with all the wisest and most accomplished scholars, where he learned all they taught him with astonishing ease and quickness. In the spring of his twelfth passage, in accord with the customs of the people, Razak Pherson went out into the countryside to seek his destiny. He collected stones of several kinds but then caught sight of a large and particularly alluring piece of color-flecked granite lying near the bottom of a deep gulch. The stone beckoned him but, alas, in trying to reach it, his foot slipped, and he fell to his death. When his companions came upon him, they well saw that he was dead and one of them, suspecting what he had sought, took up the piece of granite and placed it in Razak's left hand. At once breath came again into him and he lived.

"When he was cured of his injuries, he called all of his teachers to him and, holding up the granite in his hand, said, 'This is my destiny and yours. You need not be afraid anymore. Like the tree that gives us precious florapples, we appear to die only to blossom again. This is the will of the Creator. This is the gift of the Restorer.'

"He also taught that the rains were not forsaking the people, only congregating into their own season, and in like manner people must congregate into their own places. 'In the time of rain, you will plant your crops and in the time of sunshine you will nurture your animals. And in all things, you will celebrate and honor the sun. The sun and rain are the manifest will of our Creator, our Restorer. The sun is more powerful than the rain and will prevail over all unless he is satisfied by offerings of fire. Thus, may the sun be satisfied and rest while the rains water the land.' And so the people gathered together in large towns and cities, and on frequent occasions they built great bonfires to honor the Creator and Restorer.

"In the thirty-sixth passage of his life, Razak Pherson revealed the Sidaya, the rules of right living, and the people were overcome with gratitude. The rules were these: First, honor the Creator and the Order His creation ordains. Second, keep his temples pure. Third, respect the House of your upbringing and its lineage of fathers. Fourth, do not defile your body with impure foods. Fifth, do not defile your spirit with impure associations. And sixth, do not defile your heart with doubt. Thus it was established and they knew that those who kept the Sidaya would be forever blessed by the Creator and Restorer.

"Thereafter, they were governed wisely by Sidayens for the benefit of themselves and their kinrens. The people reveled in their congregation. For a while, some of them endeavored to tame the Shoons and teach them the ways of people and the Order of the Sidaya, but those peculiar yellow beings could not be tamed and were sent back to their forests, banned from civilized life forever."

Gerd hesitates and looks over at Brân and then at me. "I'm only reading the words as they're written here," she says.

"I know," I say. "Please go on." There's a faint smile on Brân's lips.

Gerd continues: "The people did as Razak instructed, honoring the Order of creation by paying homage and glorifying the sun. And it was as Razak had promised: The rains did come in their time. Those who lived in towns and cities built great houses and greater temples and marketplaces and they mastered all the secrets of mathematics and engineering. They harvested excellent crops and slaughtered animals for food. They also harvested more and more of the trees of the forest for building, for cooking and crafts, for paper to make books, and for fire offerings to the Creator. Only those trees that bore useful fruits or other products were reserved. Without untamed forests, they created more space for their animals to multiply in vast herds.

"Razak survived death again at the age of seventy passages and a final time as an elder of one hundred and nineteen passages. He had instructed his closest followers in the art of becoming Revelant and it was they who coaxed life back into him the third time. But at last his body was spent and before his one hundred and twenty-first passage, he died a final death and there was great mourning throughout the land.

"After many passages, the time of rains again grew shorter and more uncertain. The land became parched and crops withered in the fields. Some people began to rely more on their animals for food, while others began once again to eschew meat eating altogether. Shoons from the dwindling forests were captured and forced to labor in the fields and workshops of Sidayens. Factions arose and Houses quarreled among themselves."

Gerd turns a page and almost drops it. I wonder why it's become detached from the rest. *No, it has been added and something left out.* Brân tells me this. I glance at him. His eyes are closed, his face upturned.

Gerd clears her throat and resumes reading. "The rains became ever more uncertain. At times the rivers and streams dried up to nothing while at other times they overflowed with disease-bearing floods. Once again, they cried out for Razak to return and instruct them. Two prophets arose. Prophet Amos Quint called on the people to return to the teachings of Razak Caloyer, to honor the sacredness of water, and to treat all beings with kindness and respect. The other prophet claims to be Razak come back to us a third time. His name is Zibal Palinj and he is a false prophet. He claimed the blessings of renewal and then declared that the burnt offerings to the sun were no longer sufficient and that people must go to the great forest known as Cödweg and set it ablaze. According to his message, only then would the sun, drunk with such overtopping generosity, be able to rest so that the rains could come without floods and without fevers. And so this false prophet and his disciples the Palinjians went to Cödweg and set fire to it. But there had been many passages of drought and the forest burned fiercely. Fire spread from Cödweg into Cesta and across prairies and dry meadows and through towns and cities. There was terrible destruction, and thousands of people lost their lives, including many disciples of Zibal Palinj. No rains came. Instead the people were punished with even greater heat and dust storms and hunger for they had followed the guidance of a false prophet. The fires continue to this day, to remind us, but none rivals the Great Fires."

Gerd closes the book and lays it in her lap. "May the great Prophet Amos Quint live long," she murmurs.

Brân looks past Gerd, through her, trying to focus on something we don't see. He rubs his brow with his good hand.

"I heard a somewhat different version in Benbridge," Damon says, "from those who did not call Palinj a false prophet."

"The Palinjians tell it their own way," Gerd says. "They claim it was the Shoons who burned Cödweg, the Shoons who killed the followers of Palinj. But that's not true. We know Shoons never did such a thing. Palinjians died by the fires that they themselves caused."

"I heard some news in Blanton today," Mother says. "It may be nothing more than rumors. They're saying that Zibal Palinj himself has died in a fire at the Markham Clauster."

Brân stares out the window, nodding slightly as if Mother has confirmed something he already knew.

Damon frowns. "That could stir up the Palinjians even more," he says. "I wonder how it happened."

Brân is still thinking about the Story of Razak. *Sleep near me tonight, Meridia, and I'll tell you more.*

25.

THE FOREST RISES GREEN and majestic all around me. My feet tread the cool softness of the grassy path.

Where are we going?

We. There is a long line of us, stepping in rhythm with the bells we hold. A river of lavender light surrounds us, lifting us lightly, purpling and paling with the jangling of the bells. Another sound pulses plum-colored, bursting into the stream. *Ah, ah, ah.* The notes resound from the trees, reverberate from the hearts of the trees, from the flow of life within them.

Where are we going?

We reach a clearing in the forest. Blue sky above. Truly, deeply blue. I want to go there but Brân pulls me back. Flowers of every color line our path and surround the clearing in a perfect circle. Their colors pulse and change with our song, accompanying its rise and fall, its surge forward and back. At the center a great stone as tall as a man, the color of *Ah*, the violet color of hope. The stone absorbs our song and returns it to us. Refines it. Enhances it. We form a circle around the stone, then stand facing it, still singing. Surging forward and back. I breathe in all the images and tones. I hear a voice speaking words that are more than words.

Out there in the world, the Mundani fight among themselves. Their greed turns the land brown and dry. Their efforts to enslave us in the last Mica Meed were overwhelmed in the Lapis Meed with the great Song of Liberation. In the time of the Turquoise Meed we returned to our forest homes to live undisturbed, enveloped in our own time. Today we sing hope. Two leaders have come to the Mundani, leading in opposite ways. Children still but overflowing with hatred or hope. We choose hope. We send songs to them. Songs of hope. Some will listen. Some will join the song. This is our Song of the New Amethyst Meed, the Song of Hope.

A name seeps through the singing. *Quint. Amos Quint.*

I see another circle. The Benison at its center shines ominous black. But the song is not the one I heard from Malaki's waif. There are no drums. This is a briefer, simpler song. An urgent song. There's an acrid scent of smoke in the air. Singing is overwhelmed by confused shouts as crackling orange flames loom close. The song changes as the singers desperately try to call forth rain to quench the fire. But their song is not enough. This fire has already consumed whole swathes of Cödweg and approaches the town of Lindmor. One by one the houses erupt in flames. A great tree crashes into the sacred circle, smashing onto the Obsidian Benison, engulfing the great stone itself in searing flames. The men and women try to flee but their way is blocked by walls of fire in every direction.

Burning, burning, they shout their song as the great Benison fractures from the heat of the fire and bursts apart, shattering into a thousand shards.

I awaken and look toward Brân, my eyes full of tears, my heart full of terror.

Did it happen? I ask.

Yes, Meridia. It happened just as you saw. There's more.

"You can tell me," I say, using words. I don't think I can bear to see any more of the searing images.

His voice is a reluctant whisper. "Within the tide, Mundani arrived to verify the end of Lindmor, and when they saw what had happened to the New Obsidian Benison they went out and built fires around every Benison they could find. They followed this by smashing them into even smaller pieces, leaving them strewn in the ashes, not knowing that the song of each Benison was contained, at least in part, in every waif and particle. Melfar were once again dispersed, as they had been in the time before the New Lapis. But they carried with them the waifs and the songs. Parts of the songs."

"Thank you," I say. "What was the song I heard them singing as the fire came? Before the song about rains?"

"That was a song of healing, a song to soothe the fevers that had gripped the Mundani everywhere."

I clutch at the Jade waif I hold in my hand as I lie back onto my blankets. I beg Avienne to sing her song to me again, the song she taught me on the road to Fayredell. *Sing me the power of peace.*

26

"WHAT IS A MEED?" I ask. I know it's a sequence of passages. Returns, as Melfar say. So many questions linger from last night's vision. My thirst for clarity grows intense.

Brân and Damon are finishing their breakfast. Brân's wounds have healed more rapidly than I would have thought possible. Damon, too, gains strength every day.

Brân looks at Damon first, then back at me.

"A meed," he says, "is a full cycle of all the colors, all the stones. A new meed begins with a Marble Return in which florapple bears fruit and the snuggery petris lays eggs all in the same season."

I know the florapple. The fruit is delicious. "Florapple only bears fruit every fourth spring," I say, searching. "Snuggery petris mates and lays eggs every third spring. Is that it?"

Brân nods. He shows me the petris' bower of white blossoms, its seductive dance, its marble-white eggs.

"So that would mean that those two things would happen together only once every twelve passages," Damon says.

"Twelve returns," Brân says. "We say 'return' rather than 'passage' because it all comes back again and again in cycles within cycles. Each return is called by the name of a particular stone—Marble, Mica, Lapis, Turquoise, Amethyst, Granite, Obsidian, Jade, Jasper, Quartz, Carnelian, and Amber, in that sequence. A full cycle of returns completes a meed. And each meed is named in the same way as the returns, in the same order. A new meed always begins on the full moon closest to the start of Brightening Symmetide, a day Mundani call 'Half Sun.' The ceremony of raising a Benison declares the end of one meed, the start of another. That's what we used to do, anyway."

"Used to? Why did you stop?" Damon has good questions.

"We became too dispersed and too few. The last Benison was erected nearly five meeds ago. It marked a New Jade Meed. I'd barely completed half a meed—six returns—at the time, but I remember the ceremony well."

I see it. A towering green stone, pleasingly shaped and polished bright. Voices whisper, *Sa, Sa, Sa.* Flutes mingle with jingling anklets as dancers stamp in rhythm. The song is reflected back, unheard beyond its forest. Damon's waif—the one he got from Brân, the one I now hold for him—is a fragment of that Jade Benison.

"When the next meed arrived," Brân continues, speaking aloud, "it was impossible to erect the New Jasper Benison as we should have. Four meeds have gone unmarked by the raising of Benisons. The New Jasper, New Quartz, New Carnelian, and most recently the New Amber."

"Were there songs?" That's what it is. Each stone, each Benison contains a song. Each one *is* a song. A story. A chain of stories. A cadence.

Brân shakes his head sadly. "No. Too many had died during the fever plague and then the great fires that came in the early returns of the New Jade Meed. In the Mundani count I believe it was the early 600s."

All this makes my head spin, but like a gyroscope, seeking new orientation. A new horizon.

"As I said, Melfar had become too few and spread too far apart. Some families survived on the far edges of where the great forest of Cödweg had been. A few more scattered through the connecting forest, which was known as Cesta. There was also a community in Serani, the dense forest on the near slopes of the western mountains. We couldn't hear each other anymore. And almost all of the trees were gone. Trees had always known our songs, always relayed our songs over great distances. Nothing worked as it should anymore."

I feel Damon's body go still as he tries to let all this into his mind. "I had no idea," he says. But he's thinking of the Melfar man he knew on his farm when he was only a child. He's thinking of Chanters.

"Yes," Brân says. "My mother tried to teach Mundani how to sing. She was born in the Granite Return of the New Amethyst Meed." He holds up a purple stone.

"That's a waif of its Benison." I say this as if I know. I look, but there's nothing in his hand.

Yes, Meridia. I have a waif from the New Amethyst Benison.

He found it in a jar. No, his brother did. Abél found a large waif of the New Amethyst. And he gave it to someone. I'm confused.

Mother enters the cabin, carrying a basket half full of wilderfruit and qaji nuts. I go to the cupboard and pull out the grinder. These will make a nice lunch. In the bottom of the basket I find a few small brown eggs. Those are for Damon and Brân, to help them heal.

"There's sad news from Fayredell," Mother says. "The great Prophet Amos Quint has died."

"What?" Brân sits up straight in his bed. "How?" He finds the news unlikely. Unbelievable.

"They say it was a fire, which must please the Palinjians. They're calling it a sign of the Creator's judgment on the Quints. They do like things done with fire." Her voice is bitter.

Brân rubs his forehead with his good hand, searching his orb for confirmation.

"What else do they say?" I ask. I try to picture this man I've never seen. Tall, surely, as all important Mundani are. Old and gray, but not stooped at all. Eyes bright. I see them flash anger.

"There weren't any more details," Mother says. "It's all rumors. You know how that goes. It likely happened a few days back."

Damon has risen from his bed. "I'm sure we'll learn more in the days ahead," he says. "I'm going outside for a walk."

"I'll help you." I dry my hands on the hem of my shirt.

"No, I can do this. I'm feeling stronger. I promise I won't go far."

It's good what he wants to do. My thoughts follow him as he walks, as he settles onto the bench beside the house, inhaling deep healing breaths of freshness.

Some of the wilderfruit I'm cutting up are not quite ripe. The ripe ones will have to sweeten the rest. The qaji nuts are rich with oil. I add some dried herbs from a jar.

Mother breaks the eggs, mixing them into the dark tea I made for our patients.

Brân's eyes close. He's thinking of his Amethyst waif. Where does he keep such things? In the leather bag at his left side. I look but there's no bag there.

Malaki had an Obsidian. It was the waif that showed me the Palinjian leader, this man they call Zibal Palinj.

I smell smoke. I hear the hiss and crackle of flames.

Malaki! Malaki's set a fire. *He's burning your cart, Brân!*

"Brân?" I turn toward him.

His eyes are wide. He knows.

"Why?" I say.

"They were looking for it." *The Palinjians were after them. He's saved the waifs. Burned the cart to put them off.*

I'm not sure I believe Malaki capable of any good deed. *Where did he put them?* "Can we find them?"

Mother looks at me strangely. I'm not sure what I'm saying or hearing that she hears, not sure how much she pertanges of the unspoken.

"I can't tell where they are," Brân says. *That dark canopy of Malaki's can be impenetrable at times, even for me. And I'm not at my best yet. Let's leave it for now, Meridia.*

My stones. *Maybe my stones could help.* Mine and Mother's.

27.

WHEN THE NEWS of Amos Quint's death spread through the land, Abél, like most Melfar, hoped that the prophet's mantle would somehow pass to Amos's son Lambert. But there was no clamor for such a succession. The old prophet's followers either yielded to the mania of the Palinjians and joined their ranks, or else they went silent, unwilling to either publicly avow their allegiance to the Quints or publicly disavow it. They became sullenly apathetic and Palinjians took to ridiculing and shaming them for their cowardice. Nobody seemed to know what had happened to Lambert Quint himself.

Seeing all this, Abél was reanimated, uprooted at last from his solitary retreat at Woodclasp. Can more sadness transform sadness into action? Abél decided it was time to go back to Markham and resume his search for the Old Mica where he'd left it off. He felt a strong call to revisit the burned clauster, to search in secret through the columbarium. He wasn't sure it was only the quest for the Old Mica that drove him this time, but he didn't question. He went.

As soon as he took the Amethyst from Amos Quint's urn, Abél knew that something was amiss. He knew the stone. It was the one he'd given to Quint not even a full tide ago. It contained the Song of Hope, and Abél had thought at the time that it could be of comfort to the old man as he grieved the loss of his granddaughter Keira. And then he'd discovered that the ashes in the urn were only wood ashes and none of Amos Quint.

With the Amethyst in his own hands again, Abél knew what he had to do next; he needed to find out what had really happened to Quint. He had to seek the truth behind Quint's deception.

The story circulating at large was that the old prophet had been caught in a great conflagration in Fayredell that occurred mere days after fire had swept through the Markham Clauster, killing the disputed prophet Zibal Palinj. This second fire had consumed the Quints' ancestral home as well as the body of Amos Quint himself. Of course there had been no water adequate to battle such a blaze. What was available was splashed on neighboring properties to keep them from catching fire. The burning of the Quint home was so complete that only a few scraps of ornaments and the stones Amos always kept on his person had been recovered. A badly burned stranger from Benbridge was caught fleeing the scene and he was charged with murder and arson and summarily put to the torch himself. That was to prevent his coming back to do further harm. Meanwhile, ashes from the spot where Quint's personal artifacts were found were declared to be his and interred in the columbarium. There was subdued sorrow among the traditional Sidayens who had been devoted to Amos Quint. There was no such sorrow among the Palinjians.

Of all the stones that had been left behind in the fire, Abél wondered why they'd selected to inter this particular stone and no other in Amos Quint's cremation urn. Quietly, he hummed the song of the New Amethyst, the Song of Hope. Not the kind of song that called out to Palinjians, just as the leadership of Amos Quint had failed to appeal to them. To Palinjians, peace and hope spoke of weakness. Frailty. Impotence. They exalted strength of will over paltry hope. They'd even placed their own symbol, the image of a tree in flames, on the cover of Amos Quint's urn, as if they could claim in death one who had never been theirs in life.

Abél felt certain that if he could take the Amethyst back to the site of the burned house in Fayredell, it could connect him with the truth of what really happened.

And so he leaves the columbarium at Markham and proceeds in the direction of Fayredell. As he goes, he recalls in as much detail as he can conjure the last journey he made along this very route, when he bore the body of Amos Quint's granddaughter Keira to her final rest. He murmurs a few verses of the Turquoise Canopy of Time.

As he walks (for he now travels without cart or excuses) he catches glimpses of another traveler, a young Mundani man. The young man is anxious. Fearful. There is the scent of smoke about him. The man stumbles as he mutters to himself, distracted, arguing first one way and then another.

Abél follows this vision, trailing some distance behind so as not to put the man off his mission. Mundani are easily put off by Melfar intrusions from another time-space, although they never recognize that for what it is. The man presses on rapidly, relentlessly. He's young. But Abél is growing old and needs rest. So he stops. He'll catch up later, the nature of time-space being what it is for Melfar. He's convinced that the man is headed to precisely the destination Abél has in mind.

At last they reach Fayredell. Night has fallen dark and heavy by the time the man, breathless and agitated, knocks on the big carved wooden door at the front of

Amos Quint's house. Abél is surprised to see Amos himself open the door. He's dismissed all his servants. He believes they are no longer trustworthy. He's left alone in the immense house.

"I bring you terrible news, Prophet Quint," the man says. His breath comes hard and his mouth is dry. His eyes are red-rimmed and wide with refused sleep.

Amos Quint offers the man water and a chair next to the table. He sits. He drinks. His hands shake so vigorously that he spills more than reaches his mouth, and he apologizes for that. Amos moves a chair so that he sits facing the messenger. He refills the water glass. "What is this news you speak of?" he says, studying the man from beneath grizzled brows.

"The temple at Markham has burned. It was during a ceremony and they died in the fire," he says and then tells Amos five names. The last almost makes Amos cry out. The messenger continues, "What should we do, master? What rituals must we perform? How shall we rid ourselves of the venomous presence of the Shoons among us? Surely it is they..."

His entreaty is cut short by a swift and mighty blow to his temple. It knocks him bodily out of the chair and his head strikes the edge of the table. He slumps to the floor. Unconscious. Dead, as Amos thought at the time.

Amos Quint is beside himself and Abél understands why. He's beyond exasperated at this habit of blaming Shoons for every mishap. And he has just learned of the fire that consumed the false prophet Zibal Palinj. He knows full well who will succeed him. "From bad to worse," Quint mutters, appending a few terrible curses. "Enough!" he says. "No more."

He begins to undress, dropping his clothing on the ground next to the inert body of the messenger. He retrieves only one stone from among the ornaments he always wore. Then he removes the messenger's clothes and puts them on himself. They're a bit too small, but no matter. All they need to do is hide his person. Next he goes to the storeroom and finds a jar of precious groundfat. Not taking time to pour it out, he smashes the jar against the fireplace. Flames flood across the floor.

But Amos is already gone. Pulling the messenger's hood over his head, he has departed through the back door, disappearing into the night. Inside the house, the unfortunate corpse awakens to nakedness and a room in flames. He runs for the front door.

Abél stands amid the rubble of the ruined house.

So that's it, he says. *And where are you now, old man?*

28.

I GATHER MY STONES together. Mother has gone to work, and Damon is sleeping. I take first the Jade and then the blue stone I found on my journey, which I know now to be a waif of the New Lapis. Then the smaller waifs I pilfered from Mother. I feel a bit foolish, making such a small offering to Brân, hoping he can use them better than I can. I'm still too fearful of Malaki to try it on my own. Too afraid of my own anger. Brân has anger, too, but his has spaces in it. Mine is a solid wall, fused hard with sizzling hatred.

Brân smiles when he sees my handful of stones. He's skeptical but grateful. He will try. We will try.

I attend to Brân's verberations and his colors. I follow where he leads.

The cart has become nothing more than a black scar on the earth, covered haphazardly with sand and debris. Broken cedar twigs almost mask the burnt smell. Malaki did that.

Where did you take the waifs, Malaki?

That's what we need to know. That's what Brân asks.

Malaki is nowhere. I slide back and forth through the landscape like a lost falcon. Sometimes the trees are tall. Sometimes blazing fire. Sometimes gone, leaving only scorched rocks and charred stumps. Waifs are nowhere.

It's no use, I say.

Brân says nothing. I think he doesn't hear me. Then I pertange a dark smudge like congealed smoke. It's next to a big rock.

Is that it? Is that where the waifs are?

I think so. I think Malaki used his canopy to hide them.

And maybe to hide himself. My heart bursts anger. My orb goes dark and I see nothing more.

I collect up the stones and put them back into my deepest pocket.

29.

THE OLD MAN RECLINES in his bed, his mending leg propped up on a pillow. His hand is still rigidly contained in clay-hardened cloths. Damon, across the room, sits up on the other bed. Any time Meridia goes out, he grows restless. He keeps pushing himself every day to exercise, to recover the strength his body lost to the injuries and infection. He feels his presence within his body differently now and he tries to tell himself it's from the head injury. But he knows it's at least partly because of dying and coming back. Because of being Revelant. Again. He tries once more to piece things together, remembering how he came to be here, or at least telling himself the story as it's been told to him. He needs to remember why he was dead in the first place. He was looking for Chapling, who turned out to be Brân, this man lying on the bed across the room now.

"Where did you get the photographic plates you sold me, Brân?" That's one of the questions Damon has been wanting to ask ever since before he and Meri began their journey.

The old man clears his throat, reminding himself of the words that will answer Damon's question. "In Woodclasp, over at the edge of Cödweg. It was quite a large town before Cödweg burned." And in a different spot. Damon sees that, even though Brân doesn't mention it. "I had them for many returns before I gave them to you."

"Sold them," Damon says, then reconsiders. "No, you're right. I didn't pay anywhere near what they're worth. You gave them to me. Thank you. What else do you know about them?"

"First, tell me what you know."

"Well, I know the coating, the photosensitive emulsion, is different from what I use in my ordinary work. It has some kind of biological component mixed in with the usual chemicals. I wasn't able to identify it."

"What else?"

"I think that somehow it picked up an image from the rock. The waif, as you call it. Almost an image anyway. I was unable to reproduce that effect." He thinks he should try again. He wishes he'd brought the plates with him.

Brân sits up straighter in the bed, wincing slightly with the effort. He turns toward Damon. "Those plates belonged to my mother's brother, my Uncle Fannan. I always hoped I might find someone who could continue his work."

"What work was that?"

Brân tries to show Damon with images, but Damon finds them out of focus, pulsing into vague shapes. Muffled words behind closed doors.

"I can't, Brân. I'm still a man of words. Still Mundani, despite my recent experience. Can you please explain it to me?"

I can help you with that when you're ready. Brân adjusts the pillow under his leg. "Fannan was the brother of my mother, Avienne, born in the Amber Return of the New Turquoise Meed." He thought for a moment. "That would be in the passage 569 by Mundani calculation. Fannan was trained, like his own uncle before him, in the methods and practices of crafting Benisons." *All Melfar have the capacity; only a few are trained.*

Damon wants to ask how that is done, but mostly he's eager to learn more about the photographic plates. He tucks the larger question away for another time.

"Uncle Fannan was looking for a way to show our stories to Mundani. He thought that if he could produce physical pictures of our verberations, it might help our two communities to understand one another. He was beginning to make progress when the first Great Fire came to Cödweg. He had to flee and leave much of his work behind. He was hoping to resume the work in Woodclasp, but there was so much that had to be done just to survive in those dreadful days. He did manage to set up a workshop and produce a few prints before he died. He was caught up in the next fire that came through the remains of Cödweg, the one that swept through Cesta in the Marble Return of the New Quartz Meed."

"When was that?"

Brân pauses, reflecting. "I think that would have been Mundani passage 630."

"That's when our farm burned. When my family moved to Benbridge. I was only a boy. Barely completed eight passages."

"Uncle Fannan taught my brother and me the craft of making Benisons. But he taught neither of us how to do the photographs. I found the plates I gave to you in the remains of his workshop."

"What else was left of the workshop?"

"Quite a lot, really, but none of us knew what to make of it. So we left it." He looks at Damon, expecting something.

Damon gives him what he wants. "Could I go there? Maybe I could try and figure out what he was doing."

Brân is a little disappointed that Damon's interest is all technical. He's hoping someone will take on his uncle's mission. Could a Mundani be such a someone? A Mundani Revelant? "I could give you a map, but it's with the cache of waifs I've lost." *It's contained within one of the waifs.*

"Then we need to find your cache," Damon says. "Do you know where it is?"

"I think so," he says. "I think Meridia and I would be able to find it."

30.

BRÂN KEEPS INSISTING he's strong enough to begin searching for his waifs. I think he should wait another day or two. He's too precious to risk. Every night he shows me again the place where his stones are hidden. The smudge of darkness that envelopes them grows fainter. Weaker. The protection canopy is failing.

Today we go. Gerd has brought her equid for Brân to ride. She's rigged a support for his weak leg. It's only me and Brân and Gerd and Fergus. Damon is still too weak for such a long walk. Staying does not make him happy. I'm feeling a bit tired and unsteady, too, but I know I have to go anyway.

"Go carefully, Meri," Damon says, pressing my hand to his lips.

I caress the blue stone in my pocket and see Duende, perched on the back of the garden bench, tail bobbing up and down. He'll keep watch for us. He chirps assurance. A harsher cry makes me look up, shielding my eyes from the bright morning sun. A crow alights at the other end of the bench. Brân's crow. Where has he been all this time? No matter. We'll be well protected. I take in a couple of deep breaths. The open air steadies me.

Brân leads the way, riding on the equid. Fergus walks alongside him, and Gerd and I follow. The two birds stay nearby. Our pace is quick as we try to keep up with the equid.

This is not the path I traveled to arrive at Mother's. Brân knows a different road and when I think him and breathe with him, I find it, too. It goes beside an old stream bed where no water has flowed for many passages. Many returns. Meeds, even. I pertange the forest that once lined the stream, hear the birds calling, the water dancing around stones. The stones are still there. Beneath my feet I pertange the roots of trees. Roots hard and desiccated, almost stone. I feel a vague pulse of song through the soles of my feet. As we walk, the colors and sensations shift. Different trees. Different meeds. Different songs.

Gerd is speaking. Her words punch holes in the songs.

"Woodclasp is where my parents were from. Pilgrims used to come there from all over. I told Damon it would only take a day and a half to reach it. Do you think he's ready for such a journey? He shouldn't go alone."

"I'll be with him." Why is Damon going to Woodclasp? Where is that? I don't ask. I should have been paying attention.

I take a quick breath, searching for Duende's reassuring chirrups. I hear nothing. I look around and finally see him sitting, still and quiet, next to the trunk of a spinebranch. I chirrup to him, but he remains silent. Brân's crow has gone quiet, too.

Then I hear it. The shriek of a hawk. I look up and see it sailing high above us. Circling. Its call is plaintive. A hawk should sound more confident. This one sounds lost, almost desperate.

I catch a faint whiff of pickles and I know. This is Ann Landry's hawk. Ann Landry, who rescued me when I was alone and lost in Fayredell. I need to tell Brân.

"I know," he says. "She's just ahead."

A hundred paces on and we diverge from the path toward a place where the stream once undercut a rock face. Ann is there, huddled under the overhang, hurt. I run to her while Fergus helps Brân dismount.

"Ann?" I brush the hair away from her face. There's blood crusted in it. Purple marks along her jaw and throat. I scan her body. There are more bruises but no broken bones.

"Meridia." She remembers. Her eyes are open, and she tries to smile. She lifts a hand toward me.

I wrap her in blue light and let it pulse into the bruises, into the gash on her head. It's not a deep wound. It bled awfully as such things do and it's given her a bad headache. I try to remedy that. I turn to ask Fergus to bring water, but he's already done it and he hands it to me. I help Ann to sit up; I hold the water sheath to her lips. After a couple of small sips, she takes the sheath and drinks greedily. I take it back.

"Not too much," I say. "Go easy."

"What happened to you?" Gerd says. "Were you out here alone?"

I know she was. She was running away from her father.

"Alone, yes. I was on my way to find a friend. My mother's friend." She turns her head to look up at Brân and winces, closes her eyes. "I made a little camp so I could sleep a while. I did sleep, I think, but then I heard something." First she heard the hawk, crying a warning in the dark of night. "I saw a man walking through the bushes. I was scared and ran away. I guess I fell."

"A man? What did he look like?" Brân needs her to answer his questions not for himself but so that I'll know.

"I don't think he saw me until I started running away. He seemed… There was something wrong with him. He may have been hurt. Maybe confused."

Oh, Brân, no!

"He was Shoon." Ann glances at Brân and then at me, apologizing for the word.

Brân's eyes reach for mine. He tries to reassure me. He asks me to help him look but I refuse. I won't help him find Malaki.

"How much farther to this place you're looking for?" Gerd asks.

"I'm guessing only about half a fellspan," Brân says. "Can Fergus stay here with Ann? We can pick them up on our way back."

We do that. I follow the equid again, more nervous now. Part of me wants to return to Ann. I focus on Brân instead. I watch our two birds.

I see it up ahead. The dark cloak is barely pertangible, no more than a wisp. "I can get it," I say. No need for Brân to dismount again. He's tired and in pain.

I reach through the wisp with shaking hands and scrape away a layer of debris and then a shallow layer of earth. There's a bundle wrapped in cloth and beneath that an earth-encrusted leather bag. Brân's bag, the one containing his waifs. I pick up all the things and take them to him.

"Unwrap the bundle," he says.

I don't want to. I think I know what's inside. But I do as he asks. It's Malaki's flute. I push it aside with a finger, as if it's diseased. Underneath it is Malaki's

Obsidian waif. *Why did he leave these here?* I realize that it's how this protection canopy held its strength for so long.

Brân inhales deeply. *He left them because he was done with them. Because he's given up. I believe he's sorry for what he did.*

Do I believe that? Or would I rather hang onto my anger? Whatever has happened to Malaki, it's no more than he deserved. I wrap the hated objects again in the cloth and hand them to Brân. I don't want to touch them. "I'll carry your bag," I say.

"No, he says. You carry the bundle."

I tuck it under my arm. I try to forget about it. To forget what it is, whose it is. But Brân wants me to see what happened.

I do see.

I see Malaki follow Brân, keeping his distance because Brân has left him behind. Because Brân doesn't want him anymore. Malaki's anger bubbles orange and red with flashes of silver. He's angry at Brân. Angry at himself. Angry at his life and all the bad decisions that brought him to this. He hears the men before he sees them. They only see Brân. Malaki tries to throw up a canopy over Brân, but it's too late. All he can do is revise the cart, turning it into a hill seething with pepper ants as Brân drops it to run away. The men run after Brân. And Malaki just stands there. Watching.

I hate him even more.

I lose sight of Brân.

Malaki gathers dried leaves and twigs and stems and stacks them under the cart, builds a fire. As it begins to burn in earnest, he grabs the leather bag from inside the cart, the bag containing his father's waifs. He sets the bag down next to a big rock and digs. He digs until his fingernails are torn and bloody. He puts the bag into the ground. Before he covers it over, he places the bundle containing his flute and Obsidian waif on top of it. What is that sound he's making? Weeping? Malaki is weeping. He grumbles the protection canopy into existence and walks away. A few more steps and he's seized by the men. By the Palinjians. They strike him on the forehead and throat, and everything goes blurry.

I look up at Brân; there are tears in his eyes. There are none in mine. But the anger in my heart burns a little less fiercely.

We finally reach the place where Fergus waits with Ann. "Can the equid carry the two of them?" I ask Gerd.

"Easily," she says. She lifts Ann up to sit astride the animal behind Brân. It's painful for Ann. She buries her face against Brân's neck and cries. I send more blue light, but it isn't enough. She needs medicine.

Brân tries to reassure her with words. He's better with Mundani words than I am.

"You were running away from him, weren't you," he says. "Running away from your father Rolang."

"How did you know?" Ann says. "He'd become so angry. I couldn't take it anymore." Her own father is the cause of most of her bruises.

"And who were you seeking?" Brân knows. He wants me to know.

"My mother's friend, Vidvana. In Woodclasp."

"She isn't there," Brân says. *She's gone to Beniford to join the others.* "But I can take you to her."

31.

ANN RETURNS WITH US to Shadham where I can tend her wounds. Mother says we're running a hospital now. She sleeps in one of the other cottages in the hamlet, leaving her own house to me and our three patients. Gerd is staying with Mother.

Despite her injuries, Ann is happy to be with friends, with someone she can talk to unafraid.

"So you're the girl who helped Meri escape Fayredell," Damon says. He thanks her for her kindness.

Ann tells us about her mother's death. Her mother Keira Landry of Quint. She offers more details than when she mentioned it to me in the little shed outside Fayredell. I hadn't known then how fresh her grief was. I hadn't known her mother had been murdered in Markham. Ann tells us about her father Rolang Landry, the one who burned her mother's books. She tells us about her grandfather Lambert Quint and her great-grandfather Amos Quint. "After Great-grandfather was killed, things got even worse."

"Amos Quint was your great-grandfather? He was a respected leader. A great prophet." Damon is awed.

Ann isn't so sure. Her mother sometimes thought he was not so great. He was a leader among people who believed women to be unworthy, people who often treated women and indeed all kinren badly.

"My mother was a leader, too," Ann says. "Many women came to her to learn poems and stories. I learned some of them."

"You must recite them for us sometime," Brân says. "How did you learn of your mother's death?"

"I overheard my father and grandfather talking about it. Grandfather Lambert was sad, but my father sounded angry. When they finally came to tell me, I was already crying. I didn't want to talk to them. I didn't want to hear about it. Vidvana came the next day and told me in secret what had happened. Not all the details, because she thought I was just a child and shouldn't know. I tried to tell her I was already a woman. She did tell me that Mother was killed for being on the temple grounds in Markham. She and the other women were only reciting poetry. It's all we have as kinren. As women. But even that is forbidden on sacred ground. Their sacred ground."

"Did you know Vidvana before?" Brân asks.

"She often came to visit Mother. They chanted poetry and songs together in an old storeroom of the pickle factory. Other women were there, too. A few times they let me join them." Ann quiets her thoughts into memory.

Brân sees the woman through Ann's memory of her. Vidvana has a dignified bearing. She has an abundance of coarse hair and bright eyes behind ill-fitting glasses.

"Vidvana told us the poems came from the Shoons and that's why Sidayens hated them so much. Whenever Father caught Mother humming the songs around the house, he would scold her. Sometimes he hit her. Lots of times he did that. Vidvana taught me a song and said that I should sing it to lift my mother onto the shoulders of the Migrant. I didn't know what that meant, but she said it would be good for Mother, so I sang the song. I still sing it sometimes and it does make me feel closer to Mother." Memories arise more vividly in Ann's mind as she speaks. "While Vidvana was teaching me the song, Great-grandfather Amos came to our house, looking for Father. But Father was away so he spoke to Vidvana instead. He made her tell her own story about what happened to Mother. That's when I learned the details. She said it was the Palinjians did it. Shouted at Mother and the other women, hit them with sticks, told them to leave the grounds, saying women defile the temples. They were so angry. Then one young Palinjian took the cord from around his waist and attacked Mother with it, wrapped it around her throat." Ann chokes on the image.

Brân is alert. Breathing quietly, searching for a name. "Did she know who that young Palinjian was?"

"She said his name was Warreth Pherson."

A mutter of sparks from Brân. Angry orange, scarlet fear. They shoot out of him like seeds popped in a fire.

"I've heard that name," Damon says.

"Was he someone in the story Gerd read?" I ask this, trying to recall.

"That was Razak Pherson. Warreth is of the same House. Not much more than a boy, though." Brân looks at Ann with sadness. "Did your father Rolang know it was Warreth killed your mother?"

"He didn't care." Ann pulls her face inside. "He said Mother should never have been there. He blamed her. And Vidvana." And all the women and other kinren like them.

"Have you kept in touch with Vidvana?" Brân thinks she has.

"I've tried. She was always kind to me. I saw her a few times right after Mother's death. But since Great-grandfather Amos died, she doesn't come to Fayredell anymore. And now my father and other Palinjians won't let their kinren do anything except cook and clean and serve. They hardly let me out of the house. I couldn't stay. I have to find Vidvana. She always said if I needed help, she'd help me. You said you could take me to her. Will you?" Ann trusts no one. No one but Vidvana. She may trust me a little. She wants to trust Brân.

"We will go to where she is. Soon we'll all go to Beniford." That's where Brân was going before he agreed to help me find Damon. He wanted to take me and Malaki to Beniford.

"Where is Beniford?" I ask.

"In the western mountains," Brân says. "In the old forest of Serani."

Tall trees and taller walls of naked stone reaching for the sky.

"Near the seacoast," he says.

Nothing. What is a seacoast?

"I've never heard of Beniford," Damon says. "What's there?"

"It's an old Melfar town. Filling up again."

Brân is tired and turns toward the wall. He doesn't want to say more. He doesn't want to say that Beniford is where Melfar are getting ready. He won't say what they're getting ready for.

32.

I WAKE WITH MY STOMACH twisting. My piss has an odd smell. I try to think what foods I ate. Maybe too much onion. I find some ginger root and chew on that. I need to be strong for Damon. Today we set out on our journey to Woodclasp. We'll go slow. The fresh air will help my stomach to quiet itself.

We've borrowed a lamin from a friend of Gerd's. It's smaller than an equid and covered in soft, dark brown hair. Its neck is long and slender, and its big ears stick almost straight up. Gerd cautions that we can't ride it all day, only in shifts. It will be a help, though. There's a willingness in its large, kind eyes.

Brân has given us the Quartz waif and showed me its map. He says there was no Benison for the New Quartz Meed. Only a collection of stones like this one, sent out into the world like the Melfar.

"Are you sure this is the way, Meri?"

"I'm sure," I say. "It's a Melfar way." Not ripped into the earth like Mundani roads. I pertange it clearly and I try to show it to Damon. I show him how it's marked by a series of arrowpine trees that are no longer there. Arrowpines grow tall and thin and straight. I can just see from one to the next. Between them there's lush growth of flowers, grasses, and bushy, low-growing brassium. There's a constant hum of bees, gathering nectar. It's so long since I've tasted honey. I'm humming, too, casting the protection canopy, albeit rather carelessly. There's nothing out here to be afraid of. Duende flies back and forth overhead, keeping watch.

The heat feels unusually oppressive for the season. It's draining my strength more than it should. The toe of my sandal catches on a rock and I stumble. I try to catch myself with my hands.

I'm on the ground and Damon is beside me. Out of focus. Asking if I'm okay.

"Did you hit your head? You look stunned."

"I tripped," I say, looking around for the stone that caught my sandal. There is nothing but smooth sand. I lift a hand to my head, trying to clear my thoughts.

Damon's hands search my head for injury and find none.

There was an instant, right before I stumbled. A darkness. A gyrating darkness. It's coming back.

"Meri?" Damon's voice.

My face is wet, and I sputter.

"There you are," he says.

"What happened?"

"You fainted."

"Did I?" I try to sit up and the swirl of darkness threatens to return. I lie back down.

"You've been working too hard, Meri. Taking care of everyone but yourself. Did you eat breakfast before we left?"

"No, I wasn't hungry," I say. I don't say I felt ill. He might insist on turning back. We need to go on. We need to do this one thing for Damon.

"Well, you're going to sit right here and rest and have something to eat before we move on." He places his pack behind me for support and offers a handful of nuts and some mooli root.

All I really want is water, but I eat what he offers. He's right. I need to feed my body. We have a long way to travel. Not so far as from Temur to Fayredell. About half that, Brân said. I take small bites and regulate my breathing to help the food settle.

I squint up at the sun. It's only halfway to mid, but I feel it burning on my face. Damon maneuvers the lamin to provide a patch of shade for me. He offers the animal water and a handful of grain. I close my eyes against the sun's brightness, seeing the trees again. Feeling grass beneath my body, the fragrance of flowers in my head. The hum of bees. The taste of honey.

Damon holds my hand as we walk through the long grass. He picks flowers and hands them to me, kissing my lips. The path ahead is straight and clear. At the end of it there's a small house. Damon opens the door. Inside a few stairs lead downward. It's dark but we both see the steps clearly, as well as the room at the foot of the stairs. The room is lined with tables and its ceiling is laced with sturdy cord to which paper images are clasped. *Look, Damon*, I say. And he answers, *It's the woman, isn't it? The woman from the Jade waif.* Her picture is there, clear and sharp on a piece of paper. There are basins of strange liquids that give off pungent smells. And in one corner a glass box filled with snails.

"*Chrrr-eep!* Wake up!" It's Duende. He sounds worried.

Damon looks up at Duende and then at me. "Is it time to go?" he asks. He knows it is.

He offers me his hand and I stand somewhat unsteadily. He insists that I ride the lamin. After a while, from the lamin's back, I notice a brown line on the horizon where a sandstorm is gathering.

"Can you see anywhere we can shelter?" Damon's voice is anxious.

"There's a tumbledown house that we should be able to reach."

I worry that Damon is walking faster than he ought to. But his breath and heartbeat feel strong. I'm grateful for the lamin.

The house is right where I thought it would be, but in worse shape. Only one corner of the tile roof remains, and it looks like it might collapse if the wind is too strong. But it's all we have. The lamin refuses to go through the door. We tie her up outside, close to the wall. While Damon collects fodder for the lamin, I manage to find a couple of almost ripe guavacots. They're small and hard. The first eddies of sand kick up as we go inside and close the sagging door, wedging it shut with a couple of rocks. Damon fastens a sheet to what's left of the roof to give us more protection.

"Did you see the underground room, Damon?"

"I didn't exactly see it, but I knew we were there. Were there some steps going down? I smelled photographic chemicals. And another odor I couldn't identify. What did you see?"

We still talk about "seeing" what can only be pertanged. I tell him about the printed pictures.

"It was a clear image on the paper? Of the woman you saw from the green stone? The one you showed me?

That's amazing!" Damon's excitement is infectious. "Were there other images?"

"Yes, but I couldn't make them out. They were…complicated. More like stories." Each one had so many details. Shifting details. "The other smell…was it coming from over on the far side of the room?"

"Maybe so," Damon says. "Yes, I think so. But I couldn't see what was there. Did you see?"

"Snails," I say. "There was a big glass box with lots of snails. Live snails."

"Snails." He frowns. "Maybe that's it." His eyes sparkle with curiosity. "Can you tell me about them?"

"Oh." I squint hard and try to recall the image. "Shiny ones," I say. "Glowing?"

He grabs me all at once in an embrace. I feel him laughing. Bursting silver-gold excitement. "That must be it," he says.

"What?" I don't know what "it" is.

"How the plates capture biophotonic images. The biological ingredient in the plate coatings that I couldn't identify. I bet it's something from those glowing snails."

I'm not sure what he's talking about, but his happiness makes me smile.

He's shouting something else about the snails. Shouting partly out of excitement, partly to be heard over the wind. It's getting stronger. The lamin is restless, and the light's gone dim inside the cabin. Roof tiles rattle. Suddenly I think about Duende. Then I see he's here, perched in the corner of the house, huddled and fluffed into a gray and blue ball. How he came in I don't know.

"Magic," Damon murmurs. I'm not sure if he's talking about the snails or my bird.

33.

NO ONE GOES TO THE northern lowlands anymore, but that's where Abél is going. There was once a Mundani temple there, built, as such things often were, on the site of an older Melfar Benison precinct. This one was abandoned long ago, in the time of the floods. Long before the Great Fires. It's the only temple Abél hasn't visited yet in his quest for the Old Mica, the one that holds the song known as Calling the Rains.

The northern temple was at a place called Gorshfen, or so Abél believes. It's what he thinks he's heard in his intense communion with the tiny fragment of the Old Mica that he received from his father. He's seen the region lush with twisted mangrove and marsh grass, though it's now nothing but hard desert and salt pans. Abél knows he will have to take with him all the water he intends to drink. With the possible exception of a few well-hidden milparinkas, there will be no water in the region at all. He's figuring two days in and two days out, provided he doesn't go astray.

The sun is just nudging a hint of gold into the eastern sky as Abél lofts the heavy pack onto his shoulders and heads in the direction the Mica waif has shown him. Five water sheaths hang around his waist. He breathes slowly and evenly, humming the Lapis Song of Liberation. That song always gives him strength. It was the song that led the Melfar away from servitude among the Mundani, guiding them back out into their forest homes. Back to freedom. He knows the story not only from the Lapis, but also from his eldfather, who was only a boy then, making the journey in the arms of his mother or on the shoulders of his father or uncle.

A few hours and Abél has left the last traces of Mundani settlement behind. He finds a patch of shade beside a rocky outcrop and rests. Taking the fragile Mica waif from its wrapping and holding it at the center of his forehead, he hums the notes of its song. Sung by a single voice it lacks potency, but Abél does his best, trying to remember the song as his father taught it to him, hearing the other voices in his mind. His breathing slows. The hum goes deeper and begins to resonate from the surrounding landscape.

A breeze comes cool and moist, bending the towering grasses, releasing them, shaking them gently. A marsh wren clings to a waving stem, warbling to its mate. An answer comes on the next breeze. The wren flutters up above the grasses. Such a vast marshland. Clusters of tall ginger flowers and solitary plumpaya trees dot the green expanse. Watery roads cut through it. Where two such roads come together, the grass has been flattened and a small boat, carved from a single tree, is beached to one side, tied to a sturdy plumpaya.

The wren flutters higher and Abél pertanges the watery roads flowing together toward the far horizon, toward a vast blue lake. *Glasllyn.* The name comes in the whistle of the wren. At the far side of the lake, a rough bridge connects to a small island. On the island, a Benison. Abél wants it to be the Old Mica, but he's not sure.

He takes the waif from his forehead and dabs away the sheen of sweat that has adhered to it. His fingers and forehead and the wrapping cloth sparkle with tiny flakes of the deteriorating stone. Once the waif is secure again in his pack, he takes some food and water and then stretches out at the base of the rocky outcrop. He closes his eyes. Sleep teases him but he refuses to submit. He'll need to move on soon. He watches absently, and as the shadow of the rock lengthens toward the east, he stirs himself to resume his journey.

He treads the hard-packed earth of the way that was once all watery, wending among stands of tall grass that have long since gone to dust and ash. He feels cooler, more relaxed when he pertanges the grasses, the ginger, the plumpaya, the water. When he sees only the barren earth and rocks and the heat radiating in waves above it, he is slightly terrified.

Heat and exhaustion and ambient terror drive him to rest again after only a few more hours' walk. He tells himself the return journey will be easier. His pack will be lighter. His water sheaths will be mostly empty. He tries not to drink more than his calculations tell him he should. In the unrelenting stillness, sweat evaporates without cooling. His body is already covered in a thin crust of salt. He cringes from his task and fans himself with his hat, finding little relief.

Focusing again on the grasses and water and humming the notes of the Old Mica, he trudges on. As he nears the lake, the watery roads form a running stream. Farther on, there's a place where the stream deposited a sandy beach below a stand of rock. There's a tree there, a knobby nekosta that spreads its shade generously across the beach.

Abél opens his ordinary eyes and finds the tree. It's only a desiccated skeleton of a tree, but it's there and Abél sits, leaning his weary body against it. He's realized that the route he was shown by the Mica required circling around the lake to reach the island from the far shore. Now that there's no longer a lake, he can walk straight across. If he presses on, he might reach it by nightfall. Should he try? Or would it be more comfortable to spend the night here, next to this tree on this sandy beach?

There is no comfort here. Abél drinks. The water in his second sheath is almost gone and he knows he should save the last of it for when he arrives at the island. But his thirst is intense, and he drains the sheath dry, telling himself that now the journey promises to be shorter, he can be more generous with himself. He takes a wad of leaves from his pack and places a few in his mouth. They're meant to restore strength, to forestall pain. He rises from his brief rest and plods on, humming a few bars of the Lapis song for courage, followed by what notes he recalls of the Mica. Over and over he hums the notes of the Mica.

He's reached the edge of the lake. It's broader than it seemed from the wren's vista. Never mind. He steps into it and feels the crunch of salt underfoot. The briny crust breaks with every step and pulls at his weary feet. He hadn't counted on that. He could go back to the tree by the beach. But, no. He can feel the pull of the island. The pull of whatever Benison is there. It must be the Mica. The notes of it resound with mounting clarity.

Sunset paints the sand lavender and violet and then dizzying hues of pink and orange as the fiery disc of the sun drops behind the distant mountains. Light recedes into darkness and still Abél has not reached his destination. Trusting the Mica waif, he plods on, dragging his flagging limbs across the salt flat. The leaves he chewed have left his mind pliable and he hears sounds of boats, of fishermen, and in the distance, the sound of chanting. He joins in the chant as it expands beyond the familiar notes of the Mica. It's a chant without words accompanied by the silvered notes of tiny bells and falling rain. The syllables are images. Rain and more rain. Torrents of rain without cease. Streams rush like rivers to the lake, where waters rise and beat against the shore, waves driven by whistling winds. Thunder and brilliant flashes of fireseed. Rain coming horizontal, piercing cold rain. Water rising into houses. Over houses. Washing away roofs. Washing away men and women, children and nens. Washing away everything. All is washed. Washed clean. Washed away.

Abél awakens just before dawn. The moon reflects off the pale sands of the salt flat. He has reached his destination, though he's not sure how. He closes his eyes again, waiting for daybreak.

34.

BRÂN WALKS WITH THE CRUTCH Gerd fashioned from the root of a filiberk tree. I think it looks sturdy enough, although it's knobby and gnarled. Ann trails behind him, her eyes darting here and there, down and then skyward, keeping an eye on her hawk. She doesn't want to be afraid, but she is. Her hawk flies high. Suddenly the hawk shrieks and dives sharply as it spots another figure in the landscape.

It's Malaki. He sits between two rocks, his head slumped between his knees.

The solidness of my anger softens only slightly as I pertange his condition. One side of his head is damaged, one eye crushed into blindness. His orb has gone dark. His aurynx is thick with pain.

It's no more than he deserves.

My eyes fly open and I reach for Damon, my heart beating furiously. The sandstorm has spent itself and gone quiet. *Like Malaki*, I think. Malaki is no longer a threat. I don't know how he came to be in that condition, and I won't try to find out. I'm not sorry.

Damon stirs and pulls me closer. "Is it morning already?" he says.

"Nearly so."

"What's wrong, Meri?"

"I saw…" The name doesn't want to come out. "Malaki."

Damon knows what I mean and he kisses my forehead, strokes my hair. "Do you know where he is?"

"Brân found him. He's with Brân now." Thinking of Malaki makes me ill. I rise quickly. Just outside the door I retch. That gyration in my head again. I hold tight to the doorway. Damon's hand on my back. His voice.

"Are you okay? Meri, I'm afraid you're not well. We should go back to your mother's."

I shake my head. Not too vigorously, lest the swirling begin again. "No," I say. "We have to find the room. The underground room. I'm sure there are things there. Things you need to find. I'll be okay."

Damon offers me water and a soft cloth to clean my face. I find some herbs in my sack and break off a few pieces. They'll settle my stomach. I eat a few bites of nut-bread.

Outside, the lamin shakes herself, expelling a sizable cloud of dust. The early morning sun is soothing. Not too hot. I run my hand along the lamin's long neck, verberating gratitude. The Quartz shows me that Woodclasp is not far. Damon insists that I ride the lamin and I don't argue. We travel in silence, interrupted only by an occasional reassuring chirp from Duende.

"Do you think that's it up ahead?" Damon points toward a cluster of low buildings, barely visible on the horizon.

"That's it," I say. "Woodclasp." A few minutes later I say, "I think there's someone there."

"Brân told us everyone had left. At least that's what I understood."

"We'll soon know." What I know already is that we're on a worn path. Worn by footsteps. By individuals coming and going. Two individuals.

A little farther on and Damon says he sees someone moving about. "It looks like a woman," he says. "She looks Melfar."

My heart leaps. I've never met a Melfar woman. Not in real flesh. Not to talk to.

"There's a man, too. He's working a garden plot, but I think he's seen us. He looks to be Mundani." Damon raises his arm and waves it back and forth. "We don't want them to think we're trying to sneak up on them," he says.

A Melfar woman and Mundani man. Damon and I won't seem so strange. Of course, I'm not truly Melfar. Only half. I'm eager to meet these strangers, but I won't rush the lamin. Damon shouldn't tax his strength either. He shouldn't hurry, but he does.

I see the house. It's a low, round structure built of stones and woven tree roots. Its doorway opens downward into a semi-underground interior. The woman and the man stand side by side. They're waiting for us.

"Good day," Damon calls out.

The strangers wait for us to get a few steps closer. "Fine day," the woman says at last. She's short even for Melfar and her hair is a pale orange color I've never seen before. Her accent suggests that she's fluent in Mundani speech. But I also hear her wondering what brings us to this far place.

I tell her that my uncle has sent us. She wants to know who he is.

"Brân." I say this aloud.

"Not Brân breth Avienne?"

"Yes. Brân is my father's brother."

"So you're a child of Avienne's family! Welcome to you and your companion." *Abél breth Avienne is your father? He was here recently. Stayed most of a tide. Only left when he heard about the old prophet dying.*

Here? Why was he here? If Emba answered me I didn't hear it.

We tell each other all our names. The woman is Emba breth Gillan and her partner is Orban Pritchard. He's a lighter brown than most Mundani I've known. Emba says most eastern Mundani are like that, the ones from beyond Cödweg. They invite us in and offer glasses of cool tea. It's kept cool in a small room, dug even deeper underground. Emba knew Fannan. *Never understood his work.*

Damon does that kind of work. Work with photographs.

Emba tells me about her shama hens and promises eggs for breakfast. *Of course you'll stay. No, no trouble at all.* She shows me the sleeping ledges around the circumference of the room. *We have plenty of pillows. The sandstorm? Every return at this time. That was a bad one.*

"I'm getting confused." I feel the need to speak aloud. "I'm not used to this." I look for Damon. He's gone outside with Orban.

"We can speak then," Emba says. "Your mother was Mundani. That makes it harder for you. But I don't see how Damon is your partner but your nen is pure Melfar."

Even with words my head spins. "My..."

"Ah, you didn't know," Emba says. "Well, it's very early. I'd say only about a tide now."

A shout of dismay rises from my heart. Tears flood my eyes. One hand covers my mouth while the other clutches my belly. I feel nothing there. And yet I know I already feel different. "How is it possible? I'm barren."

"Not barren," she says. "Only impregnable by Mundani." *It's part of how we've survived.*

Anger. Dark purple desperation. Revulsion at the realization that Malaki is inside me still.

Emba kneels and takes my hands in hers. "Dear Meridia," she says. "I pertange your circumstance. A terrible way to start a life." She lays her head in my lap, her hand on my belly, and begins to sing. It's the song Avienne taught me. My tears dry as I join the song. Something deep within me synchronizes with the song.

Damon and Orban are laughing together as they come down the steps into the house. Damon is taller than Orban and he has to duck to get through the doorway. He stops laughing when he sees me. Sees my face. Pertanges my circumstance.

Emba rises, making space for him, nodding to confirm his thoughts. She speaks to share with her partner. "It seems Meridia is pregnant," she says.

Orban's face breaks into a sunny grin. "Hailjoy!" he says. Then he looks at Damon and his face goes slack. "But…how?"

"Meridia had an unfortunate encounter with another like her." Emba radiates anger and then her eyes flutter wider as she pertanges how much like me he is.

"I was raped." My words fall like hailstones. "By my cousin brother. Half Shoon like me." My revulsion toward Malaki makes me use the hated word, makes me want to flush this nen from my womb. *But it's also my nen. And Abél's grandchild. Avienne's great-grandchild.*

Emba corrects my words: "We don't say 'grandchild.' This is Abél's child. Avienne's child," she says. "Every Melfar child is a child of all of its family. Yes, it's a Melfar nen."

Damon's face reflects the quandary in mine. "It's Melfar?"

"It would have to be." Orban says.

A flash of green rises from Emba. A longing for the nen she and Orban would never have. "Definitely Melfar," she says.

Damon's arms are around me. My face hides in the soft darkness of his neck. *Emba could flush this away. She knows how.* Heavy brown sorrow spills through my head, my throat, falling heavy in my chest. Can I do this?

"It's okay, Meri," Damon says, as if words could make it so.

I try to pertange Damon's thoughts, but my own are too confused. Or is he hiding his thoughts from me? "You don't know Malaki," I say. "He's an awful man. The worst of Melfar is in him." *What if it's also in this nen?*

Damon holds me close as my gyroscope spins crazily, desperately seeking balance.

35.

DAMON'S HEAD AND HEART are full of this new situation in which he and Meridia find themselves. *I could be a father*, he thinks. *Not in the physical sense, but in the active sense.* He tells himself this as his heart aches with the knowledge of how strongly conflicted Meridia is about it all. Her anger and her hatred of Malaki run deep. Damon matches his own anger with hers, carefully directing the full force of that anger toward Malaki. He has other feelings, too, that he doesn't wish to make known, even to himself.

"Do you see it?" It's morning and Meridia shows Orban what the Quartz tells her of the location of Fannan's darkroom.

"I'm pretty sure I know that place," he says. "It's nearer the old site of Woodclasp. We should be able to reach it before midmorning."

"Shall I go with you?" Meridia asks.

"I think you should stay here with Emba." Damon's eyes appeal to Emba for support.

"Yes, that would be best," she says.

Meri holds the Quartz out to Damon. "At least take this with you."

He knows that he won't be able to pertange the map within the Quartz the way Meri can. He takes it anyway. He's not in a mood to disagree with her.

Damon and Orban take the little lamin with them as they set out, hoping they might find things too big or too heavy or too much for them to carry. Damon holds the animal's guide reins. The two men walk at an even pace. Meri's plight hangs heavy between them.

"I know it's troubling you as well as Meridia," Orban says. "You know we may return to find that she's persuaded Emba to take care of it, to cleanse her womb."

"If that's Meri's decision." Damon is chagrined at the sense of relief such a possibility seems to offer. "She showed me what happened, and it's made me despise this Malaki fellow as much as she does." Damon's breath comes hard, straining against the fire in his chest. "But… I think she also knows that if she decides to carry through, well, that would be okay, too."

"Knowing can be such a burden," Orban says. "She knows this nen is precious. She knows there are too few Melfar being born into this troubled world. Each one is a treasure. Does Meridia have a brother?"

"No," Damon says. "Not unless her father has another child somewhere that we don't know about." Surely Meri would know if such a person existed.

"A cousin? Oh…" Orban stops himself, remembering Malaki's role in the situation. Chagrined, he stumbles on. "It's just that among Melfar the mother's brother has always been important in the raising up of a child. As births became fewer, though, and so many Melfar ended up with no children or no siblings, it's been a hard custom to continue."

Orban doesn't say it, but Damon understands that sometimes cousins took on such a role. He's never been around Melfar families and he finds these customs unfamiliar. Among Mundani, fathers are the most important. Fathers and husbands are the Sidayens. Women and children, servants and employees are only kinren, subsumed to the care and authority of a Sidayen. He tries to reject such notions. But he's lived his whole life as Mundani and they're hard to shake.

Orban is pointing out mounds of upturned earth. "You can see where we've excavated tree roots for building," he says. "It was all the wood we had left after the fires came through the second time. It was because of the drought that the roots didn't rot. They dried out and got hard as stone. They make good strong walls and fences. Good for carving, too, if you've got the patience for it." He tells Damon which trees have straight roots, which ones have twisted roots, and shows him a place where even the roots burned right down into the soil.

After a while, Orban stops and says, "I think this is the place."

Damon sees nothing different from what they've been seeing for the last fellspan. Dirt and rocks and alarmingly spiny plants. He tries to remember the darkroom he saw in Meri's vision. This doesn't look like it at all. Damon's heart sinks. Of course, it's buried. It was slightly underground to begin with and suffered an intense fire, which would have burned whatever wooden structure might have existed above ground. It collapsed in on itself. They're going to have to dig. Reluctantly, he lets go of the hope of finding paper prints.

Orban takes a long piece of straight root from the back of the lamin. It's carved to a point on one end and has a slight branch forming a handle at the other. He pokes the ground with it.

Damon watches. The ground is hard, and he wonders what Orban hopes to ascertain from this procedure. When Orban finds an area where the ground is softer, the stick penetrates several inches deeper into the earth with each forceful prod. A couple of times there's a faint clunking sound, as if he's struck something.

"Yes, this must be it," he says. "This would've been the entrance, I think. And you see how this area is sunk down a little lower than what's around it? That's the extent of the place. If we had some idea about how the interior was laid out, we might have an easier time of finding something. Finding whatever it is you're looking for."

Damon takes the Quartz from his pocket and holds it in both hands. He closes his eyes and tries to call up the interior of the place as Meridia showed it to him. His vision is vague. What he's most interested in are those snails. He visualizes the entrance, trying to recall standing at the base of the stairs looking across into the room. Meri said the glass container with the snails was on the far side. Damon walks from where Orban says the entrance is to the opposite side of the sunken area.

"Can we dig here?" he says. It's only a guess. He should've asked Meridia for more details about the layout of the room. He'll ask tonight. He tries not to think of the other questions she might answer tonight.

Orban unpacks more implements. One is sharp and heavy, and he uses it to break up the earth. The other implement has a scoop on it that Damon uses to scrape out the dirt once it's loosened. They work for a while in silence.

Damon refuses to acknowledge the weariness settling heavily into his back and arms. He finally suggests that they stop for a while so that he can examine the earth they've removed more closely. "I wouldn't want to miss anything that might be important," he says. Grateful for a few moments' rest, he sits on the ground, delving through the pile of dirt with his hands.

"Mind yourself," Orban says. "I think I saw some shards of glass in there."

Glass. Could it be from the container the snails were in? "Where?"

Orban points with his digging implement.

"It's definitely glass," Damon says as he digs deeper with his bare hands. He pulls out two small shards and one bigger one. Then his fingers close around something equally hard but thinner, curved. He pulls it out. The snails must have been bigger than he imagined. He wipes the dirt away from this fragment with his shirt. The shell is striped brown and yellow. He looks for more.

Orban takes the piece of shell in his own hand and chuckles. "So that's what you're looking for?"

36.

THE OLD MICA SHIMMERS beneath the churning waters of the lake, its song rising insistently in the clashing, splashing rain. Men and women enter the water, swimming into its depths with lengths of plaited grass, seeking to bind the Mica Benison, to lift it up out of the rising water. Repeatedly they fail, fighting back to the surface breathless, breathing in great gulps of air that is mostly rain. They rest a moment, show one another a new plan, grip their ropes and descend again. This time the Mica is bound. It rises with them, almost to the surface before it slips from their grasp. A piece breaks free and settles to the lake bottom, quickly forgotten. Another brief rest and the group tries once more. This time the Mica breaches the waters. Five Melfar hold the raft in place while five more tug on the ropes to roll the Benison onto the raft. Twice it slips, first one way, then the other, before it rests at last on the floating platform. The raft itself rests several inches below the water, but they bind the Mica securely and it doesn't sink.

They know where they must go. They have to take the Mica toward the mountains, toward the high ground where the great Benison and its song can be preserved, can be, perhaps, revised and further disaster averted. The men enter their boats, three small craft guiding the raft that carries the Mica, rowing steadily westward through the pelting rain toward the mountains and the great forest of Serani.

Abél shakes the sleep from his gnosic orb. He draws his aching body up into a sitting position on the hard surface of the island. He breathes. The notes come clear as raindrops on a temple bell. He begins scratching at the ground where he'd laid his head. He searches in his sack and finds a wooden stick. It isn't much, but he digs with it, digging deeper and deeper, scooping the crusty, salty sand away with his cup. Flecks of mica sparkle in the rising sun. And then the glint of something more. He sees it now, the piece of the Benison that fell away as the men wrestled the Old Mica to the lake surface. Stopping only to drink a few sips of water, he continues digging. The piece is bigger than he anticipated. As big as his two hands together. Its song grows clearer and he answers it, finding renewed strength even as his stick breaks. At last he frees the stone from the spot where it has rested all these many meeds. And as he holds it in his hands, he pertanges at last the place where the rest of the Benison lies, once again covered in water. Saltwater this time. Encrusted with living things.

Abél asks the way. He must go westward toward Serani and the mountains beyond. Over the mountains. Beyond Beniford to Aldbeck.

37.

EMBA EXPLAINS THE PROCESS to me: First, I drink the herbal preparation. Then she injects another infusion into my womb. It always works, she says. Always in less than a day. But I know she's only done this with Mundani women, never with anyone even half Melfar like me. Never to cleanse a womb that harbors a Melfar nen. I feel her sadness, her regret for the life of this Melfar child who will never be. I share the same sadness and regret.

And so we don't do it. I cleanse my heart with tears instead. I lay my head on Emba's shoulder and let the tears flow. She shows me images of loving mothers cradling iridescent newborns against their breasts and I try to believe that could be me.

Emba's never experienced pregnancy herself, but she's cared for pregnant women. Mostly Mundani. A few Melfar. We watch the birth of Avienne's two sons together. She tells me confidence, but I'm afraid. She says a little afraid will make me mindful. She offers some herbs to help with the nausea, the swirling in my head. These I accept.

After I'm calmer, I ask her about Abél, about why my father was here.

"He was looking for a woman named Fia." *She's Orban's sister, but she wasn't here. Well, she was here, but she'd died two tides before.*

I'm sorry she died. Why did he want to find her?

To tell her that her daughter Keira had died. That she'd been killed.

Such sadness!

Yes, Abél was distraught and stayed here for quite a while. In the shed up past the spring. All by himself, he was. And then one day he came to say goodbye. It was just after we'd received the news about Amos Quint. About his death.

When Damon returns with Orban, he sees at once the decision I've made. He sits beside me and takes my hand. I lean into his shoulder. He feels stiff. Distant.

When he says he has to go tend to the lamin, I follow him.

"What's wrong, Damon?"

"Nothing," he says, knowing that I already know that's not true.

"Would you have been happier if I'd let Emba cleanse me?"

"No, of course not," he says, but what he means is that he would have felt bad about that, too.

"It's not too late."

There's a grim silence between us as Damon finishes brushing down the lamin and putting fodder into the trough. When he finally looks up at me, there's a smile on his face. Only on his face. "You know I will support you through anything, Meri," he says. He wants to mean that. He does mean it. But there's something more, something he doesn't want to say.

After supper, we lie down on our separate places on the ledge. There are blankets and pillows but no comfort. All night long I'm tormented by the edges of dreams that I refuse to enter.

Today Emba and I go with Damon and Orban to help them search for more things inside the destroyed workshop. Damon wants me to ride the lamin but Emba says the walking will do me good. Emba would've been a good mother.

"I wish I knew what kind of snail that shell belonged to," Damon says. "Do you know anything like it from around here, Orban?"

"Not anything living. We used to find shells along the edges of a pond inside the forest. They looked a little like what you found. From smaller creatures, though."

Duende flies alongside us. Carefree. He alights in bushes then soars again. We call and answer. He shows me where we're going. I see where Damon dug yesterday. A little farther left would've yielded more.

When we reach the site, I take the Quartz and sit on the ground at the entrance to the room. I try to describe it to Damon. He catches some of my verberations beyond my awkward words. When he opens to the verberations, I'm tempted to probe for more. But I don't. I need to trust that he'll tell me what's troubling him when the time is right.

Now I'm composing what remains of the room. Residue of what it once contained. It's not much. "The pans are still there," I say. The pungent smell is gone. "Fragments of the cord where the pictures hung. A few more shells from the snails. Some plates. Like the ones you got from Brân." There's something else I can't quite pertange.

"Plates? Are they intact?"

"I think so," I say.

"Can you show me where they are?"

I close my eyes again, grasping the Quartz. I get up and walk toward the center of the sunken area that was once the room. *A little to the right. Yes, right here.* Damon and Orban begin to dig.

Why am I wondering if Damon ever had a sister? He would have told me.

"Carefully," I say. "You're getting close."

As they dig, the Quartz moves in my hand, like I'm holding a pop beetle. It's pointing to a hole beneath the floor. A stone vault. I can't tell what's inside.

"We found them!" Damon uses a sweeper to brush away the dirt. He continues digging around the edges of the plates. Digging, brushing, digging some more. Finally he's able to lift them out. There aren't many, but Damon is excited to have them. He takes a cloth from inside his sack and folds the plates inside it for protection.

I show him where the stone vault lies. "It's deep," I say. "Below where the floor was."

"We should definitely have a look." He glances at Orban. They both drip sweat.

"Lunch first," Emba says. We sit in the shade of the rough canopy Orban's set up. *A Mundani canopy.* Emba laughs. It's only a piece of cloth fastened to some sticks. We rest and eat.

"Were there other houses here before the fires?" Damon asks. He's noticed other sunken spots scattered about.

"Not so many," Orban says. "Woodclasp had become a smaller town. Just a place at the edge of the forest where Mundani and Melfar could come together and learn from one another."

"A small place but very special," Emba says.

Orban continues. "Before the fires, it was mostly Mundani in the village of Woodclasp. Many of them pilgrims who came and decided to stay. Melfar kept mostly to their own places inside the forest. After the fires, we lived together in Woodclasp. Fannan always preferred to live a little apart. He died in the last fires that came through." He looks over at Emba. Asking permission. She gives it. "Emba's mother and uncle lived here in the town as healers. They left their knowledge to Emba."

"And you? What work did you have?" Damon asks.

"I grew vegetables and sweetcane. I still do, though not so much. Back when the spring at the edge of the forest still ran strong, we had plenty of water here. It kept running even after the drought had taken over most of the country. After so many fires, though, our stream became only a trickle. It's sufficient for Emba and me but not much more."

"My family were farmers, too," Damon says. "We had a wilderfruit orchard and raised cavoutis."

"We never raised animals here in Woodclasp. Well, we've always kept a few shama. For the eggs. We had to protect them from the zakis, though."

"There were zakis here?"

"They came out of the forest sometimes at night. Shama were easy pickings."

There are none of them now, Emba tells me. *No forest, no zakis.*

We've finished our meal. Damon shifts restlessly, eager to get back to work.

Emba and I drowse in the shade while Damon and Orban return to their digging. She shows me more of the history of the place. Mundani and Melfar chanting together inside the forest around great stones. *Great Benisons. At Lindmor. The Amethyst and its Song of Hope.* She shows me an Obsidian and a confusing song that seems to be about successive deaths of a Mundani prophet. Tainted by intrusions of a new prophet, a false prophet.

"What about the Jade?" I ask.

Benisons were erected in Lindmor in alternate meeds. The rest were erected to the west, in Beniford. Except in the returns immediately after the Great Floods. The New Jade was erected in Beniford, with its Song of the Calumet. Also the New Turquoise, which hid the Melfar after their liberation from servitude in the Mundani cities. The Turquoise offered comfort in the memory of happier times. The New Granite was also in Beniford. I learned its Song of Firm Resolve. I could teach you.

My orb buzzes and my head spins trying to pertange all of this. *What is a Calumet?*

A peace-bringer. A bringer of all the power that comes with a true state of peace.

Was Avienne a Calumet?

Yes, Avienne is our Calumet. She has sent many songs out among the Mundani.

She lives?

Yes, she's in Beniford with the others.

Beniford. That's where Brân is going. Where he meant to take me. And Malaki.

Since the New Jade, there have been no Benisons erected. The New Jasper was made, and it was given a Song of Burning, a song meant to protect us from future burning. But it was broken up and much of it lost. Then came the New Quartz.

Like the map I carry?

Yes. There was no Benison. No song. There were only maps and messages in Quartz waifs. The fire that came at the start of the New Quartz took what remained of Woodclasp.

And Fannan's workshop.

Yes. And your eldfather Mica, Avienne's partner. He was caught in the fires as well. The next Benison should have been dedicated at the Marble Return of the New Carnelian. But instead the Melfar of Beniford took pieces of the Old Carnelian and worked it into beads. So many beads. We wear them to keep the song of the Old Carnelian alive, the Song of the Wide Path.

Chanters, too?

Yes, we give the beads to anyone, Melfar or Mundani, who desires to walk together in harmony. Long ago, it's said that some Benisons were erected at a northern fastness as well. My mother's brother told me about that. But that was very long ago. Before the Great Floods.

A shout from Damon interrupts our communion.

"You found it?" I recoil at the loudness of my own voice. So harsh. So unnecessary. Emba makes me feel so Melfar. Almost Melfar.

"I'm sure this is it." Damon leans on his digging implement and wipes his forehead with his sleeve.

You only need to dig deep enough to open it, I tell him. *No need to take it out.* I pertange a golden flutter of gratitude.

Emba and I approach the hole Damon and Orban have dug and peer inside. Emba tells me the stone forming the cover of the vault is a piece of what would have been the New Jasper, containing the Song of Burning. *Maybe Fannan put it there for protection.* The stone is a deep blood-red, shot through with veins of a darker color.

Damon tries to lift the lid of the vault and fails. His arms quiver with fatigue.

"I can help with that," Orban says. He's older but strong. And he's clever. It's awkward trying to lift a heavy object from the bottom of a hole. He brings a length of cord and wraps it around the edges of the covering stone on each side. He hands one end of the cord to Damon and together they drag the stone to the surface.

Damon's eyes fasten on what's inside the vault. There's paper.

Pictures?

Yes, pictures. He touches an edge of the paper delicately and it crumbles into tiny flakes. He pulls his hand away. Studies the faded picture with his eyes, struggling to pertange what is there.

I pertange more. There's a group of men and women holding hands around a great stone. Some are Melfar, some Mundani. A tall Benison, deep blue. The New Lapis. Flowers of all colors are gathered into bunches and laid at the foot of the stone. Deep within the Benison the memory of servitude and the aspiration for freedom. How can all that be contained in a photograph?

"It's so faded," Damon says. "I can make out a few blurry figures but that's all."

I show him.

"You see colors," he says. "I see only monochrome. Sepia." Like the ordinary photographs he makes for customers.

Orban has excavated one of the basins from nearby and laid a clean cloth inside it. He urges Damon to place the photographs on the cloth. "We can take them back so you can study them more easily."

One by one, I tell Damon.

"Are you sure? Won't they crumble?"

This one is the most gone.

"Deteriorated," he says. He takes the first picture up, cradling it in both hands, and lays it in the tray. The edges and one corner crumble a bit more, but the picture remains intact. The one below it is clearer. I see more Melfar, more Mundani. Houses in the forest. Each photograph is clearer than the one above it. Even Damon and Orban see the colors now.

After he's taken all of them out, Damon stops. He looks at them for a moment then takes three of the pictures and puts them back inside the vault. "We can't be sure we can protect them as well as they've been protected here," he says. "We should leave some of them." It's the process of how to make such pictures that he's most interested in. Surely the stories they portray are also recorded in the Benisons.

Damon reaches one more time into the hole, this time to retrieve what appears to be a broken fragment of the covering stone. The New Jasper that was never quite a Benison.

It's approaching twilight by the time we reach Orban and Emba's house. We're all tired beyond hunger, but Emba insists on preparing a meal. Brindle beans with sweet nettles and a pickled shama egg for me. The egg tastes better than I thought it would. Emba says I should eat eggs as often as I can. To help my nen grow.

My nen. It's still so unreal. My heart reaches out toward Damon and runs into silence again. I want this to be something we do together. I want him to be the father of this child. What is he hiding?

38.

WE STAY ONLY ONE MORE night in Woodclasp. Damon has found what he came for—the photographic plates and pictures, but perhaps most importantly the snail shells that he thinks might provide the answer to how such pictures are made. I made a decision and found support for my condition. My pregnancy. Support from Emba. I reach for support from Damon, too, and find only words. They're good words, but he verberates something different. Something I can't quite pertange.

We leave early and walk mostly in silence, each of us lost in thoughts of our own making. The lamin carries Damon's treasures. Emba's medicine has banished my nausea, but my feet are heavy with doubt. Damon is stronger from our travels and from working outdoors with Orban and I struggle to keep up. As shadows lengthen, we think about finding a place to camp.

"Do you see anything that could shelter us?" Damon asks.

I shake my head and try to show him that all the places the Quartz knows have vanished into dust.

"Well?" he says, impatient.

"Nothing." Words are necessary. Why is he being so impervious? "Everything is gone. Remains of an old farmstead, too far off the road."

"We should go there," he says. He points to the sky, toward a tumble of clouds forming in the northeast. A breeze from that direction catches at my hair.

We turn toward the farmstead with me leading the way. As we walk, the sky darkens. I hum Avienne's song as the wind blows stronger. In the distance a flash and then a rumble. I look up into boiling black clouds. Fire-seed flashes between the clouds and the rumbling comes louder.

I pull urgently on Damon's hand.

"It's just a storm, Meri." His voice is nearly lost in the noise. "It won't rain. It never does."

I've experienced such storms before. Rain falls but is sucked back into the dry air, never reaching the ground.

One room of the old farmhouse remains almost intact. It will have to be our shelter for tonight. Shelter for us and the lamin and Duende.

Damon goes outside to inspect the walls and roof. "I don't want anything falling down on us in the middle of the night," he says.

I listen to his footsteps, reach out for his thoughts and find nothing. By the time he's back inside with the door securely braced, there are tears coursing down my face.

"What's wrong, Meri?" A flash of openness.

"Damon," I say, choosing my words carefully, "I can tell you don't want to do this. It's okay. You don't have to. I can stay with Mother. She'll take care of me." I take a deep breath to overcome the catch in my voice. "You can go on to Beniford with Brân and learn what you need to know about your photographs."

Damon's eyes go wide. "Is that what you want, Meri? You don't want a Mundani father for your Melfar child? Is that it?"

"Oh, no, Damon. No! Why would you say that? Why are you being this way? You've never hidden things from me before. Why are you doing it now?" My aurynx throws crazy colors and my heart swells to bursting.

Damon turns away and then sits down heavily. Slowly his head bends forward onto his knees and his shoulders start to shake.

Now I'm frightened. "Damon?" I reach out my hand for him. "Damon, please tell me."

In a rush of images, I know. It happened when he was a child. His mother was pregnant, and his parents had begun to talk of the little brother or sister that was coming. But there were uncertain feelings in him.

"I was content with my life then, too," he says. "I guess I thought that a little brother or sister would only upset things. I remember Mother's belly swelling. And then she got sick and took to her bed for a few days. After that there was no more talk of a nen. It was never mentioned again. I had dreams for a long time of a rainbow presence carrying off my little sister. Maybe I even knew where her unfinished body was buried." It was buried beneath a sheltering linden tree. "Don't you see? I thought it was all my fault. Maybe it was. I don't want that to happen to you. Being newly Revelant now as I was then, I have no idea what I might cause."

I do see. I understand how fearful he was that his own bad feelings had sent the nen away. He wants to protect me. He thinks locking down his feelings will protect me.

"That wasn't your fault, Damon." I shush the prick of doubt. "And it's okay for you to feel uncertain about our situation. You know I feel that way. But if we do this together..."

He moves closer and takes me in his arms. There's a sandy sift of apology and then a pulse the color of ripe sunberries connects our two hearts.

It won't be easy, I tell him.

He strokes my cheek and looks directly into my orb. "I know," he says. "But I'm pretty sure it will be easier if we do it together."

The storm isn't as bad as it looked. The fireseed display is spectacular, but the wind spends itself quickly and not a drop of moisture falls upon the thirsty land. We eat a light supper and sleep curled in one another's arms.

The journey on to Shadham takes another half day. The road is familiar, and we move with confidence. Duende reminds me of his presence from time to time with a cheerful *Chrrr-eep*. I think about the conversation I will need to have with Mother. I remember how angry she was about what happened with my fiancé all those passages ago.

We reach Shadham in early afternoon. "You go on inside, Meri," Damon says. "I need to look after the lamin." I know he mostly wants to give me time alone with Mother.

I take a deep breath and open the door. Mother turns from her work at the kitchen table, wiping her hands on her apron.

"You're back," she says. "And you look well. I was worried about you because you were looking a bit ill when you left. Brân and Ann are on their way to Beniford. Did Damon find what he was looking for?"

I'm trying to verberate to her, but her fountain of words gets in the way. I'll have to say it. "I'm pregnant."

There's brief joy in her eyes followed by a dark question. I know I have to tell her. I have to find words to tell her. So I tell her Malaki. I tell her Brân's son Malaki. I tell her deception. I tell her rape. I tell her so much anger until the words burn to a choking ash in my throat.

"Oh, my dear Mer," she says. "Will you…?"

"I'll carry through. Emba offered to cleanse me, but I decided not to do it. Damon and I will carry this through."

She puts her arms around me, and I try to accept her embrace, try to remember how such an embrace was all I wanted as a child. It feels awkward now. But it also feels good. Her heart pulses against my newly sensitive breasts and her face is damp against mine.

"I was too hard on you," she says. Her voice is thin, taut. "You were only a girl when that boy claimed he wanted to marry you. Just so he could rape you. I was right to be angry, but not at you. Never at you. You were always a good girl." Mother's words become a torrent of confession. "My dear Mer, why did I try to make you what you weren't? You loved poetry as much as I did. And even though you couldn't read, you could memorize a poem after hearing it only a few times and a song after only one hearing. I loved listening to you sing, and I never told you."

I'm embarrassed by this sudden outpouring, but I open my heart further and try to let it be what she wants. All my life I failed to be what she wanted. Maybe now she's different. Maybe we're both different. Tears wet my cheeks and I don't know if they're mine or hers. We've run out of words.

By the time Damon enters, Mother and I are seated at the table, working together to prepare our meal. He joins us and together Damon and I recount our journey. What we learned. Where we plan to go next, to Beniford.

"The Quartz knows the way." I have to reassure Mother. Sometimes Damon sees what the Quartz tells, too, but I always pertange more clearly than he does. He trusts me to find the way. Damon trusts me. He tries to fathom the distance, but he can only guess. We know that Beniford lies well beyond Fayredell. He says we should plan for a journey of a half-stint.

39.

MOTHER SAYS I HAVE a home here, but my home has to be with Damon. Mother's home is with Gerd. She cried when we said goodbye, longing as much for her grandchild as for me. Even though the nen is nothing of her. How could it be? It's Melfar. It's something I never wanted to be until now.

We leave before the sun breaks the horizon, night breezes cool against my face. There's no lamin or equid to help us this time. Damon carries twice as much as I do. He tried to bear it all, but I insisted on carrying at least the backsack containing his photographic plates and the paper images. "This pack isn't heavy," I told him. I didn't know what else he'd put into it.

The day heats quickly once the sun is up. We follow an old Melfar way, avoiding main roads. There were trees once. Never quite a forest here. Small glades. Low brush. Lush grasses. Flowers.

Brown and withered in the drought. Dried to dust. Animals lean and weak. Birds searching for seeds under rocks.

Birds flying. All kinds of birds together. Flying and calling alarms. A scent of smoke. A crackling and hissing. Animals leap and scurry all haphazard. Terror everywhere.

I run, too, but it's no use. The fire comes seething through the trees and brush, embers leaping far ahead. I feel it now, the heat. Go this way. No, that way.

There's no escape! Surrounded by burning, I crouch, choking, eyes watering behind closed lids, hands over my head. No protection. I rise with the smoke, fly with the birds. Below me the whole land is ablaze. Torrents and cyclones of orange flame, blistering heat. All the air a dense, dull red. As far as I can see, nothing but fire and burnt ground.

"Meri!" Damon's voice. "Meri, come back!" Duende twitters excitedly.

I open my ordinary eyes. I'm far off the path. Damon reaches out for me. I cough and my eyes still water. But not from smoke. There is no smoke. Breathless, I fall into Damon's arms.

"What possessed you, Meri? Why did you run off like that?" He clutches me tightly.

I want to show him the fire but I'm afraid. "I saw fire," I say. My eyes still burn from the smoke. Did Damon see it, too? I see that he's carrying my backsack. "Oh, did I drop it? Did they break?"

Damon sits with me and we open the sack. He unwraps the plates and finds them undamaged. I reach down into the bottom of the sack and find a stone. It's a deep blood-red with darker veins.

I hold it up to him with a question.

"It's a piece of stone that I found where we excavated the vault," he says. "I felt like I ought to keep it and nobody said otherwise. I'm sure Emba saw me take it."

"It's a waif. The same stone as the Benison. Almost Benison. Emba told me about it. It would have been the New Jasper. It was never dedicated, but it had its song, the Song of Burning."

"I didn't know," Damon says. He holds the stone, the waif, as if he's trying to pertange its song and the images that overwhelmed me. He puts the stone into his own pocket. "We can rest here a while before we go on. Are you feeling okay? We need to be careful, you know. Your condition…"

I prickle red. He's only trying to protect me. Protect the nen. "I'm fine," I say. Why do I suddenly feel as if this nen is going to try and rule me?

I take out the Quartz to determine how far off the path we've come. Farther than I thought.

We resume our journey, going more slowly. I pertange the Melfar way with increasing clarity. I see it as it was and as it is, all at once. I see the forest, the fire, the charred earth, the seeds still waiting for an awakening rain. Damon talks, tries to engage me. My words stumble over one another. The way is hard. A Mundani road goes smoother but what we seek is safety. So we keep to the road without fellow travelers. The rough road.

I hear a bird call and at first I think it's Duende. But then the song changes and I recognize it as a pilgrim finch. They're imitators, too, but only of bird song, reciting the songs of every place they visit in their travels. I listen to the finch's story. It's been to Blanton, to the clauster there. The clauster is being cleaned now, in preparation for something.

"Can you see a place yet where we can camp for the night?" Damon asks.

I grip the Quartz more firmly and press it into my palm, stroking it gently with my thumb. Asking. Rocks stacked up together. Tumbled walls. Nearby a milparinka. "Will that do?" I ask.

"What?"

"Walls of an old shed up ahead. No roof." Roofs were generally made of leaves or grass. Things that burn.

"We can fasten a sheet overhead."

And that's what we do. There are only three scorched walls and two of them have mostly eroded into dust. We stretch a sheet overhead and anchor it with rocks and Damon's walking stick. The other sheet we spread on the ground for sleeping. We sit outside, leaning against the firmest wall, watching the sun drop, listening to Duende twitter as he settles for the night.

"What do you know about this Beniford place?" Damon asks.

"Not much. Brân showed it to me when we first met. I try to see it now, but it's hidden. Likely under a canopy. I don't know how to get through the canopy to see more."

"But you do know where it is, right?" He's suddenly doubtful.

"Yes. The Quartz tells me that much."

"We should be careful tomorrow. We'll be nearer Fayredell and I'm afraid the Palinjians are a worse danger than ever."

"Our way goes well around Fayredell. Along the edges of the Northern Lowlands." He's right, though. We'll need to be careful.

We finish our simple meal as darkness settles. There's no moon tonight. Only bright stars.

"I loved watching the stars when I was a boy," Damon says. "My father taught me the names of some of the constellations and how they move across the sky with the seasons. He said there were stories about people who could travel by way of the stars, but I never understood how that works."

A way of the stars? That seems unlikely.

Damon falls asleep quickly. I lie awake. Though I won't feel the nen move for another tide or more, I feel that it's wakeful. Restless. Duende stirs, twittering softly, and then flutters away. He's joined by another bird. It's the pilgrim finch.

The Mundani road is far below. A group of travelers are on their way toward Blanton, coming from the direction of Fayredell. They're led by two men, one mature, the other young. I hover closer. The older man is slightly stooped and walks with a limp. It's Rolang Landry, Ann's father. I've only seen him that one time when I was looking for Chapling in Fayredell, but I know this is he. I breathe, attending to the words he speaks.

"Finding your destiny stone, holding it in your hand, is not enough," he says. He's speaking to the young man who walks beside him. "You must claim your destiny, possess it with your will. And you must do it without fear."

The young man nods. He struggles to suppress the fear that makes his heart beat fast, the fear that courses through his limbs. "I'm ready," he says. He's trying to convince himself of that. He hands a stone to an attendant.

"I'll be beside you, Hagan," Rolang says. "I'll renew my destiny as you claim yours. I will help you."

They walk on in silence. The young man's fear remains palpable.

Approaching Blanton, they turn toward the clauster. Ever since the days of the Great Fires, Mundani clausters and temples have gone without roofs. At the center of this one a fire burns brightly amid a circle of Sidayens. Palinjians. Near the fire, blankets are laid out like two beds. Amid the raucous din of Mundani prayer, Rolang and the young man lie down on the blankets. The clamor rises as two other men approach, holding thick bolsters stuffed with feathers and wool. One of these men is Crispin Harper. Each of the prone men takes in a deep breath, then exhales forcefully as the bolsters are placed across their faces and held firmly in place. Rolang lies still. The young man struggles, and others step forward to hold his limbs. I hear his desperate, muffled cries. And then he, too, lies still. Still and quiet.

The bolsters are removed. The prayers get even louder. Fresh herbs are thrown on the fire to make smoke. Then Crispin steps forward and places a stone in each inert hand of each man. The left hands receive a Granite. The right hands receive a different stone and I think it must be their own destiny stone.

The noise stops.

A many-colored presence roils above the scene. Opening, it seeks to welcome the two beings who have just died. A bit of brown fog hovers, then dissipates. An edge of the colored light is sucked down into one of the bodies. It detaches, and the swirl rises, expanding out into nothing. Into everything. The eyes of the men inside the temple are on their recently deceased. They don't see the Migrant.

Rolang stirs, then sits up, crying out in praise of his renewal. He turns toward the young man, who still lies motionless. Crispin presses the stones into his hands again, folding his fingers first around the Granite, then around the young man's destiny stone. I think that stone is an Amethyst. Crispin taps sharply on the young man's chest. Then he looks toward Rolang.

"It's no use," Rolang says. "It was not Hagan's destiny to become Revelant. Not his destiny to transcend fear. His vital nexus could not yoke the Restorer. His will could not defeat death. He is lost."

They pick up the young man's inert body and toss it into the flames, adding more fireblocks to make it burn hotter and brighter.

"Two times Revelant, Rolang!" one man calls out. "A man of destiny!"

A cheer rises from the crowd. The young man's body catches fire, unnoticed. From high above, it looks like any other fire.

I open my eyes. A many-colored mist quivers above my belly.

When morning comes, my mind and orb are still troubled by my vision. I tell Damon about it.

"I'd heard that sometimes Palinjians would die deliberately in order to become Revelant. I guess I didn't want to believe it really happens. You say the older man was Ann's father? These Palinjians are becoming even more dangerous now that Amos Quint is dead. We need to be careful."

I know. Their hatred of my kind burns constant and deep. Their hatred of people who befriend us is almost as strong.

40.

THE BURDEN OF ABÉL'S water and food is less now, but it's offset by the added weight of the Old Mica waif he carries in his backsack. He's moving more slowly than he'd hoped to. The weather is hotter than he'd anticipated. He needs to find water.

Nearing the edge of what was once the old western forest of Serani he squats next to a rock that would shade his whole body if the rock were a bit taller or if it were a bit later in the day. But it isn't and he feels the sun's rays burning down right through the crown of his hat. Letting the Old Mica show him cooling rainstorms doesn't help anymore. He attempts to shrink into the meagre patch of shade, drawing his stiffening legs in as close as he can. He thinks he's getting old. And then he thinks of his mother. Avienne, the beloved Calumet of the Melfar, has already celebrated the completion of seven meeds. Abél has completed little more than five meeds. Thinking of that puts him in mind of his brother twin. Abél hasn't sought out Brân in almost a tide. He seeks him now.

Brân is not far distant, traveling the way that leads to Beniford. He has two companions. One is a young Mundani girl. The other appears Melfar, but he's injured, damaged in both his aurynx and gnosic orb. In these dark days Mundani have become cruel like that. What little they've learned about Melfar they use against them. It gives them pleasure to take away from Melfar their ability to be Melfar.

This one is not even pure Melfar. Could it be? Yes, this is Brân's own son, Malaki. Brân is taking Malaki and the Mundani girl to Beniford.

Abél is pleased to see his brother twin again but concerned about the company he's keeping. His eyes close as he slips deeper into his reverie.

Brân is weary and the canopy he's thrown up grows fragile.

"Over there!" Mundani voices.

"I see him. It's that sully Shoon, Chapling."

"Got to be him. That's one that needs fixing!"

Abél is riveted by the scene he is witnessing. Before he can think how he might help, Malaki has already sprung into action.

Without speaking, Malaki gestures to the girl, ordering her to run as he grabs up a large rock and hurls it with deadly aim toward the first Mundani. The stone strikes him squarely above his left eye. The man grunts once as he falls to the ground. The second Mundani stops for only a brief instant, registers the loss of his companion, then lunges toward Malaki with a bellowed curse. His attack barely moves Malaki, who grabs the enraged Mundani by the arm, jerking downward as he sweeps the man's feet out from under him. Malaki picks up another rock and there is the sound of crushing bone as he smashes it into the man's skull. There's a faint moan from the first man. Malaki retrieves the bloody rock and smashes his skull, too.

Now both Mundani lie still. Malaki's raspy breathing is the only sound.

Tears rim Brân's yellow-green eyes.

Abél's amber eyes fill, too, as he laments the distance separating him from his brother twin.

The girl whimpers and rises from her hiding place behind a bush. She approaches Brân slowly, her eyes wide. Fearful. She's never seen men killed before. "Brân?" she says.

"It's okay, Ann. Come here." He shelters the girl in his arms, offers a soothing cloak of blue-green mist until she grows calmer.

Then the girl looks at Malaki, her eyes flashing anger. "Why did you have to kill them?"

"It was us or them." Malaki's voice is a rough whisper. Colorless.

Brân understands the truth of that statement, but he doesn't like it. Malaki has no more Melfar tricks at his disposal. All he has is his strong body and his quick mind. And the Mundani strength that rises from anger. This time it was enough, but at what cost? "They'll be searched for. Maybe restored," Brân says. "Although likely they're too damaged for that. We need to get away." He searches briefly in his sack and finds his waif of the New Granite, the one bearing the song called Firm Resolve. He pairs it with the Ancient Lapis and sings their protection into existence. It's taking all his strength. His bad leg cries out in pain as he limps along as quickly as he can on his simple crutch. Suddenly he remembers the New Turquoise and he takes that stone into his hand instead. He hums its song, the Canopy of Time. A new way opens for them. A way through a verdant forest. A way Mundani cannot follow.

Abél pertanges all of this and joins with his brother, singing the Canopy of Time as he holds his own

Turquoise waif next to his throat. *Wait for me beside the pond*, Abél tells Brân. *I'll meet you there. We'll go on to Beniford together.*

It's nearly dusk when Abél reaches the pond. The place where a pond used to be. Brân and his fellow travelers haven't arrived yet. Abél is doubly weary from assisting them. He's desiccated with thirst. Leaving the song of the New Turquoise thrumming in the back of his throat, he seeks out another tiny waif from his sack, an Ancient Amber with its song of Raising the Waters. He sits and sings. After a few minutes he goes to a nearby rock and lifts it, revealing a bubbling milparinka. He drinks deeply. He chews a few leaves to help him remain wakeful.

He picks up his waif of the New Turquoise and resumes humming the Canopy of Time. He resists the temptation to play with the song. It contains so many memories and has the power to take him to any time within the span of his memories and the reach of the song's verses. He longs for home and family, for memories of happy childhood, but concentrates instead on a verse about high forests and running streams. He doesn't want to lose the ones he's taken into his care.

Brân is in more pain now. Malaki half carries him as they proceed along the darkening path, a path the broken younger man cannot see. Brân himself has become lighter. The girl is frightened. She doesn't see the forest at all. She no longer sees Brân, only Malaki, and she's terrified of Malaki. She's even more terrified of being lost. She continues to sense that Brân is just ahead and that Malaki knows where he is. So she follows, but not too close. She startles, thinking she's heard something, a muffled sound coming from somewhere behind her on this path she cannot see.

Malaki stops and turns. He's heard it, too, and starts back the way they've come.

"Stop, Malaki," Brân says. His son requires words. "There's no need for confrontation." But Brân isn't sure. He's so tired it's hard to know. He doesn't even know if his son can pertange him at all. Or if he can hear his voice.

A man appears to Brân on the path. A Mundani man. He carries a long pole and as he walks, he whistles a tune that Brân recognizes. It's one of the Preterit songs.

"Hold, Malaki. Wait. Let him pass."

And he does pass. The travelers stand at the edge of the way and the stranger passes by without seeing any of them. Ann has seen no one. Malaki isn't sure.

"I don't understand. Was someone here?" Malaki says this aloud, or as nearly aloud as he can manage.

The Mundani man with the fishing pole arrives at the pond, where he doesn't see Abél. Abél verberates a greeting and the man turns toward him and smiles, although he sees nothing beyond his own time. Abél briefly wishes he could bring some of the fish from the pond into this time in which his stomach grumbles hungrily. But it doesn't work like that.

My brother! Brân has arrived and Abél greets him warmly. Having pertanged the state of his injuries, Abél has prepared a space where Brân can sit and stretch out his throbbing leg. Ann is relieved to be able to see Brân again and readily accepts his trust of this other Melfar man who resembles him and who welcomes them so openly.

Malaki is weary, too, and sits down heavily.

Forest and pond and fisherman have vanished into their own time.

"What just happened?" Malaki says. "Where were you, Brân? Was there someone else passing by?"

Ann waits for answers to these questions, too.

"Abél and I retreated into another time-space, a time when Serani was densely forested. We tried to take you and Ann with us, but that's difficult. Always incomplete. As for the other man, yes, he was there. But he belonged to the other time and he saw none of us. Mundani can't see beyond their own time."

Malaki's head drops forward at the realization that he is now no more than Mundani himself. His Melfar gifts are gone.

"Not unless they're Revelant," Abél adds, "and even then, it's never entirely clear to them. It looked like he was going fishing. Likely at the pond where we're seated."

Ann looks around for a pond and finds none.

"So Mundani used to come into forests to fish?" Malaki's voice is a harsh rasp.

"They did," Abél says. "Mundani and Melfar once lived in harmony. Some of them, anyway. But that was a very long time ago."

Brân sends colors of gratitude to his brother for his assistance. *I pertange that you're going to Beniford, too. And beyond?*

To Aldbeck. Abél reminds Brân of their father's charge to him to recover the Old Mica. He shows him the fragment contained inside his sack and shows where he found it at Gorshfen. But Abél cannot hide his doubts, his uncertainty about where the Old Mica has come to rest. And then Abél's deeper preoccupation seeps through.

Brân jolts in surprise. *The old prophet? Not dead?*
No, brother. Amos Quint lives.

41.

WE'VE BEEN ON THE ROAD for four days now. I look for Brân, but I keep pertanging someone else, someone hidden behind an unfamiliar sort of canopy. I think Brân and this other person are together. Brân traveled this way only recently. Or was it long ago?

I pay less attention to the Quartz. At first, I barely saw the light with all its sparkling colors that accompanies me everywhere. Every day its presence grows a bit brighter, a little more compelling. Sometimes it frightens me. When I attend to it, focus my orb on it, I pertange images sweeping along its colored paths, charming melodies and harmonies unlike any I've ever heard. I think I could easily become lost in it. I almost want to. But I need to be here with Damon, so I cling to his hand as we walk.

There's a pile of brown fog just off the path, emitting a muffled discord. I turn and point. "What is that?"

Damon sees it, too. This time he sees more than I do. He walks toward the place and then steps back quickly. "Bodies," he says. "Dead Mundani men. Two of them. Recently dead."

I see it now. Two men rushing a third. Two skulls crushed. I see who crushed them and my stomach heaves. I shove the images toward Damon and hold my hand out to him, motioning urgently. "We have to go," I say. "Someone will come for them. We can't be here."

I'm almost running, Damon at my side, holding my hand, telling me to slow down but I won't slow down. There's danger here. I see again the faces of the men in the clauster, pertange their triumphant hate. I run.

Our way changes. A forest rises up. Opalescent clouds drift high above. Breeze soft against my face, caressing me with fragrance of lemon and goldiflor.

I slow. I cling harder to Damon's hand, unsure if he can pertange our new way. I hum the colors, the fragrance. The life within me echoes every note. I lose myself.

I breathe in the breezes from the branches overhead, their melodies. Several different songs, melding together in perfect harmony; brief patterns repeated and then intertwined.

I open my eyes. There are no trees.

Damon looks at me curiously. "Where were you, Meri? You went almost transparent, but I could still feel your hand in mine."

I have no explanation.

And then I see that we've arrived.

There's Brân and Ann. And another Melfar man. I recognize him, too. It's Abél. It's my father, Abél.

There's another figure seated at the margins of the group. I choose to ignore Malaki. I tell Damon to ignore him, too, but I feel Damon's anger bubble up. Or is that mine?

Ann runs to hug me. Brân greets us with a surge of golden light and warm words. He introduces Abél to Damon. My father already knows me.

"You've grown into such a beautiful woman, Meridia. Brân told me about the nen." He's happy and sorrowful at the same time. Like me. And Damon.

Malaki's head jerks up. No one had told him. He doesn't look at me. He just gets up and stalks away, his steps heavy with maroon regret. Damon watches him go. I grip his hand more firmly. *Let him be. He doesn't matter anymore.* Damon's hand goes soft in mine, but his eyes are hard as flint as he glares at the space Malaki no longer occupies.

"What was the song I heard you humming when you arrived?" Brân asks me. "It didn't sound familiar."

"I don't know," I say. "It came to me." I draw his attention to the colorful light that has attached itself to me.

"Ah," Abél says. "A song straight from the Migrant. Perhaps a new song for a new Benison."

He pertanges my confusion. "All the songs come originally from the Migrant, Meridia. But such pure songs are impossible to share with Mundani. Mundani find them overwhelming. Sad." He continues using words, not wanting to exclude Damon from what he wants to say, speaking slowly as he struggles to find Mundani words capable of conveying Melfar realities. "The raw songs straight from the Migrant are too full of... well, everything. They overflow with an infinity that lacks any definite point to anchor it. Pointless. Melfar take such songs and transmute them, craft them into something less which makes them speak as something more. Everything is too much for ordinary Mundani awareness."

I'm confused. But it's a confusion without edges. Maybe that's what Abél is talking about.

"Melfar songs were meant to be shared with Mundani?" Damon ponders this.

"Most of them," Abél says. "Some were only for Melfar, but most were meant to be spread more widely. The waifs helped with that. A song would impinge upon some Mundani's consciousness, even though they didn't exactly hear it with their ears or see its imagery. They'd just pick up a rock, take it home, and treasure it for—as they thought—no reason in particular. Sometimes Sidayens would claim it as a destiny stone. Women collected them as healing stones. In either case, the owner of the stone would often begin to sing the song, adding their own words and then sharing it with their community. Women were better at that part than the men. We Melfar also shared our songs with the birds and with the trees, so that they could help to pass them on, help to keep them alive."

Alive. Yes, that's what it is. These songs are alive.

Brân takes up the explanation. "The songs of the individual Benisons were important stories, but there were other kinds of songs. Some were healing songs. Others were warnings," Brân says. "Some were like companion calls to hold us together. Still others were simply reminders of the existence of beauty." Beauty sparkles in his yellow-green eyes as he says this.

The songs didn't always have the intended effect. Abél tells me this.

"Emba told me about some of the songs," I say. "Like Damon's New Jade. The waif he got from you, Brân." The one I carry now.

"That one has the Benison song called The Calumet. Our mother Avienne is a true Calumet. She's brought a number of songs straight from the Migrant and gifted them to us in the Benisons and in the trees, the forests. Of course, many of the songs that resided in the forests have been lost."

"Like the forests," I say.

"We could plant new forests." Ann says. She's been listening. Thinking and wondering.

"But they'd be new forests," I say. "Different forests. Not the ones that knew the songs of my eldmother Avienne." I think of the verberations I've felt walking over the roots of old trees. Maybe some of the songs are still there. Ann thinks new forests with new songs might be good. My father Abél agrees.

"What about that large stone you're carrying?" I direct this at Abél. I don't know what to call him. I can't yet bring myself to say Father.

"You saw that, did you? That's what my own father sent me in search of many returns ago. It's a piece of the Old Mica Benison. Its song is Calling the Rains."

He found it in the Northern Lowlands. It's telling him how to find its parent Benison.

"We could certainly use that," Damon says. "The rain I mean."

"Father thought so. It's these days of scarcity and deprivation that make us enemies to one another. In times of plenty, Melfar and Mundani often lived side by side in harmony."

Abél and Brân believe that could happen again. Abél thinks Amos Quint could help.

"But Amos Quint is dead." I say this aloud.

"So he is," Damon says. "What made you think of him now?" He nudges me and chuckles.

Abél studies me with eyes and orb. *Well done, daughter.* "No," he says to Damon. "He's not. He lives. Though I'm still not sure where."

"How…?" Damon's questions trip over one other.

"I began to understand when I discovered that the ashes placed in his urn were only wood ashes," Abél says. No one asks why he was investigating the ashes of such a man. "Then later I saw what happened, how he escaped dressed in the clothes of the messenger who had come to tell him of the death of Zibal Palinj and the others. The rise to power of Warreth Pherson. But after that, I don't know. I've lost him. Still, I'm certain he still lives."

"Odd." Brân stares at my belly as if he sees something there. "Amos Quint is not Revelant. How can he hide himself so well?"

The brilliance of many colors around me pulses insistently and I'm suddenly aware how far it extends. It's everywhere. Damon's touch brings me back.

"Are we all going to Beniford?" Ann asks.

"For now," Brân says, glancing at Abél.

"I'll go on to Aldbeck after Beniford," Abél says. "And then…"

"Selbourne," I say. The name comes to me in a confluence of sound and color.

"Where?" Abél says. "I've never heard of such a place."

"Nor have I," I say. "But it's where you're going."

42.

THE DAYS OF TRAVEL are long and hard, but not unpleasant. Damon and I like traveling in company with Brân and my father. We trust the canopies they generate to keep us safe. Malaki is like a ghost, barely present.

I sense Beniford long before we reach it. Such a cacophony of song and color! And yet somehow harmonious. Can there be harmony in confusion? Symphony? So many Melfar. Mundani, too, more than I expected. And Melfar children, some still clothed in flashes of the iridescence of their birth. I remember chasing colored bubbles of laughter as they do now. I bounce one toward them and they run after it.

I remember how Brân showed me this town when we first met. I see the clusters of small brown houses shaded by tall trees, the paths with grassy margins. Blue sky! I even see a few puddles. Could there have been rain here so recently? A glow of colored light dances through it all.

A woman approaches our shabby band. She's dressed in many colors—trousers, blouse, scarf, each suffused with hues of blue, green, or purple. Her face radiates youth and wisdom.

"My sons!" Avienne's voice is as melodious as the plucked strings of a harp. "And at last my child Abél's daughter." She takes me in her arms, and I melt into the warmth of her embrace. *And my child Meridia's child*, she says.

Through both your sons, I say. But she already knows. Tears fog my eyes, blinding me to anything apart from her affection.

Then she sees Malaki and her vibrance stills into sadness. "And my child Brân's son," she whispers. She tries to absorb Brân's sadness, but he won't let her.

Avienne embraces Damon, enfolding him in gratitude. He returns the embrace with delicacy, as if he's afraid she might break.

And then I see this place through his eyes, through my own ordinary eyes.

Beniford is barely more than a rough camp. Dusty paths connect tents and travel caravans. There is no blue sky. Few houses. No trees or green grass. But the people are here. And here we are all people, a happy mix of Melfar and Mundani. Here everybody is somebody.

I see the woman Damon held in that delicate embrace. Her hair is white with age, her amber skin faded to a dull yellow, streaked with gray wrinkles like a scrap of old paper. Avienne is old. How could she be otherwise? And although she is sad, she is also full of hope. Our Calumet. The rose and gold of her embrace still suffuse me just as the light of my nen still tinges her faded garments with glimmers of color. Her eyes sparkle, youthful beyond time. Damon tries to see in her the woman I showed him, the one evoked from the New Jade waif. *She's still there,* I tell him. *Look again.*

Malaki has removed himself to the fringes of our group. Good. He doesn't belong here. Except that he does; these are his family as much as mine. They don't reject him as completely as Damon and I do. They pity his condition. But pity is not forgiveness.

Avienne introduces two women. The Mundani woman with the explosion of coarse black hair and the squinting eyes needs no introduction, as Ann has already run to her and grasped her hand. This is Vidvana. The other woman is called Zara. She's Melfar but with a bearing that betrays longtime familiarity with Mundani ways. Her speech is fluent. Her golden hair falls in soft ringlets around her face.

"I'm pleased to meet you," Zara says to Damon. "I'm always pleased to meet Mundani who respect our kind and our ways. I see the trust that Meridia has in you."

I edge closer to him. I do trust him. And I feel more at home here than I've felt anywhere ever before. These people make both Damon and me equally welcome.

"Zara is working to piece together a history of Melfar," Avienne says. "A history in words. We all know stories through the Benison songs, but none of us knows all the stories. She's collected pieces of almost all the Benisons and knows their order and their songs, all the way back through the Ancient Benisons to some of the Preterits."

"Vidvana and I are working together," Zara says. "She knows a great deal about Mundani history and together we're learning how Melfar history and Mundani history intersect. We learn from one another."

"Zara convinced me that we need to do more than send out vague songs by means of the waifs as we've always done," Avienne says. "As you know, several of those have gone tragically awry. Zara and Vidvana intend to write all the stories in Mundani words, to make a book that can encourage understanding between our two peoples."

Brân nods in agreement. "Just like Fannan wanted to make the images of our stories visible to Mundani by means of photographs." His glance edges sidewise toward Damon. "Meridia's friend has a similar interest."

"You're a photologist?" Zara says, her eyes going wide with expectation.

"Yes." Damon has never heard of a photologist before, but he readily understands how the word describes Fannan's work. And his own. "I've recovered some of Fannan's prints and plates. And now I'm looking for the snails he was using as part of his process."

Zara can barely contain her excitement, her hope that Damon might at last be someone who can bring Fannan's work to fruition. "Snails you say? How intriguing! Perhaps someone here can help with that. We have Melfar from all over. Refugees from the areas of Cödweg and Cesta as well as natives from here in Serani. Even a few whose eldpeople come from the Northern Lowlands."

"How is there sufficient water to support such a large community here?" Damon asks. "It looks hopelessly dry."

Vidvana answers. "There's a well," she says, and I pertange it as she continues to describe it to Damon. The well is large and deep, so deep that the men and boys responsible for collecting water have to descend a long staircase to reach it. It's been enclosed, although it was once open to the sky, filled with rain from billowing, towering clouds. Now it's only fed by a stone channel that brings water from the other side of the mountain. "It's good water," Vidvana says, offering some to Damon and me. "And so far, it's never run out."

"If you don't mind my asking," Damon says, "why exactly are so many Melfar gathering here in Beniford?"

Everyone is looking at Brân but it's Abél who speaks. "That was the task given to Brân by our father." Avienne's partner, Mica. My eldfather. "He believed that our songs had become too weak, too dispersed, too misunderstood. He said it was time to bring our people together. So that we could sing together once more. And in particular," Abél says, "to sing the song of Calling the Rains, the song of the Old Mica Benison. My task is the recovery of the Old Mica so that we can relearn—or rewrite—its song."

Why rewrite? I wonder.

"It was too powerful," Brân says. "Or we were too willful, too insistent. The song called forth too much rain and the lands flooded. The Old Mica itself was lost in the floods."

Abél adds what he's recently learned. "The Old Mica was not erected in western Cesta as we'd believed. It was erected in Gorshfen, on an island in the middle of the lake known as Glasllyn, far into the Northern Lowlands." He sends me a question. He's seen that Selbourne is an island.

No, that's not Selbourne.

He pulls the recovered piece of the Old Mica from his backsack.

It's the largest waif I've ever seen. Its surface appears wet, as if with the rains it once called down.

Abél continues, "Father never told me that Meridia would be helping with the recovery of the Old Mica."

Is that what I'm to do? But I know Abél has another task as well. "What about the Amethyst?" I ask. "What about Amos Quint?"

"Did you know Amos Quint?" Vidvana asks, pressing at the bridge of her nose as if adjusting glasses that aren't there. "He was…" She almost says that he was a student of hers. "He was taking an interest in Melfar stories and songs. Before he died."

"I didn't know that," Abél says. "But I do know that Amos Quint is not dead."

"No?" Vidvana sits up straighter and inclines toward Abél, her eyes wide. "How can that be? Are you sure?"

"I'm sure he didn't die in Fayredell. Where he is now, I'm not certain."

Vidvana falls silent, thoughtful.

"So to answer Meridia's question, yes, I guess I'm also searching for Amos Quint as well as for the Old Mica."

"It's all the same," I say. *When you find one, you'll find the other.*

43.

ABÉL HAS GIVEN ME the Amethyst. "For safekeeping," he says. But I know he wants me to help him find Amos Quint. He thinks the Migrant can help. The Migrant and my nen. He tells me that the colors accompanying me are from the Migrant. That they *are* the Migrant.

I ask Avienne about it. *Is this something that happens with all Melfar pregnancies?*

She gazes at my belly, her head cocked to one side. *I've seen it before, but it's uncommon.* She thinks it's as much to do with me as with my nen. *The Migrant favors you, Meridia.*

How can that be? I'm only half Melfar.

The Migrant is in Mundani as well as in Melfar. We experience them differently, but they're really the same in all of us.

I'll sleep this first night in Beniford with more comfort than I've found since leaving Mother's house in Shadham. There's a bed covered in soft blankets and even a pillow stuffed with feathers. I tuck the Amethyst under my pillow. As I drift into sleep-space, I hear Duende twitter from a bush outside the window.

Shimmering varicolored light lines my bed and my pillow. A beam of clear violet, canorous with mevelhorns reaches out to me. I slide along its oscillations toward the island of Selbourne. I slide right through the lacing of its protective canopy. The old man is surprised to see me. I think he doesn't see me so much as know that I'm there.

I can't tell what this Mundani prophet pertanges. There's a sound, a hum punctuated with clashes like beaded drums. I follow the rhythm of it, a rhythm the old prophet follows as he walks through the passageway between two rock faces. On either side I see his image reflected deep into the rock. Deep into the past.

I'm drawn into the rock. Deeper and deeper. Past days of plenty into days of scarcity far worse than we know now. A barren earth filled with starving, miserable people. I drop deeper and hear sounds stranger than anything real, colors so contorted they've become only shades of dull brown and slick gray. Flashing lights. All created, crafted lights. Words inscribed in bright, unnatural colors. Silent colors. Metal objects on wheels whiz by faster than a sprinting equid. People. So many people. Unlike any I've known. Not Mundani. Not Melfar. Some of them light brown, others an odd pink color. I walk on a long stretch of flat rock. Not natural rock. Rock crafted by people. Buildings rise around me like the faces of a canyon. Mirrors everywhere. Noise bereft of song. I hear nothing but the cacophony of noise.

"Meri!" Damon's voice cuts through to me. I feel his hand grip my shoulder.

I open my mouth to speak but there's no sound. Sound remains locked in the canyon, in the deafening silence of the canyon.

Easy, Meridia. Abél's voice? Abél is with me. Walking beside me on the stone way at the foot of the mirrored mountains. *Come with me,* he says. *Come back now. We need you to come back. Your nen needs you.*

I fall against Abél and back onto a soft bed. I'm shaking all over. "Where am I?"

"Beniford. Remember?" Damon again, sounding worried. Damon's arms around me.

"What happened?" I say. But I know what happened. The Migrant took me. What I don't know is where they took me. Or why.

Or when, Abél says.

"Amos Quint is on Selbourne," I say. I try to show Abél the canyon with its mirrored walls.

It's okay, Meridia. Don't try too hard. You could fall into the Migrant again. And I might not be able to get you back. He didn't want me to hear that part.

44.

WE DON'T STAY LONG in Beniford. Only two nights, only long enough to rest up a bit and prepare for the journey onward to Aldbeck and beyond. It will be only the four of us: Abél, Brân, Damon, and me. And Duende. Brân says his crow became lost somewhere in Abél's Turquoise Canopy of Time. Birds are not like Mundani.

Ann is happy to stay with Vidvana. Avienne has told Malaki she might be able to heal his aurynx and gnosic orb, but he's not sure he wants that. He's sullen and withdrawn. I keep telling myself it's all his own fault. I'll be glad to leave him behind.

Avienne tried to convince Abél that I ought to stay here in Beniford with her. For the sake of the nen. But Abél says he needs me. I still hold the Amethyst waif that connects him to Amos Quint. He promises Avienne that he'll guard me. Damon says the same. And Brân. They assure her that I'll be safe. All this worry. Surely I can take care of myself. Myselves. Did Abél tell Avienne about the Migrant carrying me off? However she knows such things, she knows. She reminds me that I carry the Jade waif. *I'll be with you, too,* she says.

The way to Aldbeck won't be easy. It's not a village anymore, just a place. It's on the other side of the high mountains. Brân says there's a pass, a way between the peaks. That's what we're aiming for. Reaching the pass demands a lot of climbing and I get out of breath easily. Avienne cautioned me not to chew too many of the leaves Emba gave me, but the altitude on the second day of our journey makes me lightheaded and nauseous so I chew a few extra.

I feel the Migrant so vividly up here. I keep getting glimpses of things I can't comprehend. I cling to Damon's hand or to Brân's. And to Abél's steadiness. I carry the Jade in my pocket and touch it often.

The land and air are intensely dry, and I drink water and more water.

"This area has always been dry," Brân says.

Abél explains further. "Most of the rains fall on the other side of the mountains, leaving almost nothing for this side. The forest of Serani was watered by systems of rain from farther north, slipping down between the mountains. But that's becoming dry now, too." And that's the point of this journey. We're searching for rain. And for Amos Quint.

We reach a place beyond which there never were trees of any kind and I sense their absence through my feet. The ground feels flat and colorless despite the rough terrain. We rest a bit and then after one more steep climb, we finally reach the pass. Mountains still rise on both sides. We cross through and begin descending. After a while, I hear an unfamiliar, distant sound. A bright white clash and flow. A quiescent crumbling as stone falls away, grain by grain. I inhale the sound.

Going down is almost worse than coming up. My feet slip and my tired legs quiver with the effort of clinging to the steep path. Damon goes in front of me and insists I keep at least one hand on his shoulder. He needs to know I'm still upright. Watching the path consumes all my attention and I barely see the green plants that line the way. But I know they're there. A scent of green fills my head.

"We can stop here," Abél says. "Rest and eat before going on."

I look up at last and see… "What is it?" I've never experienced such a vision. Is it really there? The surface far below us is a deep shade of silvery blue. It moves. It undulates, as if reaching repeatedly toward the mountainside where we stand, then slipping away again. It does this over and over.

"It's the ocean," Brân says. He's ever only seen it once before. He was just a child then and now he stands here as wonder-struck as I am.

"The ocean," Damon says, as if trying to convince himself this thing is real. "I've heard stories, but I never thought to see it myself. I can't seem to see the end of it. How far does it go?"

"No one knows," Abél says. "Some say it goes on forever." *Or around to the other side.*

I resist a sudden impulse to ask the Migrant to show me the other side. I rest instead with the vague "forever." Selbourne is still hidden from view by more high mountains. But I know it's there. Abél looks up at me and then directs his gaze southward. Toward where Selbourne lies.

We've stopped at a relatively flat space edged by stubby trees with oddly shaped leathery leaves. The rocks are cloaked in a soft green covering that isn't grass.

"It's moss," Brân says. "Almost everything on this side is covered in moss. That's because it's always so humid here."

"Why don't we all move over to this side?" Damon asks. "There's plenty of water and it's clear that plants thrive here."

"Plenty of water to wash us right off the hillside when the storms come," Abél says with a chuckle.

"Storms are fierce on this side," Brân says. "And frequent. Aldbeck is relatively sheltered, but even so it was destroyed repeatedly. One too many times, I guess. No one has attempted to live there for the past several meeds."

Damon wonders where we'll stay the night, but he doesn't ask. We'll find out soon enough.

"Are you okay to go on?" We've rested and Abél is eager to move again. He worries too much about me.

"I'm fine," I say. It doesn't look like it's much farther to get down to this ocean.

Our path winds back and forth across the face of the mountain, making the way down much farther than I'd thought. The wind grows stronger and the sky darkens with a thick layer of tumbling clouds.

"Looks like a storm blowing up," Brân says to Damon.

"Will there be shelter?"

"There should be some kind of shelter in Aldbeck, but we may not get that far. And we're likely going to get a little wet before we find shelter of any sort."

Abél picks up our pace. I lean into the periodic gusts of wind, struggling to keep my balance. I slip and almost fall, catching myself against Damon's sturdy back. Abél slows down again. I try to tell him not to. I try not to let them see how tired I am, but they know. They're tired, too. And there's nowhere to stop. We have to keep going.

The wind makes a terrible whistling as it sweeps between the stones along the side of our mountain. And then the rain comes. Huge cold drops of it pelt down, scattering dust, attacking the leaves. I'm grateful for my hat; it protects my eyes, but as the drops come faster and faster, my clothing is soon drenched and my hat droops.

We all walk hand to shoulder, Abél in front, Brân at the rear, Damon and me in between. A line of dripping wet people unaccustomed to mountains following a barely discernible old path that must soon lead to shelter. It must.

We're on a narrow ledge, a sheer drop toward the ocean on one side, a steep wall of stone on the other. Though I can't see it, I know that the ocean has turned brown and fierce, surging wildly, sending up plumes of gray foam. I lean into the wall of stone. My entire body quakes with exhaustion and fear. I find nothing familiar to fasten on, to calm me. Nothing except Damon and Brân and Abél. They're not calm, either.

There's a sudden flash of light and a tremendous clap of thunder as if the very earth and sky are ripping apart. I cry out and cringe closer to the wall. But the light showed us something just ahead. An opening in the wall. More than a crevice. A cave.

Inside, the cave feels dry and safe despite its musty smell. I collapse onto the floor, overcome. Exhausted. The flashes of fireseed and deafening clashes come again and again. Everything is so strange. Damon sits beside me and wraps his arms around my trembling body. I melt into him. The sheet from his backsack is mostly dry and he wraps me in it. I make my body as small as I can inside the sheet, hugging myself for comfort, too tired to think of sleeping. There's a smell of wood smoke.

"Where did you find dry wood for a fire?" Damon asks.

"Someone left a pile of it here. This cave has been used recently." Abél knows it was Amos Quint used it. Amos Quint who left the wood. They've built a fire at a spot near the center of the cave where there's an updraft toward a slanted opening in the roof.

I soak in the drying warmth from the fire and soon yield to sleep.

The storm continues to play with my mind.

I see the abandoned village of Aldbeck below us. Abél says it was a place of many storms, destroyed and rebuilt and destroyed again.

Near the village, in a clearing, a Benison lies on a wooden platform, waiting to be erected. Not a new Benison, an old one. The Old Mica, the Benison that floated on that very raft all the way from what used to be an island in a small lake, a lake that became a vast surging sea in the time of the Great Floods. The raft and its stone were dragged up the muddy hillside above the drowning community of Beniford, through the pass and down toward Aldbeck.

The storms don't stop. Every day the mud grows deeper, the line between land and sea less defined.

A noise, a shuddering of the land, and a whole mountainside slides down toward Aldbeck, barely missing the village but pushing the Old Mica ahead of a wall of tumbling rock and out into the raging sea.

Lost. I hear the lament of the villagers of Aldbeck, the despair of those who pulled the stone up from the depths of a lake, ferried it to Beniford, hauled it over the mountains. *Lost,* they cry out again. *All is lost.*

Thank you, Daughter, Abél says. *Now I know.*

45.

MY EYES OPEN TO IMPROBABLE quiet. I push the sheet aside and tiptoe toward the patch of pale light that is the threshold of our shelter. Below us, but very near, I see water, glistening like glass, heaving gently. No longer brown, the water shimmers silver gray and gold in the dawn light. There's hardly any wind, but still the water moves. Gently, rhythmically. Like breathing.

I step outside our cave and see trees. Not what you'd call a forest. They grow in protective clusters, their branches contorted into weird shapes pruned by the winds. They reach not for the sky, but for the earth. Just above the level of the ocean, a path opens out onto a broad flat space dotted irregularly with the remains of stone structures.

"Aldbeck," Abél says. He stands beside me and places a hand on my shoulder.

I'm grateful that we spent our night in the fastness of the cave. There's nothing left in Aldbeck that would have protected us from the storm. I glimpse it as it once was, with thatched roofs sheltering the rock cottages. Other structures perched high above ground on frameworks of sturdy logs buried deep. Tiny boats painted bright blue and green and red, draped with nets. Laughing children.

Near the center of the abandoned village there's a tree. It's a tree far larger than any other that we've seen, its trunk enormous, anchored into the earth with a mass of twisted roots. A few great limbs reach up but mostly outward, skimming the ground. When the wind stirs and the branches creak, I think I hear the mournful notes of a very old song.

Very old indeed, Abél tells me. *This one remembers, but she's forgotten more. Every branch shorn away takes with it not just the song, but some of the will to sing.*

Damon and Brân join us. We follow a well-worn path down through the rocks and reach a flat expanse of sand at last. I never knew there could be so much water in the world. I walk toward it with my water sheath, sensing it cold and refreshing in my throat.

You can't, Meridia, Abél says. "It's saltwater. You can't drink it."

I stop. Such a waste. All that beautiful water. Then Brân shows me the things that live in the water. There are creatures swimming there, some strong and quick and graceful. Others trudging along the bottom amid swaying branches of green and purple and orange things. There are knobby creatures cloaked in shells. He shows me how the sun takes this water up in miniscule droplets, leaving the salt behind, making clouds and rain. That's why there are trees here. And flowers. This water becomes rain.

Abél says we can eat fish for breakfast. Some of the things living in the water are fish. I feel a choking in my throat. *They don't need air, Meridia. They breathe the water.*

Mother told me about fish once. There was a poem. But something solid we can cook bind eat? I'm not sure.

Brân chuckles. "We'll eat fish if we can catch one," he says. "I've not had much experience as a fisherman." He begins whistling a low tune that reminds me of

Malaki's flute. He hums into it. A swarm of insects appears on the surface of the water and soon a swarm of fish snapping and lunging after them. The insects aren't real, but the fish are. Damon wades into the water and reaches down to grab a fish, pulling it glistening and writhing from the waves. I hear its shrill scarlet shriek. Abél has grabbed another and Brân stops his whistling and humming to quickly seize a third. This will be our breakfast.

The fish have stopped screaming and lie staring at me with eyes like polished stone beads. "They cried out so," I say.

"Fish make no sounds," Damon says. But he stops for a moment, listening, before proceeding to slice the first fish open with his blade.

Brân nods at me and I know he heard it, too. Poor fish. I'm not sure I'll like eating fish. While Brân and Damon prepare the dead creatures for cooking I watch the undulating water, trying to pertange its inhabitants. A bird glides through the sky then dives suddenly, coming up with a small fish in its beak. It swallows the fish whole and, as I smell our fish cooking over the fire, I swallow my trepidation. Brân and Abél say some colors of gratitude for the lives of our three fishes and we begin to eat. It's delicious.

Abél knows now where Selbourne lies. After our meal, we gather our things from where we'd spread them in the sun to finish drying. We head south along the beach. That's what this strip of golden sand is called. The mountain in front of us looks as high as the highest ones we passed on our journey. I'm glad we don't have to climb over it; the way around looks difficult enough.

The soft sand shifts and tries to grab my sandals with every step, and soon they're filled with sand. I remove them. The sand embraces my feet with warmth and energy.

Damon keeps looking for shells. Brân reminds him that these are all saltwater creatures and that the shells from Woodclasp would have been freshwater snails. Damon keeps looking anyway.

I'm captivated by the big white birds with blue wings soaring overhead. They call back and forth with voices like tiny trumpets, weaving a soft vocal carpet of pink and lavender. There are birds wading in the edges of the water, too. Tiny things with legs like long sticks. They pick and peck, fleeing from the oncoming water and then running back onto the wet sand to peck some more. So many new things for me. I feel like a child in this unfamiliar world.

I look again at the white birds with blue wings and think suddenly of Duende. I haven't seen Duende since the storm. No, not since the other side of the mountains. My heart reaches out, hoping he's safe. Grateful for his friendship. Not knowing if I'll find him again. Or if he'll find me.

We round the point where the beach narrows and almost disappears at the foot of the mountain. And there it is. A broad bay cuts into the coastline and far out beyond its mouth lies an island. It's really only a huge, rough stone projecting toward the sky. Its base is jagged and roils the water, sending spumes of white exploding into the air. This is the island of Selbourne.

"How can anyone be living there?" Damon asks.

Brân is busy studying the varicolored lacework canopy that shrouds the near side of the island. Abél pertanges only a faint rainbow born of mist, but he points to a series of openings along a curving path etched into the rock. "He'd be living in one of those caves, I expect."

"He does," I say. "In the one nearest the top. But he's not there now. He's in the middle chamber." The one with mirrors lining the walls.

"How will we get there?" Damon asks the practical question.

"The same way he did, I expect." Abél isn't sure what that way is, but his eye is on an inlet farther up the beach.

"I doubt that," Damon says. "If he went over by boat his boat is still on the island."

"So it would be," Abél concedes. "In that case, we may have to build one of our own. Or learn to swim."

Building a boat sounds like something that could take quite a while. I'm not sure we're prepared for such a lengthy project. I'm sure I'm not interested in swimming.

"Maybe he'd be willing to come to us," I say. "Now that he knows we're here."

"Does he know?" Abél isn't sure.

Yes, he knows, I say.

When we reach the inlet, we see the pole and rope where a boat would be tied up. But, as we expected, there's no boat there. Damon sets down his gear and starts marking out an area for a tent.

"That will do no good if another storm comes," Abél says. "We need to look for a more secure spot." He's looking up toward the mountain we've just rounded.

Looking for another cave of some sort. He points. "That looks like it might be a cave."

I resign myself to more climbing.

It's not a cave after all, only a shallow shelter beneath an overhang of rock. It will have to do. At least it affords a good view of Selbourne. We've caught more fish and I've gathered some purslane and a few handfuls of sunberries from the sandy hills behind the inlet. The berries are brighter yellow than the ones I usually find, and rather sour, but they'll help fill our bellies and do our bodies good.

I try to keep busy preparing our meal. Every time I stop, I see the man I assume is Amos Quint. He's watching us through one of those eyeglass tubes that brings distant things close. Damon showed me one of those once. I ask him if he brought it with him.

"No," he says. "I didn't think it would be useful. We were only going to Fayredell, remember? Why do you ask?"

"The man over there is watching us through one of them now," I say. He's also watching me along the path of undulating colors. He watches Abél along the violet notes. He's curious about our intent. He knows we want to meet with him. He wants to know why.

Could the Migrant take you to him? Abél wants to know.

I think so. I shrink, fearful. Where else might they take me? *I don't want to go. I don't want to get lost.*

Then send Amos Quint a message.

Saying what? Can't we do it together? I hold out the Amethyst waif.

Abél accepts the waif. Holding it between his hands, he shows me an image. It reminds me of one of the photographs we found in Fannan's workshop. It's an image of Melfar and Mundani together, circling a great Benison. In this image the stone is green. The New Jade. The Calumet. The aspiration for harmony, for peace.

I join in the dance, the singing, the joy. Avienne is here, radiant in bud-green robes. The grass is soft and cool beneath bare feet, sun gently warm on my shoulders. The fragrance of florapple blossoms scents the air with a promise of sweet fruit and new beginnings. Across the circle I see him. Amos Quint. He smiles at me and nods.

"He'll come," I say. "Tomorrow."

Abél tucks the Amethyst into his pocket.

46.

DAMON NUDGES ME AWAKE and points toward the island. Halfway between the island and the beach below our shelter, there's a boat, a small, roundish boat. The sun has not yet pushed its fire above the land's edge. The air is still and golden as I watch the man dipping a flat stick into the water, first to one side, then the other. The boat bobs crazily in the undulating waves.

We climb down the steep path to the beach, eager to meet Amos Quint, the great Mundani prophet who is coming to meet us, the prophet who clearly is not dead. Damon runs ahead and splashes out into the water to help the old man drag his boat ashore and tie it to the pole. Quint nods to Damon and then strides toward Abél, standing before him in silence, head cocked to one side, crinkles stitching the corners of his eyes and mouth.

The man is beautiful. He's no taller than Damon, but he moves with a bearing that makes him seem to tower over all of us. His skin has faded to a mellow brown from so much time spent inside his chambers. His hair is mostly white and hangs in a careless plait down his back. The hair on his chin is also grayed, as are his marvelous brows, which reach outward and together, sheltering his sparkling black eyes from the sun. On his wrist he wears a wrap of knotted cloth and Carnelian beads.

It's been more than a tide since Amos Quint has spoken any words other than those of his chants. I pertange his awkwardness, his absorption in the colors and imagery of the Migrant. Even so, he's Mundani and born to be a man of words more than images. His verberations remain vague without the focusing power of words and there's a dance as we struggle to understand one another.

Abél reaches into his pocket and pulls out the Amethyst, holding it in his open palm, offering it once again to Amos Quint.

A bubble of laughter rises in the old prophet's throat as he reaches out to receive the waif. "Is that how you found me?" he asks. His voice is a deep rumble.

"That's part of the story," Abél says. "Come sit with us and share our simple food and we'll tell you more." Abél hopes that Quint will reciprocate with his own story.

Damon and Brân build a small fire. I prepare the eggs I pocketed from a nest we passed on the way down the mountainside. I took only a few of the freshest ones, leaving the others to their parents. I stir the eggs with some nut meal and crushed herbs and wrap the mixture in leaves to cook in the edges of the fire.

"How long have you been living here?" Damon asks. He can bear the image-splashed silence no longer.

Quint clears his throat and inhales deeply. The chant forms in his chest but he pushes his intended words past it. "Ever since I died," he says. There's a deep peal of laughter. He's pleased with his joke. Quint sees that Abél already knows something of what happened to him and suggests that he share this with the rest of us. He's curious to find out just how much Abél knows.

Abél reviews the story of the messenger who brought Quint the news of Zibal Palinj's death and Warreth Pherson's claiming leadership of the Palinjians.

"Warreth Pherson is too young," Quint says. "And too full of hate. He was the one who took my granddaughter's life, you know." Quint nods toward Abél as if to thank him one more time for having brought the body of his granddaughter Keira back to Fayredell.

"What made you decide to disappear?" Damon takes the question from my mind.

There's a vivid rippling along the colors of the Migrant, pulsing crimson amid a sweep of turquoise. "It had all become more than I could bear." Quint's words come slow and deliberate. "The direction the Palinjians were taking was wrong. Warreth Pherson was only going to lead them further astray. I was learning so much from Vidvana. I'd come to doubt the prerogatives of Mundani over Melfar." *And of men over women.*

"You studied with Vidvana?" The image of a leading Mundani man, a recognized prophet, learning poetry from a mere woman astounds me.

"And with Zara. Though I only met with her a couple of times when she came into Fayredell to meet with the women." Quint grows sad, remembering. He remembers his granddaughter.

I see how he cloaked himself in women's garments to slip into their meetings unrecognized. "Ann is in Beniford now, with Vidvana," I say. Somehow that makes me feel brave and I venture something more. "Will you let us come to your island?"

"Yes, of course," he says. "You've already come all this way." He's not happy about breaking his seclusion.

"However, my little boat is barely adequate for one. You'll have to wait for the bridge."

And suddenly I see it: A line of stones projecting above the water, leading from this beach to the sunrise side of Selbourne. I crane my neck, looking out over the water. There are no stones. No bridge.

Quint chuckles from somewhere deep in his chest. "The stones are there, Meridia. But at the moment they're underwater, as they are almost all the time. Impossible to negotiate with the current being what it is. You can see a few of them a bit at any low tide. But when we get a full moon tide as we will tonight, you can walk right across." On such nights Quint eschews sleep, keeping watch with an armory of rocks and huge shells, in case some unwanted visitor should approach. We'll not be greeted with any such barrage.

"How can the moon make the stones appear?" I say.

Quint tries to explain that the moon, being a large object circling around our planet, pulls the water in different ways when it's in different positions. During the course of a full cycle, as the moon gets bigger and then smaller, it intensifies the effects of daily tides.

Damon adds a few comments to the discussion. "I've only read about it in books," he says. "I've never been near the sea to watch how it works."

Quint doesn't stay long with us. He says he needs to return to his island before the tide comes back in. Mostly he wants to get away from us, to digest what he's learned, what he's experiencing with this unexpected influx of outsiders into his world. To contemplate what it might mean. He's unaccustomed to all this conversation and eager to return to his chanting in his chamber of mirrors.

He longs for the company of the Migrant. Damon holds the little boat steady for him as it bobs and jerks on its rope with the water rising beneath it.

I'm fascinated by this idea of the comings and goings of water, so as I sit on the beach watching Quint row away, I also watch the water and see it lap a little closer to my feet with each wave. Damon wanders up and down the beach looking for shells. Soon I have to retreat from the encroaching water.

Quint has arrived at his island, going ashore on the far side, just out of sight. He climbs up a long staircase carved into the rock. Who carved such a staircase? Surely not this old man who's been here little more than a stint. He climbs past the first chamber, entering the second. He stops at the entrance and washes his hands and face with water held in a metal basin. Then he closes his eyes and steps forward one, two…six steps. He opens his eyes and inhales as he looks deeply into the images reflected and reflected and reflected in the mirrors lining his sacred space. He begins chanting. I hear him clearly, though it makes no sense: *Sa, sa, calumet. Say-may key-na eye-matta, sa.* Over and over he intones the same syllables. In my mind I hear the sound of flutes and jingling anklets. And then the tune comes, the notes of the song Avienne taught me, the one from our green waif, the New Jade. It blends perfectly. I walk a while with Quint, supplying melody to his chant, intensifying the images inhering in his syllables.

I'm aware of Damon sitting beside me. Quint's chamber dissolves.

Damon lays out some shells he's found. "What do you think, Meri? Are they all the same?"

I pick up the shells, turn them in my hands. They vary in size and in certain qualities of color, but they all look like they've been constructed by the same sort of creature. "Yes," I say.

Damon rocks backward, his hands around his knees, and cackles like a shama that's just laid an egg. "I think so, too. And the only way I can tell which ones came from Woodclasp and which ones I picked up here is to look inside and see if there's wet sand. Don't you see, Meri? These aren't from freshwater snails. They're from the sea. They're from here. Or some other place like this. Fannan must have kept a saltwater environment for them in his workshop."

"Can you do that?" I ask. "Keep a saltwater environment, I mean." I'm trying to visualize a vessel big enough to contain an ocean.

"If Fannan could do it, I can do it."

"You'll also need to know what they eat," I say, "if you intend to keep them alive."

Damon spends the rest of the day splashing about, sticking his head into the water, looking for the living artisans of his shells, studying all the things that live and grow in this salty bay. He shows some of the plants to Abél, who says he once spent some time near the coast, in a fishing community down past Markham. Abél claims that some of the sea plants are good to eat and helps Damon find them. I try to figure out how to prepare them. They're very salty. And tough. They smell like fish. Or maybe the fish smell like these strange plants. If I cut them up into small pieces, I can boil them in a pan with a heated rock.

As the sun drops toward day's end, the water in the bay continues to recede. After supper, we gather on the beach to watch.

"How long will it take?" The shoreline has moved farther away, but it goes very slowly.

We look to Abél for an answer. He points to where the moon is rising over the water and gestures about halfway up the sky. "About that long," he says. "But the rocks may appear before the tide reaches its lowest. We should be ready to go as soon as the bridge is available."

We wait. The sea grows calmer as the air cools. There's an occasional soft breeze. Clouds play with the moon, hiding it from view for a while and then revealing it again, slightly higher up in the sky. A bank of particularly heavy clouds drifts across the moon and I'm dismayed at how dark it gets. Will we have sufficient light to see our way across the bridge? I huddle closer to Damon. My gaze keeps returning to the spot where I last saw the moon.

Suddenly Damon leaps to his feet. "Oh!" is all he says. I look in the direction his eyes are fastened, and I see it, too.

Unexpected.

The rocks have appeared. They're just breaking the surface. Even without the moon we see them clearly, cloaked as they are in something luminous. Damon splashes toward them. He's seen something more. There are snails with glowing green shells feeding on the luminous coating of the rocks. He's found both his snails and their food source. I feel his triumph, bright and golden as the song of a clapperbill. He picks up one of the snails and brings it to me, letting it crawl along through the water he holds in the palms of his hands. He coos to it like a nen.

"Do you want to hold it?" he asks me.

I don't. It looks sticky. I watch as it sucks its way slowly across Damon's flesh, its feelers waggling in all directions. "Put it back," I say. It isn't happy to be out of the water. Its color and vitality are already fading.

When the rocks protrude above the surface of the bay sufficiently to offer safe passage, we venture out. Where they've mostly dried on their tops, the rocks no longer glow so brightly. Abél leads the way. Damon is concerned about my safety.

Yes, I'll be careful. The stones are evenly placed and almost flat on their surfaces.

Damon turns to face me and leans over, holding my hand as I take each step. Then he moves on to the next and does it again. Slowly we make our way across. Brân comes last.

Quint has come down to meet us. Without speaking, he guides us up the stone stairway and, after a moment of hesitation, leads us into the first chamber. He picks up an oddly shaped glass jar and it begins to glow, casting soft light. My eyes quickly adjust, and I'm mystified by what I see. The walls are coated in a thick black dust and there's a pile of dull black rocks heaped against one wall. A huge oven of some kind is located near the entrance. Containers line the stacks of shelves. They look like glass containers. There's a stone table that's dotted with dribbles of a silvery substance.

"My workshop," Quint says. "I make glass." And mirrors.

"What kind of rocks are these?" Damon has picked up one of the dull black rocks and sniffs it. I could have told him that they smell like groundfat.

"I don't know what it's called, but I found a huge mound of it buried under some rocks. Because of the smell, it occurred to me that maybe it would burn. There are old stories about black rocks called fahm that could burn in a fire. I always doubted there could be such a thing."

"Does it burn?" Damon pokes through more of the rocks in Quint's stack.

"Indeed it does. It makes a very hot fire, hotter even than charcoal. Hot enough to melt sand, as I discovered when I built a fire with it on the beach. That's how I started making glass."

"And the mirrors?" I say.

"You've seen that, have you?" He knows I have. "That took a little longer to figure out." This fahm can also melt some metals and soften others so that they can be worked. Some of the mirrors were already there. How is that possible? "Come with me. I'll show you my reflection chamber."

I'm not certain I want to go; I've already been there once. But I follow.

We walk up some more stairs. The clouds have blown away, and the moonlight reflects off the polished surface of the steps and sparkles on the shifting surface of the bay. My feet are heavy, my legs wobbly as we proceed. But this is more than weariness. I'm apprehensive.

The chamber has a narrow entrance. We follow Quint, going in one by one. It's dark beyond the little patch of moonlight falling across the threshold. We gather in a pile, waiting for Quint to guide us. I blink as a lighted pathway emerges. I look more closely and see that Quint has dug trenches on both sides of the chamber and filled them with water and with rocks covered in the luminous substance. He lights another lantern and its glow is taken up, reflected and amplified by the mirrors. The room is almost bright.

I look down at the glowing trenches. I don't want to get lost in the mirrors again, to fall into them. I reach for Damon.

Quint turns to face us and his deep voice echoes through the mirrors with his image. "I came here to this island," he says, "knowing that we can never learn if we only go about blaming others when things go wrong. I knew I needed to examine myself. The mirrors became an obsession, I'm afraid. But they taught me to…" He shakes his head and gestures toward the mirrors, not sure how to express it in words. He wants to talk about opening up to the Migrant. He wants to show us how his mirrors help him to meet the Migrant, to walk with the Migrant.

The images that lurk behind his words frighten me.

Quint wrests his gaze from the mirrors and fastens it on me. "I was afraid, too, at first," he says. His voice shivers with age and wisdom. "My people call it the Creator and Restorer. I believe you call it the Migrant," he says. "I like that better. It comes and goes, doesn't it? Always moving. Always present. It can be anywhere and is at home in all of us. Whatever it is, it's well beyond what any name can capture. So much more than my simple understanding. And they called me a prophet!"

He looks down and gestures toward the doorway, indicating that we should leave. Then he stops and looks back over his shoulder. "I knew so little. Now I know only one thing: That this Migrant contains all we need to know if we only take the time to listen. And I know that our selfish attempts to hold onto our little fragments of it here in this earthly existence are wrong. And worse when we grasp at it again and again when we ought to let go."

There are tears in Brân's eyes.

"Avienne wanted me to finish my work," Brân murmurs. I pertange how he yearned to be at one with the Migrant. How he heard me calling his name. How his mother urged him to take renewal, rebirth. To become Revelant, to continue being a Token, as all Melfar are, but more so. She wanted him to complete the task given to him by his father, Mica.

"And what about you, Abél? I think you came here for something more than to renew the acquaintance of an old so-called prophet." Quint's face crinkles into a smile as we leave his chamber of mirrors and continue climbing upward to his living space. "You can tell me about that over tea," he says.

Quint's living chamber is simple. He's brought the glass lantern and sets it on a low stone table carved out of the center of the room. Again I wonder who lived here before him. We gather around the table, sitting on woven mats on the floor. He brings five drinking glasses and a jar of tea.

"How did you find this island?" Brân asks Quint.

"That's hard to say." The grizzled old prophet pushes a strand of white hair behind his ear. He really doesn't know, but he has his suspicions. "My destiny stone is a Mica," he says. "It's the only stone I brought with me when I left Fayredell."

"Would you mind letting me see your stone?"

The old man reaches into a pocket of his cloak and takes out the stone, cradling it for a moment between his hands before dropping it into Abél's outstretched palm.

Abél begins to hum.

"That's it," Quint says. "That's what I keep hearing when I carry it with me into my mirrored cave. But it was only a few notes and I couldn't do anything with it. I just continued with the chant Vidvana and Zara taught me. It was the only thing I felt certain of."

Vidvana taught him different words. The syllables, which he prefers, he learned from Zara.

"This is a waif of the Old Mica," Abél says. "And I have no doubt that this is what led you here. Its Benison is what I've been seeking these many returns. I'm convinced that it lies somewhere on or near this island."

Quint drums on the table with his fingers. "I can assure you that I've not seen any great Benisons here. There are a lot of rocks. This whole place is nothing but rocks. But I've seen nothing that would qualify as a Benison." Vidvana is the one who explained to Quint about Benisons. He's never seen one.

"I believe it may be in the water. Submerged." Abél describes his vision to Quint. Still water. Not too deep. Many living creatures. Not the kind that swim about like fish.

"There are pools on the morning side of the island," Quint says. "Enclosed pools that fill with water at high tide and become isolated at low. Perhaps in one of those?"

Abél wants to go and investigate at once, but Quint urges caution.

"The rocks around the pools are treacherous. Doubly so in the dark of night. And when legs are tired, and minds clouded for want of sleep. We'll have another low tide tomorrow. Stay with me here. There's room enough though not great comfort. We can go in search of your Benison by morning light."

The stone floor of the cavern is worn smooth and, with the extra blanket Damon insists I take instead of him, it proves to be an acceptable bed. I sleep. My dreams are filled with song and color beyond images and all night long I dance. I wake once and see, beyond our sleeping chamber, the moon dipping into the silvered waters of the sea and something like the wings of a butterfly floating on its distant surface. I inhale the beauty and wrap myself in the colors of my dreams, sleeping soundly until morning.

47.

I WAKE REFRESHED. I feel anchored to this strange place. *It's not a place, Meridia. It's a portal.* A breach? The Migrant can take me anywhere from here. Or hold me as I sleep. I send golden waves of gratitude for sleep.

I offer to help Quint prepare our breakfast, but he insists there's nothing to prepare. "All I have is what I find here," he says. "It isn't much, but it keeps me alive." So we eat a few berries and scraps of dried fish and some slices of a root he says grows deep underground in a valley beside the bay.

The way down the stone mountain keeps turning toward the rising sun and I pull my hat down over my eyes. The steps have pleasing shallows in the centers of them that help me keep my footing. Any time I falter, Damon's hand is there, reaching for me.

We pass by the place where the bridge emerged last night and turn along a narrow beach of black sand strewn with large, rounded stones that glisten in the sunlight. A little farther on it's all stones and my feet slip and slip again. I remove my sandals and let my feet shape them-selves to the stones, my toes grasping with each step.

Quint stops next to a place where the rocks form a sheltering pool. It contains a lot of water. It's still and I can see into its depths. There are living things there. So many living things. A few small fish but other things with strange shapes I never knew could harbor life. Some shelter in hard containers like Damon's snails. But this pool is too small and not deep enough to hold a Benison. We move on.

Abél hums a tune and it quickly absorbs my awareness. It's only a fragment, but I know it must be the song of Calling the Rains. I breathe the notes to myself, deep silver and gray, soft as a dove's breast. Brân picks it up, too, and then Quint. Even Damon's voice finds a note here and there.

I see this island rainswept and I catch my breath. Howling, shrieking winds and so much rain. Cold, harsh rain. Percussive against the stone. I back away from that vision, straining to see the Old Mica itself.

We pass several more pools, but none of them is the one we seek. None contains the Benison. We keep moving. The sun reaches high in the sky, the rocky beach growing broader as the water recedes. We continue, singing as we go.

My legs are stiff and ache from our journey over the mountains. Walking on this uncertain ground makes my feet and ankles weary. I take an awkward step, and a foot slips. I lose my balance and crash onto the rough rocks, failing to catch myself as my arm buckles with a sickening snap. "Aaahh!" I cry out as crimson pain sweeps through me.

The song is broken; everyone clusters around where I lie sprawled across the stones.

"Meri!" Damon kneels over me. "Are you hurt?"

I want to say "no" but that would be a lie. "Just my arm," I say, ignoring the pain that radiates from my right hip and shoulder and my left ankle. The arm is the only thing broken. "The nen is fine," I say. My left hand lies protectively across my belly.

"There's a small beach ahead where she can rest," Quint says. "We can carry her there."

"I'll walk," I say. Damon has helped me to sit up. I've scanned my ankle and my hip. There will be bruises, but I'm okay to walk. I wrap my wounds in blue light and soothing sound. No, that's coming from Father. Even so, every step sends a bright flash of pain through my body. I concentrate more blue light around the nen.

I'm grateful for the tiny patch of sand where I can sit, legs stretched out before me, almost in the water, back resting against a smooth stone. Father takes my broken arm in both his hands and gently massages the bones back into position, absorbing much of the pain into himself. He takes his own shawl from his sack and binds my arm tightly against my chest.

Thank you, Father. That's already much better. "I'll be okay here," I say. "You need to keep searching. Go, Damon. You go, too." But he won't go.

There's a sudden cry from Brân, just out of sight from where I sit. "I think this is it!" he says.

I see it, too. This pool is deeper and broader than the others. Despite the low tide, it still contains water. Deeper water that can shelter a large object at its heart. An object encrusted with shell creatures and colorful living things waving their tiny arms and branches in the gentle current. A vibrant object.

They've found the Old Mica.

Abél enters the pool and squats. His hands reach out to the Benison and his incomplete notes merge with a grander song, a fulsome song of rich harmonics and soaring melody. He stops.

The song subsides.

"We can't be consumed by this song. It's one of the deepest songs Melfar ever put out into the world. Its power did great harm. We need to be cautious." He hums instead the New Amethyst song, the Song of Hope.

Although he pertanges clearly what lies in front of him, he wants to see. Gently, with sepia waves of apology, he dislodges the living things from a small area of the Benison's surface until he sees the very mica it's made of glinting in the water. A small piece of it falls away in his hand.

"Recovering this Benison and its song will be difficult," Abél says. "But I promised my father to do this and so I shall. Our people—all our people—need the Old Mica. Without the rains, we won't survive." He gazes at the old stone and ponders its future. Our future.

We gather on the tiny patch of beach to decide what to do next. The excitement makes my pain almost bearable. Abél hands the fragment of the Old Mica to me. The waif.

We eat a few handfuls of nuts and drink fresh water laced with bitterroot.

"We could build a raft," Brân says. "With the aid of Quint's boat, I think we could safely get the Benison to the other shore at low tide."

Abél recalls the raft that took the Benison from Gorshfen across to Beniford in the midst of the Great Flood and he nods in agreement. "I think I know the sort of raft that could work," he says. "There will be wood enough on the other side to build it there."

"If we're going to do it, we should go across now, while the bridge is available," Brân says. "I'll go. But I'll need help. I can't do it alone."

"Damon can go with you," I say. Then to him, "I'll be fine here. My father can look after me." *I can look after myself.*

Damon protests. "I won't go without you, Meri."

"But I'm injured. I need to stay here and heal. Brân needs you." *We need the raft.*

Damon knows the task of building a raft will require the work of someone younger and stronger than Brân. He gives in. He holds me in his arms for a while. Kisses me. We know that after today the bridge won't be available again until the moon once more shines full at low tide. It will take that long to build a sturdy raft. And to heal my broken arm.

I refuse the tears that sting my eyes as I watch Damon go.

48.

QUINT GOES EVERY NIGHT to walk among his mirrors and to let the Migrant carry him to places and times I don't want to see. But I do see. I see the flat stone roads and the wheeled machines that flash noisily along them. Does Quint see all this? I see machines that soar across the sky. I see the air turned acrid as it burns the clouds away and turns the land hard and dry.

And one night I pertange something more.

I'm sitting at a table staring anxiously at a brightly lit rectangle with moving pictures and lines of words. I'm someone else and she's crying. The room begins to shake. It jerks and bucks like a crazed equid. Things fall all around me, bouncing and rolling into cracks opening up in the earth's surface. The shaking goes on and on and I roll and fall and fall and fall. I sense the whole surface of the earth buckling and breaking and sliding into different configurations.

I wake with my hands over my face and a scream in my throat. Quint runs in the door and comes to my side. "You saw it, too, didn't you, child? Come with me. There's more to see."

"No! I've seen enough. It's terrible."

"This isn't like that. Please come."

I'm afraid, but I go. Abél is awake, and he comes, too. I'm sure he knows. We follow Quint into his chamber of mirrors, and he walks quickly past them, back farther into the cave, beyond the last mirror. Even farther back we go, where the ceiling slopes so low that even I stoop to walk.

"Here," he says. "Look at this." He shines his lantern toward a place on the wall where an odd shape protrudes. Is it metal? Or glass? Maybe both. The piece of dull glass is oddly shaped and rimmed with a stone-swathed lace, like rust-eaten metal. A piece of red glass is embedded below.

"It's from one of the machines with wheels, isn't it?" I say. "How did it get here?"

"The earthquake," Abél says. "Yes, I saw it, too. The Migrant took all of us there. They wanted us to see. To see the end of that world. And maybe the beginning of ours?" He speaks with quiet awe. He studies the strange object. "It's all here in the rocks, isn't it? In the layers of the rocks. Not stories so much as messages. Things we ought to know about."

I don't understand, I say.

Nor do I, Abél replies. "All I know is that the past is right here. Locked in this stone just as Melfar have always locked our stories in stone." He wonders if, somehow, the future might be here, too. *Or maybe the future depends on how well we read the messages.*

Quint guides us over to a chest that rests against a wall. "I've found a few other things," he says as he opens the box. "I never suspected where they came from until now." He lays a bundle on the table and unwraps it, spreading out his small collection of objects. Strange objects. The ones of glass and ceramic are almost familiar. But others are of an inert, more pliable substance that I've never seen.

"These came from the people before," I say.

The three of us stand in silence, eyes wide as we study the strange objects. Their stories surround us.

49.

THE WORK IS HARD. Damon and Brân scrabble through sparse hillside stands of trees in their daily search for branches—thick branches, straight branches—suitable for construction of their raft. Brân won't allow the felling of entire trees. At first they use only the small saw lent to them from Quint's toolbox, but then Brân crafts an axe of sorts from a large piece of stone he dug from the earth and shaped to a sharp edge. The sharpened stone is bound to a sturdy wooden handle and Damon uses it to hack the branches from their trunk. Brân trims and finishes with the saw.

Every night Damon walks with Meridia along the sandy beach. How they do this, he doesn't know and doesn't care. He feels her hand in his and it is enough. Almost enough.

"We have another helper arriving tomorrow," Brân says. He has that look on his face that he gets when he pertanges something beyond the mundane time and space available to Damon. "Or tonight."

"I'd be grateful for that," Damon says. His arms ache from chopping. They've been at this for many days and have prepared not even half the number of branches they'll need. Every day they have to go farther afield. And every day they also have to search for the food that will get them through to the next day. Some days they've had to sit inside their rock shelter for hours at a time, watching rain and wind. Whenever the clouds make it visible, they watch the moon growing smaller. It's down by half already.

"Their arrival will depend on whether this next storm decides to come here or go farther up the coast," Brân says.

At least the rainstorms mean that there's no shortage of drinking water. The two men secure their building materials between and beneath the safety of some large stones and trek up the hillside to the rock shelter where they spent their first night beside this bay, when Meridia was with them. They've accumulated a stock of fuel with the smaller branches cut from the large ones that will form the raft. Tonight they have fish and a couple of the roots Quint taught them about. Digging the roots out of the ground is almost as taxing as chopping off branches. Brân prepares more food than usual.

The travelers arrive just as the first raindrops spatter against the entrance to the shelter. "Welcome!" Brân says, extending his hand in greeting to the Mundani man and woman who enter.

Damon recognizes the woman as Vidvana, the scholar. Had she always had that many gray strands in her thick hair? She introduces her partner, Willem Učen.

"Avienne thought you two could use some help, so she sent us," Willem says. "I've had some experience in wood crafting." He's carrying a sturdy-looking metal axe over his shoulder and there's another saw protruding from his backsack.

"I can help find our daily food," Vidvana says. "And I'm good at making ropes and weaving poles together to build things." She carries a length of plaited rope looped over her shoulder.

Both Damon and Brân murmur gratitude and shift their positions to make the travelers welcome around their small fire.

"How is everyone in Beniford?" Brân asks, mostly for Damon's benefit. He already knows. He also knows these guests have come for more than woodcutting and raft building.

"More arriving every tide," Vidvana says. "From all over. A few days back a whole Melfar family arrived from over south of Brightlea. Zara told us about a community that used to exist over there. It was called Túl, but she thought it had died out long ago. Zara hopes to learn more of the history of the Cesta Melfar from these new arrivals." She supplies a brief review of what she's learned of Melfar geography. Melfar used to form three intertwined groups, identified by the forest they called home—Cödweg Melfar in the east, Cesta Melfar to the south, Serani Melfar at the foot of the western mountains. "Some say there was a fourth group to the north, up past the lowlands. But they wouldn't have been forest Melfar. There's never been forest there."

"Much of that area was taken over by Mundani even before the Great Floods," Brân says. "Abél told me that."

Vidvana has been poking at the fire with a stray stick. She watches the stick catch fire and then fade to a soft glow as she withdraws it. "Ours is an ancient and complicated history," she says.

Ours? Damon wonders. Vidvana is Mundani, but isn't she speaking of Melfar history?

"Avienne says you've found Amos Quint. Does he have something to do with the Old Mica?"

Brân recounts their journey over the mountains to Aldbeck and Selbourne. At first, he tries it with only a few simple words, augmenting with images that pass too quickly even for Damon's Revelant sensibilities. Then Brân remembers he's telling a story to three Mundani, and he uses more words.

"Avienne also told me a little about your adventures before coming to Beniford. About your encounters with the Palinjians," Vidvana says.

"Yes. I'm afraid I come away with regrets from that journey."

"How so? Avienne says you became Revelant. That must have been a remarkable experience. One rarely experienced by Melfar."

"Because we believe it's wrong," Brân says. His eyes are downcast as he pokes the fire with one of the still-green sticks from the day's work. "Melfar death has always been about the fulfillment of being absorbed into the wholeness of the Migrant. This was taught in the Song of Embracing Death. But occasionally, even we Melfar find ourselves called back, asking for the Migrant's permission to continue. It's often the thought of others that brings us back. For Damon here it was Meridia. She called me back as well, she and my mother, who reminded me of my unfulfilled promise to Father. We see ourselves afterward as a more purposeful Token of the Migrant and it makes us humble."

"That would seem to be a good thing," Damon says. "The desire to help, to complete a promised task."

"Sadly, it's not that way for all Revelants," he says. "With the Palinjians it's the lust for power that brings them back. The desire to make themselves greater, to be more than a man. More than Mundani. They think it's a way of exerting willful control over their Creator, their Restorer. But that's impossible. All they've learned to do is pinch off a bit of the Migrant and imprison it in their dark hearts."

"And I guess it's worse when they invite death deliberately." Damon stamps on an ember that has escaped the fire.

"What do you know of that?" Vidvana says.

"Only what Meri saw one night." Damon recounts what he remembers of Meridia's vision.

"I've heard that phrase before," Vidvana says. "The one about the vital nexus yoking the Restorer. It really is an effort to control, isn't it, Brân? Not the Melfar way at all. And not your way, Damon."

Damon wants to ask about what precisely this vital nexus is. He feels a glimmer of its meaning in his heart. The conversation calls him in another direction.

"What stone did Meri say it was that they put into the hands of Rolang and the boy?" Brân asks.

"A Granite in one hand. A different stone in the other. She thought that one was each man's own destiny stone."

"A Granite." Brân muses, toying with the stick he uses in coaxing the fire.

Vidvana squints expectantly at Brân, then offers her own thoughts. "Zara says there was an Ancient Granite endowed with a Song of Regret. She says it was one of the songs that went sadly wrong."

"That's true," Brân says. "In the words given to it by Mundani, it became a Song of Revenge."

"This is the sort of thing that motivates us to find better means of communication between Melfar and Mundani." Vidvana directs her words at Damon. "We need work such as Fannan was engaged in. We need to continue that work."

Damon feels a surge of warmth. What began as mere curiosity for him could become something greater. His heart swells with determination.

At last they let the fire die away so that weary workmen and exhausted travelers can rest. Damon lies awake another hour or more contemplating what he's learned, trying to recall all the words so that he can share them with Meri. And then he feels her hand in his and knows her voice: *I heard, Damon. Sleep now. We'll be together.*

50.

EVERY DAY I WATCH the myriad colors knotting and plaiting and stitching all the sounds and objects and events into existence. I feel safe here with my father and Amos Quint. Every night I fall into the arms of the Migrant and walk with Damon along the beach. Even so, I miss Damon terribly.

Abél and Quint go most days to where the Old Mica lies at the bottom of the tidal pool. They say they're learning its song. So far, I've only observed from a distance. But today I insist that I'm well enough to go with them. My bruises and scrapes are fully healed and even my broken arm is almost well. The moon has shrunk to a mere sliver of light so I know we're halfway to the time when Damon and Brân will return.

"You know your own body best, Meridia," Father says. "But watch your footing as we go. Don't be distracted by anything." He smiled at me like this when I was small, when I would come back from playing outside, humming to myself. Or when he'd notice me chasing colored hoops and bubbles. How different my life would have been if he'd remained in it.

Amos Quint takes the lead and Father follows behind me, worrying too much along the rocky parts of our path. On the easy parts, where we walk on the narrow sand beach, I let my eyes drift to the water, feeling the way it pulses against the shore, caressing the cacophony of life within its depths. I yearn to enter it. Before I was born, life felt like that. I hum quietly, perhaps silently. I'm not sure. I'm only singing to the nen.

When we reach the tide pool, I sit back and watch as Quint and my father enter the water. The song emerging from the Benison sounds different. I'm less fearful. I let it wash over me in a gentle shower of notes like plucked strings and tinkling chimes. The melody sounds the same, but it's become less harsh, softer. Not so percussive.

How is this possible? I ask.

Quint continues singing as if he didn't hear. Father reaches toward me, inviting me to enter the pool, too. As soon as I sink into the water up past my belly, I feel the song change again. Abél falls silent and signals for Quint to do the same. I breathe. There's still singing, and I don't know where it's coming from.

It's coming from the stone itself. From the creatures clinging to its mass. From my nen. From the Migrant.

The notes come silver blue etched with golden green and clear rosy lilac, showering the landscape with their dance. The showers come and go like breathing, leaving arcs of all the colors in between. The land grows green and lush with plants of every kind, flowers of every color. Trees shoot up and grow heavy with fruit. Children splash in the puddles, roll in the grass, climb up into the trees. Two of the children are mine.

I follow the song to its end and join in as it repeats. On the second repetition I hear Abél's voice joining mine, then Quint finds a deep harmony and joins in as well. Finally the song drifts away, merging into the squelch and sigh of the sea.

"That's what we were looking for," Abél says. "That's the new song. The new song of the Old Mica."

"How can that be?" I ask. "I thought once a song was embedded within a Benison it was fixed."

"Stones are not so inert as people think, at least not Benisons. This one has communed with these sea creatures for many meeds. And now, with your help, the stone and the Migrant have composed a new song. Not altogether new, I guess. The melody, the theme is much the same. It's still a song of rains."

"We three can learn this new song and teach it to others," Quint says, his voice buoyant with wonder.

"We four," Father says, smiling at me.

"Five," I say. "I carry two nens."

"No wonder the presence of the Migrant is so strong," he says. "Oh, my dear Meridia." *There have been so many twins in our family. And now it's happening again.* He smiles so broadly I think his face might break.

"I'm thinking," Quint says, "that maybe we should leave the Benison where it is. Let it rest in its cloak of sea creatures. We could bring others here to learn its song."

Father looks thoughtful, doubtful. "Perhaps," he says. "Although the ceremony of dedication of a new Benison has always been a powerful thing for us. The rededication of this one would be profound. And it could be done together with Mundani. With Chanters like yourself, Amos."

Amos Quint has never been called a Chanter before, at least not to his face. He doesn't mind it at all. "Yes," he says. "I can see how that might be best."

Still he's afraid the old stone could break when we try and raise it. Break into two. Could two be even stronger than one?

51.

THE MOON WAS NEARLY FULL as it dropped toward the horizon at nightfall. In the predawn, I walk down the steps, pausing on the terrace in front of Quint's chamber of mirrors to watch for Damon. Surely this morning they will launch their raft.

I strain to see, but there's no sign of activity yet on that distant beach. Only the pulse of the surf. Soon the sun glints off the water so brightly it makes my eyes hurt. I sit down in the chamber's doorway and close my eyes. I hear the echo of Quint's chant from the mirrors behind me. I've felt his mirrors calling me from time to time, but I've resisted. The Migrant may have more to show me, but am I ready? I think I'm not.

Father joins me on the terrace. "They're about ready to launch," he says.

I'm sure he's right. We watch for a while in a silence patched with undulating colors and images.

You have a question? he says.

Of course he knows. "Brân told me about the aurynx and gnosic orb." I think this requires words. I need to know the words. "But what about what I feel in my chest? Isn't that something, too?"

"It seems that you have the Mundani gifts as well as the Melfar," Abél says. "They call it the vital nexus and say it is the seat of life, the root of the mind." *The source of emotions.* "It's not so strong in Melfar, just as the aurynx and orb are not so strong in Mundani. Apparently, all of these are strong in you."

I want to ask more questions about this vital nexus, but suddenly I see something bobbing across the water along the path of the stones. My heart swells within my chest and a series of bright pink spheres races toward Damon, toward the physical presence of him moving toward me across the water. An unexpected ululation escapes my lips as I scramble to my feet and begin descending the stairs.

Not so fast, Meridia. It will be a while before they get here.

I slow my steps. My two nens flutter like tiny fish within me. I tell them this is their father coming.

I pace back and forth along the little beach as the raft draws nearer and nearer. Finally, I can contain myself no longer and I splash out into the water, running toward Damon. The water grows deeper sooner than I thought it would and I'm suddenly in water up to my chest. Another step and it's up to my neck. A wave comes and washes over me. Damon leaps from the raft and plunges into the water toward me. Then his arms are around me, lifting me above the water, and we're both laughing and kissing. Salty wet kisses, eyes stinging, full of tears and the sea. He holds a rope in one hand and helps pull the raft onto the beach, never letting go of me with his other hand. Me never letting go of him.

After the raft is securely on land, we go back up all the steps to Amos Quint's quarters. I cling to Damon. His arms and shoulders are muscled hard from all the work of the past tide. I see that he wears a wrist wrap with beads. Beads of the Old Carnelian and its Song of the Wide Path. He strokes my arm, the one that was broken and is now fully healed. He lays a hand on my belly.

"It's twins, Damon." I whisper the words and try to show him that these may not be brother twins like Brân and Abél, but could be simultwins, each exactly like the other. But he's too excited to grasp any of that. He hugs me and looks into my eyes and orb, seeing the contentment there.

Malaki thought he was the thief, stealing his pleasure from my unwilling body. But I'm the thief now, stealing from his physical substance to make not one but two Melfar children. Two children who belong to me and Damon alone.

Our clothes dry into a salty crust as we drink our tea. I look around at our group: Two Melfar. Four Mundani. One pregnant woman who always thought she was neither but now knows she's both. All afternoon we laugh and talk together, sending and receiving and sharing colors and images and sounds and words all at once. This is how we should be. The Palinjians seem a world away.

"The next problem will be raising the Old Mica from the pool without breaking it." Abél paces toward the doorway and back, eager to begin the work.

"I have a couple of old ropes," Quint says, "but I'm not certain they can hold so much weight."

"I've brought along some new ropes that I plaited." Vidvana keeps looking at Quint with unabashed reverence. "If we twist them together with your ropes, that should be strong enough."

They continue discussing their plan and I suddenly realize we'll be leaving this place soon. Maybe tomorrow. I've come to feel so at home here. But is it the place or these people? The people will all be leaving together, except for Amos Quint. The Old Mica and its song will come with us. We leave behind only Quint and whatever deep stories are still lodged in the chamber of mirrors.

Eventually we all settle down to sleep. A few more words are exchanged. A few images float in the air. And then silence, lapped by the silver-blue colors of the waters that surround us.

I glide across the waves and around the mountains. Avienne is calling me. Her song reaches for me. I try to touch the remembered strength and peace of it, but something is wrong. The notes break into discord, the colors go brown and heavy. People shout, some in anger, some in fear. Terrible sounds of bodies slashed and bones crushed. Flames crackling.

Avienne? Avienne! I need to find her. The angry men, the Palinjians, are setting fire to everything, lashing out with sharp iron at anyone in their path. So much smoke. I can't see.

"Meri?" It's Damon.

I want to show him, but he can only see the terror in my eyes as I turn and see that my father and Brân and Quint are also sitting up, staring at me and at one another.

Quint gets up and, with trembling hands, lights a lantern. Vidvana and Willem stir and rub their eyes. Quint has begun a chant and I see that it's this chant that wove his extraordinary canopy of protection over Selbourne. Brân and Abél see, too, and add their own song, manifesting a second canopy, interlaced with Quint's.

"Why do I feel so afraid?" Damon whispers. "What has happened?"

"Beniford," I say. "The Palinjians have attacked Beniford."

52.

"FORGET THE BENISON for now," Vidvana says, after the situation has been explained to her. "We need to get to Beniford and help the people. Whoever's left. Willem and I will go."

Brân and Abél aren't sure. They're also uncertain how long the canopies can hold if the Palinjians come searching here. If they found Beniford, they might also find Selbourne. Brân is afraid our work with the Old Mica and with building the raft has been incautious, leaving us open and vulnerable.

Quint is silent, thoughtful. "We only have the one small boat and the raft," he says. "Wherever we go, we'll need to go together. All of us. For safety." He would rather stay here, alone on his island, slipping back into anonymity and isolation. But it's too late for that. He will come with us.

"How long would it take to raise the Benison and get it on the raft?" Damon asks.

Abél recalls how it was raised from the waters of Glasllyn. At least this time they won't have to dive underwater to bring it up. "A half day or less," he says. "Should we take the time?" His voice comes from a distance. Not Glasllyn. He's searching for his mother, for Avienne.

Brân and I look, too. The Palinjians are gone. Beniford has gone quiet. Too quiet. There's a brokenness to it. Fragmented voices of pain and terror lie silenced in a landscape of congealed chaos. Splotches of heavy brown and dull orange and gray. I can make no sense of it. Even the Migrant feels withdrawn, inaccessible.

Should we go to the mirrors? I ask. Father says maybe. Brân says no. Quint scowls at the three of us as he frets with the Carnelian beads on his wrist.

Bring the stone.

The voice is so clear, I look around to see who spoke, even though I know the voice could have been none other than Avienne's. There are startled looks on Brân's and Abél's faces. They heard it, too.

Quint takes in the three of us and says, "So?"

"We take the stone." Abél speaks with the kind of authority that defies challenge, precludes questions.

"We take the stone," I say, with whispered awe.

We troop to the place where the Old Mica lies submerged. Vidvana brings her ropes and Quint retrieves his from his workshop. As we walk, we hum the new song, petitioning the Old Mica to agree to be moved. Apologizing for our urgency.

The work proceeds quickly and efficiently. The stone is tilted, first one way, then the other, as they deftly fasten the ropes underneath it. It groans with every shift. Damon and Willem bring the raft and moor it securely. Then they stand with Brân in shallow water next to the raft, each man with a rope wrapped around his forearm and grasped firmly in both hands. Abél and Quint and Vidvana stand in the tide pool to urge the stone from its resting place and to position it as it rises. I watch, continuing to murmur the song like a lullaby.

"Easy, now," Abél says, as they begin to heave on the ropes. The plan is for the stone to be guided along the lengths of rope and onto the raft.

The stone rises. There's a clatter of dissonant notes as it's wrenched from its resting place. And then, suddenly, a deafening chord, a chaotic explosion of horns and drums like thunder. The ropes go slack and everyone stands erect, peering into the pool.

They don't need to say what happened. Their faces and the purpled blackness of defeat emanating from Brân and Abél tell me that the Benison has broken. Not just broken in two, but into many pieces.

Suddenly Abél's face breaks into a smile. "Well, I was wondering how we would get it over the mountain," he says. "And now I know."

Brân sees it, too. The Benison has broken into exactly seven pieces. One for each of the seven members of our little band. No single piece is too large for one of us to carry.

As the workers lift the pieces out of the pool, one by one, we each receive our cargo. The largest pieces go to Damon and Vidvana and Willem. Then Brân and Abél. Finally Amos Quint and I receive our fragments. Our waifs. But all of these waifs will remain united within our group and will one day be restored to wholeness. I exhale soft green longing: *May this day come soon.*

By day's end, we have crossed the bay and left Selbourne behind. I rode in the little round boat with Quint, trying not to be sick as it bobbed and twirled across the waves. The raft barely stayed afloat with its five pieces of the Old Mica. The five custodians of those five pieces swam through the water, guiding the raft along the partially submerged stones of the bridge. Tonight, with good weather, we'll rest in Aldbeck. Tomorrow we go to Beniford. To whatever's left of Beniford.

Avienne's voice still resonates between my brows. *Bring the stone.*

We're bringing it, Eldmother. We're bringing it.

I want her to be there to welcome us. I want her to be okay. But I'm not sure. I look for her, but I can't find her. I nestle closer to Damon and silently hum myself to sleep with the new song of the Old Mica.

53.

THE JOURNEY BACK over the mountains is less taxing, even with the extra weight of the Old Mica. Living for a tide on Selbourne, traversing its steepness many times a day, has made me stronger. Vidvana and Willem set a challenging pace, but I manage to keep up. There's an odd mixture of urgency and hesitation in our steps. We're desperate to know, but we're afraid of what we might discover once we arrive at Beniford.

I keep getting glimpses of smoldering houses. Blood-soaked earth. Silent, frightened children. All in shades of brown and gray. Pulsing muted colors. A muffled cadence of angry drums.

I'm afraid to look too closely, so I concentrate on my feet, on stepping carefully along these narrow paths with their loose rocks and crumbling margins. We talk very little among ourselves. We've grown colorless and blank and quiet, too troubled for thought or conversation. We carry our respective burdens, our pieces of the Old Mica, our anxiety.

At last the steepest paths are behind us and our way is easier. We've hardly stopped all day, eaten little, drinking water as we walked. At the crest of the next rise, Brân stops. His shoulders slump, and he turns with outstretched hand to bring the rest of us into his purview. We gather alongside him and we see what he sees. In the distance we see Beniford. We see where Beniford used to be, a spot now marked only by scorched shadows.

We cluster on the hilltop in mute despair.

I must have heard it first, because when I look at Brân and Abél, they are still draped in ashen grief.

"She's here, Father." I must have whispered it, because Abél turns toward me only slowly, and I have to repeat it. "She's here. Avienne is here. Listen."

And then Abél hears it, too, the one note shimmering above the blackened ground, glistening clear green like the fluting voice of a lulark. We answer with a lilac harmony and suddenly there's a whole chorus of sound and color rising from the hillside above what was once Beniford, calling us to a new camp farther up the mountainside.

Laughing with relief that obliterates exhaustion, we run in the direction they show us. Our Mundani friends aren't entirely sure what's happening, but they trust us. Damon is caught up in the array of shifting colors. Vidvana and Willem are happy because we are.

There are more survivors than we'd dared to hope. Avienne is here, and Zara and Ann Landry. Ann is overcome at the sight of her great-grandfather, alive and well. He envelopes her in a rosy embrace and lets her cling to him. She's ashamed that her father was one of those who attacked Beniford, one of those who survived the attack. As I look around at the group, I notice that they're mostly women and children. A few older men and youths. The camp is rough, sparse. They left most of their belongings behind when they fled. How did they know?

Mundani are not good at being secretive, incapable of hiding from Melfar. "So of course we saw them coming," Zara says, trying to remember to put things into words. "But it wasn't much warning. We got Avienne to safety and tried to throw up denser canopies, even some New Turquoise Canopies of Time and an Old Amber Song of Turning, but the Palinjians charged on blindly and finally found our village, setting it on fire and killing the men who had volunteered to stay and defend it."

Avienne's sadness is not only for those who died, but for those who were killed by those who died. For those who did the killing. "Most of the defenders were Chanters," she says, "Mundani who believed they could protect our ways by killing our enemies." Her voice quivers with doubt and remorse as she turns toward Brân. "And Malaki. He died in our defense, too."

I'm chagrined at the wave of relief that washes over me with these words.

"He was so broken," Brân says. "The Mundani in him was all he had left to offer."

Vidvana bristles. "Don't suggest that being Mundani is all so regrettable," she says. "Our capacity for anger holds space for our capacity to love, you know."

I didn't know. I think she's talking about the vital nexus and I think I need to learn more.

"I didn't mean…" Brân falls silent as Vidvana places a hand on his arm and her head against his shoulder.

"I'm sorry for your loss." Her voice is gentle.

We sit down to share a meal together in a little clearing that's been supplied with a rough table. As we eat, colors and sounds and images and words fly back and forth with such speed that I grow dizzy trying to follow. No more than a dozen died in defense of Beniford. More than that many Palinjians died before the remnants of their group fled.

"Won't they come back?" Damon asks.

A Melfar youth who says his name is Jalu answers Damon's question. "Not likely," he says. "They believe that our settlement and all its inhabitants were utterly destroyed. They believe they accomplished the final defeat of the evil Shoons." There's laughter in Jalu's eyes. Laughter and triumph. The triumph of having deceived someone into believing that those they call enemies have been decisively defeated. This young man was one of the group that conjured the trick. I know whose trick it was. They even duped the Palinjians into carrying back with them large chunks of ordinary stone, believing they had also captured the last of the Benisons.

"What now?" I'm wondering how long a group of this size can stay in hiding, even with the considerable array of Melfar trickery.

Avienne sits with Amos Quint and Vidvana and Zara to her left, me and Damon and her two sons to her right. She looks at each of us in turn. "That is what we have to decide," she says.

54.

BUT WE DIDN'T DECIDE. It was decided for us. Avienne and Father and I pertange it. Or maybe each of us pertanges our own piece of it. And when we put it together, we know it's right. So do Brân and Quint and Vidvana and Zara and Damon.

And so we proceed toward the healing of our shared environment. We sing the new song of the Old Mica and, one by one, others learn it from us, learn their parts of it. Abél works to restore the wholeness of the Benison. I watch his work, studying how the structure of the stone shifts as the images from the new song penetrate its depths.

And then I see that my father is instructing me, passing on our family craft. I learn about the clay-like material that encases a Benison, sometimes holding pieces together, sometimes merely a penetrating wash, permeating the stone with its properties. The clay contains two substances in particular. One of them Father calls pointing-stone, because of its ability to orient itself to the energy pattern of the earth. Pointing-stone is also affected by fireseed. He shows me how fireseed comes, in differing intensities, from all living things, but most powerfully from aurynx and from lightning storms. I think it can also come from the vital nexus. The other substance he calls ecphorite, a mineral energized by sound itself and having the ability to preserve imprints of sound. Father shows me how singing—the kind of singing done with the aurynx—can generate not just the patterned photons that Damon seeks to capture, but also incandescent arcs of fireseed. I'm not yet clear exactly how that is accomplished. For now it will have to be enough to know that it does happen.

As Abél works, inevitably fragments of the Mica fall away. He hands them to me.

"What are those for?" I ask.

"Waifs," he says. And then I see how there have always been waifs created during the crafting of a Benison, kept near it while it is being imbued with its song so that each waif also knows the song, or parts of it. So that people can carry the song with them, out into the world.

Avienne declares that on the next half-moon the Old Mica will be rededicated with its new song. That is when we will gather to sing in concert. Until then, we murmur our own parts of the song in private as we go about our daily work.

Damon has crafted a saltwater container inside our cabin. It's where he cares for the snails he brought back from the ocean in one of Amos Quint's glass jars, which miraculously did not break during our hurried journey. He only has a few snails, and he's uncertain whether the single rock covered with the luminous slime will be able to feed all his snails and keep them alive. "The slime needs to propagate," he says. "I expect I'll have to go back eventually to get more, but I can try a few experiments with what I have." He can do that because in the flight from Beniford, Zara brought his photographic plates and prints, the ones we excavated from Fannan's workshop in Woodclasp. Damon is humbled to see how important this work is to Zara. And to Avienne, our Calumet.

I take long walks with Ann Landry in the patches of woods that still dot this remote hillside. We like listening to the birds. We can't go far, only as far as the farthest reach of the canopies. In the northern distance, woods merge into stands of true forest and I long to go there. The forest looks dry and brittle, but it's still forest. I wonder if Duende is somewhere among those trees. Every time I hear the call of an echo thrush, I answer, but none of them answers back. None of them is Duende. "What became of your hawk?" I ask Ann.

"Brought down by a hunter," she says.

I know it was one of her father's men, one of the Palinjians, but there's no point forcing her to say it. Her pain is too heavy. "Zara says you have your mother's gift for poetry and song." I say that instead.

"I'm learning," she says. "Zara is a good teacher. Mother only knew the tunes for a few of her poems, but Zara knows them all. And I'm teaching her the words to a couple of them that she didn't know."

I'm reminded that the songs are only given Mundani words once they're adopted by Mundani.

We walk on in silence; the only sounds are the twitters and trills of the birds. We gather some berries and eat most of them.

"Is my grandfather Revelant?" Ann asks.

"No."

"Then how does he see and hear the kinds of things he does? He's almost like a Sh… Melfar."

"He's worked at it. For a couple of tides living on Selbourne and chanting with the Migrant in his chamber of mirrors." And before that, too, studying with Vidvana. "He's learned to listen. To breathe with his mind. To hear."

"Can I learn, too?"

I think she's already learning. There's a faint aura of rosy desire around her heart, her vital nexus. My heart resonates with hers. "I'm sure you can. You should talk with your eldfather Amos about it."

"I used to be so afraid of him. Everyone calling him a great prophet made him seem so distant, like someone I shouldn't touch or talk to. But now he smiles at me like he just wants to be my great-grandfather. My eldfather? I like the Melfar word."

I didn't know him before, so I can't speak to how he might have changed. But I see how Ann is changing. "He's a good man," I say. I wonder what he'll do, whether he'll go to Fayredell again or return to Selbourne.

"I hope he stays here with us," Ann says.

"He'll be here for a while, anyway." I say this, knowing that Ann is the one who won't be staying.

55.

DAMON HAS BUILT a small shelter where he and I can sleep at night. We call it a cabin. I've made a sort of mattress that we call our bed. It's only a sack filled with grass, but it's gentler than the bare ground.

"Do Melfar have a ritual to unite life partners?" Damon asks one evening as we lie together, his arm draped across my belly.

I don't know. I know little more than Damon does about Melfar customs. "Are you saying you want to go through such a ritual with me?"

"I do, Meridia. I know we both feel united already, but wouldn't it be nice to stand up and say that we are united in front of a gathering of people?"

I'm not certain about doing anything in front of a gathering of people, even if most of them would be Melfar. And all of them friends. But I like that he wants this, and I nestle closer into his arms, stirring our bed of grass to release its sweet fragrance. "We could ask my eldmother," I say.

The next morning, we ask.

"Yes, we have such a ritual," she says. "It's a simple one. Wouldn't you like to have a Mundani ritual as well? I'm sure Amos could do that."

"I'm not sure about a Mundani ceremony," I say. "I believe it's not so much for partnership as to subsume a woman to a man's House and kinren."

"Ask Amos anyway," Avienne says. "He can probably alter it in some way." *Or perhaps you and Damon can start something new.*

Amos writes out the script of the traditional Mundani subsuming ritual and gives it to us. "Read through it," he says. "Then we'll talk. I'd be happy to make changes for you."

In the afternoon Damon and I rest outside, next to our shelter. "Read me the script," I say. "I want to know what it says."

Damon pulls out the paper and looks at it and then at me. "You won't like it," he says.

"I know. But read it anyway."

Damon clears his throat and smooths the paper. "Dear Sidayens," he begins.

I know only Mundani men are recognized as Sidayens, so that part won't do.

"We come to tie one House to another through the subsuming of this woman." Damon shakes his head and lays the paper in his lap. "Well, we won't be saying that part," he says.

"Keep reading." I try to suppress the scarlet lumps bumping against the inside of my chest. "I'm curious," I say, as scarlet softens to rosy pink.

"The unity of Houses through the love of two people is the foundation of peace." Damon looks up and we nod at one another.

We find a few more things we like about the Mundani ritual. But most of it is composed of words we could never say to one another nor permit others to say on our behalf. We are not two Houses; we are only one woman and one man who love each another. One man and one woman who take each other as equals.

The Melfar ritual, naturally, has no words, only a pattern of colors and images and cadences and melodies. Colors blend and separate and blend again until there is only the purest of white light. Cadence and melody alternate, briefly counter one another, soar with a descant, and then combine into two rhythm patterns and two melodies playing counterpoint to one another. These are the words Zara uses to describe it to Damon. I begin to hum a harmony, a third part and then a fourth.

"Of course," Zara says. "Of course we will add the nens into the ceremony. They have their part in this union as well. If you'd like, I could take the words you find agreeable from the Mundani ceremony and set them to some of the tunes from the Melfar ritual."

Damon and I readily agree. Avienne suggests that we perform the rites on the same day as the rededication of the Old Mica. At first I resist, not wanting to draw attention to myself on a day so important for the community. But then I realize that there's a practical reason for her suggestion. We are a community with scarce resources and assembling what is needed for one festival, one feast, is easier than trying to provide for two.

56.

EVERY DAY WE TAKE TURNS maintaining the protection canopies, maintaining the semblance of Melfar absence, the lie of our demise. It's an orchestrated performance for the benefit of the Palinjians. Day after day we find no evidence that they even suspect there might be survivors of Beniford's burning. No movement of anyone else anywhere near our sheltered hideaway. We're tempted to relax our vigilance, until the day Jalu interrupts his singing to warn us that someone is coming.

"It's no more than a couple of people," he says, "still at some distance. But it could be Palinjian scouts. They're definitely Mundani. I've got to go back and help maintain the canopies. We could probably use more voices."

Avienne quickly advises all of us to stop what we're doing and generate whatever canopies we know. Damon and I sit next to our tree as I hold the Lapis next to my throat and hum its protection canopy. I remember how a canopy felt the first time Brân showed it to me and so I hazard a look through its tracery to see if I can pertange who's coming.

The man is a lighter-skinned Mundani, like the eastern people.

My eyes fly open. "It's Orban!" I say. In an instant Avienne knows, too, and she instructs Jalu to walk outside the canopy and bring Orban and his companion in under its protection.

When he arrives, I run to him. The woman with him isn't Emba. It's Gerd. My heart trips wildly, muddling the words I want to say.

Orban is relieved to be safe at last but exhausted from the terrors of his journey. His face collapses into sorrow as he turns to look at me and sees that I know Emba is gone. "The Palinjians have gone mad," he says, fighting back tears. "They're killing every Melfar, trying to rub out every trace of your existence. They leave a few sympathizers as warning to the rest." He was forced to watch as Emba was tortured and finally killed, her body too damaged to be restored. Not that she would have wanted that.

"What about Mother?"

Gerd has a pained expression on her face. "Your mother was captured and taken to a Palinjian camp to do their bidding," she says.

I don't want to think about what that means. At least she's alive. Or would it be better if she weren't? My heart is shredded by doubt. Fear. Anger.

"Gerd here barely escaped," Orban says. "I'm sure they never expected a Mundani woman to fight so hard or so well. It would've taken more than the three they sent to capture her."

"But I couldn't save Maddie." Gerd doesn't look like the zaki she must have been while fighting off the Palinjians. She looks defeated and tired. There's regret, too. At first I think it's regret that she had to kill three Palinjians. Then I see that her regret is that she didn't mutilate them sufficiently to keep them from seeking renewal.

"And Fergus?"

Gerd's regret deepens as she shakes her head. "He was absent on an errand when the attack came, and I don't know what's become of him." She waited in hiding for him to return, waited until Orban came through on his mournful flight from Woodclasp. She's hoping maybe I can tell her something.

"How did you find us?" Damon asks Orban. We'd all like to know that. Could there be some flaw in our canopies?

"I saw the way in the Quartz when Meridia was showing us the map of Woodclasp and she mentioned Beniford. I knew there would be canopies, so I had to trust that my memory wouldn't lead us astray. I almost gave up when I saw the place where Beniford used to stand. That's when we began to wander, hoping to find survivors."

Avienne quickly assigns lodging to Orban with an elderly Melfar man and to Gerd with a young family. Orban would have preferred being with a family. Gerd would have preferred to be alone. But they're grateful for a safe place to rest and for food shared graciously, food that they don't have to scrounge from a barren landscape.

Damon and I accompany Orban to his quarters. We have more questions. Ann Landry tags along, bringing questions of her own. We sit and drink tea while Orban devours a good meal of roasted quamash roots and a shama egg, finishing off with a dish of wilderfruit cooked with oberanth. People here are generous with the little we have.

Orban paints a bleak picture. "I can only say what I've seen and what I heard from a few people we encountered along the way. But I will tell you, it's not a land any of us would want to live in anymore."

"Do you know anything about Rolang Landry? Or Lambert Quint?" Ann is concerned about her family.

"That Landry bastard is one of the worst," he says, oblivious of Ann's connection. "He's become leader at one of the clausters where they do their ridiculous suicide rituals. As for Lambert, no one seems to know. He's either dead or gone into hiding. Either way, he doesn't seem to matter anymore and hasn't ever since Amos Quint died."

"Amos Quint isn't dead," Ann says, a note of belligerence in her voice.

Orban's head jerks up and he looks to me and Damon for confirmation.

"He's here," I say. But I let Damon tell the story of how Brân and Abél found him at his retreat on the island of Selbourne.

"Well, it's good to know old Prophet Quint is still alive," Orban says. "But I doubt even he can make any difference anymore. I tell you, those Palinjians act as if they can do anything they please with no fear of reprisal. Who's going to stop them? And their treatment of women…" His voice fails him, and he looks away. When he turns his face toward us again his eyes harbor a steely sadness. He chooses his words carefully. "Their subjugation of women has become brutal." He can say no more. I try to send healing to him, but his wounds are too deep.

I still want to know about my mother and so I excuse myself and go in search of Gerd. When I tell her what Orban said, she shakes her head vigorously, her eyes flashing like sparks off flint. "There's more to it, Meridia. We haven't been defeated. Not yet." She tells me that Chanters have become more organized, although working deeper underground, more clandestine than ever. "The organization is built on the foundation of the weftreds. Some Mundani men are joining weftreds now. Sidayens and not just kinren. Also, some Sidayens are leaving the Palinjians to go back to their farms or shops. They say the Palinjians demand too much."

I tell her about the Old Mica, about the song that we hope will soon bring rains. "Will you stay here with us?" I ask.

Gerd is unwilling to accept the hopefulness of the Old Mica. "No," she says. "I'm going back to fight. I came here hoping to learn the truth behind all the rumors."

"What rumors are those?" I don't ask what she means by "fight."

"The stories about Beniford being utterly destroyed, all the Shoons obliterated, and the last of the banestones either captured or ground into dust. I guess that wasn't really a rumor, since it was the news spread far and wide by the Palinjians themselves." Gerd confirms much of what Orban said, telling us how, in the wake of what they styled their great victory, the Palinjians became even more arrogant and brutal.

But she confides that there were quieter voices as well, rumors passing in whispers at secret meetings of the weftreds and in brief encounters in alleyways and at back doors. These rumors claimed that there were survivors, that some of the Melfar and Chanters had taken refuge in the mountains. "We were careful not to let the

Palinjians hear about this," Gerd says, "but we shouldn't have worried. When they did hear, they only laughed and told each other even more outlandish tales about the foolish things believed by gullible Shoon sympathizers."

"What can you tell me about Mother?" I ask. I know I could look, but I'm afraid. Let Gerd tell me first.

Her voice goes soft. "As Orban said, she was captured and taken to the Palinjian stronghold at Blanton. To the clauster there. The Palinjians have taken to living apart from women, except for a few servants. They're mostly in camps outside the towns."

I know the place she means. It's where I watched the renewal ceremony. The suicide ritual. Mother is there now. So is Rolang Landry.

"They think they're protecting themselves from our bad influence, but what they're doing is making it easier for the weftreds to organize and plan. It's safer with fewer Sidayens around. We've recruited quite a few of the male kinren they left to guard us. They, too, are sick to death of the Palinjians, yearning for something better." Gerd squares her shoulders and looks away. "We'll bide our time. Collect our resources. Let them keep killing themselves." She nods almost imperceptibly, as if affirming what she's said. Or acknowledging something left unsaid. "If you're able to learn more about Maddie, you'll tell me, won't you, Meridia?" Her heart wrenches a lilac-tinged silver.

"Yes," I say. "I will." I don't say how uncomfortable I am with what she's told me. It all sounds so dangerous. I don't know how there can possibly be a good outcome from all of this. I try to think about the ones returning to their farms and shops. That's the only part that seems hopeful.

As I prepare for bed, I tell Damon what Gerd said. I try to tell him how worried I am. For Mother, for Gerd. It's hard for me to put into words. I fall asleep with the notes of the Old Mica's new song drifting in silent colors around me. Hopeful colors full of gentle rain and sprouting seeds. Opalescent clouds drift high above. Amethyst breezes caress my face.

The song shifts.

I hear deep sonorous sighs embellished with a shrill sweetness. There's a fragrance of lemon and goldiflor and it reminds me of the song that led me to my father and Brân when Damon and I were traveling to Beniford. I hear again the several songs, how they melded together in perfect harmony. Brief songs repeated and then intertwined, rich melodies dancing red and green and blue across the sky. Some tones too deep to be uttered by Melfar, the kind of sounds only Mundani are able to produce. Other tones join with intricate melodies and harmonies. Above it all, a descant soars, vaulting and trilling in a way only Melfar voices can accomplish. What was it my father said? *A new song. A song straight from the Migrant.* I'm drawn into it. I breathe with it. All night long, I walk with the Migrant, dancing the colors of this new song.

Near morning, I hear Avienne's voice. *This is our new song, Meridia. Our Song of All Songs. Learn it so we may learn it from you.*

57.

GERD SAYS SHE'S LEAVING tomorrow. She only agreed to stay this long so she could witness the rededication of the Old Mica and see me and Damon united. She's helping the other women to dress me in preparation for the ceremony. I'm wearing new trousers and a billowing shirt made of far more material than was necessary. It's soft, flowing stuff and they tell me I'll be grateful for its ampleness in another few tides. There's a little pocket where I've hidden the gift that I will offer Damon at the appropriate point in the ceremony. The women have plaited two garlands of fragrant herbs and colorful ribbons, which they drape over my shoulders, crossing them front and back. Avienne has given me one of her scarves to wear, and the women wrap it around my head, letting the extra length float down behind. They tell me I look beautiful and for once I feel it might be true.

Gerd hugs me and whispers in my ear, "When I find Maddie, I'll tell her everything. I'll tell her how happy and beautiful you are." I nod and rise on tiptoe to offer her a kiss that aims for her cheek but falls at her jawline.

Since early morning our camp has been filled with the aromas of food preparation. Simple food prepared with care into delicious concoctions. A central clearing is swept clean and lined all around with fresh branches of arrowpine brought over from the other side of the mountains. Avienne declared that our union ceremony has to come first, before the raising of the new Old Mica.

The company gathers and begins to chant and sing. There are only a few instruments, some salvaged from the destruction of Beniford, others newly made. Mostly drums and flutes. Avienne and Amos Quint stand together at the center of the circle and motion for Damon and me to come forward. Orban stands next to Damon as his witness and Ann Landry stands beside me.

The chant stops. Drummers continue to tap with their fingertips, creating a pleasing whisper of sound as Amos speaks.

"Dear people of the earth," he says, "we gather today to celebrate the love uniting these two, Meridia breth Madelyn and Damon Mikelson. Love such as theirs is the foundation of peace." I lose his words in the surge of colors as Avienne raises her voice in song. Zara joins her, adding words to the music. The sounds and colors bear me up and I fly, clutching Damon's hand in mine, soaring as the song soars, breathing to our nens, who laugh together in my womb. As the colors merge into vivid white we settle again into our earthly spaces. We exchange our gifts—single Quartz beads on simple strings. A joyous shout rises from the gathering as Damon and I lean together and kiss. Hands reach toward us in shared happiness as we join the circle to await the entry of the Benison. I stand next to Ann Landry. Damon will be one of the bearers, as will Gerd.

They come forward, the restored Old Mica resting on their shoulders. They step with measured pace toward the foundation prepared for the stone at the center of our circle. The Benison is wrapped in a soft gray cloth adorned with spiral patterns like clouds, worked in silvery threads. There's silence except for the cadence of the bearers' measured tread and then the grunted instructions: "Lift. Turn. Set."

Zara and Avienne step forward for the recitation of meeds, their voices catching a few notes of song as they mention each Benison that is still remembered—the Preterits, the Ancients. I watch their hands moving with the images they evoke. When they reach the Old Mica and its Song of Calling the Rains, Abél unwraps the stone. Sun glints off the bright surfaces of the rejoined seven pieces as Avienne begins singing the new song. The notes come silver-clear, tinged with blue. We join in and our chorus showers the landscape with a buoyant dance, notes bouncing from singers to the Benison and back again, sparking across its surface. The stone becomes incandescent, alive, arcing the notes of our song high into the sky, where a circle of clouds forms. We watch, continuing to sing the clouds into existence, pulling miniscule droplets from the air, gathering them to the notes of our song until by their own weight they fall, soft and wet on our upturned faces and washing like joyful tears across the face of the Benison. Laughing children dance and splash as puddles form.

The rain keeps falling, caressing the land as the clouds drift away toward the east, leaving our little band washed clean under a brilliant arc of all the colors.

"Can you see it, Damon?" I whisper.

"It's a rainbow," he says. "It's not Melfar colors, Meri. It's a rainbow." He hugs me close as we continue to sing, sending the rain we've called up out across the parched land.

58.

GERD LEFT THE DAY AFTER our ceremonies, as she said she would. She came to me in the early morning to say goodbye.

"I saw Fergus." I'm not sure I want to tell Gerd this, but I don't know how to avoid it.

"Yes?" There's a mix of expectation and fear in her voice.

"He's at the Blanton Clauster, the same one where Mother is."

"Is he safe?"

"Oh, Gerd, I can't tell. It looked like he was safe, but only because… Gerd, he wouldn't really join with the Palinjians, would he?"

A groan escapes her lips as she turns her face away from me.

I reach out and take her hand in mine. "I'm sorry, Gerd. I'm sorry I can't tell you more. I don't even know what Mother is doing. I know she's alive, but I can't quite reach her. Everything about that place is all blurred and confused." I suspect Mother may have learned some tricks. She is Revelant, after all. But then, as Amos Quint has demonstrated, being Revelant isn't the only way of accessing some of the powers the Migrant offers.

Gerd looks at me, her face set into a calm mask. "Well, once I get there we'll know more, won't we?"

I watch as she disappears down the path, heading for places our protection canopies cannot reach. I try not to be fearful for her. I send a few more blue waves of protection, and some pulses of orange to keep her aware and alert to anything that might threaten her. I wonder briefly if I could send something to Gerd on the rains, the rains our singers call up every day, sending them to all the dry places, never too much in one place at one time. This, in addition to keeping our protection canopies intact, keeps everyone busy.

Every morning I sit for a while with Avienne and Zara and Vidvana as we work with the new song the Migrant has been showing me, the one Avienne calls the Song of All Songs. She's declared that it's time to revive the practice of erecting new Benisons to mark the transition into a new meed. At the next full moon it will be time to celebrate the Marble Return of the next Marble Meed. So Avienne and I learn this song together, while Abél and Brân search for the physical marble to fabricate the Benison.

"About this new meed." Vidvana opens a notebook and adjusts her glasses. Then she takes the glasses off. These days she thinks she sees more without them. "How will we refer to this meed?"

"It will be the New Marble," Avienne says.

"But what about the last Marble Meed? Don't we call it New Marble?" I say this.

Zara answers. "That one will become the Old Marble. We call the Marble Return of a Marble Meed a Great Turning. All the meeds of the previous sequence shift their references. So it's not only that the previous New Marble becomes Old Marble, the previous New Mica, New Lapis, New Turquoise and so on right through to New Amber become Old Mica, Old Lapis, Old Turquoise, and so on. You see?"

I think I do, although it makes my head spin. "And what about the old Old Marble?"

"Ancient Marble. And the previous Ancients become Preterit, like all the meeds before that."

Falling into a time before time. One more shift in an ever-turning cycle. I think about that the rest of the day.

Abél returns in the late afternoon with good news. They've located an outcrop of finest white marble just beyond the next mountain. He plans to assemble a group of our strongest men and women to go where Brân waits for them, ready to extract the marble for the new Benison and carry it back to Beniford.

"I need to go to Temur," Damon says. We've finished eating supper at the common table and have returned to our cabin. "I think I've figured out the answer to how Fannan made his pictures, but I can't test it properly without the equipment and some of the chemicals from my workshop in Temur."

"That's not safe." I tell him what he already knows. Am I being selfish? Avienne and Amos Quint and my father and uncle all think Damon's work is important. But Damon himself is important to me. I'm already worried over Mother and now Gerd out there among the Palinjians.

"I'd be careful," Damon says, placing an arm around my shoulders. "We're never apart really. I know you'd protect me."

I'm not sure I could protect him at such a distance, though I don't say it. I only say I don't want him to go. And so he doesn't. Not right away. Instead he goes with those who will help extract the marble for our new

Benison. He'll be gone for several days, but he'll be safe under the protection canopies Brân can generate. Abél stays here with us.

             59.

ZARA AND VIDVANA ARE teaching me more
about the sequence of Benisons in Melfar history and I
think that may be what led me to dream last night about
a pattern of twelve stones, one for each kind of Benison.
Avienne insists that it was the Migrant showed me the
pattern, and she suggests that it should be incorporated
into the New Marble Benison.

"If it's to carry a Song of All Songs, it would be good
for it to contain the stones of all the different kinds of
meeds as well. We can do this, Meridia. We can make a
pattern of all twelve stones on the face of the New
Marble."

Abél asks me to draw the image I saw in my dream,
the design of the twelve stones.

"I don't know how to draw," I say. I never learned to
write and surely drawing is harder than sketching letters.
"Can't I just show it to you? Verberate it?"

"You already have," he says, as he places a piece of
paper in front of me and a drawing implement in my
hand. "But I want to be able to show it accurately to
Amos and Vidvana. Try."

The implement feels awkward and I adjust it until it
feels more comfortable. I close my eyes and call to mind
the image I saw in my dream. I see the stones arranged
in the four directions and the four intervening directions.
Another stone north, one south, one east. And one at the
center. I open my eyes and see the pattern on the paper.
Maybe I can draw after all.

"Now, tell me which stones go in which position. We need to make sure we get this right." He thinks he's never done anything that was more important to get right. "Let's start with the four main directions. Which stone is in the north?"

I close my eyes again. I know what this is. I carried a piece of it over the mountains. "Mica," I say.

"East?"

There's a purple stone. It's the one Abél gave to Amos Quint, the one he found in the jar filled with wood ashes.

"New Amethyst," Abél says. "Now south."

My head fills with the sound of it, the vision of Avienne from the stone Damon got from Brân.

"New Jade. And west?"

I don't want to look. I hear the drumbeats again and see the angry man with the sash stitched with so many stones.

"New Obsidian." Abél barely murmurs the words.

I open my eyes and see that he is arranging waifs from his own leather pouch onto the pattern I sketched on the paper.

"Now the intervening directions," he says. "Start with northeast…"

I see it easily, rosy and clear, showing me the way to Woodclasp and to Beniford.

"Quartz. Now southeast."

The beads on the wrists of Chanters. On Damon's wrist and on Amos Quint's.

"Old Carnelian. Southwest?"

I see a blue-green color and suddenly I'm back in Temur, holding a tiny turquoise pebble in my hand and my heart aches for my mother and my birds and my eyes well with nostalgia. "I don't understand," I say.

"It's the New Turquoise. Its song is the Canopy of Time. Now show me the northwest."

I shudder and my eyes fly open. "I don't want to see that again," I say. I don't want to think about that horrible ceremony where Rolang and the boy died and only Rolang came back.

"It's okay. I have it. The Ancient Granite." He's not sure about this one. Why would the Migrant want us to include something that has gone so dreadfully wrong? "What is at the far north position?"

A tree rises in my vision, covered in white flowers…purple fruit…brown and orange leaves and then no leaves at all.

"Ah, the Marble." Abél stops for a moment as if to fix this vision in his own mind. "Far south?"

A spring bubbling up in the depths of a lake.

"Ancient Amber. Now the far east."

My hands fly to my face as I cough. "No!"

"I see. The Jasper. The Song of Burning. Odd, since this was never dedicated as a Benison. One more, Meridia. What's at the center?"

Spaciousness and the sound of bells. Release like water bursting from a broken jug. Duende at my shoulder.

"Lapis. The New Lapis with the Song of Liberation. You had a bird?"

"Yes," I say. "I lost him on the journey from Beniford to Aldbeck. I keep hoping he'll come back. Will you place your own waifs onto the Benison?" I notice that the pattern he's made has a few empty spots.

"I'm certainly willing to do that. But first we have to be certain which songs need to be included. Most of them are clear enough, but I'm not sure about the Marble and the Jasper." He's also uncertain about the Mica. He thinks I may be too steeped in the Old Mica and its song. He looks up at me expectantly.

"I don't know the song of the New Mica," I say. There are so many of the songs I don't know.

"The Migrant knows," he says. "We'll have to trust the Migrant to show us."

Damon and Brân and the others have returned with the marble for the new Benison. It's a marvelous piece of brilliantly white stone. Father is given responsibility for carving it, crafting it. As he does so, he continues teaching me. I sit next to him and study his hands as he taps and scrapes at the huge piece of stone. I try to feel what he touches. Any large chunks of marble that he removes he places into a basket.

He hands me one of the waifs and shows me how to work with it, shaping and smoothing it, bathing it in the clay mixture, letting it take up the song not just from my verberations but from my hands as well, from the sparks of fireseed in my palms and at my fingertips. Have those always been there?

I describe our work to Damon, and he reminds me that his own destiny stone is a New Marble.

"That Benison had the Song of Falling Leaves. I don't know that song," I say, even as a few mournful notes drop one by one into my awareness, drifting pale yellow and deep orange.

Every day, Father and I continue our work. Every day we sing. Or at least we sing the parts of the song that we know and that we can manage. Some parts are too low for Abél's voice, some too warbling for my abilities. So sometimes we invite Amos Quint to sit with us and contribute his resonant bass notes to the song. At other times we invite Zara or Jalu. Both of them are gifted singers, with aurynxes that can produce the most intricate and vivid sonic ornaments.

In my head, between my eyes, and sometimes in my vital nexus, I know the whole song in all its intricate harmonies and cadences and counterpoints. And I pertange how the stone shifts and reorients its elements around the images the song actuates, how the images and sounds are imprinted there, but not in a fixed way. Rather in a way that continually works with us, adapting and even— I swear this is true—suggesting subtle revisions in the song itself. As Abél and I work, the song and the stone evolve together into something beyond either.

The Marble Benison itself is taking shape and Abél says it will be ready for its dedication at dawn on the first day of the Marble Return of the next Marble Meed, less than a tide from now.

It will be ready for the Great Turning.

60.

"I'M LEAVING FOR TEMUR today," Damon says. We're still lying in bed with the rosy gold of morning seeping between the twisted roots that form the frame of our little shelter.

"I know," I say. I've known it for days. We just didn't talk about it. I reach under the edge of our bed and fumble for a little package I stashed there for this moment. It's a tiny leather pouch attached to a sturdy plaited cord. I hand it to Damon.

"What's this?" He holds it in his left hand, feeling the weight of what it contains, feeling the smooth length of the cord.

"Open it."

He expands the mouth of the bag and reaches inside. "It's amber," he says.

"Old Amber. The Song of Turning. I think it can help if I need to send danger away from you. To protect you. Brân has been teaching me the song." Brân gave me his piece of the Old Amber. Zara also gave me a piece, which is the one I'm giving to Damon.

He puts the stone back inside the pouch and sits up to loop the cord over his head. The pouch falls at the level of his heart. He tucks it inside his shirt next to the Quartz bead from our ceremony and leans over to kiss me.

My Mundani heart overflows with love for my Mundani lover, my life partner. The nens leap and turn in response and I reach for Damon's hand so that he can feel them, too.

He leaves after breakfast and my heart goes with him.

I've become more accustomed to the presence of the Migrant and I'm learning to ride their colors with a little less fear, a little more trust that I'll be borne back again to this time and this place, to these people, and to the future we're building together for one another and for our children. Sometimes I feel like I'm almost in control of where the Migrant takes me. No, that's probably wrong.

Today I'm tired after so many hours working with Abél, crafting waifs and singing to the New Marble Benison. I walk to the edge of our canopy, to a small glen I've claimed as my own. Its stones sprout moss from the recent rains. I'm worried about Mother. I've tried several times to find her. I'm afraid that Gerd hasn't found her, afraid that she hasn't found Fergus.

I don't like thinking of the place where they told me Mother is being held. It forces me to remember the vision of Rolang Landry and the young man who died and was cast into the fire with never a thought or feeling. The place was once a fine clauster, filled with so many bowls of water offered up every day to the Mundani Creator. There's a cottage in one corner of the walled grounds where a spring still bubbles feebly. Once this was the place where the monk who was the clauster's caretaker collected water for offerings, back when the spring ran fresh and copious.

That's where Mother is.

My heart beats faster and I try to calm it with my breathing, opening the space between my eyes, humming a single note of surrender to the vision.

"Woman! Why have you not brought the fireblocks? Have you forgotten again?" The surly Palinjian turns to his companion. "Why do we keep this one here? She's worse than useless!"

Mother stares at him with blank eyes. "Come in," she says. "My name is Maddie. What's yours?"

The man grumbles again as he and his companion grab an armload of fireblocks and stomp away.

A sly smile steals across Mother's face as she watches them go.

She's pretending! But what a dangerous pretense. They seem ready to rid themselves of her presence. Doesn't she know that?

I know, Meridia. Come back tonight and I'll show you how much I know.

Her coldness makes me shiver even as I settle back into the warm embrace of my green glen. I should tell Gerd. Maybe Gerd can get her out of there before she does herself serious harm. But there are so many men there. So many Palinjians and only a few women. The women are all servants, all overworked and weary. All of them angry.

Gerd is there! She's been captured. No, she's let herself be captured. The women have a plan, but I can't pertange what it is. Mother said to come back tonight. I quiet my fear and resolve to do as she asks.

I'm not hungry, but for the sake of the nens, I eat a light supper. I don't know the taste of it. I visit with some of the women for a while, biding time in the Mundani way, and then, as the last of the sun's light fades behind the mountains, I retreat to my little cabin.

I wish Damon were here.

I take out the bag where I keep my collection of waifs, including the ones I pilfered from Mother's jar back in Shadham. I arrange them on the table with my Lapis at the center, the one whose song is called Liberation. I'm uncertain where to put the Jade with its Song of the Calumet, so I put it back into the pouch and tuck the pouch inside my blouse, between my breasts.

I pour a cup of calming tea and sip.

Colors flicker around me.

I sip. I breathe out an Amethyst note of hope.

The colors flash brighter. A band of crimson reaches toward me and I slip willingly along its tone.

Mother has slipped into a room where she shouldn't be. There's a tray set out on one of the tables and something on it is covered with a richly embroidered cloth. She looks furtively about and then lifts the cloth. She takes a vial of liquid from inside her blouse and pours a few drops from it into each of the six wine cups on the tray. The vial she restores to its place and then she carefully pulls the cloth back over the cups. She turns to leave but before she reaches the door, someone enters.

"What are you doing here, woman?"

"Have you come for your breakfast?" she says cheerily. "It's not ready yet. You boys will have to wait a bit longer." She chuckles madly and shakes her finger at the man.

"Just get out," the man says, exasperated. "Go back where you belong and no more trouble."

"It's time to feed the chickens," Mother mumbles. "Get some eggs for breakfast."

She shuffles off and the man picks up the tray and heads into the inner courtyard where a crowd of Palinjians are assembled as if for some great feast. The attendant places the tray on the head table and offers a cup of wine to each of the men seated there. I see Rolang Landry, Crispin Harper, and a young man whose face I don't recognize but who I know at once has to be Warreth Pherson. He shifts uncomfortably in his chair, as if he's unaccustomed to this full-grown adult body that still seethes with youthful energy. Altogether there are six men at the table.

Mother is with Gerd. Three other women follow them as they steal through the darkness. Behind them a corpse lies next to the house where they're supposed to be. Gerd is sorry. They head for the gate in the wall, where a solitary guard drowses. As they approach, Mother moves ahead while the rest huddle in the shadows. Mother sings a nonsense song as she shuffles forward.

"Good morning," she calls out brightly.

The guard laughs. "So it's you, old woman. What have you brought me this time?"

"Some sweet nutcakes and a whole basket of ripe florapples!" The words come out singsong as Mother holds out her empty hands.

The man reaches toward her as if to accept her gifts.

"Too much for one hand, my young friend. So many nutcakes. Wouldn't want to bruise the florapples!"

He puts down his weapon and holds out both hands. In that same instant Gerd pounces on him from behind, smashing in his head with an iron implement so swiftly that he utters not a sound. He drops like a stone, gushing blood.

Gerd signals with a jerk of her head and all five women scurry through the gate to freedom. And behind them a man. Fergus is there.

The rising chorus of chaotic Mundani prayer draws my awareness back inside the clauster. In the sacred space, six beds are laid out and six men stand by with their fat bolsters of wool and down. The six honored guests lie upon the six beds and exhale. Bolsters press into their faces, stifling breath as the Migrant swirls above them unseen. One by one, six clouds of brown fog dissipate into the night. The Granite stones—broken into small pieces so that there are enough of them—are pressed into each man's left hand, each one's destiny stone in his right. The crowd waits in silence, barely breathing.

They wait.

Someone wails.

There's a murmur of disbelief as they notice that none of their leaders has yet resumed breathing. There's frantic activity as hands are pressed around stones, chests tapped furiously. And then a howl of dismay as they realize that these six men will not breathe again.

The Migrant caresses my shoulder, touches my heart and my orb as a pale sigh escapes my aurynx. *Mother, what have you done?*

61.

AS SOON AS I MEET ABÉL the next morning, I see that he knows. He puts an arm around my shoulders and draws me to him, caressing my matted hair. "She's a brave woman, Meridia," he says.

Did she kill them?

He frowns and then turns so that we're face to face. *They killed themselves. She only prevented them from coming back again.*

But how? As soon as I form this question, I know the answer. It's one of the herbs we both knew. We only used it when hunger drove us to kill an animal for food, so that we could kill it without violence.

I don't think she was even sure it would work, Father says.

It quelled their will, didn't it?

Yes, Daughter, I think that's what happened. Have you seen where Maddie and Gerd have gone?

And Fergus. I don't know. And I think it's better not to know for a while. In case there are Palinjians who are also searching for them.

I try not to think about Mother as we return to our work on the New Marble. Abél is setting the waifs of the other Benisons into the polished face of the Marble according to the pattern the Migrant showed us. I'm hopeful that Damon will be back for the dedication. I try not to think about Mother.

I go to Damon every night, when all has gone quiet. During the day he's too far away to reach through the chaos of Mundani voices and activity. His experiments have gone better than he dared hope and he's bringing back equipment as well as containers filled with the substances that he needs in order to continue his work here at our camp. We've begun to think of it as New Beniford.

Damon thinks he'll be here the day after tomorrow. After what I saw happen in the temple near Blanton, I'm more fearful for his safety. Who knows how the Palinjians will react to the loss of all their leaders at one stroke? I'm ashamed of the flush of pride I feel when I think about what Mother did. I trust the Migrant to protect her. The Migrant and Gerd.

When I tell the nens not to worry about their father or about their grandmother, I know I'm talking to myself.

I settle into my bed of grass, listening to rain pattering on the roof. I let the beat of my heart synchronize alongside the faster beating of the two hearts of my two nens. Together we look for Damon. I think where he ought to be now and I fly high, searching.

What I find causes me to catch my breath. I open my eyes for a moment, blinking into the darkness, breathing hard. Damon is in danger. I can't tell exactly what it is yet, but I know he needs my help. I reach for my pouch of waifs. First, I hum a deep blue canopy of protection around the nens. I leave that tune thrumming in the back of my throat and return to Damon. I take a tiny Turquoise waif, a gift from my father, and, holding it between my hands, I hum the Canopy of Time.

Suddenly I'm back in Temur, engulfed in the suffocating despair I knew then. The sense of being nobody. I force my mind away from that, seeking Damon.

An old man confronts Damon at his workshop. "I know you," he says. "You used to follow after that sully Shoon whore." The man turns and spits in the dust.

Damon stifles his anger. "I hear she's gone away." That's all he says.

The old man wants him to say more and when he doesn't, says it for him. "Good riddance, I say. I hope she was obliterated with all the rest of 'em up in the mountains there." There's menace in his grin.

Damon's anger almost overwhelms him. He verberates curses but his words are calm. "That seems likely. Did you have need of my services?"

"I do," the man says. "My son is going off to Fayredell to join up with Pherson and that lot. I'll want a picture of him before he goes."

"You can bring him in tomorrow," Damon says. "Just past midday." He knows he'll be long gone by then. He only wants the old man to go away so he can finish packing up his gear.

Now the old man and his son are following Damon as he approaches New Beniford. They're suspicious of where he's going, thinking maybe he knows more about "sully Shoons" than he was willing to admit. Mostly, they need somewhere to direct their anger since word came of the deaths of Warreth Pherson and Crispin Harper and Rolang Landry and the rest.

I take out my Old Amber waif and begin humming its Song of Turning.

I see Damon's hand go to the leather bag holding his piece of the Old Amber. A golden bubble shimmers into place around him, expanding out until it almost reaches the place where the old man and his son follow Damon's trail. The bubble pulses a few times and then starts to revolve. It wobbles as it turns, carrying the weight of the entire landscape with it, luring Damon's pursuers farther and farther astray. When they're finally headed off into wilderness, I stop. They can wander there for hours before they realize they've lost their quarry. And they'll never know how they got there. Most importantly, they'll never know what became of Damon.

Satisfied, I tuck the Old Amber away. I touch the Turquoise lightly, brushed again by the memory of being nobody. Knowing that here in New Beniford I am not that.

I feel Damon's presence growing stronger. He'll arrive tomorrow.

62.

THE DAY FOR DEDICATION of the New Marble is nearly here and its existence in our midst is palpable. Everyone has learned their part of its song and we're eager to finally join our many voices and verberations, our words and colors and images, and lift up at last the Song of All Songs.

Abél tells me I have a gift for the crafting of waifs. He tries to tell me that the next Benison may have to be made under my guidance. I try not to hear that. Surely Abél and Brân will still be around in another twelve returns for the start of a New Mica. I imagine my two children celebrating its song. If one of them is a boy, perhaps I'll name him Mica, like his eldfather. He'll be Mica breth Meridia. Or he could be Damon breth Meridia. A girl could be Avienne or maybe Madelyn. I asked Avienne one day if she could tell whether my nens were boys or girls and she said there was no way to tell. There will be indications at birth, she says, but there's not much real difference until they complete at least eight returns.

Brân and Abél and I have located Mother and Gerd and the others. Orban has gone out beyond the canopies to guide them to us.

I'm going in a different direction, to the southern edge of our canopies to meet Damon. I see him before he sees me, and I restrain my impulse to run to him. *Wait until he's inside the canopy, here where we're safe.*

As soon as he sees me, he tries to run, but his tired legs and the mass of things on his back weigh him down to a brisk walk. I run. He wriggles out of the constraints of his backsack and takes me in his arms, our hearts joining in crimson joy as we kiss.

"You brought back so many things," I say, trying to imagine what all those bulky objects might be.

"Everything I could carry," he says. "Maybe more." He rubs his shoulders and flexes his back before picking up the burden again.

"Give me something. Make it lighter."

"I've made it this far. I can make it a little farther."

I start to insist so he hands me his empty water sheath and we laugh.

"Did you have any trouble along the way?"

He gives me a sidewise glance. "Only that old fellow in Temur. But I guess when the news about the deaths at the Blanton temple reached Temur, he lost interest in me. I'm sure you'll tell me more about that."

He doesn't know he was followed. "Yes," I say. "Later." For now I want to relish the joy of being together. I wish we could prepare a meal at our cabin so that we could eat alone, just the two of us. Instead we deposit Damon's burden at the cabin and head for the common table.

Mother and Gerd have arrived and are seated at the table with Fergus and the three other Mundani women who came with them. I'm relieved to see that Mother looks well. She does look weary, though. Her pretense of dementia worried me more than I wanted to admit. Was it only pretense? She jumps up and strides toward me. We embrace and then she backs away, looking at me, still holding both my hands. Her eyes are hard and dull as they meet mine. I remember that dullness.

"I had to do it, Mer," she says. "I don't know what will happen now, but we had to get away." She wants forgiveness. I'm not able to offer it. Not yet. Not with my whole heart.

She gives Damon a hug, too, and then the three of us go to the table for our meal.

Damon doesn't ask the questions that cloud his face. I don't know how I'll answer them.

When we're finally alone together in our cabin, he asks, "What was it your mother meant? What did she have to do?"

So I tell how she poisoned the six men at the Blanton temple. "Not poisoned exactly," I say. "They would have recovered except for the ceremony. They couldn't recover from that. She and the other women only wanted to get away. It was all she could think of." *Yes, she learned about that poison from me.*

Damon presses my hand between his. A sepia cloud of sadness engulfs his heart. "Why does it have to be so hard, Meri? I keep wondering if all these deaths, all this killing, can possibly lead to peace. Won't the Palinjians come looking for revenge? Isn't that what they do?"

"They do blame the women. Mother and Gerd and the others." They saw how all the women fled at the same time the men died and took that as a sign of guilt.

"If the Palinjians are to continue, they'll need new leaders," Damon says.

He's right. Could new leaders be any worse than Warreth Pherson? When I looked, I overheard some men talking in Temur. Or rather arguing. They couldn't seem to agree about who ought to take over leadership. Warreth was so young that he had no sons. His younger brother is not even a man yet. And blind from a childhood fever. One man thought they should ask Lambert Quint to lead them away from their extreme practices, but he didn't share his thoughts with the others.

I have to try and believe that the New Marble and its song and the book Zara and Vidvana are writing will shift things.

63.

LAST NIGHT WAS THE FULL moon that welcomes the Marble Return of the New Marble Meed. Today we dedicate the Benison. We've been busy gathering and planning and preparing. A light rain always falls just before midday and it's brought forth an abundance of flowers. Today there will be only sunshine.

The Benison stands in the center of a new clearing, cloaked by an intricately embroidered cloth worked on by several men and women for most of a tide. At its foot there's a covered basket filled with the Marble waifs that are my own work.

We gather in silence in another clearing nearby. I'm wearing the clothes I wore on the day Damon and I were united. He wears a new shirt Mother stitched for him. Each of us carries a small ceramic bell, newly crafted for the day. We wait.

As the first sunbeams leap into the sky, the drummers begin their cadence and we file forward through dew-wet grass dotted with blossoms of every color. Upon reaching the clearing where the Benison stands, each of us rings our bell, keeping time with the drums. The sound rises as more and more of us enter, encircling the New Marble, treading out the rhythm of drums and bells. Three times around the Benison and we stop. The drums stop. The bells stop.

Three children go forward as the drummers cease playing. Zara and Avienne perform the recitation of meeds, the full cycle this time. They even mention the names of the recent meeds that had no Benisons.

There's a moment of silence and then, on the first beat of a new cadence, the children fling the covers away from our new Benison and from the basket of waifs. The Marble gleams in the morning sun, smooth and white and shimmering with all the colors.

The pattern of waifs on the Benison pulses and flashes. Our voices rise, and for the first time, the music of our new song, the Song of All Songs, surges forth in all its fullness into the world. In the beat of the drums I hear the Obsidian song, in the bells the Lapis joy of liberation. Flutes join in, tracing the melodies of Amethyst's hope, Jade's power of peace, Carnelian's wide path. Now trumpets made of great shells from the sea sound the nostalgia of the Turquoise, the rising waters of the Amber. I'm surprised to hear the Mica Song of Reflection entwining with the Quartz's reconciliation, the apologetic sorrow of the Granite, the Jasper's notes of warning, and all the seasons of all the Marble Benisons. Notes tumble and turn, weaving this new Song of All Songs as the air around us glistens with colors and a brilliance engulfs our New Marble Benison, showering it with a thousand sparks of fireseed.

Voices surge forth as the song evolves. Bass notes dig deep and lift while high notes soar upward and outward. Mundani voices add words and poetry. Zara and Vidvana sing the opening words of their book: "Light is the essence of all things. Light comes from song and song from light. Singing all the colors, all things come to be."

And then I hear Amos Quint's gruff bass join in with a chant: "We are the myriad expressions of the singularity of existence. We are one."

I rise with the song, floating on the sounds and colors that reach out beyond our fastness and into all the land. Canopies are abandoned so that all voices may be dedicated to this new song. The landscape crackles with possibility, and glints of bright, hopeful color spark amid the gloom outside our space. We join the Migrant with all our powers of heart and voice and mind and sing new possibilities into existence.

Abél and Brân go forward and take up the basket of waifs. They walk around the circle, placing a waif into the upturned hands of each adult. I pertange how the stones gleam with the different colors of their songs in each pair of hands. Some of us will bring peace, others liberation or hope or refuge, according to our gifts and our own stories. As Avienne's dancing hands pause to receive her waif, I'm sad to see an Obsidian song rise from the stone, the song of Embracing Death.

We file out of the circle at last, each voice and each bell going silent as we depart. Finally only the drummers are left. Their cadence slows to a single steady beat and then stops. We stand in silence for a moment and then our voices rise again, this time in a chaotic eddy of happy hugs and tears that still sparkle with song.

"Do you think it will work?" I ask Damon as we wander toward our cabin, sated from the feast. "The new song, the book?"

He doesn't answer directly. "They've decided to call it the Book of All Time," he says.

64.

THE FIRST MORNING of our New Marble Meed dawns all purple and orange. After yesterday's sunshine, the rains will resume in another hour or so.

Quint refuses to go with Abél and Brân to Fayredell. He'll stay here in New Beniford for a while and then he insists he'll go back to Selbourne. He's eager to learn all he can from the Migrant while he still lives. He's promised Vidvana that he'll write what he learns in a book and leave it there for her.

Ann will go to Fayredell to help them search for her grandfather, Lambert Quint. Gerd is going to Fayredell, too, but separately, accompanied by her son Fergus and his new friend Jalu.

Father hopes that if they give Lambert a waif of the New Marble and tell him about all that has happened, he will agree to join with us. But we still don't know where he is. Orban told us that he had disappeared, gone underground. Gone very deep, it seems.

"I'm sure the Migrant can show us where he is," Abél says. He looks directly at me as he says this.

Will you come with me, Father?

He nods and my eyes close as a vortex of color rises up around me. I whisper the name of Lambert Quint, while visualizing Amos. Abél offers an image of Lambert. He's a younger man than his father, of course, but still old. Not so gray, though his hair seems thinner. Wispier. He has a more delicate face, paler eyes. But he's taller, straighter. Amos was taller once.

I see Lambert, seated at a small table, leaning forward on both elbows. His head rests on his two open hands as he looks down at something on the table. A mirror. A hand mirror like the ones used by women when they arrange their hair or dab color on their lips. The image in the mirror is unclear, the silver on its back scorched by fire. A droplet of water falls on its surface.

I see him, Meridia. Now take us outside. Let's pertange where this house is.

Such a small house. No more than a broken-down cabin, its earthen walls near collapsing into the surrounding soil from which they were taken. The door lies just behind the place where Lambert is sitting. A gnarled meskie tree tries to shelter the doorway. On one of its twisted branches a rock sparrow sways and then leaps skyward, taking me with him.

I've never seen a more dismal landscape. It seems to contain nothing at all, only flat ground, shining hard and slightly pinkish in the blazing sun, still unaffected by the recent rains.

Bird turns and flies the other way. Greening fields and in the distance a town.

Fayredell. One more turn, Meridia.

We fly in a high circle. Sun illuminates distant mountains to the west. Barren flatness to the north. Fayredell to the south.

I open my eyes, dizzy with my sudden descent to earth, still held in the eddy of color that embraces me.

"I know that mirror," Amos says. He saw, too. The Migrant showed it to him. "It was his mother's. He knows. I think he'll be ready to lend his help."

"Do you know this house then?" Abél asks.

"I saw only my son and the mirror. My powers for such things are limited to what I already hold in my heart."

"It seems to be somewhere north of Fayredell, up near where the land gives way to the Northern Lowlands. I think we should be able to find it. There are so few houses of any kind out there."

I recall that Abél traveled that way on his journey to Gorshfen. I'm certain he'll be able to find Lambert Quint.

Tomorrow they begin. They'll be accompanied by Vidvana's partner, Willem. I'll show them the way. Or rather, the Migrant will show them. Avienne and Amos Quint and Damon and I stay here.

Damon resumes his work with Zara and Vidvana. Their Book of All Time will be carried to completion, and Damon promises that it will have pictures. It will tell the story of all our people in a way all can comprehend.

The work goes forward in a world already changed by the existence of a new song.

But the story isn't finished, Meridia. There's more. We'll show you.

APPENDIX 1

EXPERIENCING TIME

MELFAR do not think linearly, but rather conceptualize all time in terms of cycles. They utilize a lunar calendar overlaid on a solar one, measuring time in *tides*, *returns*, and *meeds*. A tide is a full lunar cycle. The only consistently named tides are Darktide, Brightening Symmetide, Suntide, and Darkening Symmetide (corresponding to periods encompassing winter solstice, vernal equinox, summer solstice, and autumnal equinox, respectively). Other tides receive descriptive labels, which vary from one return to the next (e.g., Fogtide, Budtide, Fruittide). A return is a cycle of all the solar seasons, with a new return always beginning on the full moon closest to the start of Brightening Symmetide. There are twelve named returns corresponding to the twelve types of stone from which a Benison is crafted to mark the start of each return (see below). A full cycle of returns comprises a meed, and meeds are named in the same sequence as returns. The completion of a full cycle of meeds is known as a Great Turning. Returns of the current cycle are called New, with previous cycles referred to as Old, Ancient, and Preterit, in that order. To the Melfar, "Preterit" means both "before" and "after." To "date" a particular event, one might say that it happened during a Cloudtide of the Amber Return of the Old Turquoise Meed.

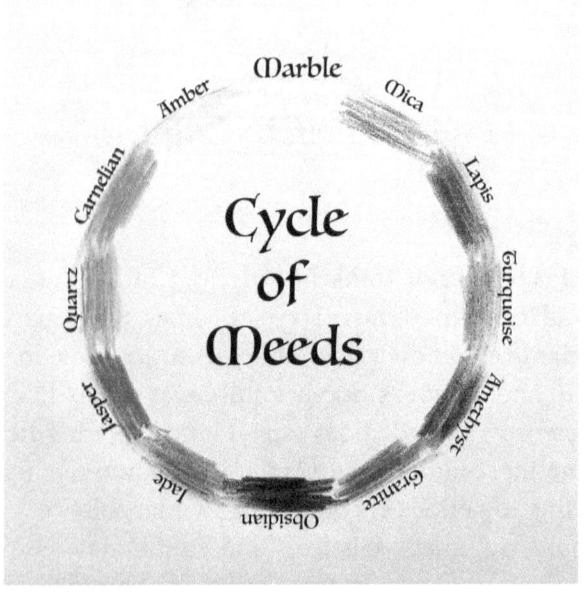

MUNDANI, on the other hand, utilize a rigidly linear solar calendar. Their equivalent of a Melfar return (our year) is a *passage*. Passages are sequentially numbered, beginning with the birth year of Razak Caloyer, a revered prophet. Each passage is divided into twelve *stints*, each with exactly thirty days, comprised of five *sixes*. These stints are not named, only numbered. To regularize their calendar, they observe a period of five (sometimes six) days at the conclusion of Twelfth Stint. These days are called the *Binder*. The new passage begins on the longest day (our summer solstice), which they call Full Sun.

358

APPENDIX 2

THE MAP on the following page represents the Mundani world. Melfar don't use maps as such (see Chapters 12 and 32). The eastern "Wasteland" is what was once the Melfar Forest of Cödweg and the southern "Wasteland" is where the Forest of Cesta once stood. The Melfar Forest of Serani lay at the foot of the western mountains. For the benefit of readers, the map shows the approximate locations of the following places that are important only to Melfar:

1) Beniford

2) Aldbeck

3) Lindmor

4) Woodclasp

5) Gorshfen (on the lake called Glasllyn)

6) Selbourne

7) Túl

8) New Beniford

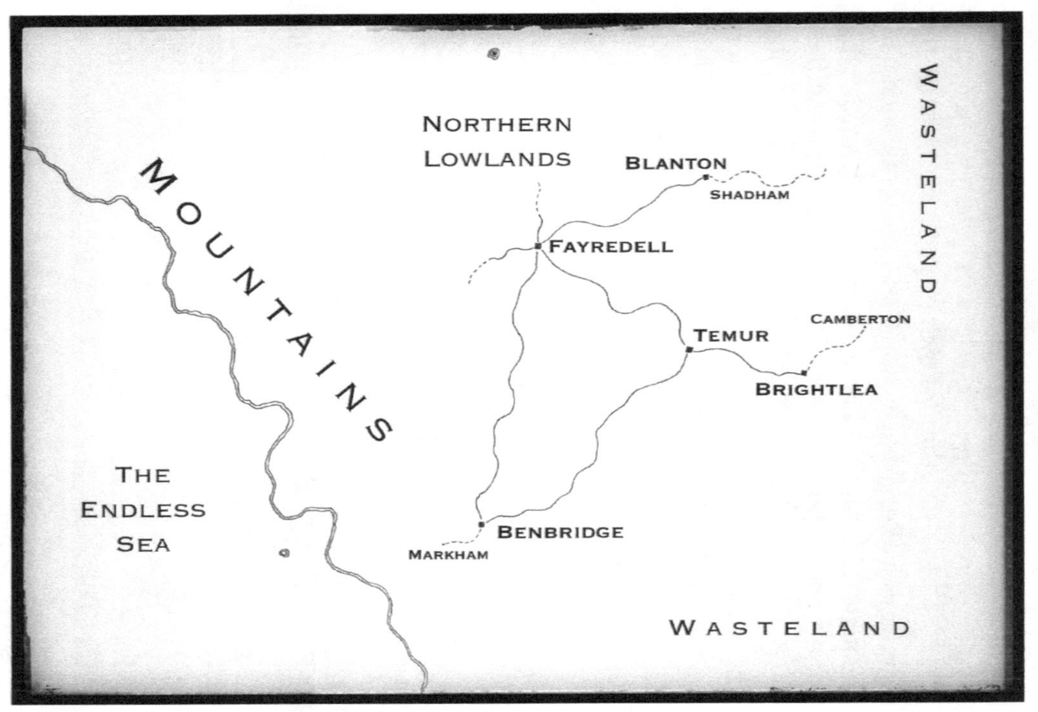

MOUNTAINS
NORTHERN
LOWLANDS
BLANTON
SHADHAM
FAYREDELL
WASTELAND
CAMBERTON
TEMUR
BRIGHTLEA
THE
ENDLESS
SEA
MARKHAM
BENBRIDGE
WASTELAND

APPENDIX 3

GLOSSARY

aurynx: The organ that sonically verberates biophotonic patterns. It is located in the throat near the larynx.

Benison: A stone monument crafted by Melfar to commemorate the end of one meed and the start of the next. Each Benison contains the imagery of a song.

billbug: A biting insect similar to a mosquito or horsefly.

cabra: A goat-like mammal sometimes kept for milk.

Calumet: A "peace-bringer" who serves as a respected social and cultural leader among the Melfar.

cavouti: A species of large rodent raised for meat.

clauster: A sacred space often associated with a Mundani temple.

equid: A horse-like mammal kept as a draft animal.

fahm: Coal. Deposits of fahm are found mainly in the remains of ancient storage facilities.

fellspan: The distance to the horizon on relatively flat ground. Approximately 4.2 miles.

fireblock: A fabricated fuel made from waste material soaked in groundfat.

gnosic orb: The sensory organ that pertanges biophotonic patterns. It is located in the center of the brow just above the eyes.

groundfat: Petroleum, raw or refined. Found mainly in the remains of ancient storage facilities.

kinren: Any of the employees, servants, clients, apprentices, and women attached to a particular Sidayen.

lamin: An alpaca-like animal kept as a beast of burden and draft animal.

Migrant: The ineffable presence that, according to Melfar belief, motivates and empowers everything.

Palinjian: A devotee of Zibal Palinj.

patkány: A very large species of predatory rodent.

pertange: To sense in a tangible way the biophotonic and sonic verberations of people and natural things.

Revelant: An individual who has died and come back to life in the same body.

Sidaya: A code of moral conduct among the Mundani.

Sidayen: One who adheres to the Sidaya. Alternatively, a high status exclusive to Mundani men.

Token: An individual who recognizes the indwelling of the Migrant.

verberate: To sonically generate biophotons.

vital nexus: The energetic network centered around an individual's heart.

waif: A stone associated with a Benison and sharing some of its properties.

zaki: A large predatory feline.

CHART OF FAMILIES

```
                    ┌──────────┬──────────┐
                    |          |
            Mica  = Avienne   Fannan        Amos Quint  =  Nahla
                  | b.575     b.569         b.568          |
            ┌───────────┬────────────┐                ┌───────────┬──────────────┐           ┌──────────┐
            |           |            |                |           |              |           |          |
  Mindrel = Brân       Abél = Madelyn               Rahmond    Lambert = Fia Pritchard    Orban    =   Emba
          | b.600      b.600 |                      595-610    b.600   |  b.607           b.612        b.615
          |                  |                                 ┌──────────┬──────────┐
        Malaki            MERIDIA                              |          |
        b. 628                                          Rolang = Keira   Nollag
                                                        Landry | b.625   640-655
                                                               |
                                                           Ann Landry
                                                           b.649
```

ACKNOWLEDGMENTS

The world of *EarthCycles* has been germinating in my mind for many years. As an anthropologist, I've always been intrigued by those periods of early human evolution when two (or more) varieties of us—species, subspecies, "races"—lived in proximity. What would that have been like? Through the years I've also speculated occasionally about what the end of human life on earth will be like. Will we be completely obliterated? Or might there be one or more pockets of us who survive? And then what would happen?

As this story sent out its earliest roots and stems, I harked back to conversations with fellow anthropologists like Debra Schumann and James Nations and Nancy Singleton. As the manuscript came to fruition, I pruned and edited with the advice and input of readers Teresa Roberson, Cheryl Rooke, Ana Cristina Rudholm, and Claire Villarreal. There were also words of encouragement from an anonymous reader at Writers' League of Texas and early input from a critique group at ArmadilloCon40 led by William Ledbetter and Bonnie Jo Stufflebeam. Katherine Catmull at Yellow Bird Editors helped me in uncounted ways to shape the story into something worthy of publication. I extend gratitude also to Elena Sandovici (who continues to be my go-to for those moments when the stresses of being an indie author threaten to overwhelm) and to Rebecca Pheasant-Reis (who talked me through my quandary about how to present my readers with a map depicting the world of people who hate maps).

I hope my readers will find the *EarthCycles* world as submersive as I have. And as I still do, as I continue exploring Meridia's story in the next two installments of the trilogy.

I'm online at *donnadechenbirdwell.com* and you can also find me on Facebook, Twitter, and Instagram.

OTHER BOOKS BY
DONNA DECHEN BIRDWELL

Not Knowing, 2019

THE RECALL CHRONICLES

Way of the Serpent, 2015

Shadow of the Hare, 2016

Flight of the Owl, 2016

COMING 2021

EARTHCYCLES, BOOK TWO:

BOOK OF ALL TIME